THE BOY NEXT DOOR

When childhood sweethearts are reunited, will the same sparks fly?

Terri Mills is going home to London. With only a battered mini and a bankruptcy order to show for her life in Devon, she's not feeling particularly proud of herself. At least her nine-year-old daughter Sasha sees their trip as an adventure. Terri's Gran is keen to lend a hand and has already found Terri a flat and a job. If only the job wasn't at the local flower shop. Growing up, Terri had two passions: flowers, and Martin Blake, the boy next door. Now she's about to walk into his florist's ... and straight back into her past.

THE BOY NEXT DOOR

THE BOY NEXT DOOR

by

Cathy Woodman

Magna Large Print Books
Long Preston, North Yorkshire,
BD23 4ND, England.

British Library Cataloguing in Publication Data.

Woodman, Cathy
    The boy next door.

    A catalogue record of this book is
    available from the British Library

    ISBN   978-0-7505-2834-4

First published in Great Britain in 2007
by Headline Publishing Group

Published in Large Print 2007 by arrangement with
Headline Publishing Group Ltd.

Magna Large Print is an imprint of Library Magna Books Ltd.

Printed and bound in Great Britain by
T.J. (International) Ltd., Cornwall, PL28 8RW

To
Tamsin and Will,
Ben and Jessica,
Rachel and Adam,
and Charlotte and Millie.

Acknowledgements

I should like to thank my family, my agent Laura Longrigg at MBA, my editor Sherise Hobbs, and the team at Headline for their encouragement and support.

Chapter One

How did I let it come to this?

I glance down at the official letter in my hand. It is addressed to me, Terri Mills, ex-proprietor of the florist's shop known as *Flower Power*, in Paignton, on the South Devon coast, and now an undischarged bankrupt. I might have excellent flower-wiring skills, and an enthusiasm for scrubbing buckets. I might be highly creative, especially when it comes to updating my CV (the less said about that, the better), but my instinct for colour and design and my individual style of combining flowers and foliage with natural materials, such as weathered driftwood, pebbles and shells swept up onto the beach by the tides, were not enough to keep my business afloat.

I post the keys through the letterbox of the shop door, take one last glance at the flat above which used to be home, and turn back to the mound of black binliners heaped up on the pavement. My nine-year-old daughter, Sasha, is perched on top, wrapped up in fleeces, a lilac raincoat and gloves against the January cold. She pulls her hood down, in order to see me better, and her long dark hair tumbles free.

'When are we going to get there?' she calls.

'We haven't left yet, Petal.'

Sasha's lips curve into a smile, and my heart soars. Whatever happens, I am and always will

13

be, Sasha's mum. All the creditors and County Courts in the world can't take that away from me.

I place the last bag at the foot of Sasha's mountain just as a small, rather battered red car pulls into the parking space I have managed to preserve with a couple of traffic cones that I 'borrowed' from the roadworks in town.

The driver's door flies open, and a woman dressed in a long coat, wide-legged trousers and heels, stumbles out.

I was trying to slip away quietly, but with Sharon turning up, there is no chance of that. Sharon, my best friend, doesn't do quiet.

'Terri!' She rushes up and flings her arms around me. Her glasses clash with my shades. 'I thought I was too late to give you two a lift to the station. One of the twins kept me up for the first half of the night, and the other, for the second. I overslept.' She takes a step back. Her hair, of an indeterminate colour that is best described as grizzle (she has been dyeing it since I can remember), is out of control. Her lippy is smeared across her teeth.

'You're looking great, Terri. When the Official Receiver asked you for a list of your assets, you should have mentioned your figure, your long legs, and the fact that your teeth are all your own.' Sharon smiles. 'He might have looked on your petition more favourably.'

I'm tall – over a head taller than Sharon anyway – passably good-looking, and unreasonably slim for someone who lives on a diet of thick and creamy yoghurts and Galaxy bars. I wear contact lenses for distance vision, and I can still read bedtime stories to Sasha without needing glasses, as long as I hold the likes of Roald Dahl and Jacqueline Wilson at arms' length. I have hazel eyes, freckles and auburn hair which, although short, has a tendency to curl.

'The only interest the Official Receiver had in me was the fact that I had no money, and very little in the way of seizable property that my creditors hadn't already seized.' It was my fault that my business failed. I concentrated on arranging flowers, not my finances.

'What's with the sunglasses?' Sharon enquires. 'Are you planning to travel to London via the Costa del Sol, or have you been shedding a few more tears?'

I pull the faux-fur-trimmed hood of my jacket down, and slip my shades up onto the top of my head. 'I'm past crying,' I tell Sharon. 'I decided to leave in disguise. Incognito.'

The smell of cold fish and chips wafts from the shop next door, and seagulls cry from the roof of the clubhouse on the playing fields opposite.

'You could be Dick Whittington in those boots,' Sharon teases.

'Mum bought them for fifty pee in the charity-shop sale.' Sasha's big brown eyes spark with mirth. 'She calls them her kinky boots.'

'You should be very proud of your mum, the way she can pick up a bargain.'

'Let's just say I'm grateful for boho chic.'

A dustcart comes rumbling down the road between the two rows of parked vehicles and draws up level with Sharon's car. One of the dustmen walks towards us.

'We can't take all of that, my lover,' he calls out in a rough Devon accent. 'You'll have to put some of it out next week.'

'It isn't rubbish,' Sasha calls back. 'It's our stuff, and we're taking it to London.'

I am thirty-nine years young, and all my worldly goods fit into eight binbags and a couple of suitcases. I was so desperate to hang on to *Flower Power* that I sold the furniture, lamps and toys, and even the rugs from beneath our feet. I scratch my head as the dustcart passes by. 'It isn't much, but how am I going to get it onto the train?'

'You don't have to.' Sharon grabs my hand, and presses a set of car keys into my palm. 'South London is three hours' drive away. My little old banger doesn't do much more than sixty with the wind behind it, but it'll get you and Sasha to your gran's by teatime. I've filled the tank.'

I picture myself trying to heave eight binbags up onto the overhead luggage rails in a crowded carriage on the Paddington Express. Trundling along with them in the back of Sharon's car would be easier, not to say loads cheaper for Sasha and me.

'Thanks, Sharon, you're a pal. I'll bring it back next weekend.'

'Only if you can't find anywhere to park it in Addiscombe. Terri, the car is yours. And before you start arguing about it, Chris agreed that you should have it. He's bought me a new one.' Sharon wiggles her bum, and sings a snatch of Groove Armada's 'I See You Baby (Shakin' That Ass)' from the car ad on TV. 'Guess which model.'

'Your husband is very generous, but I can't accept it.'

'Chris said that you wouldn't take it as a gift, so we've agreed to sell it to you.'

'Sharon, you've forgotten that Mum hasn't got any money,' Sasha observes.

Sharon pulls a purse out of her coat pocket and takes out a coin. 'Yes, she has. I'm lending her a pound.' She gazes at me. 'Take it. You can pay me back when you start work.'

I hold out my hand. Sharon drops the coin into my palm. I hand it back. The deal is done.

'Come on – I'll help you load up,' Sharon says. 'How many black bags do you think you can get into a Supermini, Sasha?'

My daughter, possessing the optimism of youth, guesses all eight. Sharon says six, while I suggest four. Sharon is right. We squish six bags and the two suitcases into the back, leaving the front seats clear for me and Sasha, then abandon the remaining bags on the pavement for the dustmen's return. I check them, and they only contain a lumpy duvet and some clothes that have seen better days.

'We're just like the Famous Five, setting out on an adventure, Mum, except that there are only two of us – at the moment.' Sasha sweeps her hair back, twists it into a ponytail then lets it go, so that it bounces back around her shoulders. 'Have you packed the ginger beer?'

'Lemon squash and a flask of tea. Will that do?'

'You'll be the Terrific Two,' says Sharon. 'You *are* the Terrific Two.'

Sasha climbs into the car, leaving me and Sharon facing each other.

'I'll miss you,' Sharon begins.

Tears prick my eyes and my throat constricts. 'I feel as if I'm missing you already.'

'Most people move from the city to the country. Trust you to do it the other way around! Keep in touch.'

'I promise.' I am just about to get into the car, when Sharon stalls me.

'I almost forgot to give you these.' She hands me a set of pink furry dice. 'Good luck, and don't forget to give me plenty of time to choose a hat.'

I tie the dice to the wing mirror, not wanting to be caught for dangerous driving, and slide into the car where I turn the key in the ignition.

'There are three and a half million men in London,' Sharon says above the sound of the engine, which is more tractor than Supermini. 'Even if you don't meet Mr Right, you'll have fun looking.'

'I'm not looking!' I shout as she stands and watches us pull away. She simply grins and waves.

'Are there really that many people in London?' says Sasha from beside me. 'It must be very crowded.'

'They don't all live in Addiscombe where we're going. Addiscombe is just a small area of South London,' I explain. It's also the place where I grew up. I turn right at the crossroads and Sharon has gone.

'It would be great if you found yourself a boyfriend,' Sasha says wistfully as we head for the motorway. 'As long as he isn't like the last one, who used to steal my chips,' she qualifies, 'or the one before him – Russ. The man who drives the ice-cream van thought he was my brother!'

Okay, the fast-food freak and the toyboy... I don't have much luck with men.

'I wonder how many ice-cream vans there'll be in Addiscombe,' I say, changing the subject. I am not looking for someone special any more. It takes time and emotional energy, and I am determined to concentrate on creating a new life for my daughter, moving into the flat which my grandmother has found for us, settling Sasha into a new school, and starting a new job where I am an employee, not the boss.

Can I get through it? At least the place will be familiar... Smiling to myself, I switch on the radio and adjust the tuning. It is a good omen. Gloria Gaynor is singing 'I Will Survive.'

The tune keeps replaying in my head, falters a little when I have to park the car several roads away from our new address, and fizzles out completely when our landlord shows us around our home.

Pat is in his fifties or early sixties. He is dressed in a blue-and-white striped shirt, and suit trousers held up with red braces (very 1980s), and introduces himself as a property developer and general entrepreneur.

When he unlocks the front door and lets us into the flat, Sasha's immediate response is, 'Where is the furniture?'

'My grandmother said that the flat was furnished,' I say.

'Part-furnished,' Pat corrects me.

'Which part?' asks Sasha.

Pat demonstrates the 'as new' sofa that he has acquired for the living room, the bare expanse of carpet, and the wastepaper basket strategically placed to hide a cigarette burn. There are no beds. If I wish to purchase a double bed for the tiny, one bedroom in the flat, Pat says, he would be willing to re-hang the door so that it opens outwards into the hallway. I decline, allocating the room to Sasha.

Pat enthuses over the neutral colour of the kitchen units. It isn't any old beige, apparently – it is 'Cancun' beige. Finally, he hands over a bath-plug and keys.

When I tell him that I will pay him on receipt of my first wage, he informs me that my fairy godmother i.e. Gran has sent a cheque to cover both the deposit and a month's rent in advance.

'You mean Great-Granma hasn't seen the flat?' Sasha says later, once Pat has gone.

'Apparently not.' However, by the time I have finished cleaning our new residence, using a combination of bleach, vinegar and lemon juice, it looks and smells much better, although it could still do with something else to cheer it up, something that I consider an essential, not a luxury; fresh flowers.

'It was very kind of Great-Granma to find this place for us, but it isn't quite how I imagined it,' I observe later.

'Don't worry, Mum,' Sasha says brightly. 'We'll pretend that we're on holiday.'

On the morning of her first day at school, I find

20

a hand-drawn map in Sasha's room, entitled *Tourist Information for Addiscombe by Sasha Mills*.

There are pictures of the red and white trams that run through Addiscombe between East Croydon and Elmers End. A plane with a pilot, resembling Biggles in goggles and a scarf, marks the site of the Croydon Aerodrome, the original London Airport, and the twin towers of IKEA lean precariously towards each other. Three other shops are marked *Vinyl Resting Place, Prawnbrokers* and *Toys 'R' Us*.

'We'll put this up on the wall with your other pictures – if we can find room.' The bedroom walls are already covered with my budding Gainsborough's signature landscapes of the English countryside, populated by black-and-white striped cows, and children flying speckled kites.

Sasha is standing beside her new Argos folding bed. Her long dark hair frames her elfin face. Her dressing-gown, open to reveal an uncharacteristically cheerful Eeyore on the front of her pyjamas, barely covers her knees, and her toenails are decorated with scuffed pink polish.

'What would you like for breakfast? Cornflakes or cornflakes?' I go out to the tiny kitchen without waiting for Sasha to argue that she would prefer Cheerios, and I take a box of cereal and a bowl from the cupboard beside the window.

I look outside, letting my eye follow the line of the fence which runs away over one hundred feet between two narrow strips of overgrown lawn that are white with frost. Whoever divided this Edwardian terraced house into flats in the first place made an odd decision, dividing the rear garden

21

into two lengthwise plots.

'What are you doing, Mum?'

I turn away from the worktop to find Sasha in her school uniform, a green jumper and black trousers that fit perfectly. I refuse to become my mother, buying my daughter clothes to allow for growth. I never did grow into the summer dress that Mum bought for me when I started at the very same school Sasha is going to, Havelock Primary.

'I'm admiring the vista,' I say.

Sasha frowns.

'The view,' I explain.

'No, you've poured orange juice onto my cornflakes, and milk into my mug.'

'Have I?' I pick up the mug and examine its contents. Sasha decorated it herself. There is a family holding hands around the circumference; mum, dad and two little girls, beneath a blue sky and yellow sunshine. It's her dream and, although I'd never tell her in case I should raise false hopes, it has always been mine too.

I throw the cornflakes into the bin under the sink and start again. We are going to be late. I am beginning to regret not asking Gran to take Sasha to school, but I wanted to do it myself on her first day.

'What is your new boss like, Mum?'

Martin. I can hardly bring myself to say his name aloud. 'Martin?' Over twenty years ago, when I left Addiscombe with my parents, for a new life in Devon, he was tall, wide-shouldered and narrow-hipped. His brown hair fell wildly across his forehead in waves, above piercing blue

22

eyes. I recall his playful smile and sexy laugh. Martin was definitely a vista to be admired, but that was way back, and looks aren't everything. 'I haven't seen him for years,' I say, and clear my throat.

Sasha drips milk across the worktop as she spoons fresh cereal from the bowl into her mouth.

'Be careful, Sash. I've just cleaned everything.'

She giggles. 'You can hardly tell me off about my table manners when we haven't got a table, or chairs.'

'Very funny.' I plant a kiss on top of her head. 'Love you.'

'You too.' Sasha crunches back her response through a mouthful of cornflakes. 'Do I *have* to go to school?'

'You know the answer to that. You have to learn to read and write.'

'I can write already. Pneumonia is a very long word, how do you spell it?'

'Ha ha. I, T.'

'No.' She dips her finger into the spilled milk and scrawls the word *pneumonia* across the worktop. 'Tricked you!' She grins, revealing a set of teeth that seem too big and too many for her mouth.

'Clever clogs.' I smile back. 'Now will you hurry up, please.'

'Can we go by tram?'

We walk. I stroll along, weighed down by Sasha's backpack because I agreed to carry it on condition that she zipped up her coat and wore her gloves, and Sasha jogs beside me, breaking into hopscotch mode wherever she can find paving stones in the appropriate orientation.

23

The school – my old school – looks a lot smaller than I remember it. The Junior and Infant sections are on the same site: a collection of buildings, old and new, and prefab; a muddy playing-field and a playground surrounded by a high railing fence. The metal climbing-frame from which I used to dangle upside down by the backs of my knees, with my skirt down around my ears, and my navy-blue knickers exposed to the world, my head a few precarious feet from the tarmac, has been replaced by a wooden fort with chips of bark beneath it.

As we approach the gates, Sasha, who for some months has refused any physical contact between us that might be construed as embarrassing or babyish, slips her hand into mine. The width of her hand is such that I have to spread my own palm to accommodate it, and my throat tightens as I realise how quickly my daughter is growing up.

'I can't go to this school,' she says suddenly. 'It's mingin'.'

'I wish you wouldn't use that word. I don't like it.'

Sasha clings more tightly to my fingers when I walk her past the gaggles of mums and their child-ren, through drifts of fresh perfume and fabric conditioner, across the playground. Once inside the school buildings, we track down the secretary who directs us to Sasha's classroom and intro-duces us to Miss Hudson, the class teacher, before the bell rings to bring the rest of the children in from the playground.

I'll bet with her cropped blonde hair, blue eyes and baby-pink lips that Miss Hudson has all the dads queueing up to buy her flowers. However, Sasha doesn't seem all that impressed.

'I'm not staying,' she says firmly, keeping her coat on.

'You can help me with the register.' Miss Hudson holds out a pot of pens. Sasha wipes her nose with the back of her hand then pulls out the first pen she touches. 'You'd better try it, see if it works.' Miss Hudson hands her a scrap of paper.

'What shall I write?' Sasha kneels on a chair and leans across the table closest to her.

'Whatever you like.'

'Pneumonia is a very long word,' Sasha begins, and Miss Hudson shoos me out of the classroom.

How will Sasha settle in? In my experience, it is more difficult to make friends when you arrive at a new school in the middle of an academic year than at the beginning, when friendship groups haven't yet been established. I can only hope that someone takes her under their wing, like Sharon did to me when I moved to Devon. Yes, I survived, but it was different for me. It was a secondary school, and I was sixteen.

As I walk the ten minutes or so towards the park, I find myself glancing over my shoulder, looking out for potential creditors – force of habit, I suppose. A biting wind chafes through my jeans, and my toes are numb inside my kinky boots, as Sasha describes them, on account of them having tassels and skyscraper heels which wreak havoc on my tendons if I don't wear them every day.

As I turn the corner, passing the traffic that jerks along bumper to bumper in the rush-hour queue into Central London, the wind drops and sleet-laden clouds part to reveal a weak, wintry sun.

Ahead of me is the Parade, a terrace of three-storey buildings, shopfronts with two levels of living accommodation above. Their red-brick walls seem to glow through layers of grime, and the pavement shines silver from the last shower.

For a moment, I wonder if I have taken a wrong turning, for there is no red-and-white striped awning outside the newsagents where I spent my childhood with my parents. However, there are still newspapers displayed just inside the open door, and posters in the window advertise extra services, including hot sausage rolls, a drycleaning service, and late-night opening.

There's an electrical shop where the grocer's used to be: an austere display of equipment behind a pane of smoke-effect glass, instead of crates of veg and apples on the pavement.

I glance at my reflection in the window. The glow in my cheeks makes my freckles appear less distinct, yet my hair is ruffled, making me look slightly wild. I try to smooth it down. I will have to do.

The fourth shop in the Parade is as I remember it – *Bickley & Bickley: Funeral Directors & Monumental Masons* – but the third stands out like a single bright bloom from an urban jungle of drab foliage. Gold lettering on faded green paint reads *Posies: Flower Sellers since 1949*, the year in which Martin's grandfather opened his shop. I never met him. He died suddenly in his forties, and left *Posies* to Martin's parents. I try to peer inside, but a screen of condensation trickles down the windows on either side of the door, making it impossible to see anything except indistinct shapes and splashes of colour.

I hesitate, my heart beating in my throat, and the palms of my hands damp with apprehension. Why on earth did I agree to come back? Because I needed a job, because of Gran, because I was tempted by the idea of seeing Martin again...

I place my hand on the brass plate on the door and push it open. The bell jangles, making me start. I step inside, and the door swings closed behind me, shutting out all sound apart from my heartbeat. I take a deep breath of the startling heat and stifling humidity, of the sharp scent of leaves and moist peat.

To my left are rows of staging, much of them obscured by flowers: roses massed in porcelain vases; single orchids in elegant glass stems: house-plants in terracotta pots; exotic ferns and yuccas; hyacinths in baskets – all blue.

Beyond these, the shop opens up into a space containing a desk with a till, and a small round table with three chairs. On one wall, painted pale green to show off the plants to their best advantage, is a series of framed certificates and awards. Opposite them are shelves crowded with greetings cards, cute teddies and unicorns, bottles of brandy and champagne, and boxes of Belgian chocolates.

Like Doctor Who stepping out from his Tardis, I have stepped straight into my past.

'Is anyone there?' I call softly. I hear footsteps before a figure emerges from the shadows at the

27

rear of the shop. A man. Light slants through the glass behind me so that I can't see his face, but I recognise him from the width of his shoulders, the slight stoop to one side and the way that he moves, slow and taut like a prowling tiger. I catch my breath. 'Martin?'

He moves towards me until I can see his face. It shocks me because his brow is deeply lined in a questioning frown, the corners of his eyes are creased and his hair, cropped very short, is flecked with grey.

I almost laugh out loud. What did I expect? That he'd stay young forever like Peter Pan? Martin is two years older than me, which makes him forty-one. He is a middle-aged man, just as I am a rather foolish middle-aged woman, imagining that I could come back to Addiscombe to work for Martin as if nothing had ever happened between us, as if twenty-three years apart was long enough to heal old wounds.

'Terri?' Martin says slowly. Although the square-ness of his jaw has softened, his voice is the same, like nut cracknell breaking into shards; sweet and hard-edged, sometimes cutting.

'I'm sorry I'm late.' I look him up and down, taking in the navy cords and pale blue sweater which complements his tanned skin. He looks me up and down in return, and I wonder what he sees. 'Sasha – she's my daughter – didn't want me to leave her at school. It's her first day, you see.'

'It doesn't matter.' Martin holds my gaze. His eyes are blue, not speedwell or cornflower, but shadowy and changeable like the sky at dusk, and ringed with dark lashes. A shiver runs down my spine. 'You've had your hair cut,' he observes.

'Many times since I last saw you.' I try to make light of his comment, but Martin blushes as if he too recalls the last time that we met. He was eighteen. I was sixteen. We were cuddled up on the bed, listening to music in his room, with a chair propped up against the inside of the door. Martin gave me a ring, a heart-shaped green stone set on a plain gold band. I told him that I loved him. He said that he would love me for ever.

'I must fly.' Martin turns away abruptly, and picks up a file and notebook from the counter. 'I have an appointment up in Town about a commission for an art gallery that's opening next month. My mother will look after you.' He calls back into the shadows, 'Mum, are you there?' then heads out of the shop as if he cannot get away from me fast enough.

He might well be embarrassed at seeing me again, and it doesn't surprise me that he is running away. He didn't have the courage before to meet me, and tell me face to face that our relationship was over. He didn't bother to write or phone. Why should he have changed?

'Well, if it isn't little Miss Chocolate Orange.' A woman comes bustling towards me, stops and stares.

'Good morning, Val.' When I was Sasha's age, I used to invite myself to play in the shop. I pretended that I was the florist and Val was a customer, and made up bouquets of roses, with spray carnations and gypsophila. I remember Val as being taller than me, but now she is a couple of inches shorter. She must be in her sixties. She has grown heavy and her shoulders are rounded as if she's borne years of disappointment; her cheeks are flabby and her eyelids hooded. Her hair, dyed a peculiar shade of burgundy, is cut severely around her ears, and left longer on top.

Like a chameleon, Val stands camouflaged against the flowers on the staging in a chintz tabard, rose-print blouse, striped skirt and opaque green tights. 'To this day, I have been unable to understand how a parent could inflict the name of a piece of confectionery on their child.'

'You can't choose your parents,' I say lightly, wondering whether or not Martin would have opted for Val being his mother, if he had had a choice.

'Now that you're here, I suppose that we'd better find you something to wear.' She looks down at my boots. 'We like to keep everything very traditional.'

'Old-fashioned, you mean?'

'It's what our customers want.'

'I don't think that you're allowed to tell me what to wear, Val.'

'Oh Terri,' she sighs. 'I think that I can – unless you don't want to stay for your week's trial.'

'Trial?'

'Your grandmother didn't mention that, did she?' Val smiles for the first time. 'Let's find you a uniform.'

I follow her out to the back room through the door which has been left propped open with a bucket, following the sound of a radio: Bruce Springsteen sings 'Dancing in the Dark', from the year when I last saw Martin.

I remember the table that stands in the centre of the room with its scrubbed pine surface covered with pieces of plastic foam and wire. I remember the flight of stairs that leads directly from the room to the flat above; the double draining-board that is partially obscured by a forest of foliage; the porcelain sink that is filled with pots of scented hyacinths, all blue like the ones on the staging in the front of the shop; the worktop beneath a wall-mounted boiler.

The fridge, the ribbon dispenser on the wall, and A4 files with their spines labelled *Inland Revenue*, *Extortion* and *VAT* on the shelf are more recent additions.

I watch Val step around the buckets of lilies and curling stems of bamboo, carnations and gypsophila, which form a frothing flood of colour across the tiled floor. She reaches for one of the tabards hanging from the door that leads onto the alleyway behind the shops in the Parade.

'No, you can't possibly wear this one. It belongs to Letitia.' Val examines a second tabard. 'This will do you.' She hands me the garment, a riot of pink and purple chintz cotton. I slip it on over my head.

'I can't wear this,' I object. 'I feel like a marquee.'

Val purses her lips and exhales a perfume of coal-tar soap and cold bacon. 'That, Terri, is one of mine. Keep it on.' She tips her head to one side and gives me a sly smile. 'Corporate branding. It's Letitia's idea.'

She's challenging me to ask who Letitia is, but I'm not going to rise to the bait. I already know.

Gran might have failed to mention that I had the job at *Posies* on a probationary basis, but she has told me about Letitia.

'There's the broom,' Val says. 'You'd better make a start. Martin isn't paying you to stand around yakking all day.'

'I'm not a cleaner. I mean, I didn't think...' My voice trails off.

'Floristry isn't all about making up pretty bouquets and chatting up the customers, is it? You should know that by now. And anyway, I can't do it, not with the state that my poor old knees are in.'

Out of deference to Val's knees, I start sweeping the floor in the back room, wondering what on earth I have let myself in for. One of my grandmother's favourite sayings is, Beggars can't be choosers. Neither can bankrupts, it seems.

'Customer, Terri,' Val calls from the front of the shop. I pop my head around the door. 'One hand-tied bouquet; a dozen pink long-stemmed roses, some of those scented lilies that came in fresh today, and plenty of foliage. Five minutes... Let's see what you can do.'

I select a single rose from one of the buckets in the back room, and hold it up to the light that streams through the window. It is the palest pink, unblemished, and the petals are just beginning to unfurl. Perfect. I collect up roses, lilies and foliage and lay them across the table.

I pick up stems of Eucalyptus and Pittosporum, and hold them in my left hand. Turning the growing bunch, I add a rose, a lily and some pink gypsophila, repeating the sequence of foliage, flowers and filler until I run out, creating a spiral arrangement of stems. I bind a piece of string around them to secure them, then trim the stems so that they are all the same length, before taking them through for Val's scrutiny.

'Thank you, love.' Val's manner is positively tropical compared with the Siberian conditions I experienced on my arrival. She takes the bouquet from me and wraps it in a sheet of clear cellophane printed with a pink and white pattern to coordinate with the flowers. She hands them over to her customer, an elderly man in a trenchcoat and scarf. 'There you go, Nigel. Tell your ladyfriend that all she has to do is cut the string and pop them in a vase of fresh water with a sachet of flower food.'

'My Betty swears by lemonade.'

I can hardly see Nigel's lips moving through a dense moustache which seems incongruous compared with the sparse grey hair on his head.

'This is Terri, Len and June's daughter.' Val casts me a glance. 'Do you remember the Mills who ran the newsagents next door?'

'Indeed I do.' Nigel stares at me. 'I used to pop in there for my copy of *Buses Magazine*. What do I owe you, Valerie? I imagine that your George could do with a nice pair of moccasins for when he's dining at the Captain's Table. Or perhaps you'd like a summer dress for your round-the-world cruise.'

'What chance have I of going on that cruise while I'm stuck in here, working my fingers to the bone?'

'Terri can stand in for Martin's partner. I

33

expect that she's just as capable of running the shop as Letitia is.'

'I shan't abandon my son and his family until Letitia comes back. I promised her that I'd look after them.' Val plucks at her sleeve. 'You couldn't get me another blouse like this one, could you?'

'I'm doing a great line in winceyette night-gowns at the moment, but I'll see what I can do.' Nigel smiles, and turns to me. 'I run a stall at the Surrey Street Market, within touching distance of the trams. Come along sometime when you're in Croydon, and I'll see if I can do you a deal.'

I thank Nigel for his tip, silently resolving to stay away from his passion-killing sleepwear, and return to my sweeping.

Val interrupts me once Nigel has gone. 'I wonder how long you'll stay with us – *if* you should survive the week.'

'I haven't made any definite plans.'

'I'm sure you'll soon be off running your own floristry business again, an ambitious woman like you. Do you see what I mean?'

I see exactly what she means: she doesn't want me here. When my parents and I left Addis-combe, Val put the flags out – literally. She hung a decrepit Union Jack, like the ones you might see in a cathedral, so moth-eaten that it was almost transparent, out of the first-floor window of their flat. George insisted that it was to give us a good send-off, to wish us the best of luck in the future, but Mum was livid.

'Silly cow,' she said, as we drove away. 'How could she do that to us when we've been such good neighbours, Len?'

My father silenced my mother with a glower and the grating of a gearchange, as we lurched into our new lives.

Val doesn't like me, does she? I'm not sure when she turned against me, or why.

'Perhaps you could get started on making up the rest of the day's orders. I can't do any wiring nowadays – my fingers aren't up to it.' Val pauses. 'I hope that your grandmother explained that this job is only temporary. When Letitia comes back, we won't need you here any more.'

When Letitia comes back, I think as I soak a ring of plastic foam. Gran gave me the impression that Martin's long-term girlfriend had gone for good. I push single leaves of ivy into the foam, then pin small pieces of moss between them to conceal the gaps before I insert white roses evenly around the ring to form a wreath for a funeral.

Have I really laid all my regrets and resentments to rest? And have I made the right decision, returning to work for Martin Blake, the boy-next-door, my childhood sweetheart – and the man who broke my heart?

Chapter Two

Who cares if I look like a blown rose when I feel like a sixteen-year-old bud of a girl inside? I rub half a tube of revitalising moisturiser into my skin, just in case it should make any difference.

'Mum.' Sasha joins me in the bathroom, peering underneath my armpit so that I can see the reflection of her eyes in the mirror. 'I need a cardboard box, a squeezy bottle and a balloon.'

'What on earth for?'

'We're doing a project in Design and Technology. I'm going to use air pressure to make a rabbit hop into and out of its burrow.'

'Miss Hudson doesn't ask for much, does she?' I head for the kitchen where I unload our eggs into the tray in the fridge and pour the washing-up liquid into a small bowl so that Sasha can have the bottle.

'She's going to have a baby in the summer.' Sasha grabs the bits and pieces and stuffs them into her rucksack without saying thank you.

'Oh thanks, Mum.' I'm being sarcastic. 'I hope that Miss Hudson's baby grows up with better manners.'

Sasha apologises. I walk over and give her a hug. 'It's time for school.'

'I don't want to go. The boys call me names like Old MacDonald, because I don't speak like they do.'

'You'll soon be speaking like Ray Winstone – remember Mr Beaver in the film *Narnia*?'

On the way to school, Sasha and I recite 'the rain in Spain falls mainly on the plain' in something resembling a Cockney accent.

When I arrive at the Parade for work, there is a green van with *Posies* printed in gold lettering along the side, parked on the double red lines outside the shop. A man in his late sixties, a couple of inches shorter than Martin but with the same tilt of the shoulders, is unloading boxes of flowers.

'Hi, George.'

He stops and stares at me, open-mouthed. He touches his chest with his fingers peeking from the frayed cuff of a forest-green sweatshirt, and whistles through his teeth. 'You gave me a shock just then – you look so much like your mother. How is she?'

'She's fine, thanks.' At least, I haven't received any reports to the contrary.

'I was sorry to hear about your father.'

I nod, because even though fifteen years have passed since he died, I still find it difficult to talk about my dad. I shall always regret that he didn't live to see his granddaughter. I'll always miss him.

'Your mother married a millionaire, so I hear.' George sighs. 'I must get a move on. Martin will shoot me if I get another parking ticket.'

'Can I help you with those boxes?' I offer.

'These are the last ones, thanks, love.'

I follow George through the shop to the back room where he places the boxes with the rest on the table.

'Those roses are gorgeous,' I observe.

'Times have changed, Terri, and not for the better. You can buy flowers from Spalding to Bogotà down at New Covent Garden Market now. These foreign roses might look like topnotch blooms, but they have no scent. Give me a traditional English rose any day.'

From the twinkle in his bloodshot eyes, I'm not sure that he is referring to roses of the Genus *Rosa*. George always had an eye for the women. He is, in spite of the grey moustache, whiskery sideburns and the veins that thread across his nose, still a charismatic man.

'A year ago, I thought that I had retired for good. Then I returned to work, thinking it would take a couple of months for Val and me to find someone else to run the shop, but six months later I was still here. That's when Martin said he was coming back from Spain with the kids. I said, "Son, I'll help you out for as long as you need me. Family's family".'

It seems that George hasn't changed all that much since I last saw him. Once he starts talking, he can't stop.

'Actually, it's a blessing in disguise. Val wants to book us on a world cruise, but I've always reckoned that you can learn far more about the world from inside your own local than you can from a deckchair on the high seas. All you'd get to see is water, and dolphins, maybe, and icebergs if your captain wasn't paying attention to the steering.' George snorts as he glances at his watch. 'I've been chinwagging for too long. See you soon, I hope, Terri.'

Once George has gone, I turn my attention to the boxes. I assume that all the fresh stock needs conditioning – to prolong the life of the flowers – so I get started. I run cold water into clean buckets, then work through the roses, removing all the lower leaves from the stems so that there is nothing soft to rot under the waterline, and cutting the stems at an angle to allow them to take up as much water as possible.

As I snip and discard, I become aware that I am being watched.

I turn to find a small boy in pyjamas and slippers at the foot of the stairs that lead up from the back room into the flat. He's about five years old, with thick fair hair that sticks up from his head, and blue eyes that glitter from a grubby face. He waves a light sabre, a small stick of coloured plastic that you might find in a cereal packet.

'You must be Obi-Wan Kenobi,' I say politely.

He takes a deep breath and blows it out slowly. *'I am Darth Vader...'*

'Is that you, Dad?' I hear Martin call from upstairs. 'Come on up!'

'It's Princess Leia,' the boy calls back and ducks behind the banisters.

'Will you stop messing about, Elliot. I must have told you to get dressed a million times this morning.'

'Only three times actually, Mr Skywalker.'

'We're supposed to be at school by now!' Do I detect a touch of hysteria in Martin's voice? 'Hurry up, Cassie!'

I make my way up to the flat. The third step creaks under my feet, and the seventh and the

39

fourteenth. I used to count them as a child, running up ahead of Val to find Martin. Today, I follow Darth Vader through the small hallway which is still stamped with Val's taste – or lack of it – in décor; floral wallpaper and a pink carpet pricked out with gold fleur-de-lys.

There are three photographs on the wall. The first one is a giant studio portrait of Martin with his arm around a woman's waist. It has to be Letitia. Martin is looking down at her face, while she gazes out of the frame. A lump catches in my throat. They make a beautiful couple.

There is a picture of Martin's family on a sailing boat: two children in sunhats, holding out ice creams; Martin frowning, in Bermuda shorts and sandals; Letitia flashing a length of tanned thigh. The third photo is of Letitia on her own, standing against a backdrop of sea and sky, her breasts thrust out and barely covered by a red bikini, and her legs dusted with sand, like Pamela Anderson on *Baywatch*.

Why isn't Letitia here with her kids? What business is so pressing that she can't keep them with her? I couldn't contemplate the idea of me and Sasha living apart, no matter how brief the arrangement. As it is, I can hardly bear to let my daughter out of my sight.

I step over a set of handlebars, a pair of wheels with spokes, tyre levers and spanners – parts of a dismembered bicycle, and the tools to reassemble it, I guess – and follow Darth Vader into what I remember, before Val and George gave the property and the business to Martin and moved to nearby Woodside, as a cosy sitting room with a roaring fire.

The boy perches on the arm of a cream leather sofa. He aims the remote control at an enormous widescreen television, and Jerry Springer is in the room with us, mediating in a row between a young woman and a heavily tattooed man. The woman is hysterical and the audience is screaming, *Who is the dad?*

'Elliot, will you switch that thing off!' Martin rushes in.

'No.'

Martin lunges towards the boy and snatches the remote. Elliot rolls down onto the sofa and bursts into tears.

'You've hurt my hand,' he wails. 'You're the meanest daddy in the whole wide world and I'm going to get you with my light saver.'

'You're the stupidest brother in the universe,' crows a girl whom I assume is Cassie. She stands in front of the bowl of pebbles which flicker rather feebly in the fireplace, with her arms folded tight across her chest. 'Everyone knows that it's a light sabre with a B. B, b, b, b!'

Elliot stands up and runs at his sister with his light sabre outstretched in front of him. Martin tackles him just before he can make contact, whisks him up in the air, and drops him on the sofa. 'You stay there!'

'But Daddy, I've got to get dressed,' Elliot wheedles.

I don't think that Martin has noticed me. I clear my throat. Twice.

He turns, eyebrows raised. 'Terri?'

Some men can't do rough and ready. Martin is

41

one of those who can. Think Hugh Jackman. There are crescents of shadow under his eyes. One cheek is smooth and streaked with blood where he's nicked his skin shaving, and the other is dark with stubble. His shirt is spattered with milk, or toothpaste, and unbuttoned down to his navel, revealing the hair on his chest.

'I thought you might be able to go through today's orders with me, but I can see that it isn't a good time.' I become aware that my fingers are at my throat, stroking the skin exposed above the neckline of my top. Blushing, I let my hands creep slowly down to my sides, and clamp them firmly against my hips.

'I can't go to school today.' It is Cassie who breaks the awkward silence. She must be a couple of inches taller than Sasha. She is wearing a grey skirt, tights and a green jumper. Her shoulder-length brown hair is in tangles.

'Well, you can't stay here,' says Martin. 'I've got four weddings and a funeral on today.'

Tears fill Cassie's eyes. 'How can I go when I am so ill?'

'Where?' Martin bends slightly. A mistake, I suspect, because Cassie makes a theatrical gesture of rubbing her forehead.

'I've got such a headache.'

'You sound just like your mother,' Martin says.

'Where is Mummy?' Elliot pipes up.

'She's in Spain,' says Cassie with authority. 'How many times do I have to tell you?'

'I want my mummy,' Elliot says wistfully.

Martin glances at me, his lips curving into the slightest smile. I know what it's like. You love your children, but sometimes they can drive you mad. Some of the awkwardness of the previous day evaporates. We connect ... as parents.

'Who'd be a single parent?' Martin sighs.

'Tell me about it.' I hesitate. 'Why don't you stick a syringe of Calpol in Cassie's lunchbox so that she can take it if she needs it during the day?'

'No way,' Martin says sharply.

'I've done it several times, once when Sasha was going down with chicken-pox, and again when she had tonsillitis. When you have masses of work on, and no alternative childcare arrangements, what can you do?'

'I don't want some interfering dinnerlady accusing me of planting drugs on my kids.'

At that point, I leave Martin to it, following the sound of the bell downstairs and into the front of the shop. I breathe in the scent of crushed chrysanths and dried lavender, keeping a discreet eye on the customer, a woman of about my age in a long black quilted coat, as she browses along the flowers on the staging.

'Can I help you at all?' I ask eventually.

The woman looks up and smiles. 'It's so peaceful in here. You must love it.'

'Yes, I love working with flowers,' I say, uncertain yet exactly what I think of my position at *Posies*. 'Are you looking for anything in particular?'

'A gift for my aunt. It's her birthday, and I'm fed up with buying her vouchers.'

'A bowl of scented hyacinths makes a lovely present. They come in all shades of white, pink and blue.'

'Pink – it's her favourite colour.'

I look along the pots on the staging. As I have noticed before, the hyacinths that have burst into flower are all blue, and those that are about to are tinged with a cyanotic hue. 'I'll see if we have any pink ones out the back.'

Martin is working in the back room. I can hardly see him for flowers and foliage. His sleeves are rolled up, revealing the sinewy strength of his forearms.

'Are you looking for something special?' he asks.

I suppress the urge to say that I thought I had already found it, many years ago, and lost it. 'Pink hyacinths,' I say.

'Oh dear. My dad bought a job lot of bulbs cheap from one of his mates down at the Claret, and they all came up the same colour. What about pink roses or carnations instead?'

'I'll ask.' I send my customer out of the shop with a potted pink orchid, just as Val turns up for work.

'I notice that you haven't had time to slip your uniform on yet,' she says.

'Er, no.'

'Go and fetch your tabard then. I'll look after the till while you give Martin a hand.' She smiles. 'You don't mind, do you?'

I don't mind at all. It's what I've been waiting for, an opportunity to talk to him, to ask the questions I have been carrying about in my heart and my head for the past twenty-three years, and more besides.

'What can I do?' I pull up a chair opposite Martin across the table in the back room. There

44

is no way that I am wearing Val's tabard – I have my pride.

'You can wire those roses.' He waves at a pile of flowers at one end of the table. 'I'm about half-way through today's orders. My dad's taken the first batch – the hatch and despatch. There are just the matches to go – four bridal bouquets, a pedestal, table and some pew-end arrangements.'

I pick up a pair of scissors while Martin continues, 'I'm sorry if I was snappy with you earlier.'

'If? You *were* snappy with me.' I pick up a rose and snip it off, leaving a small length of stalk. 'Apology accepted anyway.' I cut a piece of wire and push one end through the side of the rose's bowl-shaped base, or to use the technical term, the hypanthium, so that it penetrates the other side. I wrap the wire around the stalk several times, then straighten it and wrap it with green tape to create the illusion of a natural stem. I can wire roses in my sleep.

Martin turns his attention to a pair of metal stands on the table. 'I was surprised when your gran said that you were planning to come back to Addiscombe after so many years. Would you pass me the glue-gun? It's beside you.'

'Not exactly planning.' I hand over the gun, making sure that our fingers do not touch. 'She told me about the advert you placed in the *Croydon Guardian*.'

Martin frowns. 'Lil happened to mention that you were looking for work up this way, and considering my situation, wondered if I could put a few hours your way.' He flashes me a brilliant smile. 'I must have been mistaken. Your gran's

45

quite a gossip – I can't always keep up with what she says.'

'So she's told you every embarrassing detail of my life?' I say ruefully, wondering if Martin asked Gran about me from time to time, or whether she volunteered the information. The latter, I assume, considering the way that he treated me – no, ignored me – at the end.

Martin chuckles. 'There's no need to look so worried, Terri. I'm sure Lil's told you just as much about me as she's told me about *you* – not that I've had such a colourful love-life as you have.' Abruptly, he falls silent. He runs his hands through his hair. 'I'm sorry, I didn't mean to insult you.'

'All those stories about my exes?' I try to laugh it off. 'It's the way Gran tells them.'

Martin inserts a skeleton of dark foliage and trailing ivy into the oasis in the top of the stands, then adds heads of ruby-red roses and much larger scarlet Amaryllis flowers which always remind me of the tubas in the brass band in which my father used to play, to flesh it out.

'This is the second order for wedding flowers that I've made up for this lady.' Martin looks up. 'She dumped the last groom at the altar. Changed her mind at the last minute in front of her friends and family.'

'How cruel.'

'Not exactly. The groom's wife turned up at the critical, "is there any impediment" part of the ceremony. You see, there are two sides to every story,' Martin says quietly. 'Judging from the number of arrangements that she's ordered this time, the bride-to-be has found herself a groom with deeper pockets.'

'Talking of money...' A thorn pricks into my finger and embeds itself there. I squeeze it, but it shifts deeper. 'Is there any chance you could give me some of my pay in advance? I wouldn't normally ask, but–'

'You're bankrupt,' Martin interrupts. 'Your gran told me that too. I don't think that she meant to – it slipped out.'

I can see my face turning the same colour as the roses, in the reflection in the stainless-steel kettle on the draining-board opposite. So Martin knows that I embellished my CV, that 'running a successful floristry enterprise' was a cover for 'my business went belly-up'.

Martin pulls a pen and chequebook out of his trouser pocket, and starts scribbling on a cheque. He tears it off and holds it out to me. 'Go on, take it.' He waves it at me, like Chris Tarrant on *Who Wants To Be A Millionaire*, except that I have no aspirations to be wealthy. All I need is enough of my wage to buy some groceries.

'I don't want to sound ungrateful, but when I said money, I meant hard cash. I haven't got a bank account at the moment, and anyway,' I gaze at the figure, 'it's far too much.' What does Martin think he is doing? Trying to make up for what happened between us, all those years ago?

'I'm not going to apologise this time,' he says. 'I know what it's like to be short. I'll give you the equivalent when I cash up at the end of the day.'

'Thanks.' I decide to accept Martin's advance gracefully. 'Money is tight at the moment.'

'Didn't your mother marry the Billy Butlin of the South Devon coast?'

'I'm not a charity case,' I bridle.

'I'm not suggesting that you are. I'm just saying that if I was your mother, and I had money, I'd want to offer some financial assistance to help you get back on your feet.'

'My mother *had* money, that's true, but she hasn't now. She sold the B & B to pay David's divorce settlement to his most recent ex-wife, and they've had to remortgage the holiday park, and their house.'

'Sasha's father doesn't contribute anything either?'

I shake my head. I don't want to talk about him, but Martin presses on. 'Don't you worry about Sasha not having contact with him, and how it might affect her later on?'

'I think that Gran might have misinformed you about the kind of relationship I had with Sasha's dad.'

Martin gazes at me, and my pulse falters. 'Is that because you misinformed *her?*' he asks slowly.

I watch him stand up and count out ten shallow bowls and ten pinholders from the shelf beneath the tax files. He places them in front of me.

'If you do the table decorations, Terri, I'll start the bride's bouquet. Follow the same theme as the pedestal. Five stems of Amaryllis for each one.'

I fix a pinholder into each bowl and cover them with water. I choose five stems of Amaryllis, and press the fleshy stems onto the pins, putting the taller stems and larger flower-heads in the centre of the display to draw the eye, and the shorter ones at the edge, followed by some spiky foliage. I repeat each action ten times. That is the difference between flower arranging as a hobby and as a business. You don't make up one of a design, and sit back, saying, 'Wow, that's fantastic.' You make several, sometimes more, until your fingers ache.

I finish off by hiding the tops of all the pinholders with handfuls of glass marbles. Why should I hide anything from Martin?

'I've never been brave enough to admit the truth to my grandmother, that I conceived Sasha in a one-night stand.'

'Why not? Lil would have called you a hussy and lectured you on how people's sense of doing right has changed over the years, but she would have forgiven you.'

'I think she'd have felt very hurt, that I'd let her down in some way. You see, Gran never slept with anyone else except Grandad. You didn't mess about in those days.'

Martin's eyes twinkle with amusement. 'That's because it was too risky, not necessarily because people had higher moral standards.'

'In Gran's youth, there was a stigma attached to having an illegitimate child. I didn't exactly lie to her. I led her to believe that Sasha's father was the baddie, and that he left me when he discovered that I was pregnant.'

'He did abandon you, if he never arranged to pay any maintenance, or send his daughter birthday and Christmas cards.'

'He couldn't.'

'You didn't tell him?' Martin secures the stems of a shower-style bouquet of roses, Amaryllis and ivy trails with raffia and ribbon.

'I did sort of tell him – about the pregnancy. I caught him at the bus-station, just as he was about to set out with his mates on a rugby tour.' I pick up a stray glass marble, drop it back into the jar with the rest that I haven't used, and screw the lid back on. The memory of my second encounter with Sasha's father flits back into my mind like a toxic moth...

'Hi,' I said, trying to draw Robbie away from the crowd of young men in rugby shirts who were assembled beneath a shelter at the bus station to avoid the rain.

'Er, how are you?' Robbie said.

'I think I'm having a baby.'

He held out his hand as if he was about to shake mine. 'Congratulations.'

'If I am, it's yours.'

His complexion paled; he swayed and fell back onto the ground, catching his head on his backpack. If he'd hit the paving slabs, I might have been telling Martin a very different story about Sasha's father. Three of Robbie's team-mates slapped his cheeks, and squirted a bottle of Lucozade at him to revive him, then helped him onto his feet.

'What on earth did you say to him?' one of Robbie's mates asked me.

'That I might be pregnant with his child. I mean, I haven't done a test yet, but...'

He laughed and clapped Robbie on the back.

'Well done, mate. Not only did you score, it seems that you converted the bloody try.'

'She isn't sure,' Robbie said weakly. 'Do the test, and we'll talk about this when I get back, Tessa.'

'It's Terri.' A bus drew up beside us, spewing black fumes. Morning sickness? I had all-day sickness, and the stench sent me running for the toilets. When I returned to the shelter, Robbie and his mates had gone.

The rugby tour gave me time to think. I didn't want a relationship with Robbie, but I did want a baby – desperately. Perhaps the tick-tock of my biological clock deafened me to the voice of my conscience, which should have been urging me to consider contraception.

I tried to tell Robbie about our child one more time, just after Sasha was born. I wanted him to see how beautiful our daughter was; I wanted someone to share her with, but when Sharon found out through her brother that Robbie was engaged to be married, I decided not to make contact.

I was selfish – I can see that now. But, as Gran says, what the eye doesn't see, the heart doesn't grieve over, and I guessed that Robbie would have more children with his wife...

'You should have told him,' Martin says, bringing me back to the present.

I take a quick guilt trip across the back room to rinse my hands in the sink as he continues, 'What about Sasha? Didn't you consider her feelings at all?'

'Of course I did.' I bite my lip. 'I did what I thought was best for her – at the time.' I want to tell him off for making judgements when he doesn't know anything about me any more, apart from what my grandmother has told him, but for the sake of harmony, and the fact that we are going to be working together, I restrain myself.

'I'm not judging you. I'm just saying that, if I had a child, I'd want to be involved with bringing it up in some way.' Martin rubs his forehead. 'We haven't done very well between us, have we?'

'What do you mean?'

'Letitia and I... I can't believe that we've ended up living apart.'

'Gran said you'd taken your family to Spain to settle there,' I say because, according to my rules of gossip, one confidence deserves another. 'A few months later, you were back.'

'When Letitia suggested that we moved to Spain, I pictured matadors, mountains and olive groves. She was attracted by the sunshine, siestas and sangria. Anyway, we sold our house and used the equity to buy a bar, with living accommodation above, on the Costa del Sol. I didn't want to burn our bridges by selling up completely, so I decided to let my parents run *Posies* for a while. Letitia accused me of lack of commitment, but I called it commonsense. I mean, I'd never been to Spain before. How did I know if I was going to like it?'

Martin pauses. 'It turns out that I was right – I'm a florist, not a bar manager. I can do tulips in a trug, but not chicken in a basket. And Letitia's idea of hard work is a couple of hours behind the bar, followed by a siesta.' He stops suddenly as if he realises that he has said too much, and regrets sounding disloyal. 'Our *Place in the Sun* turned out to be more like the soap, *El Dorado*, except that it didn't last as long. I missed England, the cold and the rain, *Posies*, and my friends at the Cycling Club.' He tips his head to one side. 'What's so funny, Terri?'

'I can't imagine you in goggles and cycling kit.'

'Lycra is great for disguising the spare tyre – I'm referring to my stomach, not the bike.' Martin grins. 'I must do some work on it.'

'I noticed that it was in pieces.'

'I meant that I should get down to the gym sometime. I haven't been since I returned from Spain. I can't keep asking my mother to babysit.'

'I bet that you can't wait to have Letitia home.'

'The kids are desperate to see her.'

But what about you? I want to ask.

'We have a buyer for the bar, and Letitia's staying to sort out the money and the paperwork,' Martin goes on. 'It shouldn't take much longer.'

'How did you two meet in the first place?'

'I was out with some friends, celebrating a divorce, funnily enough.'

'Gran didn't tell me that you'd been married.'

'It wasn't *my* divorce.' Martin smiles. 'Anyway, there was this young woman working behind the bar in the pub. I remember joking that she looked like a weathergirl, and it was indeed a whirlwind romance. I asked her for a date, and within a week, we were a couple. Two months later, she was pregnant. I asked her to marry me, but she turned me down, and moved in instead. I didn't mind – there was no one else,' he adds softly, and my heart twists. Is he – could he possibly be referring to me? 'I could see us running *Posies* together.'

Continuing the Blake dynasty, I think.

'Letitia was quite a catch, and she loved me, so she said – whatever love is.'

Whatever love is... The words echo in my mind. What is love? A reassuring squeeze of the hand? A secret smile? The offer of a crumpled tissue? Shared jokes? I glance towards Martin. History?

'Terri!' Val calls through from the front of the shop. 'Put the kettle on, Michael Schumacher's dropped by.'

'Do you still take three sugars in your coffee?' I ask Martin, assuming that, as well as being the ancillary florist and cleaner, I am also expected to adopt the role of tea-lady when required.

'Just one. Your gran says that I'm sweet enough already, don't you, Lil?' He looks up and my grandmother walks through the doorway, all five foot nothing of her.

Gran suspects that she is shrinking, vertically at least, but she is no shrinking violet. A startlingly turquoise mac that might well have come from the same market stall as Val's blouses, hugs her matronly curves.

'Can I take your coat?' Martin offers.

'Oh no, I'm not stopping.' Keeping a grip on her stick, Gran turns to me. 'Where's my Sasha?' Her teeth slip on her gums, yet the piercing expression in her sharp blue eyes belies her age. I can never quite remember whether she is eighty-four or eighty-five, and when I ask her, she claims to have lost count of her birthdays years ago.

'I told you – Sasha's at school today.'

'Oh?' Gran grips the sleeve of my sweater with twisted fingers. I give her a brief hug. Looking down, I can see the pink of her scalp through the white hair that waves across the top of her head. She smells of talc and rose-water.

She steps back in her brogues and beige nylon trousers that are cut too short, revealing folds of fluffy pink sock at her ankles.

'It's lucky that I have such a useful grand-daughter, isn't it, Martin?'

'Lucky for whom?' Martin winks at me.

'Don't you cheek me, my lad.' Gran's voice is sharp, her manner flirtatious. 'I can remember you going to school with your knobbly knees sticking out from your shorts.'

Did Martin have knobbly knees? I can't remember his knees. His thighs, yes. In shorts, not Lycra. Long, hard and lean, tanned and fit from hours of cycling. I can see him now, riding towards me at great speed across the park, then skidding to a halt sideways on, laughing at my assumption that he was going to hit me.

'I'd never hurt you,' he said, dismounting. He balanced his bike with one hand and tentatively reached for mine with the other. 'Can I walk you home?'

'All the way?' I was teasing – it was only a few hundred yards back to the Parade – but then I realised that Martin was gazing at me, his eyes flickering with uncertainty. He swallowed hard, then spoke so quietly that I could hardly hear him.

'All the way,' he said. 'With me? Would you?'

I squeezed his hand and moved closer, leaned up and kissed him on the lips...

'Are you and Sasha free for lunch at the weekend, Terri?' Gran brings me back down to earth.

'You've invited us already.'

'Have I?'

'We agreed to arrive at yours at twelve on Sunday.' I hesitate. 'You are still all right to pick Sasha up from school tonight?'

'Of course I am. You can collect her at six, after I've given her some tea.'

'You don't have to do that.'

'I want to,' Gran says. 'Allow me to spoil my great-granddaughter a little. Oh, listen to me going on. I'll leave you two to it. To your work,' she adds hurriedly, with a wicked glint in her eye, and suddenly I realise that she thinks she's set me up.

'Come back to Addiscombe, Terri,' Gran had said on the phone, the day that I finally plucked up the courage to tell her that I was about to go bankrupt. Actually, I didn't put it quite like that. I recall using the term 'seriously financially challenged'. It was the Fifth of November last year, and I had just returned to the flat above *Flower Power* with Sasha after the firework display at the footie ground across the road.

'There's a job going at *Posies*,' my grandmother continued. 'You must remember Martin Blake?'

Bang! Fireworks started going off in my head. How could I forget Martin? How could anyone who met him, even the most amnesiac of goldfish, forget Martin Blake?

56

It was my parents who provided the fireworks for the Guy Fawkes-night party that the Blakes and the Mills held jointly every year from when I was four until I was fifteen. Val and George supplied the food – sausages, baked potatoes and bonfire cakes, decorated with Matchmakers chocolate sticks from our shop.

I can still recall the last party. My bright red trousers glowed almost as brightly as the flames of the Roman Candles as I stood close to Martin, imagining that I could hear his heartbeat, and yearning to feel his arms around me. How though, was I going to make this gawky, but gorgeous guy notice me, especially as his eyes were fixed on his father and my mother in the distance, level with the first line of bushes and a row of five milk bottles in the park?

'You keep holding that torch for me, June,' said George.

My mother giggled and the light of the torch she was holding bobbed up and down. Too much vodka, I suspected.

'Closer, June. Much closer. I can't see a thing,' George went on.

'You'll have to do it by feel, Georgie-boy,' Val called out from where she was standing with my dad, writing in the air with a sparkler.

'Get on and light the bloody rockets,' my dad grumbled. 'I told you, you should have left it to the expert.'

'You, you mean?' my mother shouted back. 'You can't get a fire going without half a box of lighters and a can of petrol.'

I smiled at my mother's reference to the open

fire in the living room of our flat. Dad insisted on making it up with wood he acquired on the cheap from a friend. It was invariably damp, or green, which meant that once lit, it spat, fizzled and smoked in the grate, and went out again.

The torch blacked out, George shouted in triumph, and a rocket shot out from the darkness. Not upwards into the sky, but straight at my father. Dad ducked and the rocket swooshed past his head, catching one side of his glasses. Mum's torch came back on, its beam sweeping across my father's face.

'You could have damn-well killed me, George,' Dad yelled, heading towards the line of milk bottles, clutching his mangled glasses. 'I know what you're up to. I'm not blind!'

'No thanks to my husband,' added Val, following him.

I shivered as my mother and Val restrained my father from popping George one on the nose.

'Terri, you're upset,' Martin said from beside me.

Of course I wasn't. It was an accident. My dad wasn't hurt, but I was frozen in my tight trousers, cotton shirt and thin jacket. 'I'm petrified,' I whispered back, and the next thing I knew, I was in the alleyway behind the Parade with Martin's lips on mine. It was dark. It was cold. It was heaven...

How could I ever forget the boy next door? Although I've tried, believe me.

'He's desperate for help from someone with experience of the industry,' Gran had continued on the phone. 'His girlfriend is stuck in Spain, so

58

he has to look after his children single-handed, poor lad. Val and George have come out of retirement to help him, but Val's suffering from those knees of hers, down to her having been on her feet running that shop for nigh on forty years, and as for dear George ... with his fondness for a tipple, I don't think he'll last much longer.' Gran sighed deeply. 'I'd love to have a chance to get to know my only great-grandchild properly before my heart gives out on me.'

'Your heart?!'

'I have a touch of angina, that's all.'

'Mum didn't mention that you were ill.'

'I haven't told her.' Gran paused. 'You mustn't tell her. I don't want to worry June when she lives so far away. You know, I dream of taking Sasha down to Waddon Ponds to feed the ducks, like we used to when you were little.'

I realised with a twinge of guilt that Sasha was no longer little enough to enjoy such simple pleasures. I should have made more effort to visit my grandmother when Sasha was younger.

I watch Gran leave the shop and make for the mobility scooter that is parked outside on the pavement. It has racing-green bodywork, and a tent-like cover to protect the driver from the elements.

Gran climbs stiffly into the seat, fiddles with the controls and shoots off in a series of jerks along the pavement. She never did learn to drive, except from the back seat.

'I've always fancied a convertible,' Martin says. 'Lil's a feisty lady.'

I can think of other ways to describe my grandmother, like 'nosy' and 'interfering'. 'She isn't well,' I say instead. 'It's her heart.'

'I didn't know,' Martin says, and I wonder if he is a little hurt that my grandmother didn't confide in him. 'That's typical of her. She doesn't like to worry anyone.' He stretches and rubs the back of his neck. 'It's strange how things work out, isn't it, Terri?' He looks at me directly. 'I didn't think I'd ever see you again. It must be down to the Hand of Fate.'

I smile to myself. Martin and I meeting again has more to do with the Hand of Gran.

Sharon likes to consider herself as my personal dating agency, having fixed me up with two of my former boyfriends and, indirectly, with Robbie.

'It's for you, Mum.' Sasha hands me the phone on the evening of my first day at *Posies*. 'Sharon wants to know why you haven't been in touch with her for two whole days.'

'Thanks, Sash.' I picture Sharon with Holly, her daughter, beside her, and the twins toddling about at her feet.

'I wish I could pop round and share a full-bodied Australian with you,' Sharon says.

'I'm not into threesomes.'

'I was talking about a Shiraz or a Pinot noir.' Sharon's voice is teasing.

'Sure.'

'So, how is it going?' she asks.

'Hang on a mo. I've barely been here long enough to chat up the postman.'

'I'm not asking about your love-life,' she giggles. 'I'm asking about your new job.'

60

'Oh, that. I'm on trial. And the position, if I do get it, is temporary, not permanent.' Aware that Sasha is eavesdropping, I wave her away, and lower my voice to a whisper. 'Val is a slavedriver, and I have to wear a tent.'

'What about Martin? What is it like to work for your childhood sweetheart?'

'It was a little awkward at first, seeing him again after all this time.' My face grows warm. Martin has seen me naked, and not just when I was three and he was five, and we were playing in the bath...

'Has he apologised for dumping you?'

That is what Sharon and I have always assumed. I can almost hear our conversations, sitting on the bus in Paignton on the way to school, endlessly analysing the possible reasons for Martin's lack of response to my letters. We knew that he wasn't dead, because Gran would have said so.

'Whether he dumped me or not, Martin is still an attractive man.'

'His girlfriend might be in Spain, but he's still involved with her. They've been together for over ten years,' Sharon reminds me. 'Martin is as good as married.'

'I didn't say I was going to do anything about it,' I say huffily. 'Give me some credit!'

'What? More? I thought you'd learned your lesson about asking for credit.'

I smile ruefully, recalling that piece of paper confirming my bankruptcy.

'How's the flat?' she goes on. 'Have you settled in?'

'I wish I hadn't signed a six-month tenancy

agreement. Do you remember that television series, *The Young Ones?*'

'About the students who shared digs?'

'Yes. Well, our place is like that. Festering.'

'Can't you have a word with the landlord?'

'I'm just about to, as I can't get the boiler to work. It's packed up. I hope that he isn't still asleep – it sounded as if he and a ladyfriend were practising for *Strictly Come Dancing* for most of last night.'

'Mum, you said you were going to have a *quick* chat with Sharon,' Sasha says when I eventually put the phone down and stand up. 'You've been nattering for over an hour. Where are you off to now?'

'To have a word with Pat.'

'I'll come with you.'

We stand outside the upstairs flat, waiting for Pat to answer Sasha's knock. When his head appears around the door, his hair is untidy, his complexion a dusty salmon-pink, and there is a strange tideline at the level of his Adam's apple. He doesn't invite us inside.

'I sense,' he says, 'that I am in hot water.'

I relax slightly. 'You would be if I had any.'

'Have you checked the pilot light on the boiler?'

'It won't ignite.'

'Ah, there's a knack to it.' Pat doesn't appear to be about to make a move.

'Are you going to demonstrate this knack?' I ask impatiently.

When our landlord informed me that he occupied the flat upstairs, I wasn't sure whether to be relieved that he was on the spot to deal with any problems that might arise, or concerned that he'd be forever popping in to keep an eye on his new tenants. In his more conventional mode of dress, he reminded me a little of Michael Douglas, but I am no Catherine Zeta Jones to succumb to the allure of an older man.

'Let me slip into something more comfortable and I'll be right with you.' Pat returns in a T-shirt, joggers that are too short, and red patent shoes with stiletto heels. 'I'm an Am Dram fanatic, by the way, a founder member of the local society.'

'You must have been practising last night,' I comment, wondering if Pat will accept a subtle hint about the noise rather than a blunt approach to ensure good neighbourly relations.

'Did I keep you awake?'

'I'm finding it difficult to sleep,' I explain. 'It's being in a strange place...'

'And not having a bed, I imagine.'

I hesitate. 'It's a bit late for panto, isn't it?'

'It's a one-off performance of *Cinderella*,' Pat announces, rather glibly in my opinion, as if he has been practising that line, as well as the lines of the play.

'You must be one of the Ugly Sisters,' Sasha says, and I wince at her frankness. I don't think that she means to be rude.

'Oh no, I am not. I am the leading lady.' Pat performs an ungainly pirouette in his heels before heading downstairs. Sasha and I follow him into our flat, where Pat makes a quick inspection before he examines our boiler. 'I expect you to repair any damage that your Blu-tack does to the walls,' he says, observing Sasha's artworks.

'As long as you don't blame me for the stiletto marks in the lino.'

Pat looks down at my fluffy lilac slippers. 'I don't think you'll do much damage in those.' Grinning, he fixes the boiler and leaves. When the water has had time to heat, I run a sink of hot water for Sasha to wash her face in, and a bath for me.

Sasha hangs around at the bathroom door.

'Thank goodness Pat's gone and left us in peace,' I say as I search for a new bottle of bubblebath. I find my landlord's presence unnerving, when he is sporting stilettos, even if it is for the sake of performance art.

'He hasn't gone,' says Sasha. 'He's behind you.'

Apprehension pricks up my spine. I turn sharply. 'There's no one there.'

'Oh yes, there is,' Sasha giggles.

'You're pulling my leg.'

'Oh no, I'm not.'

'Oh yes, you are! Come here, you cheeky minx.' I grab for my daughter and catch her, pulling her into my arms in a wriggling hug.

'If Pat is Cinderella, why isn't he wearing a glass slipper?' Sasha asks when I finally release her.

'Good point, Petal.' I smile to myself, thinking of the stilettos. But I have far more pressing concerns than the details of Pat's costume. I lean over the bath and flick my hand through the water running out of the hot tap. It has gone cold again.

Just my luck. I am beginning to feel that if I were to audition for panto, I would be chosen to be the back end of the horse.

Will I have any more success mending my confidence, which has been shattered by bankruptcy, than Pat has had, repairing the boiler? And can I fix it for me and Sasha to lead happy lives in Addiscombe, in spite of Gran's interference, Val's antagonism and Martin being in love with somone else?

Chapter Three

I'd love a home of my own to share with Sasha, but who will offer me a mortgage now? If I should play and win the Lottery, I would choose a house like my grandmother's, full of character and in need of some TLC.

Gran has lived in the same three-bedroomed terrace in one of the narrow roads off Lower Addiscombe Road since the 1960s. The porch runs the full width of the house, across the door and living-room window, creating the conditions that you might find inside a furnace or freezer, depending on the time of year. Today, it will no doubt feel like the Arctic.

'If we'd been at home in Devon,' Sasha says pointedly, as we stand outside, waiting for Gran to open the door, 'I'd be playing with Holly at Sharon's house.'

'It'll make a change to see Nan and Great-Granma for Sunday lunch.'

'It isn't the same as having friends of my own age.'

'You'll soon make friends at school.'

'I have already, but some of the other girls tease me because we have dinner at lunchtime, and tea at dinnertime.'

'Would you like me to have a word with Miss Hudson?'

'No way, Mum. I can handle it.'

'As long as you're sure.' I recall my mother trying to reassure me in the same way when we moved from Addiscombe to Devon to follow my parents' dream of an easier life at the seaside. It wasn't my dream though, and it didn't turn out quite as they expected either.

I recall my first sight of Highcliffe View, a rambling detached house, rendered white with black windowframes. I half-expected Basil Fawlty himself to leap out of the laundry basket that the previous occupants had left at the bottom of the stairs in the hall.

The sea views that my mother had bragged about to Val turned out to be in the singular, from the attic room. The remaining windows looked out on cypress hedges and the Redsands Holiday Park across the road, rows of caravans tumbling down the hillside to the edge of the cliff. How I envied those holidaymakers in their caravans! No one so much as raised their voice in the B&B, apart from my parents and the occasional guest complaining about the watered-down tomato ketchup.

My mother bleached her hair and performed for the visitors, a caricature of a pub landlady in a soap. My father remained in the background, laying the tables with stiff linen cloths and cleaning the ashtrays. Even when I escaped to my room, I couldn't get away from the smell of fags, black pudding and floor polish. I wore Martin's ring, and wrote love-letters to him, outpourings of passion and hope. A soul laid bare in gold ink on purple paper, pre-sprayed with my mother's Chanel No 5.

Before I began to compose each letter, I would

count all the seagulls that I could spot from my seat in the attic room, since there weren't that many magpies on the coast, and look for an omen of how my letter would be received. One for sorrow, two for joy...

Dear, or *My Darling Martin? Luv,* or *All my Love?* I agonised over the nuance of every word. It sounds pathetic now, but Martin was my first love, and I wasn't brave enough to press for a resolution in case it should turn out to be the one that I didn't want.

Mum said that I was wasting my time – Martin wouldn't write back. There was no point brooding in the attic, waiting for my prince to come. She bought me a black skirt and lace pinafore, and sent me to the four-star hotel along the road to learn the art of Silver Service waitressing. I returned to serve cod and chips to the B&B guests.

'There are plenty more fish in the sea,' Mum said, which was true for her. Her fish swam up in the form of David from the Redsands Holiday Park. After Dad died, David became my mother's second husband, twelve years her senior. He attributes the success of his business to the creation of his mascot, Marky the Mackerel. Dressed in his scaly costume, he compères the karaoke nights, organises the kids' entertainments, and judges the disco-dancing competitions.

'Here's Nan,' Sasha says happily as a sleek silver convertible pulls up outside my grandmother's house.

Long legs in shiny black opaque tights and high-heeled boots slide out from the car, followed by a red pencil skirt and the rest of my mother. She leans back across the driver's seat, and lifts out a cardboard box.

My mother's hair is frizzy and fake-blonde. Gold hoop earrings tremble against her high cheekbones, and her eyes and lips shimmer in the pale sunshine. A thick layer of coppery foundation cannot disguise the blemishes and creases in her sun-damaged skin that reminds me of elephant hide. Of course, being a reformed suntan addict myself, I shouldn't be so critical of her complexion. That'll be me in a few years' time.

'Hi there, Sasha,' Mum says, kissing her.

'Haven't you forgotten someone?' I say.

'I'm sorry. Morning, Terri.' She gives me a brief hug.

'I meant, where is David?'

'He's playing golf at his club just outside Torquay. He's probably at the nineteenth hole by now.' My mum shivers, in spite of her fur-trimmed cardigan. 'Come on, Mother, hurry up and open the door.'

Sasha stretches up and keeps her finger pressed on the doorbell. 'Do you think she's gone out?'

'She would never leave that electric chair here if she was going out.' Mum turns to me. 'If I should ever consider buying a mobility scooter, you're to take me to the nearest vet to have me put down.'

Alongside the scooter that is parked inside the porch, there are two terracotta pots – one empty, the other holding a flourishing Christmas cactus that has flowered late. There is also a row of shoes, and a mousetrap containing neither cheese nor mouse.

69

Gran finally arrives at the door, then takes another couple of minutes to open it, struggling with various bolts and locks that she had fitted after my grandfather died. She holds her arms out wide to greet us, showing off her apron with *Come and Get It* embroidered on the front. Underneath, she is wearing her Sunday best: a pleated skirt, blouse fastened at the collar with a paste jewel brooch in the shape of a butterfly, and Black Watch tartan slippers.

'How's my darling great-granddaughter?' she says fondly.

'Fine, thanks.' Sasha hands over the bunch of daffodils I brought back from *Posies* yesterday and made up with a ribbon. 'What's for dinner, Great-Granma? I'm starving.'

'Didn't your mum feed you breakfast?'

Sasha shakes her head.

'Oh, Sasha,' I remonstrate, with a smile.

'Only toast,' she says, 'and cornflakes and a banana.'

'Not much then for a growing girl.' Gran winks at me. 'I wanted to do you some nice lambshanks or pig trotters in jelly, but since all these celebrity chefs like Gordon Ramsay and Antony Worrall-what's-his-name started cooking them, you can't get them for love nor money. I had to buy a joint of pork and some fresh veg.'

'I'm not keen on veg,' Sasha says immediately.

'I'm sure that you'll be able to find something that you like.'

'Another present for you, Mother.' Mum hands over the cardboard box.

'What on earth is this?' says Gran.

'It says *Digibox* on the side,' Sasha points out.

'Thank you, June, but I can't see what use I'll get out of it. Perhaps you should take it back to the shop and ask for a refund.'

'I can't do that,' says Mum. 'David won it in the Golf Club raffle.'

'I'll hold on to it then. I might be able to swap it for something more practical down at the Lunch Club.' Gran shuffles off to leave it in the sitting room before returning to the kitchen where four saucepans steam and rattle their lids on the hob. There are not two vegetables, but six different varieties. I cringe when I see Gran add salt straight from the container into the pans. She pours a heap into the palm of her right hand, and tosses it over her left shoulder.

'What did you do that for?' Sasha says.

'To hit the Devil in the eye.'

'It's a silly superstition,' says my mother, but she collects up a few grains of salt from the worktop and follows suit. 'Just in case there is some truth in it.'

'Lunch will be served in the dining room,' Gran announces. 'Follow me.'

The room appears to have been shut up for some time. It smells of mothballs and polish. The furniture is dark with age, the shelves above the sideboard crammed with mementoes. Gran shows off the photographs before she fetches the meat in from the kitchen.

'That's your great-grandad, Sasha.' Gran points to a soldier in uniform. Then: 'That's me, picking hops in Kent one summer. That's Nan when she was a girl, in her school uniform.'

Gran hacks at the joint with a carving knife which can't have been sharpened since my grandfather died. After shaving a curl of skin from the side of his thumb to test the blade, he would carve the joint at the table, slicing the meat into translucent slivers because there was never enough to go round. By the time he'd finished, the vegetables would be cold.

'I'm so glad you and your mum came to London, Sasha.'

'Mother, this is Surrey, not London,' Mum says sniffily.

'It's both,' says Sasha. 'The postal address for Addiscombe is Surrey, but it's also in the London Borough of Croydon.'

'Thank you for that.' Mum turns to me. 'I don't know what possessed you to agree to work for the Blakes.'

'I lost my business, and have no money. I didn't want the job – I *needed* it.' I glance across at Sasha's face and realise that I've said too much. The concept of being poor has worried her since she saw children forced to eat gruel in *Oliver, The Musical*. 'Now that we're here, I'm very happy.'

'David was quite willing to keep you on the Holiday Park staff.'

'I know. It was very thoughtful of him, and I'm grateful.'

'Mum likes working with fresh flowers, not plastic ones like the ones in the caravans,' Sasha butts in.

'Well, if you've made a mistake, Terri, I don't suppose that you'll admit it.'

'You be mother, June.' Gran passes the plates

round and hands over a serving spoon for the vegetables. 'I'm expecting a representative to call about a chain next week. It has some built-in massage system that helps to keep you feeling youthful. I appreciate that it isn't going to make me look like Gloria Hunniford though – those days are long gone.'

'You never looked anything like Gloria Hunniford in the first place,' Mum says, before returning to the subject of the Blakes. 'I don't understand how you can demean yourself, Terri.'

'You never did like Martin, did you?' says Gran.

'Well, he'd hardly have won Newspaper Boy of the Year, would he?' Mum counters.

'I don't suppose that they're called newspaper boys any more,' Gran complains. 'Not with all this newfangled, politically correct thingummy-what's-it-called.'

'You mean sexual equality.' Mum's voice lingers on the word *sexual*. 'In my opinion, Women's Lib didn't do us any favours.'

'It means that we're no longer subservient to men,' I say. 'We don't have to depend on marriage to survive.'

'Hooray for liberation,' my mother says with sarcasm. 'Look at you with no man and no money. You'll never be able to afford to retire. You'll be working on the supermarket checkouts when you're in your seventies, unless you find yourself a wealthy husband.'

'Like David, you mean?' I ask.

'Time lifted the scales from your eyes, didn't it, June?' Gran smiles.

'You may mock, but David and I are perfectly

73

comfortable, in spite of the demands of his ex-wives.'

'All four of them,' Gran says gleefully.

'He's a popular man. I was lucky to meet him when I did. He was such a comfort to me after Len died, but I'm afraid that you, Terri, have left it too late. Who will look at a single mum of forty?'

'I'm not forty yet.'

'When is your birthday?'

'It shouldn't be that difficult to remember. You gave birth to me. I am your only child.'

Mum smiles. 'Such a fiery and artistic temperament. You're a Leo, your birthday is in August, so, yes, you are closer to thirty-nine than forty.'

'I *am* thirty-nine.'

'I should have loved to have gone to college,' says Gran wistfully. 'I didn't have that opportunity. In my day, a girl was expected to marry young and have children – until the war, that is.'

'I'm not going to get married, *or* work in a supermarket,' Sasha says smugly. 'I'm going to be an Egyptologist.'

My mother stares at her. 'You won't earn much studying mummies, darling.'

'Did you know,' Sasha goes on, 'that the Ancient Egyptians used a hooked stick to pull the brains out through dead people's nostrils?'

'Not at the table,' I interrupt.

'How did you know that, Mum?'

'No, I don't mean *not at the table* – I haven't a clue where they carried out that unpleasant practice. I meant, that it isn't a subject for dinnertime.'

'Miss Hudson says that they embalmed the bodies at the Pyramids.'

74

'You'll end up with some fusty old professor,' my mother interjects. 'Men of learning work for love, not money.'

'A bit like florists,' I say drily.

'The Blakes have always done well out of flowers,' says Gran, bringing the subject back to *Posies*. 'That shop of theirs has been a little goldmine. Not that they haven't worked hard for it. Look at Martin: as soon as he was old enough, he came round to you, June, and begged for a job as delivery boy – I mean, person.'

'It was Len who took him on,' says Mum. 'Poor Len, I told him there was no point in employing a cynophobe to deliver papers.'

'A what!' exclaims Sasha.

'Someone who is afraid of dogs,' says Mum.

Sasha giggles. 'You sound as if you've swallowed a dictionary, Nan.'

'Martin was bitten more than once,' Gran says.

'There you go, defending him again.'

'I've always liked him. He's a charmer. Anyone for more carrots?' Gran plonks them on Sasha's plate before she can refuse, and Sasha bravely struggles through a slice, as if it is a raw fish-eye on *I'm a Celebrity Get Me Out of Here*.

'How's George?' My mother stabs her fork into the meat on her plate. 'And Val? Is she still as stuck-up as ever?'

'I haven't had much to do with her,' I respond, aware that Sasha is listening.

'I should keep it that way, if I were you.'

It is what am I planning to do anyway. I shall work hard each day, then go home each night and leave the Blakes playing their own version of

75

Happy Families. After all, I have a family of my own.

After lunch, when my mother has driven off on the long journey back to Devon, Gran wraps some meat and potatoes up in greaseproof paper for Sasha and me to take home. She also slips a two-pound coin into Sasha's hand as we leave the house.

'You've done enough for us already,' I say, but Gran insists.

'I had a small win at Bingo. The prizes were better this week, better than the talcum powder and the corn-plasters that I won last time. There's some for you, and I've put the rest away for a rainy day.'

On the way back to the flat, we divert to the park across the road from the Parade. There is a light on in the Funeral Parlour, and there are billboards outside the newsagents, but both *Posies* and the electrical shop are shuttered up. Sasha and I head towards the children's play area that is railed off in one corner of the park. There aren't many people about; two kids playing on the multi-coloured climbing frame, and a man in a long dark coat and a Crystal Palace scarf, watching them with his back to us. I stick my hands in my pockets and prepare to freeze while Sasha has a run around.

'Can I give you this?' Sasha tries to hand me the money that Gran gave her.

'You want me to look after it while you're on the swings?'

'I want you to have it, Mum.' Sasha bites her lip. 'You can put it towards the groceries.'

'Oh, Sasha.'

'Why are you laughing?'

'We aren't that poor. Really, we can manage.'

However, neither Val nor Martin have mentioned the outcome of my week's trial. My situation is precarious. For a moment, I picture myself selling flowers from the back of Sharon's old car in some layby off the A23, on the way out of London.

Sasha tugs on my coat-sleeve. 'One of the girls in my class at school is here. She's called Cassie.'

'Cassie who?'

'Cassie Blake, of course – she's the only Cassie in my class.'

'Pardon me for not having a detailed knowledge of all your fellow pupils,' I say, wondering at Sasha's sudden sharpness with me. Is she subconsciously taking it out on me for removing her from all her friends back in Devon?

Before I can suggest that we walk straight home, Sasha slips through the mini-gate in the railings and runs up to the climbing frame. I follow.

The man with the children turns as I draw level with him. 'Hi, Terri.'

My heart skips a beat. It is Martin. He looks down and twists up the top of the plastic bag he is holding. The awkwardness that exists between us has returned – mistrust on my part, and dare I hope, a sense of shame on his?

'I can only stand so many episodes of *Pingu*,' he says. 'The kids are driving me mad, Elliot especially. We had to get out.'

'Sasha and I are on our way back from my grandmother's.'

'Push me, Daddy,' Elliot calls from where he is dangling helplessly on a swing, his legs too short to touch the ground below.

'In a minute, Ells.'

Elliot kicks his feet at the air, making the swing wobble. 'Now!'

'Okay.' Martin sighs, and I follow him to the swings, my hands in my pockets, fighting the biting cold.

Now, if Elliot was mine, I'd tell him that I was involved in a conversation and he would have to wait until I had finished, and then I would push him on the swing, not pander to him. Is Martin afraid of Elliot making a scene, or is he trying to compensate for his mother's absence?

'Push me higher, Daddy!'

'If you go any higher, you'll fly right over the top.' But Martin continues to push, while the girls try out every piece of play equipment in the park. Eventually, they skip back to us and sit on the empty swings, one on each side of Elliot.

'Our mum never brings us to the park,' Cassie complains. 'She says that it's Dad's job.'

'My mum takes me everywhere,' says Sasha.

'What do you think of London so far?' Martin asks her.

'It's okay. There doesn't seem to be much to it, just houses and shops, more houses and more shops.'

'Have you been on The Eye yet?'

Sasha shakes her head.

'What about the London Aquarium, the Science Museum, or Buckingham Palace?'

'So your mum doesn't take you everywhere,'

Cassie says triumphantly, and soars on an upswing while Sasha and Elliot go down. It makes me giddy, watching them.

'When we went to see the Wombles of Wimbledon Common, they were asleep in their burrows, weren't they, Dad?' she goes on.

'Wombles have a siesta every day.' Martin winks at me, confirming his role in the Womble deception.

'And when we visited the Queen, she was out, and Elliot was scared of the soldiers.'

'I wasn't,' Elliot shouts.

'Was.'

'Was not.' Elliot lets go of one chain on the swing. 'I'm getting off now.'

'Wait!' Martin warns, but Elliot jumps off anyway, the momentum from the swing propelling him forwards at great speed and force at the so-called 'safe' surface beneath. Martin dashes across and sweeps him up in his arms. 'I told you to wait,' he snaps, and Elliot, who was trying to be brave, bursts into tears. 'I'm sorry, Ells. I shouldn't have yelled at you. Daddy's worn out.' Martin caries his son across to a bench against the railings and sits him down.

Elliot lifts his trouserleg and stares down at his knee. 'I'm bleeding.'

'I have a packet of wipes and a box of plasters in my bag.' I dig them out.

'My mummy has plasters with pictures on them,' Elliot says.

'I have plain ones – they're much more grown-up.'

Elliot sits back, and smiles. 'My mummy was

on the phone this morning, and she said she will be back next week.'

'That's wonderful news.' I think regretfully of my job. A week, and that will be the end of it.

'I shouldn't get too excited, Ells,' Martin cuts in gently. 'Mummy said that she *hoped* to be back next week.'

Elliot's face falls, and I find myself wanting to give Letitia a piece of my mind. What kind of mother is she, keeping her children in suspense?

'Do you want to carry on playing, or shall we go home?' Martin asks. 'You must have had enough of the park by now,' he adds hopefully.

'I'm going to fly to Spain to tell Mummy to come home right now.' Elliot slides off the bench and jogs away, apparently forgetting the pain in his knee. He clambers into a spring-mounted aeroplane which reminds me of the de Havilland Heron that stands on stilts outside Airport House, the former air terminal for Croydon Aerodrome.

Elliot rocks the plane back and forth, flying away into his imagination.

'We should be going, Sasha,' I call, but from the way she fixes her eyes on the horizon as she continues to swing beside her new friend, I can tell that she is pretending not to have heard me.

Martin holds out a bag of jellybabies.

I shake my head and say, 'I've just eaten a roast dinner.'

'Go on. I won't be upset if you take the last red one.' He grins suddenly. 'They're your favourite.'

'When I was six!' I take a green one, and some of the awkwardness of the past dissolves, at least for now. 'Can I ask you something?' It's time to find out what I did wrong. I nibble one arm from the jellybaby. 'This is all rather embarrassing,' I say, hardly daring to look at his face. 'I contacted the Post Office many years ago, just after I left Addiscombe, to trace some letters I had sent that had gone missing. At least, I assumed they had gone astray, but it turned out that they had been delivered to the right address.'

'What on earth are you talking about?'

I nibble another limb from the jellybaby. 'Is your memory as bad as you make out? I sent you several letters.'

Martin frowns. 'I didn't receive any.'

I bite off the jellybaby's head and chew it fiercely, as if it is Martin's.

'When I moved to Devon, we promised each other that we would keep in touch. I've always wondered what happened, what changed your mind.'

'I assumed that you had made a new life for yourself, met new friends.' Martin looks down. 'More interesting and exciting boyfriends than an aspiring florist.'

'I planned to come back. I told you so in my letters.' My voice falters. 'Which you didn't read because you didn't receive them.'

'What about my phone calls? You didn't respond to any of them.'

A pulse beats in my throat as I begin to suspect that persons, not unconnected with me and Martin, have conspired against us. My mother always took the phone calls at the B&B in her posh receptionist's voice, in case they were from people enquiring about bookings. That is what she said anyway.

The sky darkens and starts spitting rain. The lights go off in the Funeral Parlour.

'Your mother promised me that she'd ask you to phone me back,' says Martin. 'She didn't, did she?'

'No.' Oh my God! Both of our mothers had been working against us. But why? 'What motive did they have for keeping us apart?' I say.

'They?'

'Our mothers!'

Martin pauses for a while as if deep in thought.

'They weren't speaking,' he says eventually. He looks me directly in the eye. 'Your mum and my dad had an affair.'

'Never!' I don't believe him. 'That isn't true.'

'I thought you knew – I caught your mum in bed with my dad. *That's* really why your parents moved away.'

Old memories begin to resurface. That last firework party, and other occasions. I came home early from school once, having bunked off Games, feigning period pain. I remember the sickly scent of barley sugar and newspaper print, and strange noises in the storeroom, as if someone was struggling to move a heavy box across the floor.

'Do you need any help?' I dumped my school-bag on the counter.

'George is managing very well,' came my mother's voice, and I didn't think any more of the incident. Why should I? According to my mother, Val and George had the perfect marriage. She always maintained that George would never leave his wife for anyone else.

My hands ball into fists in my pockets. How

could she have lied to me? She let me believe that it was my father who was the unfaithful partner, not her. She wrecked my life.

'Are you all right, Terri?' Martin's voice is tender, caring.

I turn to him, my throat tight, and manage to say, 'How long was my mother carrying on with your father?'

He shrugs. 'A couple of years or so.'

So that's why my parents moved away. I can see it now. It was a deal brokered by my father. 'Finish with George. Move away from Addiscombe. Live *my* dream of running a B&B beside the sea.'

Martin's voice breaks into my thoughts. 'I shall have to bribe Cassie and Elliot with a comic from the newsagents to persuade them to come home – I can't have Letitia blaming me for them catching pneumonia. I'll see you tomorrow, Terri. And thanks for the plaster.'

'No worries.' I call Sasha over, and we walk across the park with the Blakes, leaving them at the corner of the Parade to walk home. A plaster might help Elliot's grazes to heal, but nothing will heal the wound that my mother's lies have inflicted. To think that I have been living in blissful ignorance for over twenty years... As soon as I have Sasha out of earshot, I shall be having a few words with my mother. A few *last* words, because I don't see how I shall ever forgive her for what she has done, for what she has denied me through her selfish behaviour.

'Mum, you've just said that I can have a trampoline,' Sasha pipes up from beside me.

'No, I didn't.'

'You haven't been listening to me, have you?'

'I'm sorry, Sash. What were you saying?'

'You know, you're the best mum in the world,' she says. *But.* I can feel a *but* coming on, and if Martin's revelation about my mother was a right hook into my chest, Sasha's follows it up with a left. 'But I'd really, *really* like a dad as well.'

A dad? Why now? I can guess – she has seen Martin with his children, and it's reminded her of her father, the fact that she has never met him, that he will never push her on a swing, or give her jellybabies.

Haven't I always been enough for Sasha? I thought I was. I've tried so hard to be the perfect parent. The metallic taste of blood replaces the flavour of jellybabies in my mouth – I must have bitten the inside of my cheek.

'I love you, Mum.' Sasha takes my hand and links her fingers through mine.

'Love you too.'

'Love you three,' she says brightly.

'Ha ha.' I squeeze her fingers.

'What's for dinner?'

'Tea, you mean? Sasha, you've just had dinner at Gran's, or was it lunch?' Sasha is growing up. It is natural for her to want to know where she came from. I had just hoped that it wouldn't be so soon. I dismiss the question of what I should do about it from my mind, for now at least. 'We'll have crumpets,' I decide.

Sasha eats crumpets dripping with butter in front of the radiator in the living room, but I cannot eat. I wait until she has gone to bed before I try my mother. Her mobile is switched off so I dial her home number.

'Redsands Holiday Park, home of Marky the Mackerel.'

So she got back safely. 'Mother?'

'Oh, it's you, Terri. They've put the phones through from the holiday park. There's been such a to-do which I could have done without after such a long day. Jeff, our resident manager, is no longer in residence, having decamped to Baytor Manor with Cleo, no less.'

Baytor Manor is a relatively new set-up, a former stately home converted into a spa retreat for adults only. Cleo is Miriam the Mermaid to David's Marky. Meeter and greeter, qualified First Aider, retriever of lost teddy-bears, and creator of Redsands' exclusive cure for hangovers. (Her combination of Effervescent Vitamin C tablets, fruit juice and a raw egg doesn't work for everyone – I've tried it.) Cleo is all singing, all dancing, in more ways than one.

'If you fancy a permanent change of career,' my mother goes on, 'David and I will welcome you with open arms.'

'I wouldn't be seen dead in a blonde wig and a tail.'

'You're right – you aren't a sunny, summery character like Cleo. You remind me of winter, especially when you're using that cold, Snow-Queen tone of voice. What's wrong?'

'Cast your mind back to the first few weeks after we left Addiscombe with Dad,' I say. 'Why didn't you tell me about Martin's phone calls?'

'What phone calls?' My mother feigns inno-cence.

'You know what I'm talking about,' I continue fiercely.

'Darling, that was years ago. Martin wasn't right for you. I thought you could do better.'

'That's pathetic. Who did you think you were, trying to run other people's lives? *My* life?'

'I'm your mother,' she says simply. 'Bringing up a daughter is like driving a car; you have to steer her in what *you* know – but she doesn't – is the right direction. You had a lucky escape.'

'How do you work that one out?'

'It didn't take much to put him off, did it?' I can feel my mother's words knifing through my chest. She pauses, then turns the knife. 'If Martin had loved you at all, he would have turned up on our doorstep, demanding to see you.'

'He promised me...' I can hardly speak.

'That's what they all say,' Mum says triumphantly. 'Men are all the same. Look on the bright side: at least you avoided ending up with Val as your mother-in-law. I can't think of anything worse, can you?'

'Yes,' I spit into the receiver. 'Ending up with a spiteful old cow like you as my mother, but you are not my mother any longer. I shall never speak to you again.' I cut her off, but having the last word is no consolation.

Why *didn't* Martin make more effort to contact me? Why *didn't* he turn up, tossing handfuls of gravel at my attic-room window, like some lovestruck Romeo with a scarlet rose between his teeth?

Chapter Four

My mother – my *ex*-mother – is wrong about men, of course. I have met enough of them to know that they are all very different. In fact, if I were so inclined, I could write a book on the subject of diversity within the male species.

I don't know who to believe – my mother, who claims that it was Martin's decision to break off our romance, or Martin, who explained about the affair and its repercussions. Although I hate to admit it, my mum does have a point. If Martin really hadn't been able to live without me, he would have either made the trip to Devon, or died of a broken heart.

When I get into work, Martin is in the back room at *Posies*, making up the orders for the day. Looking up from a bouquet of yellow ranunculus and mimosa, he says, 'I hope that you didn't take too long to warm up after your visit to the park. I'm in agony.'

'What's wrong with you?'

'Chilblains.'

After yesterday's revelations, I am not sure how I feel about him and his afflictions. However, Martin dumped me by default, not by design, therefore I find myself advising him to buy a thicker pair of socks for his next outing to the children's play area.

The bell at the front of the shop jangles. 'I'll

go,' I say, glad of an excuse to make an escape.

'Hey babe, what can I have for fifty pounds?' The man approaching the till flashes a cheeky smile that dimples each side of his mouth. His eyes are dark, his hair darker, almost black. He's young – well, younger than I am by a few years – which means that I can forgive his suggestive remark.

I rest one hand on my hip. 'We'll see, shall we? What's the occasion?'

'I owe my girlfriend an apology.' He leans across the desk beside the till. 'What do I get for a hundred?'

'That's some apology.' I glance behind me, aware that Martin and Val, who have been talking at the door to the back room, have stopped their conversation to eavesdrop. 'What did you do?'

'It isn't so much what I did, as what she *thinks* I did.'

I smile to myself: the greater the blunder, the bigger and more magnificent the bouquet.

I bend down to pull Martin's book of bouquets and arrangements out from under the till, wishing that I'd chosen to wear either high-waisted trousers with big pants, or hipster jeans with a thong. Hipster jeans with big pants isn't a good look, especially when those pants are shocking pink.

I am beginning to wonder whether I left the wrong bags out for the dustmen when we left Devon. I could have sworn that I unpacked all my decent clothes when we arrived in Addiscombe, but some of them have disappeared – odd items here and there, like a pair of black popsox, and a bra and pants, as if the washing machine is swallowing them up.

With one hand behind my back, trying to tuck the pants down beneath the waistband of my jeans, I flick through the pages of Martin's brochure, checking the prices.

'How about this one?' I point to a funky arrangement of tropical flowers. 'You can add a box of chocolates or a teddy bear. Or champagne.'

'What do you recommend?'

'If I were your girlfriend, I'd expect to receive one of each.'

'I'll stick with the chocolates.'

'What message?' I ask.

'How long can it be?'

'As much as I can fit onto this card.'

'How about a poem?' he suggests. 'That should impress her.'

'Depends on whether it's in the style of Byron or Pam Ayres.'

'I'd like flowers for my old mum too, so if you'd like to choose a couple of bunches for her...'

I pick some daffodils out of one of the buckets in front of the staging, the stock we have had the longest. They are still okay. I love their scent and colours, the pale petals and contrasting tiny, deep-orange trumpets. Narcissi. They might have been named for this customer who preens himself, stroking his hair, as he decides what to write in the cards for his mother and girlfriend.

I sneak a glimpse at the notes as I tuck each one into an envelope: ...*buttocks ripe for spanking*, and *To the love of my life, still young at heart*.

Narcissus hands over a credit card. 'I can't stop long. I have patients queuing in the corridors for me.'

'You're a doctor?'

'Cardiac surgeon.'

'You don't want to listen to him. He doesn't mend hearts – he breaks them,' Martin interrupts, as he walks towards the counter. 'Hi, Kev. How is life as a hospital porter?'

'I'm a patient transport facilitator, if you don't mind.' Kev taps in his PIN number for his card, and waits for the receipt to print.

Martin peers out of the window after him once he has left the shop, his face acquiring a green tinge, reflected from the ferns that curl from a crock on the staging. 'Kev is an ex of Letitia's. I can't stand the bloke.'

As I record the delivery addresses in the book for George's round later, I wonder about Martin's reaction to Kev. If I were looking for clues as to the state of my boss's relationship with his partner, which I am not (liar!), because it is none of my business, I would deduce that Martin's feelings for her are very much alive, since the ex-boyfriend Kev is capable of inspiring such bitterness. I wonder too about Letitia – how she would react if she knew that Martin had employed one of his ex-girlfriends. Does she know? Has anyone told her?

I am about to follow Martin into the back room, leaving Val in charge of the till, when she confronts me in the passageway between the staging and the table.

'Who would have thought that such a lovely child would grow up to be such a stubborn woman? *How* many times do I have to ask you to wear your uniform? I can't have you flaunting yourself in front of our customers like that. I'll order a couple of tabards in your size, but extra long.'

I don't argue. I can always turn them up, like I used to do with my school skirts. 'Does that mean that I have the job?'

'For as long as it lasts.' Val turns towards the door. 'Here comes your grandmother and young Mr Bickley. Be a dear and put the kettle on.'

'I'll make the tea,' Martin calls through from the back.

Young Mr Bickley is the son of Mr Bickley, who long ago availed himself of the services of his family business at the end of the Parade for the despatch of his mortal remains. According to Gran, his two sisters assist young Mr Bickley part-time to run the enterprise. Occasionally, he ropes Martin in as a pallbearer.

Having left a hearse parked on the double red lines across the pavement from *Posies*, Mr Bickley joins Gran, taking a seat at the table behind the counter. I stand beside the staging. Water trickles down the back of my neck. I reach up and turn the offending fern so that its fronds curve towards the wall and drip down that instead.

'Have I missed anything?' Martin joins us.

'Give me a chance to warm up first,' says Gran.

'Popped in to save on your heating bills again, Lilian?' says Val.

'Don't worry about little old me, Valerie. I'm illegible to receive extra allowances on top of my pension.' She taps the end of her stick against the floor. 'Hasn't that kettle boiled yet?'

'Not yet.' Martin's arm brushes lightly against

91

mine, creating tiny crackles of static on my sweater. The hairs on the back of my neck prick upright with antagonism.

It is ridiculous. It is ancient history, yet it still matters to me, although I now have a better understanding of what happened. Martin and I were too cowardly to make a definite end to our relationship, so I drifted on, reluctant to commit to anyone else, and always comparing them with my childhood sweetheart.

'It's wonderful to see you again, Mrs Parkin.' Young Mr Bickley, who is at least fifty-five, nods obsequiously towards my grandmother. His receding hair is slicked down with some product that gives it a bluish sheen. His eyes are pale and grey behind dark-rimmed glasses. I wonder if he keeps his weight down consciously, as if he doesn't want anyone thinking that he's grown fat on the profits of death.

'You are a picture of health, as always,' he continues.

Gran smiles and shows me off, which leads Mr Bickley into reminiscing about the time he last saw me, jumping into the hire van with my parents to drive off to our new home in Devon. I was sixteen, dressed in torn fishnets, a short dark skirt and combat boots. My hair was red and green, and spiked up in the style of what Sharon later termed 'punk hedgehog' to annoy my mother.

I don't want to hear any more. My face burns with embarrassment. It wasn't me, not the 'me' I am now.

'I waved, but you didn't wave back, Terri,' Mr Bickley says.

It is true. I didn't notice Mr Bickley. My panda eyes, smudged with eyeliner and tears, were for Martin alone.

'I always thought you'd end up marrying Martin,' Mr Bickley goes on. 'I was dead envious of him, the way you were always in each other's homes. My father's shop, God rest his soul, wasn't the kind of place you'd want to pop round to visit when you were a kid.'

'I didn't realise,' Martin murmurs as Del turns to my grandmother.

'Perhaps you'd like to make that appointment to come and choose your funeral plan, Mrs Parkin.'

'Gran, you don't have to think about that yet.' I glare at the undertaker.

'I like to be prepared,' she says calmly. 'Death comes to us all, doesn't it, Mr Bickley?'

'I'd like to say that unfortunately it does, but death is my bread and butter, and I can't afford to knock it. If you'd like to come into the parlour one day soon, I'd be delighted to give you some ideas.'

Gran dithers.

'I keep a bottle of brandy, the finest cognac, to treat shock,' he adds.

'Your prices are that high then, Del?' Gran says coolly.

'You can't take it with you.'

'I never – almost never – drink and drive,' says Gran. 'A poor gentleman from the Lunch Club had a drop too much, and drove his scooter into the Wandle.'

'He drowned,' Del remarks mournfully. 'I remember. There wasn't a mark on him.' He pulls a grey handkerchief from his pocket and mops his brow. 'I don't understand how you can work in here, Martin. It's so stuffy compared with next door.' His mobile cuts him short, the ringtone, *Pie Jesu*. He presses the phone to his ear, turns away and holds a brief conversation.

'I hope it isn't another of my circle,' Gran worries. 'They're all popping off now.'

'It was my dentist,' says Mr Bickley.

'It can be very difficult to find a new one on the NHS when you can't afford to go private,' Gran says. 'Terri knows all about that, don't you?'

'He isn't dead. He wanted to rearrange my next appointment.' Del smiles – at least, the corners of his mouth rise a fraction relative to the rest – and turns to Martin. 'I hear that one of our neighbours in the Parade is closing down.'

'It isn't me.'

'John has gone into liquidation.'

Martin nods sagely. 'What is the point of driving here, and struggling to park within walking distance, to buy your electrical goods for three times the price you can order them for on the Internet?'

'How times have changed,' says Val.

'You'd better run around there quick and get yourself a new kettle, Martin. It's taking ages to come to the boil, if it's working at all. You must have blown the element, or burned out the fuse on that one out the back.' Suddenly, Gran nudges Mr Bickley with the end of her stick. 'Forget the tea,' she hisses. 'The Gestapo are on their way. Shift that hearse, double quick!'

Del flies up from his seat and runs out of the

shop. Martin and I follow and wait side by side, taking shelter in the doorway from the sleet that has begun to scurry from the dark sky. Two traffic wardens plant their big feet between Mr Bickley and his hearse. Both wear uniform. The woman is small and bolshy. She is accompanied by a West Indian man who towers above everyone else.

'To whom does this vehicle belong?' She waves her hand-held computer in the direction of the hearse.

Flakes of snow settle like dandruff on Mr Bickley's shoulders. He is not so respectful now.

'You know very well that it's mine.' He swears. 'You can't ticket a hearse. We have a gentleman's agreement with the local council.'

'As you can see,' the woman thrusts out her chest, 'I am no gentleman, and your hearse is parked on a red route. Now, move it.'

'Gone are the days when you could park where you liked,' Martin observes.

I smile ruefully. Like Del parking his hearse on double red lines, I fear that I have made a mistake parking myself in Addiscombe. If it wasn't for Gran, I would be miles away by now. I glance at Martin. Or would I?

Big pants, high-waisted trousers, flat shoes, and a close-fitting tabard over a polo-neck jumper. My mother would be ashamed of me. If you've got it, flaunt it, is her motto, and if you haven't got it, let it all hang out anyway

Val seems pleased with my demure appearance when I turn up for work, although I feel my jaw tightening when she reaches out and tweaks the side of my tabard.

'That's much better. You look more like a florist and less like a call-girl. Look after the till, will you, while I get the phone.'

When I look up from rearranging the leaflets on the counter at the sound of the bell inside the door, I recognise the next customer as the man who came in the day before; it's Letitia's ex-boy-friend.

'Hello, Kev.' I like the way that *Posies* has so much repeat business. I tried to encourage it at *Flower Power*, but the shop was so out of the way that people who did discover it on taking a wrong turning out of town, struggled to find it again. However, according to Sharon, my old premises have been converted into a kebab shop. The new proprietor can hardly keep up with the demand for chopped lettuce and chili sauce. It's funny how people can find it now, even in the middle of the night, when they're so drunk that they can hardly stand, let alone walk.

'Are you able to arrange counselling for post-traumatic stress as well as flowers?' Kev's voice rises as he speaks, and although he isn't smiling, I can't help wondering if he is trying hard not to. 'My girlfriend – my *ex*-girlfriend – has received a bunch of daffodils with a note referring to her advanced age, while my mother is so disgusted at my base, animal instincts that she has disowned me. I have never been so embarrassed.' Kev rests one elbow on the desk, and the smile he was holding back escapes. 'Apart from the time I was caught *in flagrante* in the nurses' locker room. Now, what about my compensation?'

How do I handle this? I take a deep breath. Contrary to popular opinion, the first rule of customer service is not that the customer is always right; it is *grovel*.

'I am sorry that you haven't been satisfied with our service.' I pull the delivery book out from beneath the counter. Did I transpose the addresses on the orders? Did I slip the cards into the wrong envelopes? 'Excuse me a moment.'

I have a word with Val, who is sitting in the back room with her feet propped on an upturned bucket, her fingers not so worn out that she can't turn the pages of a novel. I can just make out the title: *The Greek Tycoon's Bride*.

I clear my throat. She looks up across the top of her reading glasses.

'Val, I have a problem.'

'I dare say you have lots of problems, but I don't wish to be privy to them.'

'I'm not sure how you would prefer me to deal with a customer complaint.'

'Complaint?' Val raises one rather straggly eyebrow, which doesn't match her vibrant hair colour. 'Oh dear, oh dear. I hate to say this, but I told Martin that this wouldn't work out.'

'You don't hate it at all,' I observe. 'You're loving it.'

'You've had enough experience of life to know that it's almost impossible to repair a reputation once it's been damaged.'

My fingers tighten around the scissors in the pocket at the front of my tabard as Val stands up and moves past me. The thought of snipping her flowery blouse into little pieces makes me feel

97

slightly less aggrieved.

'It's Kevin, isn't it?' Val takes cash from the till. 'Our Letitia is a popular lass. Lovely girl. Such a shame that you missed out.'

'According to the rumours, it appears that I had a lucky escape, disengaging myself when I did,' says Kev. 'I hear that she is living in Spain.'

Val hands over three twenty-pound notes and bangs the till drawer shut. 'She'll be back.'

Kev holds the notes up to the light, one by one, then purses his lips and shakes his head. 'I've had to buy shares in Thorntons.'

'There is no more,' Val says.

'My girlfriend has dumped me. She's pregnant, and I'm trying to win her back.'

'Go on then.' Val hands over another twenty quid. 'Take her out for dinner. Never let it be said that I stood in the way of true love.'

Kev pockets the cash, winks at me, then walks out. I watch him head for a red BMW sportster parked on the double lines opposite the shop. Two traffic wardens, the regulars, are just about to slap a ticket on the windscreen, but something that Kev says stops them. They back off. The indicator lights on the car flicker on and off.

'How does he do that, the flashy so-and-so?' says Val.

'With the key, I expect.'

'I meant, how did he persuade the Poison Dwarf and her assistant to forget the fine?' Val turns to me. 'You know, you really should be more careful, Terri. We can't afford to give money away like that. You must have written down the wrong instructions.'

'I didn't.'

'I shall have a word with Martin about your pay. I think it's only fair that you accept some responsibility for our losses. Don't screw your face up like that – you'll make those crows' feet so much more obvious. You look as if you've swallowed a pinholder.'

'You're assuming that it's my fault.'

Val banishes me to the back room because Martin has an appointment to discuss wedding flowers. The bride-to-be and her entourage of three other women – matron of honour, bridesmaid, and mother-of-the-bride, I guess – join him at the table behind the counter, while Val bustles about, tidying the staging and answering the phone.

Feeling like Cinderella, left out of the excitement of planning for the ball, I prop the door open with a bucket, so that I can listen to Martin while I carry on conditioning the fresh stock. I watch him slip off his jacket and cast it carelessly across the counter. The bride-to-be keeps touching her face, and fiddling with her hair, as she compares scraps of dress material, magazine pictures, and a flamboyant cerise hat, with samples of fresh flowers, and photos in Martin's scrapbook. She blushes and giggles, and Martin flirts back with great charm and chivalry, until she makes a firm order.

I am torn between admiration and envy. Before I went bankrupt, I was in Martin's position as salesperson and florist, confident and professional, and in control. In control of my business – or so I thought – and in control of my life outside work. I had friends, although most of them drifted away once the notice of my insolvency was published in the local papers, as if bankruptcy was somehow infectious. Sasha was settled in school. We were happy.

Now look at me, back among the buckets with someone else's scissors in my hand, because I mislaid mine during the move.

A mass of bright flowerheads catches my eye, yellow roses which add cheer to a dull winter's day. I select a handful of stems, taking care to avoid the thorns pricking into my gloves, and prepare to cut an angle across the first stem with my scissors. My hand slips, the blades catch my glove and pierce the soft cloth.

'Damn!' I drop the scissors and tug off my glove with my teeth. A line of blood wells up across the skin between my finger and thumb.

'Someone wasn't concentrating.'

I jump at the sound of Martin's voice from behind me. Slowly, I turn round to face him as he stands in the doorway

'I haven't cut myself like that for years.'

'Let me see,' he says softly.

'It's nothing – I'll live.'

Martin approaches and bends forward across the table.

'Let me see,' he repeats, and takes my hand in his. His touch is gentle, yet his skin is rough. A man of contrasts. As are my reactions to him. Regret at the memory of the last time he held my hand, on the day before I left Addiscombe with my parents. Resentment that he apparently feels quite comfortable with our renewed physical contact. Why can't I stop dwelling on the past?

'Martin! Oh, there you are. What's going on here?' Val's voice is taut with suspicion. What is she worried about? Does she think I am about to seduce her son, when he has made it perfectly clear that he thought so little of me that he didn't make more effort to stay in contact once I left Addiscombe? Out of sight, out of mind. Well, she is wrong. I'm not a bloody martyr.

'Terri's had an industrial accident.' Martin looks up. 'She's nicked her finger.'

'Is that all? Anyone would think she'd lopped it off from the way you're carrying on.'

'Would you fetch the accident book and first-aid kit from the flat, Mum?' Martin examines my wound very closely. I wish that he had paid as much attention to the wound he inflicted on my heart, over twenty years before...

Just as the tension is about to become unbearable, I notice a pink object stuck to his cheek. It's tiny, a sugary sprinkle that you might pour onto ice cream, or cupcakes. A giggle wells up in my throat. I bite my lip. Hard. And withdraw my hand from Martin's grasp.

'My boy is always so popular with the girls.' Val stares at me as if I am slightly touched. 'Look at that lovely bride who was in just now – you made her forget that she was about to get married.'

'I don't think so,' Martin says modestly.

'I've always sworn by iodine.' Val heads off upstairs then returns, smiling as she hands me a wad of cottonwool and a brown glass bottle. 'It's a great antiseptic, and guaranteed to sting.'

'Do you remember when I rescued you from

the school bully, Terri?' Martin asks.

'I would have dealt with him myself if you hadn't interfered.'

Martin grins. 'I held your hand while Mum picked the gravel out of the grazes on your knees, and then you promised not to cry when she swabbed them with iodine, if I gave you some Polos.'

'Not Polos. You gave me Parma Violets.'

'Polos.'

'I distinctly remember the soapy flavour of Parma Violets.'

'We'd better agree to disagree.'

I nod, my throat tightening with disappointment that we don't share the same memories. However, it only goes to prove that Martin never did feel the same way about me as I did about him. I clung on to the details, like a limpet clinging to a rock along the shore, fighting the tide of passing time. The scent of liquorice on Martin's breath, the white blemish at the base of his thumbnail and the flake of red paint on his top lip from where he had chewed the end of a school pencil.

'The sweets didn't make any difference,' Val adds, before she bustles away to serve a customer. 'You cried anyway.'

'I don't remember you crying,' Martin says, and this time I believe that he is fibbing out of a sense of gallantry, of respect for my feelings, because I did cry. I bawled my eyes out. 'I'm sorry about my mother,' he adds in a low voice. 'She doesn't always think before she speaks.'

'She gives me the impression that she doesn't

like me working here.' I choose my words tactfully. She doesn't like me at all.

'She's been under a lot of stress recently, what with being dragged out of retirement to look after the shop again when she was planning to go on a world cruise. She worries about my dad's state of health, about how Letitia is coping alone in Spain, about me, about her grandkids. I owe her so much.'

'I wouldn't have become a florist if it wasn't for your mother,' I say grudgingly. It was Val who inspired me. 'I know I keep harking back to the past, but did she ever mention that I came to see you?'

I was sixteen. Three months had passed since I left Addiscombe, and I couldn't stand not knowing what had happened to Martin any longer. I asked Gran, but she was consumed by caring for my grandfather who had become bedridden with what she described as 'kiddly failure', and had temporarily lost contact with the Blakes.

I had earned enough waiting tables at the B&B to pay for the train fare to London. Encouraged by Sharon, I bunked off school for a day, assuming that Martin would be working in the shop, but when I arrived, it was Val who was serving behind the till.

'Have you come to visit your grandparents, Little Miss Chocolate Orange?' she said, which I thought was strange at the time, since she knew of my relationship with Martin. 'Your grandmother might appreciate some flowers.' She selected a rose from one of the buckets beside the counter, and cupped the bloom to demonstrate its quality. 'Look at that. The palest peach, like the blush of a maiden.'

'Er,' I stammered. 'I've come to see Martin.'

Val's mouth formed a tight 'o'. 'You should have telephoned first.'

'I did, and you said that Martin would ring back.'

'Yes, but he didn't, did he? I thought that might have told you something, Terri, but then you Millses have never been good at taking a hint.'

As she stared at me, my blood ran cold. My hands began to shake. My whole life, my dreams of marriage and children, of working alongside Martin in *Posies*, shattered into tiny pieces like a glass vase dropped from a great height.

The sound of a chair scraping across the floor brings me back to the present. Martin sits down opposite me, straddling the chair and resting his arms across the back.

'Lil told me of your visit several months later when she came into the shop to order tributes for your grandfather's funeral. I was furious with Mum at first, until I gave her a chance to explain. She had seen how gutted I was when you left, and then, when you didn't get in touch...' His voice tails off.

'If you were that devastated, why didn't you make more effort to contact me?'

'I assumed that *you* had changed your mind. That you had chosen to make a clean break. I wanted to believe that you made that decision out of respect for my feelings.'

'I felt exactly the same.'

'Well, we were a right pair of numpties, as

Cassie would say.' Martin's mouth is smiling, but his eyes are not. 'I doubt that it would have worked out anyway. You and me. You lived too far away.'

'I could have come to stay in the holidays. You could have spent time with us. There was always plenty of room at the B & B.'

'My parents needed me here at *Posies*, but if they had been able to afford to let me go, your mum would have baited my full English breakfast with rat poison, and your dad would have had me running errands to keep us apart.' Martin smiles. 'I don't suppose that I shall approve of Cassie's first boyfriend.'

An ache grips my chest as I think of Sasha's father, and how he has missed out on all of Sasha's firsts so far: her first words – *Muma* for Mummy and *Ook* for Look; her first shoes – which were soft and properly fitted with room for growth, essential when Sasha refused to take them off for the first week; her first day at nursery, when she screamed when I left her and screamed when I arrived to take her home.

'Looking on the positive side,' Martin continues, 'if you hadn't gone away, you wouldn't have had Sasha, and I wouldn't have had Cassie and Elliot.'

I suppose that this concept is vaguely consoling. It is sensible and realistic, hardly the stuff of the fairytales that my mother used to read me. The prince and princess met, but didn't marry. They had children with other partners and lived relatively contentedly ever after, or at least, until their paths crossed once again.

And then what? The prince revealed that he did care for the princess – but that was once upon a time – and now he is as-good-as-married, and whether happily, or not, it makes no difference. It is too late.

'You don't want to use that iodine, do you?' Martin says. I hand over the bottle. He hides it behind the tax files, and scribbles in the accident book, *Terri Mills – violent altercation with pair of scissors*, before Val appears with a request for a dozen red roses for a customer to give to his fiancée.

'If you wouldn't mind, Terri. My fingers are killing me today. What a lovely young man,' she coos, 'in spite of the earring. So romantic. Don't you adore a love story with a happy ending!'

Chapter Five

Does Martin believe that I talked about the past with a view to renewing our relationship? Is that why he blushes when I turn up to work with Sasha in tow on the Saturday morning a few days later, or is the colour in his cheeks caused by the reflection of the scarlet carnations against his skin?

Val and Martin are on their feet in the back room, surrounded by pedestals, baskets and bouquet arrangements, masses of colour, reds and golds, pinks and creams, interspersed with sparkling diamanté pins. Martin greets me and Sasha with a nod of the head.

'Why don't you run upstairs and tell Cassie to hurry up and finish her breakfast and clean her teeth?' Val says to Sasha.

Sasha glances at me, her expression sheepish.

'Don't tell me,' I sigh. 'You forgot to clean yours this morning.'

Grinning, she races off up to the flat.

Although he didn't say it in so many words, Martin expressed enough remorse the other day to convince me that he really did love me, way back when I was sixteen, and the barrier of anger and resentment that kept us at a distance has been replaced by one of deep regret, on my part anyway.

It was wrong of me to have raised the subject of our parting, to have raked up the past, to have reminded Martin of past intimacy when he is an as-good-as-married man. I thought that it would make it easier for us to work together, but I sense from the awkward silence between us that I was mistaken.

Val turns to me. 'How's your poorly finger?' she says slyly.

'It's fine now, thank you.'

'I knew that a splash of iodine would do the trick. Right – I must take a break. My arthritis is playing me up again.' Val pronounces her affliction 'Arthur-itis', as though it is the name of a person, a familiar friend. 'I adore these spray orchids that came in yesterday,' she goes on, hoisting herself to her feet. 'Exotic, showy, dare to be different – they remind me so much of dear Letitia. Don't you agree, Martin?'

'Uhuh,' he says.

'Our Letitia is such a talented woman, Terri. She's given birth to not one, but two babies, yet she still has a wonderful figure. She turned her hand to floristry – in a small way, admittedly – and now she's running a bar.'

And she's abandoned her children, I want to say, but I bite my tongue.

As if reading my mind, Val goes on, 'Letitia has always put Cassie and Elliot first. She could have kept them with her in Spain, left them with strangers while she put the bar on the market, but she knew that they would be better off here, at home, settling back in their old school.'

I glance towards Martin. His expression is unreadable.

'Has Letitia finalised the sale yet?' Val asks. 'She was too busy for a chat the last time the children and I called her.'

'As far as I know, the bar is off our hands,' Martin says.

'I still don't understand why you didn't stay out there for longer,' Val says. 'You didn't give Spain a chance.'

'There's a difference between having a couple of weeks' holiday on the beach, and living there,' Martin observes quietly. 'I was bored.'

'It's such a shame. Your dad and I were planning to join you one day. You could have run the bar with Tish, opened one or two more down the coast, and expanded into nightclubs ownership. Son, you could have been the next Peter Stringfellow.' Val pauses. 'We could have shared a villa – I could have looked after Cassie and Elliot, while your dad looked after the pool.'

I notice the muscle in Martin's cheek tautening and relaxing. His reaction to his mother is restrained. 'I can't see my dad as a pool boy,' is all he says.

'I'd better be off,' I say. 'Where are Cassie and Elliot? Are they ready?'

'You know, I could have taken the children,' Val says.

'Terri's happy to do it today,' Martin says. 'It's Sasha's first class at the dancing school.'

'Oh?' says Val. 'Our Cassie has been dancing since she was three.'

'So has Sasha,' I say, unwilling to let my daughter be outdone by Val's competitive grandmother act. 'I signed her up for lessons at the age of two and three quarters.'

'Cassie's working towards her Grade Three

ballet exams.'

'So is Sasha.'

'Ah, but Miss Cora, the dancing teacher, says that our Cassie has remarkably flexible ankles.' Val sashays towards the foot of the stairs that lead up to the flat. 'Cassie and Sasha!' she calls. 'Elliot!'

The children arrive downstairs, Sasha and Cassie dressed for dancing, and Elliot in a *Bob the Builder* sweatshirt, cord trousers and a green cagoule tied like a cape around his neck. Elliot points at me.

'I'm not going with that lady. I wanna go with Granma.'

'Granma is going to work in the shop this morning, while I deliver the wedding flowers,' says Martin. 'If you go with Terri, I'll let you take your light sabre.'

'The big one?' says Elliot hopefully.

Martin glances at me. I nod. Anything for an easy life.

'You'd better go and find it,' Martin says and Elliot skips away, only to return brandishing a light sabre that is as long as he is tall. He jams his thumb against a button on the handle, triggering a display of light and sound.

'Can I take my other light sabre too?'

'If you put your coat on. See you later, Terri. May the Force be with you.' Martin looks towards Elliot and grins. 'You're going to need it.'

It is quicker to walk the twenty minutes to ballet and, as Sasha points out, more environmentally friendly than taking the car and driving around for ages trying to find a parking space. I follow Sasha and Cassie, who skip along side by side

110

with their pale-blue voile skirts peeking out beneath their coats. A disgruntled Elliot scuffs along behind me, carrying a light sabre in each hand.

'Hurry up, Darth.'

Cassie pirouettes and drops back. Sasha joins us.

'So Sasha,' Cassie says, 'I haven't got a mum, and you haven't got a dad.'

'You *have* got a mum,' Sasha scolds. 'She's on her way home from Spain.'

'She said that she was,' Cassie says sadly, 'but she hasn't arrived, has she?'

'Oh?' I wonder about the wonderful Letitia. How cruel can she be, making a promise to return to her children, then breaking it, apparently without giving any explanation?

'It's different for me,' says Sasha. 'I've never had a dad.'

'You must have done,' says Cassie knowledgeably, 'otherwise you wouldn't have been born. Would she, Terri?'

'Cassie is right. Sasha did have a dad,' I begin. 'It's just that he isn't around any more.'

'Why not?'

My fingers, numb with cold, tighten around the shoulder-strap on my bag. Why am I still in denial? It was ten years ago, yet I always find myself wanting to claim that Sasha's existence is down to a virgin birth.

'What was my dad like, Mum?'

Sasha loves hearing the story of how I met her father, the edited version, in which a one-night stand becomes a series of romantic, moonlit encounters. I do admit that I didn't know Robbie

111

very well. 'Robbie was very handsome.'

'My dad is handsome,' Cassie interrupts, and much as I try to deny it to myself, it is true. 'What job did Sasha's dad do?'

'He was a policeman and he played rugby.' It makes him sound as if he could have been anyone, but how can I be more specific when I hardly knew him? A casual invitation to a party to celebrate the thirtieth birthday of Sharon's brother's friend. A summer barbecue. A warm, velvet evening. Glasses of soft Merlot and Pinot noir. I'd like to say that I know exactly what happened, but to this day, I can't remember. Not exactly.

Thinking back to that shameful episode makes me feel bad, but it doesn't make me a bad person, does it? Two consenting adults. Both unattached. Just a pity that the subject of safe sex slipped our minds.

Later, I find myself sitting in an austere and draughty kitchen which is attached to a church hall, while Sasha and Cassie join their ballet class in the room above. There's a fridge, a small oven and hob, a sink with a dripping tap, and stacks of green china, like my grandmother has, on top of a range of cupboards.

Upstairs, a piano strikes up the staccato notes of what sounds like the tune of 'If You Should Meet A Crocodile'. I can't help it – I find myself thinking of Val...

Elliot wanders around, opening and closing each cupboard in turn. I can't relax my guard for a second. It is as if he's powered by one of those longlasting batteries.

112

'Come and sit down.' I ask him nicely three times, then weigh up the pros and cons of forceful action. If I were on my own, I might pick him up and plonk him on a chair, but there is another mum sitting at the Formica-topped table opposite me, and I'm not sure how Elliot will react, whether or not he'll scream the place down and interrupt the class upstairs. I can't see him doing meek acquiescence.

'If you don't sit down, I'm going to take away one of your light sabres.'

'I don't care.' Elliot holds out the smaller of the two.

'I'll have both of them then.'

Elliot hesitates, but instead of objecting, or handing the light sabres over, he wrinkles his nose. 'What's that smell?'

'Disinfectant, I think.'

The other mum observes that the smell isn't disinfectant at all. It's gas. 'I'll bet that little horror of yours has turned the knob on the stove.'

'He isn't mine. I'm looking after him for a...' I wonder exactly how to describe what Martin is to me '...a friend.' However, the other mum is too busy checking the oven and hob to notice my correction.

'He hasn't turned the gas on. There must be a leak.' She hesitates, as if she is uncertain as to what to do, whether to do anything at all, whereas I am thrown into a panic, picturing Sasha caught in an explosion, me having to tell Martin that his children have perished whilst in my care.

'Gas is explosive. One spark... We must get everyone out of the building,' I say. 'You get the

113

dancers out. I'll raise the alarm and stop anyone else coming in.'

I try to force the window in the kitchen, but the catch is painted shut. I open the door that leads straight outside, letting in gusts of icy air and a horde of older girls who have been trying to open it, apparently for some time.

'You can't come in.' I try to push them back. 'This is an evacuation.'

Someone at the back calls out, 'Everybody out. There's a fire.'

'There isn't a fire,' I say, but no one is listening. A young man in a dog collar and dark jacket appears from the corridor behind me, giving the address of the church hall as he talks on a mobile phone. The younger ballerinas, flushed with their elephantine exertions, descend the stairs ungracefully, followed by a hefty woman in a pink leotard and tutu who jétés about like a jellyfish, rounding her babies up and escorting them outside.

'Elliot, hold my hand.' He shakes his head, so I grab his arm and lead him out to join the melée in the car park.

'What's happening?' Sasha darts out from the group of ballerinas with Cassie. 'I can't see any smoke.'

'Or flames,' says Cassie.

'Where is the fire?' Elliot asks excitedly.

'There isn't one. The building is being evacuated as a precaution.'

Not one, but two fire engines pull up, one behind the other. A fireman who is still pulling his protective coat on over his vest, jumps out and heads towards me. He is tall, broad-shouldered, and followed by several equally hunky colleagues.

I step aside, a casual onlooker, my face on fire even though the church hall isn't. In fact, I believe I know what triggered the whole fiasco. Elliot may well have turned on the gas at the hob in the kitchen. Unfortunately, I suspect that he also turned it off again afterwards.

'Let's go,' I say quickly. 'We're in the way.'

'Why are we walking so fast?' Cassie complains as we march away from the church. 'My legs are *soooo* tired.'

'Why did the firemen come when there wasn't a fire?' asks Sasha.

'Why are you making me hold your hand?' grumbles Elliot. 'I wanted to stay and watch them put the fire out.'

'For the last time, there is no fire! What did you do in your ballet lesson, girls?' I try to divert them, and this time, it works.

'We danced to the *Sorcerer's Appendix*,' says Cassie. 'We were brooms whizzing around Miss Cora's room.'

'Pirouetting, not whizzing.' Sasha giggles. 'Cassie went so dizzy that she fell over.'

'I did not.'

'You fell over.'

'I did not! I made a beautiful position on the floor.'

'That's enough, girls. You're arguing just like a pair of sisters.'

They laugh and skip along together through a faint haze of traffic fumes. I smile to myself. Money cannot buy love, but it does help advance friendship, and if the four quid I have just spent on Sasha's ballet lesson helps her settle in at school here in Addiscombe, it was money well spent.

When we return to *Posies*, Elliot abandons his light sabres for the rest of the day, acquiring several buckets – with water – to become a fire-fighter. I catch him extinguishing a 'fire' that he has created with a bundle of flame-coloured birds of paradise in the middle of the floor in the back room.

'What is going on here?'

'London's burning.' Elliot jumps up and down, crushing the flowers into an unrecognisable mess.

'There's water everywhere! We'll have to mop it up before it floods the shop. You can help, Elliot,' I add, before he can run off.

'I'm not Elliot.' He picks up an empty bucket and tips it upside down over his head, covering his face. 'I'm Fireman Sam.'

'Well, Fireman Sam,' I rap the bucket, 'your helmet is too big.'

Elliot giggles.

'I don't suppose that Fireman Sam is strong enough to use a mop,' I begin.

Immediately, Elliot whips the bucket off and drops it on the floor. 'I've got 'normous muscles.' He jumps around and flexes his biceps. 'Look!'

I shake my head doubtfully. 'Mops are very heavy, especially when they're full of water...'

'They aren't.' Elliot marches over to the mop that is leaning against the wall in the corner of the back room, and picks it up. 'Not for Fireman Sam.'

'How did you persuade him to do that?'

I turn at the sound of Martin's voice.

'I've just got back with the van,' he says. 'Are you Supernanny, or what?'

'It's called reverse psychology.' I help Elliot wring out the mop in the sink and send him upstairs to join the girls.

'Elliot would never have done that for me. He's been a nightmare recently with his attention-seeking behaviour.' Martin's eyes are ringed with dark shadows, and seem to have lost some of their spark over the past few days. He must be shattered, looking after two kids, and running a home and a business, but even so, I feel that Martin is being unreasonably harsh on his son.

'He must be missing his mum,' I say gently, standing up for Elliot. 'When you're five years old, your parent staying away for even one night can seem like an eternity.'

The lines on Martin's forehead deepen, and I begin to regret offering my opinion. What gives *me* the right to lecture anyone on the art of parenting? After a moment's silence, he changes the subject.

'I'm going to drop Mum home, if you're okay here. I left Dad outside the Cricketers.'

'I can stay, Martin, love,' Val interrupts, coming into the room behind him.

'There's no reason for you to work any longer,' Martin says rather more firmly than I've noticed him speak to his mother before. 'Terri is here now.' He collects his keys from where he has left them on the counter, and fetches his mum's coat from the hook on the back door. He wraps it around her shoulders and gives her a peck on the cheek, before escorting her out to the van.

When Martin comes back from dropping his mother off, I catch the sharp scent of aftershave and cold air on his fleece jacket as he takes it off and throws it across the table in the back room.

'I had a word with my dad about those deliveries that went awry. It was his mistake – a kerfuffle, as he likes to call it, so as not to accept any blame.'

Like father, like son, I think, recalling my mother's view that Martin was a hopeless delivery boy.

'My mother shouldn't have jumped to conclusions and accused you,' he goes on. 'She sometimes finds it difficult to remember that she is no longer the boss.'

That isn't the impression that Val has given me, but it is reassuring to know my future here depends on Martin's opinion, not his mother's.

Martin heads off upstairs to do some paperwork, and keep half an eye on the children while they play. Much later, as I am locking up the shop, he reappears.

'Quickly, Terri, you have to see this.' Martin grabs my wrist and leads me back through the shop to the foot of the stairs. He puts his finger to his lips and slides in front of me. I follow him up the steps, aware of the afterburn of his grip on my skin, and the neat curves of his buttocks, sheathed in close-fitting cords.

Nice bum, I muse, giving myself a metaphorical slap on my own bottom for thinking such a thing about my boss, and an as-good-as-married man, at that.

Martin stops at the top of the staircase and squats down. The living-room door is open. There is a sign stuck to it: *The Baeeauty Sallon*, scribbled in purple felt-tip pen.

Martin moves forwards into a commando-style crawl. Just before the doorway, he turns and waves me across to join him. I drop down to my knees and follow.

Martin looks around the edge of the door. I stay back, keeping space between us.

'You can't see from there,' he whispers. 'Come closer...'

Come closer... A shiver of desire, of regret, tingles down my spine. It was so much easier to deny any attraction that I felt towards him when I was upset and angry with him for dumping me in my teens.

I close the distance between us, my heart thumping above the sound of Sasha talking in the next room. I press myself against the wall to avoid contact with Martin's long legs, but I can still feel the heat radiating from his body.

I peer through the crack between the door and the frame. The smoked-glass coffee-table glitters with stickers and blobs of spilled nail polish. Cassie is lying on her back on the sofa. Something glistens on her upper lip. A strip of Sellotape. Sasha bends over and examines it.

'Your mum doesn't have a moustache.' Cassie's voice is slightly muffled, down to the restriction of the sticky tape, but the words are clear enough for us all to hear.

'I told you that's because she waxes it,' Sasha says wearily. 'My great-granma's got one because she doesn't. Simple.'

I can feel Martin's body shifting beside me, and hear his stifled sob of laughter. My blood runs hot.

'Thanks, Sash,' I murmur.

'Ouch!' Cassie writhes around on the sofa. Sasha has ripped the tape from Cassie's lip and is holding it up to the light and examining it for hairs. Do I do that? I stand up. Do I really do that?

'You can't keep anything a secret around here, Terri,' Martin chuckles. 'Give us a hand up, will you?' He stretches out his arm. Reluctantly, I take his hand, just the tips of his fingers in mine. 'It's my back.' He grins. 'I must be getting old.'

He doesn't look so old now, I think, as he links his fingers through mine, and takes a firm grip.

'Pull me,' he says. I wish...

'Heave ho,' says Cassie, appearing as a silhouette in the doorway.

Martin struggles up, grimacing. 'Do you have anything for men at this beauty salon?'

'Men don't have beauty treatments,' Sasha says scathingly from behind Cassie. She looks towards me, her confidence and my conviction that I have done my best bringing Sasha up without a father, a male role model, suddenly snatched away by doubt. 'Do they, Mum?'

'Where is Elliot?' says Martin. 'You girls are supposed to be looking after him.'

'He's in the tanning cubicle,' says Cassie.

'No,' Sasha contradicts. 'He's in that place where you have your wobbly bits removed with electricity.'

'You haven't rigged him up to the mains?'

120

Martin asks.

'He's in Mum's wardrobe upstairs,' says Cassie. 'He was being a pain.'

'Go and let him out,' Martin sighs.

When the girls run off, giggling, to release Elliot, Martin turns to me. 'If you'd like me to babysit Sasha any time, in return for looking after the children this morning, just ask.'

'Thanks.'

'I'd better rustle up some tea. Would you and Sasha like to stay?'

I decide to go home. If I was Martin's girl-friend, I wouldn't be terribly impressed by the thought of a stranger, a single woman particularly, sharing my man's company over sausages, chips and spaghetti hoops.

Actually, I don't know what Martin gives his kids for tea, but that is what Sasha and I have. Once I have washed the dishes, I settle down to watch one of the soaps, and their stories of family relationships that are far more complicated than mine. Sasha wanders through with the *Yellow Pages* in her arms, and switches the television off before joining me on the sofa.

'What did you do that for? I was watching *EastEnders*.'

'With your eyes closed?'

'They weren't.'

'Were.'

'Well, would you mind turning it back on?'

'Your programme had finished. I heard the theme tune,' Sasha argues.

'I might want to watch the programme after that one.'

'You shouldn't watch TV for the sake of it, Mum. How are we going to save the world, if you're always wasting electricity?'

'Where have you been learning all this stuff about caring for the environment?'

'On TV.' Sasha tips her head to one side, then grins, seeing the funny side. She bounces down on the sofa and opens the *Yellow Pages* out on her lap, instead of doing her homework.

'What exactly are you looking for?' I ask her.

'The number for the Missing Persons' Bureau.' She smiles gamely. 'They'll be able to help me find my dad.'

'I've always done my best for you, Sash.' I reach out and curl her hair back behind her ear.

'Yeah,' she says, but I know what she is thinking: that my best isn't good enough. 'Why do you think that my dad never wanted to see me?' She gazes at me, her eyes wide with appeal, and my heart clenches into an aching ball of guilt. Not only have I kept Robbie in the dark about his daughter, I have misled her into concluding that her father chose not to meet her.

'It wasn't, I mean, it *isn't* a case of not wanting to see you, darling. Your dad doesn't actually know that you exist.' I hold my finger to my lips very briefly to silence her next question. 'I told him that I might be pregnant, but I didn't let him know when you were born. I did try, but–'

'I thought you were good at arranging stuff,' Sasha interrupts.

'Flowers, yes. Stuff, as you call it, no.'

'Please, will you find my dad for me?'

I swallow past the lump in my throat. 'I'll see

122

what I can do. No promises, though,' I add, as my daughter's face lights up. 'It could take some time to find him – if he wants to be found, which he might not. I'll do my best.' I'll do my utmost to make up for those missing years.

After a long silence, Sasha says, 'I've seen Tiegan's dad come to collect her from school.'

'Who is Tiegan?'

'She used to be Cassie's best friend, but now she's Brooke's, and Brooke is really horrid. Anyway, I wouldn't want a dad like Tiegan's – he's bald and he keeps racing pigeons, and he makes her mum wash the pigeons' bowls in the dishwasher. That's what Cassie says.'

'Is everything all right at school now?'

Sasha hesitates before responding. 'It's better, but I still prefer my old school.'

The rain patters against the window, the streetlamp flickers outside, and the traffic swishes along the wet city roads. I miss the sea, the cries of the gulls and the taste of the salt spray. I miss my dad.

'There is trouble and strife in the family,' Gran says, opening the door to me and Sasha on Sunday.

'How do you work that out?' I kiss her cheek.

'The gravy has gone into lumps. That's a sure sign.'

'Is that another silly superstition?' Sasha says brightly.

'The last time I can remember this happening, Nan and your Grandad Len moved away from Addiscombe.'

'So, who is moving this time?'

Gran looks at me. 'It isn't a move. It's a falling-out.' She turns. 'This way, my loves.'

I wanted to cook lunch for Gran, but she insisted that Sasha and I came to her house to help set up the Digibox. She decided to hang on to it when the best deal she could come up with at the Lunch Club was a swap for a set of ceramic hair-straighteners and a steam facial.

'I planned to dish it straight onto the plates as there are only three of us. You carve, and I'll sieve the gravy,' Gran says as I follow her into the kitchen. 'Sasha, there's a present for you on the dining table, a notebook and pen. I won them at Bingo. I've had another lucky week.'

My grandmother starts to press gravy through a sieve with a wooden spoon, while I pick up the carving knife and fork to carve the beef.

'I hear that you've fallen out with your mother,' she goes on. 'I realise that it isn't all that difficult. I've lost count of the times that I've fallen out with my June, but what is it all about?'

'What did she tell you?' I apply the edge of the blade to the meat. It slides off. I press it in harder, and get hacking.

'That you accused her of ruining your life. She said that she thought you should get over it.'

'How can I, when I've only just discovered the facts?'

'Forget the facts,' Gran says. 'I'm asking you to hold out the hatchet.'

'Bury it, you mean? Or hold out the olive branch?'

'Oh,' scolds Gran, 'you've got me all confused.'

124

'Do you know what my mother – my *ex*-mother – did?'

'I don't need to know. Everyone is allowed a few secrets,' Gran says enigmatically

'What's that, Mum?' Sasha pipes up from down the hallway.

'Nothing, Big Ears,' I say lightly, then lower my voice, and go on. 'I am sorry, Gran, but I shall never forgive her.'

'Never forgive who, for what?' Sasha interrupts from the doorway into the kitchen. When she realises that neither Gran nor I are about to enlighten her, she continues, 'Thanks for the notebook, Great-Granma. I'm using it to write my birthday list.'

We sit down for roast beef and Yorkshire pudding. Afterwards, Gran's black-and-white jigsaw puzzle of a cat jumps onto Sasha's lap, pushes its head through the crook of her elbow and starts licking at her empty plate.

Gran has shared her life with a series of cats, calling each one, male and female, Old Tom. Like many people who live alone, Gran sometimes finds it easier to address critical remarks to her pet than directly to the person concerned.

Gran grabs a teacloth and flaps it at the cat, which takes no notice.

'Old Tom doesn't mind the lumps in the gravy.' Sasha smiles.

'Your nan considers that this cat lives here for its own convenience. She calls it cupboard love. Well, Old Tom,' Gran says fondly, 'I fancy that your motives are purer than some people's. *Some* people' (I assume that she is referring to my mother), 'are always on the make.'

'Guess what, Great-Granma?' Sasha tickles the cat behind the ears. 'Mum is going to arrange for me to meet my dad.'

'If I can trace him after all this time,' I say quickly.

'And if he wants to see me,' Sasha adds.

'He's bound to want to see you,' says Gran. 'One day, you will have a father. Whether he is, like a washing powder, of the biological or non-biological kind, remains to be seen. Whatever happens, you can be sure that it will all come out in the wash.'

Gran offers us dessert. Sasha has a slice of apricot tart. I decline. Gran shuffles through some papers in the top drawer of the sideboard, selects an A4 booklet, and hands it over to me.

'This might take a while.' I flick through the instructions for setting up and using the Digibox. It isn't as bad as I thought; the procedures are duplicated in ten different languages.

'It's in the living room, along with my flash new telly. I had the sofa removed to fit it in. My June,' Gran says, and I wonder if she is regretting what she said about her daughter over lunch, 'said that I'd need a scart socket, so I had a word with Nora from Bingo. You might remember her, Terri – Nora Fulbright, the school nit nurse. She's ninety-two, so she's been retired for a long time, and to supplement her pension, she dabbles in selling secondhand electricals. Lo and behold, she turns up with her nephew this afternoon, with a choice of two televisions.'

'How much did you pay for it?'

126

'About a hundred, but I can afford it. I have a bit put by, and I've applied for an extra allowance for a regular supply of inter-continentals.' Gran lowers her voice, but I suspect that Sasha can still hear her. 'I haven't got any problems down below...'

'You mean incontinence pads,' I interrupt.

'As I was saying, a person from one of the charities for old-age pensioners visited the Lunch Club, and suggested that we made sure we claimed everything we're entitled to. We had a chat about it afterwards, and decided that after all our generation did for this country, we deserved a bit of luxury.'

'Exactly what kind of company are you getting into?'

'You can joke about it, but although I have you and Sasha, and my June, my circle of friends is diminishing as, one by one, they pass away. There is no one left of my generation that I was close to.' Her eyes mist over. 'I have lost them all.'

'I'm sorry. I didn't think...'

'I have had to make new acquaintances at the Club, and I'm proud to count on some of them as my friends. We can talk about anything and everything: gout, the price of Eccles cakes – I do like a nice Eccles cake – and bedsocks. We understand each other because we're going through the same...' She pauses, frowning.

'Stuff?' Sasha says helpfully.

'That's right. We're going through the same stuff together.'

'I didn't mean to make light of it.'

'You'll be old soon enough,' Gran says gently.

'Now, can you get this digi-mi-thingummy box working, or am I going to have to sell it to Nora for a knock-down price?'

Once we are settled in Gran's living room, which would be better described now as the television room as it is dominated by a 42-inch widescreen TV, I remove the Digibox from its packaging. Immediately, Old Tom jumps into the cardboard container and curls up, purring.

'I'd like a pet cat,' says Sasha.

'We can't have one in the flat. Pat wouldn't allow it.' I examine the cables, and the back of Gran's television set. The instructions in English for the Digibox turn out to be Double Dutch to me. I hand over to Sasha who plays with the cables and the remote controls, while Gran and I drink tea.

'I'm good at the techie stuff,' Sasha says smugly, calling up a twenty-four-hour news programme on the television screen. 'Mum doesn't have a clue.'

'What would you like for your birthday, Sasha?' Gran asks.

'First of all, I'd like a pet even though Mum says that we can't have one, a trampoline, two beds and, most of all, a dad.' Sasha produces a birthday list on a piece of paper torn from her new notebook, and hands it over to me. She has drawn a picture of a man with a toothy smile and fat legs, dressed in shorts, socks and sandals. In one hand he holds a can of beer, and in the other, a football.

'What would be on your birthday list?' I ask Gran, trying to divert her from Sasha's mention of the beds.

Gran's face creases into a grin. 'Health, happiness and jellied eels. What about you, Terri?'

'The same, but without the eels.'

'I wish you hadn't mentioned the beds,' I say later to Sasha, when we're back at the flat, with me standing over my daughter while she cleans her teeth.

'I don't think Great-Granma heard me.'

I hope not. My grandmother has done more than enough for us already.

'You'll have to give me a list of things that I mustn't say in front of her because I can't remember them all,' Sasha goes on, dribbling toothpaste. 'By the way, can I borrow your shades, the ones you were wearing when we left *Flower Power?* Cassie and I need them for dressing up.'

'As long as you don't lose them.' I find my sunglasses in my handbag where I left them, and hand them over to Sasha, before giving the flat a quick once-over with a duster. When I am folding up the clean clothes, I notice that one of my blouses has a pink smear across the collar. I scratch at it with my nail. It smudges like lipstick. In fact, it probably is lipstick...

Why should anyone want to come into our flat while we're out and interfere with my clothing? I try to shrug off my sense of outrage and disgust with a little more tidying up, whistling the tune to 'Always Look on the Bright Side of Life'. When I ring Sharon, she tries to make light of it, saying, 'You should be grateful, Terri. It's the first time you've had your clothing interfered with in years.'

Chapter Six

I can't remember when I last had my clothing disturbed, at least not while I was wearing it, nor can I recall when I last received a Valentine. However, love is in the air, and even if it isn't destined for me, I am lighter of step, and since Martin paid me my second month's wages, somewhat heavier of purse than I have been of late.

Last night, I helped Martin and Val to dress *Posies* for Valentine's Day, and make sure that everyone receives their gifts: traditional bouquets; baskets of roses and acid-green spray chrysanths; roses and lavender, tied with ribbon which has been pricked out with heart-shaped decorations.

This morning, bunches of helium-filled balloons bob up and down outside the shop, brightening a cloudy day. Inside, you can hardly move for red roses.

Sasha follows me through to the back room where Martin is busy with the order book. He's taken to printing instructions from a routefinder on the Internet to help George find unfamiliar destinations, and colour-coding the bouquets with the list. Will it prevent further errors? We'll see.

Sasha drops her schoolbag and coat on the floor, and shoots off towards the stairs.

'Where do you think you're going?' I demand.

She turns and tips her head to one side.

'You haven't got time to play. It's half past eight. School starts soon.'

'I'll fetch Cassie and Elliot.'

'I'll fetch them.' Martin looks up. 'I know what will happen if you go upstairs, Sasha. You'll all find some game to play, and your mum will end up going to school without you.'

'Stick your coat on while we're waiting, Petal. It's starting to rain.'

'The rain in Spain falls mainly on the plain,' Sasha intones in a Cockney accent worthy of Chas and Dave.

Martin rounds up Cassie and Elliot, and hugs each of them in turn.

'Now you behave yourself today, Ells,' he warns. 'If I hear from Terri, or Mrs Britton, that you've been naughty, I shall take your light sabres away for a week.'

'You can't, Dad,' says Cassie. 'You put them in the box yesterday after Elliot wrote that rude word on the bathroom wall with one of Mum's old lipsticks.'

'What rude word?' Sasha joins in.

Cassie whispers into Sasha's ear, loud enough for the rest of us to hear. 'B-U-M.' Both girls dissolve into giggles.

'Let's go,' I say. 'Sasha's great-grandmother is going to collect you all from school this afternoon.' I checked before we left the flat. Gran sounded slightly breathless on the phone; she blamed it on an energetic Salsacise session before breakfast.

'Are you sure that it won't be too much trouble?' I asked her.

'It's nice to be needed, Terri,' she told me.

131

'Thanks.' Martin looks me in the eyes. His face relaxes into a smile, and I become aware of a tiny pulse thrilling at my temple. Now that I have recovered from the shock of discovering that Martin is no longer a handsome teenager, I am beginning to realise that he has matured into an incredibly attractive middle-aged man. I wonder if Letitia realises how lucky she is.

On the way to school, Sasha walks beside me with the piece of artwork that she insisted on bringing with her, covering it with her coat to protect it from the rain. I caught her working on it by torchlight under her bedclothes last night, giving her duvet cover a funky makeover with orange gel pen in the process.

'Martin's very strict,' Sasha says. 'Do you think my dad's the same?'

'I don't know, darling.'

'You don't know very much about him, con-sidering that you had a baby together.'

I change the subject. 'Why don't you walk with Cassie?'

'She's in a mood.'

'She wasn't ten minutes ago. You couldn't stop giggling, back at *Posies.*'

'We've had a disagreement.' Sasha falls silent, and sets her mouth in a straight line. That is all she will say on the matter. There is no point in pursuing it.

The rain falls harder. I take shelter under my umbrella while Elliot splashes in fresh puddles.

'Do you mind?' I ask, dodging the spray.

'No.' He lands in another and another, sending a shower of black water up my legs.

I raise my umbrella, give it a twirl, and leap into the next puddle. I am not sure who is the wettest, me or Elliot. Laughing, he jumps again.

'Why don't you two join in?' I call, but the girls refuse, apparently having more serious matters on their minds.

'Mum, you've been eating too many of those good bacteria. You're just like Mary Poppins,' Sasha says. 'Will everyone look out for Jacob? I have to see him.'

'Jacob is Cassie's boyfriend,' Elliot interrupts. 'Cassie's got a boyfriend,' he goes on in a singsong voice, designed to wind his big sister up to maximum effect. 'Cassie's got a boyfriend.'

Cassie aims a kick at her little brother.

'Leave her alone, Elliot,' I intervene.

'Jacob isn't my boyfriend any more, and it's all Sasha's fault.' Cassie glowers at her. 'I wish you'd stayed at your old school.' Then tears spring to her eyes. 'I wish that my mum was here.'

'Oh, Cassie.' I drop back and slip my arm around her shoulders, giving her a squeeze.

'Mummy will be back soon,' Elliot says.

'That's what they all say – Dad and Granny – but I don't believe them any more. Mum said she'd be home last week, and that was ages ago. She's never coming back.'

How can I console her? I haven't a clue when Letitia is supposed to be coming home. Or *if...*

I send Cassie and Sasha into school, and make sure that Elliot is safely delivered to his teacher, before I return to *Posies* where I find Val holding the receiver of the phone in one hand and thumbing through the Wedding Brochure with the other, while a queue of four customers wait in a tidy line at the counter.

'We don't do plastic. If you're looking for fake flowers, try the garden centre.' Val rolls her eyes towards me. I know what she means. It is like asking for a Pot Noodle in a Michelin-starred restaurant.

I leave my brolly in the sink in the back room and put on my new tabard. Martin is loading the van through the back door from the alleyway. George is sitting on the step at the rear of the van with his head in his hands. He peers out between his fingers, and groans.

'The landlord forgot to call time on Happy Hour last night,' Martin says, as if reading my mind. 'Don't mention this to my mother. She'll hold the fort at the front, while you make up the orders as they come in. I'll drive, and Dad will deliver today's bouquets to the door – the parking in Croydon is impossible, especially now that the traffic wardens turn up out of the blue on mopeds.' Martin is holding a cushion with *Be Mine* piped across it in white lettering. He glances down, looks up at me and quickly turns it around so that the plain side is showing.

A wave of warmth rushes up my neck.

'Did Elliot behave himself?' Martin asks.

'Apart from antagonising his sister. Cassie was upset about not seeing her mum. She seems to be under the impression that Letitia will never return.'

Martin frowns. 'I'll have a word.'

'It does seem a little unfair, keeping the children on tenterhooks.'

134

'I know. Sometimes I'm so wrapped up in the situation myself that I forget what the kids are going through.' Martin sighs. 'We haven't sold the bar, after all. The buyer pulled out at the last minute, after he had an accountant look over the books. Letitia put it back on the market with six property agents, advertised it online, and had vests printed with *Bar Tequila For Sale* printed on the front, so that even when she's on the beach, she is doing something. We've had three more offers since, but when she eventually twigged that they were in euros, not pounds sterling, she decided to hold out for more money. I've suggested that we cut our losses, but she insists on staying. I'm not sure how much she wants to come home.'

'What, with her family waiting for her?' I say, aghast. 'I'd be desperate to see Sasha by now if it were me.'

'You and Letitia are very different. I don't blame her. I'm not Mr Perfect. Letitia began training as a beauty therapist when Cassie started school, but gave up halfway through the course because my parents decided to retire. It made financial sense for us to move into the flat above the shop, and for Letitia and me to run the business together. At first, it worked out well. Letitia is great with the customers, but...' Martin nods towards the front of the shop where his mother is serving customers, 'there was always a certain amount of interference in our affairs: how we ran *Posies*; how we brought up the children. It was meant well, but Letitia couldn't always see that.'

I smile ruefully. I know all about parental interference, well-intended or otherwise.

'I do have the occasional celebrity client, but Letitia imagined *Martin Blake* becoming an internationally recognised name, and our flowers appearing in *Hello!* and *OK!* magazines.'

'Terri!' Val calls.

'She is very young, twelve years my junior,' Martin goes on hurriedly. 'She should have seen the world before she settled down with two kids and a grumpy old man.'

'We aren't paying you to stand about gossiping,' Val calls again.

'I'd better go.' On my way to join Val at the front of the shop, I stop to rescue a bear that has fallen from the shelves. It has blue fur, a smile and a squint. I am aware that Val is watching me. She doesn't like Martin paying me attention, does she?

As I set the bear back on the staging, I feel rather sorry for it, being left on the shelf. I know the feeling, and the fact that it is Valentine's Day makes it more acute.

However, I refuse to mope about feeling sorry for myself. The atmosphere is buzzing with rumours of proposals, new love affairs, and life-long romances. It gives me great pleasure to think that our flowers – there, I am beginning to feel like one of the team at *Posies* – help to bring people together.

Val introduces me to Maureen and Ella, two elderly ladies from the local church, with tartan shopping trolleys and leather handbags.

'You look after them, Terri,' she says.

'No Martin today?' Maureen asks.

'He's busy.'

'What a pity.'

'Have you any preference?' I ask.

'Tall, dark and handsome over short, fat and blond,' Maureen giggles.

'Terri's talking about flowers, not men.' Ella apologises on her friend's behalf.

'I shall be giving them up for Lent,' Maureen says solemnly, but she is one of those people who cannot remain solemn for long. 'Except for Martin, and our nice new vicar.'

Eventually, they leave the shop with their trolleys filled with lilies.

At three-thirty, Gran turns up at *Posies* on her scooter, having collected Sasha, Cassie and Elliot from school. Elliot is perched in front of Gran on the buggy, while Carrie and Sasha jog along behind. Gran parks, and brings the children into the shop.

'The poor little chap was tired,' she mumbles. 'I gave him a lift.' She smiles fondly at the children. 'Hey, girls and boy, what do you call a group of florists?'

'A bunch,' says Sasha.

'Clever clogs.' There is something different about my grandmother, and it isn't just the emerald-green trousers which clash with her turquoise mac. Her lips keep receding into her mouth, and she seems to have some difficulty forming her words.

'Where are your teeth?'

My grandmother's eyes widen. She pats the pocket of her mac, then rummages about in her handbag.

'Allow me to help you, Lil,' Martin says chivalrously. He takes her handbag gently from over her shoulder, and empties it out on the table behind the till. He turns away discreetly while Gran examines her belongings which are full of little bits of foil and paper wrappers.

'Have you been buying the children sweets?' I ask sternly.

'We shared a packet of mints, that's all.'

'That's all,' Cassie says.

'That's all, isn't it, Mrs Parkin?' says Elliot very politely. 'See? I did it.' He grins. 'I said what you told us to say.'

Gran resumes her search of the contents of her bag. There are keys, a dog-eared photo of Sasha, a lace-trimmed hankie, and a pair of knickers! (If I thought that *my* pants were large, these are enormous.) Gran sidles them off the table and into her pocket.

'They're spares, in case I should meet with an accident and end up in hospital,' she mutters in explanation. 'My old mum, bless her soul, taught me to be prepared for any eventuality.'

'Have you got a mum then, Mrs Parkin?' Cassie's eyes are like saucers.

'She died a long time ago,' says Gran. 'I come from a long line of mothers, generations of them.'

'Everybody does,' says Sasha.

'You're a clever girl. I don't know where she gets her brains from, Terri.'

'She didn't inherit them from you, did she?' I tease. 'Where on earth are your teeth?'

Sasha giggles and blurts out what the rest of us have been too polite to say. 'You do look funny without them.'

'I look pretty funny *with* them.' Gran starts to repack her handbag. 'I must have left them at home.' She stops for tea and a piece of Val's latest sponge creation, a Victoria sandwich filled with jam, and decorated with pink fondant roses. It's nice and soft for her to eat.

'Can I have a word?' Martin draws me aside. 'I have three weddings booked for next Saturday, and I wondered if you could come in early to help me make up the arrangements. One of the brides is having flowers with everything: orchid corsages and buttonholes for two hundred guests, and a porch decoration for the church.' He smiles. 'You can bring Sasha with you.'

'Are you sure?'

'Quite sure.'

I congratulate myself on having a boss who understands the logistical problems of having sole responsibility for childcare, while holding down a job which entails working flexible hours. 'Thanks, Martin.'

'You can say no. I don't want you to think that I'd take advantage of you,' he presses.

'I don't mind.' The bell jangles, and on the staging just behind Martin's head, a group of potted narcissi tremble in the draught as the door opens. A long-forgotten emotion, desire perhaps, flutters down my spine. Take advantage? I am beginning to think that I'd quite like him to – hypothetically, of course.

When we arrive home at the flat at five-thirty, Sasha presses the piece of artwork that she has been carrying around with her – an orange heart on a piece of yellow card – into my hand. 'You'd better have this, seeing that you didn't receive anything in the post. Happy Valentine's Day.'

I hug her, touched by her thoughtful gesture.

'I'll cross out Jacob's name later,' she adds, 'and make it out to you.'

I smile to myself. 'What happened to Jacob?'

'I changed my mind.'

A woman's prerogative, I muse. I thought that I hated Martin. Now I am beginning to like him. Note the word 'like', as a friend. I believe that he could become a friend again, nothing more, because I am no longer a naïve and innocent teenager, and Martin is in a long-term relationship, equivalent in status to a married man. I don't do married men. Never have done. Never will.

All things in moderation: that is my strategy for a balanced lifestyle. Martin appears to have made lifestyle choices that are rather different from my own. At five o'clock the following Saturday morning, when it's still dark, and freezing cold, I find him sitting on the stairs at *Posies*, eating vanilla ice cream topped with sugar sprinkles.

'Why can't *we* have ice cream for breakfast, Mum?' Sasha asks immediately.

'Because it isn't good for you.' I gaze at Martin. 'Haven't you heard of Jamie Oliver?'

'He campaigned for healthy eating in schools,' he says sheepishly. 'This is home.'

I don't suppose that Martin will ever change. He's eaten ice cream for breakfast since I can remember. An only child, his mother indulged him, and apparently, he still indulges himself.

'You can't imagine how pleased I am to see

you.' The effect of Martin's sultry smile is spoiled slightly by the way the dyes in the sprinkles have leached across his lips, giving them a blue hyacinth-like tinge.

The feeling is mutual, but for different reasons, I suspect.

'Come on, Sasha – let's get in the warm. You can play with Cassie later, when she wakes up.' We go into the back room and I look around. 'What shall I do first?'

At that moment, there is the sound of a key in the lock, and Val marches in. Taking off her coat, and dropping it on the little table behind the counter, she comes into the back room, puts on her tabard and rolls up her sleeves.

'Terri can do the bridesmaids' baskets,' Val decides for her son. 'We need six.'

'Just a moment. I've got something for you, Terri.' Martin hands me a small blue bear. 'It's the last of the Valentine's Day bears. I thought you took a fancy to him.'

'Thanks.' I clutch the bear to my chest at the point where my heart is beating hardest. It would be true to say that he wasn't the only item in the shop I took a fancy to. Okay, so I am a love-starved single mum with a fervid imagination. I think that means I'm allowed the occasional moment of weakness.

'I thought you were supposed to be helping your father unload the van, Martin,' Val says curtly. 'Put that bear back on the shelf – we can always use it next year.'

'It belongs to Terri,' Martin interrupts.

'I hope she's paid for it.'

'I gave it to her.'

'Oh, Martin.'

'As a token of our appreciation for all the hard work she's been putting in.'

'As long as that's all that you're giving her.' I think that is what Val says, but I am too shocked and angry to respond. 'Martin! A word!'

Ignoring both mother and son, who disappear into the dark alleyway behind *Posies* to continue their discussion, I sit down at one end of the table and get started. I line six baskets, stapling plastic sheeting to their willow frames, then fix a piece of foam that Martin has already soaked in cold water, to the base of each basket with tape.

Meanwhile, Val returns, makes more coffee and sits down opposite me. 'You need the white ribbon for those,' she says bossily. 'It's a white wedding. Quite unusual, these days...'

I try to concentrate on tying the ribbons, wiring the bows and wrapping the handles of the baskets, but Val seems determined that I should hear exactly what she has to say.

'I'd forgotten that you'd met Del Bickley before.' She cups her chin and leans her elbow on the table top. 'Who knows what passion lies re-pressed beneath a funeral director's black coat?'

Who wants to know, I wonder.

'I don't know another man who pays so much attention to personal grooming. He has lovely hands, doesn't he?'

'I can't say that I've noticed.' I glance at mine, at the creases engrained with dirt, at the peeling nail polish – blue with a sparkle – that Sasha painted on a few days before.

'So smooth.'

'Some people age better than others. It's in the genes.'

Val's lips curve into a small smile. 'As with flowers, one never knows the consequences of unplanned breeding until it is too late.'

'I suspect that Del's state of preservation has more to do with all that embalming fluid that he uses. You should ask him if you can try some – unless it's too late for your skin.' Good. I like to get a dig in of my own, every so often.

'It is never too late to make changes to your life and lifestyle.' Val's nostrils flare as she looks me up and down, more dragon than crocodile. 'Have you shopped at Harrods or strolled across the Millennium Bridge?'

I shake my head, wondering where Val's conversation is heading, as she continues, 'Del could show you the sights. You should encourage him a little.'

I see. Well, I won't be flashing my loins at Del, tabard or no tabard.

'I can't understand why he hasn't been snapped up,' Val goes on. 'He was engaged for many years to a complementary therapist. Rachel was a lovely girl – she found something to admire in everyone. Anyway, in the end, she begged Del's sisters to persuade him to put his father in a nursing home, so that they could have a life of their own, but he refused to do it. He cared for his father until he died – and afterwards, of course.'

'I hope that you're not suggesting that I go on a date with Del Bickley.'

'Why not? You're young-ish, free and single.' Val

pauses, then says, 'I've never seen a romance entitled *The Funeral Director and the Florist*, but it does have a ring about it, doesn't it?'

A hollow one, I think, trying not to laugh at the idea. It is ridiculous. 'Why do married people assume that all us singletons are after a relationship?'

'In my opinion, there should be no single women in this world to go around distracting attached men from their partners. Singletons should be banished to another planet.'

Of course! Val isn't worried about *my* happiness, never has been. She is concerned for Martin and Letitia.

'I don't need your help to find myself a husband, thank you.' The cheek of it!

'You don't appear to have done very well on your own, ending up as an unmarried mother of a child without a father.'

'It wasn't an immaculate conception. Of course Sasha has a father.'

'Yes, but where is he? I'm not criticising you,' Val goes on. 'I'm merely making a helpful observation. I often felt sorry for you, lacking as you were in parental guidance.'

'Parents don't always know what is best for their offspring,' I say coolly, recalling how both Val and my mother had a hand in breaking up my relationship with Martin.

I begin to build the outlines of the basket arrangements with golden privet and stems of tuberose, and finish off with freesias, recessing some of the heads to give the impression of depth. I smile wryly to myself, doubting very much that

144

the six bridesmaids will concern themselves overly with the techniques I have used to create their pretty baskets.

By eight-thirty, my fingers are aching, but the buckets and boxes of flowers that were scattered haphazardly across the back room, have now metamorphosed into regimented lines of dazzling white and gold displays that brighten the winter's day.

Much later, at the end of the day, I tidy up. I pick out the best of the discarded and fallen petals and put them aside, then sweep the rest into the bin. At home in the flat, I tip the petals into a spare cereal bowl and mix in some moss. I add a few drops of essential oil of lavender onto the moss so that I don't discolour the petals, and park the bowl on top of the television in the living room to banish the musty odour of Pat's old carpet. My pot-pourri won't last too long, since I should have dried the petals, but soon I'll be able to replace them with the roses I have hung upside down over Pat's dodgy boiler to air-dry.

I also borrow a pair of decent secateurs from work, and cut some foliage from the garden to create an arrangement for the boarded-up fire-place. The flat is beginning to feel more like home, and after tea, I put my feet up on the sofa and read the paper.

'Are you looking for a bed, or a secondhand trampoline?' Sasha asks over my shoulder. 'I'd like a trampoline.'

I shut the paper quickly, as if reading the news has suddenly become illegal. Why do mums do that – feel guilty for taking a break?

'If I can't have a trampoline, I'd like a sister. Elliot's so lucky.'

'I don't think Elliot always sees it that way, do you?'

'He has someone to talk to and share with.'

'You can share with me.'

'That's different, Mum.' Sasha falls silent.

'Life doesn't always work out the way you want it,' I say softly. 'I thought you were supposed to be doing your homework.'

'I've finished it.' She plumps herself down next to me and thrusts her book under my nose. 'See!'

I scan her sentences.

I threw *a brick through a window. Please note that no windows were smashed during the making of this sentence.*

I can't help laughing. 'How was school this week?'

'Miss Hudson was really grumpy.'

'I was grumpy when I was pregnant with you.'

'If we packed our things, we could be home by midnight,' Sasha says suddenly, changing the subject.

'We *are* home.'

'I mean home to Devon.'

'You know we can't go back there.' I reach out and stroke her hair, and wonder if my mother felt like the Wicked Witch when she sat me down to tell me that we were moving.

I'd just come home from school, with my tie dangling around my neck and my shirtsleeves rolled up over my sunburned arms. In those days, we didn't realise that sitting out in the hottest part of the day, smothered with cooking oil, isn't all that great for your skin.

'Come out the back and sit down, love. We need to have a little chat.' My mother has always had a knack of making 'a little chat' sound ominous. 'Don't go making excuses that you have homework to do. You never do your homework.'

I grabbed a packet of Opal Fruits off the shelf, and followed her to the room out the back where I sat myself down on a pile of newspapers.

'Your dad and I have decided to get out of the newspaper business,' Mum began. 'We're going to look at a property at the weekend that might be suitable to run as a B & B.'

'Oh.' I started thinking that, if it was just around the corner, I could stay at school and still drop round to see Martin. Nothing would change.

'It could be perfect.' Mum's cigarette smouldered. 'It has six bedrooms, two en-suite, off-street parking and sea views.'

Sea? Since when had this place been Addis-combe-on-Sea? I guessed that she was talking about the South Coast. There were plenty of trains that ran direct from East Croydon station to Brighton. It wouldn't be so bad.

Mum took a drag on her cigarette, and expelled several uneven rings of smoke. 'So we're going to Devon on Saturday,' she continued eventually. 'I've arranged for George to run the shop for the day.'

'Devon? We can't!' I yelped. It might as well have been Mars. 'What about my exams?'

'There are schools in Devon.'

'What about Gran and Grandad?'

'They can visit,' my father said, appearing in

147

the shadows behind Mum at this point. Unlike her plucked and pencilled eyebrows, his were bushy, like nests of spiders. 'Out of season.' From his tone of voice, I detected that, just for once, it was he who was calling the shots here, not my mother, so it was no use me appealing to his better nature.

'What about Martin?' I blurted out.

Ash trembled on the end of my mother's cigarette. A clump dropped, hit the cardboard box at her feet, marked *Cash & Carry*, and scattered.

'What about him?' she said casually.

Dad scowled at her. He didn't approve of her smoking, but what could he say when he made a living as a purveyor of tobacco? I was aware, though, of a new tension between my parents. Something had changed. My father was the strong one. My mother could hardly bring herself to look at him.

'Did you hear that, Len? Terri's worried about leaving the boy next door.' Mum turned to me.

'I don't have to go anywhere,' I said stubbornly, but what were my options? Val would never let me stay with the Blakes. How about a bench in the park across the road from the Parade? Or a sleeping bag in the newsagents shop doorway? I didn't possess a sleeping bag. I had no choice.

The sins of the mothers shall be visited upon the daughters. It is true. My parents uprooted me because of my mother's affair with George. I uprooted Sasha because of my bankruptcy. Did we really believe that we were off to embrace new and happier lives, or were we running away in an attempt to leave our shame behind?

Lying here on the sofa now, next to my beloved daughter, I wonder what I can do to help Sasha settle down. Would she be happier about staying in Addiscombe if I did manage to organise some contact with her dad?

Eventually, I send her to bed, and wait for her to fall asleep before I can call Sharon. I don't want Big Ears listening in to what I have to say.

Much later, an hour after she is supposed to have switched out her light, I catch her making an 'I'm sorry' card for Cassie under her duvet. It reads, *You can have Jacob for your boyfriend, because I like Hayden better anyway*. The fickleness of youth!

'Go to sleep,' I say. 'Per ... lease.'

Sasha's face peers over the top of her duvet. 'I can't fall asleep to order.'

'Count sheep, or something,' I say in exasperation. By the time I'm free to ring Sharon, she'll be tucked up in bed with Chris and a nice cup of cocoa. I make to leave the bedroom, but Sasha calls me back.

'Yes?'

'I've decided that I'll count trams.'

'Good idea.' I resolve to try counting trams the next time I can't sleep, because Sasha is out for the count within minutes. Pouring myself a large glass of wine, I phone Sharon.

'Thanks for repaying the loan on the car,' she says, once we have caught up with family news, 'but you needn't have sent that pound in the post. You know that I'd never turn up on your doorstep to demand my money back.'

'One thing that losing my business taught me is

149

how much I hate being in debt. I don't do older men, married men, or credit. They are my three new rules for a happy life.' Sharon chuckles as I go on, 'Did I tell you that Val fancies herself as a matchmaker? She's only trying to set me up with Del, the funeral director next door to *Posies*.'

'What is he like then? I'm picturing Gomez from *The Addams Family*.'

'I'm sure that he's a very nice man, but we have nothing in common. I arrange flowers; Del arranges funerals.' I pause, staring out of the kitchen window. There are no blinds or curtains, and the tremoring striplight illuminates the lawn just as far as the first pole of Pat's washing line, where I catch sight of a flash of pale satin. A woman in a flowing dressing-gown, headscarf and pink wellies, is unpegging the clothes from the line at last, and bundling them into a basket.

'Can I ask you a favour?' I say, my voice trembling a little. 'It's about Robbie, your brother's friend.'

'And Sasha's father,' Sharon continues for me.

'I've decided to get in touch with him.'

The line falls silent for a moment. 'Why now? After all you said about keeping your lives separate?'

'Sasha has been asking if she can meet her dad.' A lump catches in my throat. 'I knew that this would happen one day...'

'If Chris suddenly announced that an ex-girl-friend had contacted him to tell him that he had a daughter, I don't know how I'd react.'

'I know you – you'd be fair and reasonable.'

'Before or after I'd tipped a couple of jars of

150

chili powder into his portion of chili con carne? I'm not sure. Is it fair, after all this time?'

'Is it fair on Sasha?'

'I'll have a word with my brother and see what I can find out,' Sharon says eventually.

'You won't rush in and scare Robbie off?'

'I'll be as tactful as I possibly can,' Sharon promises. 'Like Mama Ramotswe of The No. 1 Ladies' Detective Agency, I shall be the soul of discretion.'

I check on Sasha again before I go to bed. It is as if her room has been hit by a tsunami which has picked up all her belongings then deposited them on its retreat from the shore. As I wade through pencils, dirty socks and hairclips to her bed, I come across a ball of screwed-up paper. I pick it up, but before I chuck it in the bin that I bought to help Sasha keep her room tidy (ha ha), I notice my name scribbled on it: *For the attention of Ms Mills*.

I unscrunch and smooth the paper out. It is a letter from school. The Headmaster requests that I attend an appointment to discuss the matter of Sasha's unacceptable behaviour. My heart plummets. My daughter? There must be some mistake.

I look down at Sasha. She smiles in her sleep, and I wonder if she is dreaming about her father. What on earth will I do if Sharon can't find him?

Chapter Seven

'I'd expect Gran's memory to fail occasionally, but not yours, Sasha. What is this?' I wave the letter from school in front of her as she eats her cornflakes the following morning. 'When were you going to remember to give it to me? I've had to ring Martin to make last-minute arrangements so that I can keep this appointment. Is there anything that you'd like to tell me before the Headmaster does?'

'Not really,' Sasha says through a mouthful of cereal, 'except that everything he says is not true.'

'If I find out that you're in any trouble, I'll be inclined to cancel your birthday treat.'

Sasha shrugs. 'Whatever.'

'Have you been borrowing my pants?'

'No way.'

'I wondered if you might be using them as rags for your painting, only I can't find a single pair this morning.'

'I don't care.'

'What is wrong with you?'

'Nothing.' Sasha's lip wobbles, suggesting otherwise.

I slip my arm around her shoulders, lean down and kiss her on her cheek.

'Love you,' I whisper. 'I'm sorry that I've caused you grief, moving you away from your friends.'

'I'm fine,' Sasha says abruptly. 'Can I borrow

your shades again, for a Science project this time? I would explain, but you wouldn't understand.'

That's me been told, I think, and it isn't for the last time today.

I feel about six years old when I emerge from the Headmaster's office later the same morning. My cheeks are stinging as if he has thwacked me with a cane.

'Terri?' Martin is pacing the corridor outside, his jacket damp with rain. 'So this is why you wanted time off. I had hoped that you were going out shopping, or to have your hair done, something like that.'

'Is my hair that much of a mess?'

'I didn't mean...' Martin swears softly, and my pulse flutters as he continues, 'You look great. You always look great.'

I am not sure how to respond, whether to laugh off his compliment, or accept it gracefully. I choose the latter, and change the subject. 'What are you doing here?'

'Well, I haven't come back to update my knowledge of Maths and Geography.' Martin smiles, and I wish that we could go back to the classroom and revise our history. 'The last time I went to the Headmaster's office, it was for the slipper, because he couldn't find his cane. I have an appointment.' He glances at his watch. 'I shouldn't be long. Wait, and we'll walk back to the shop together.'

'I'll go on ahead. Your mother is looking after *Posies* on her own.'

'She'll cope. Stay, Terri, it's raining, and you haven't got a coat.'

I don't mind rain – it rained a lot in Devon. I

can recall many hours walking on the beach in the rain, waiting for Martin to get in touch, hanging about like the oil tankers that sat on the grey horizon.

'You can have my umbrella.' Martin grins and adds, 'When I'm finished in there.'

'Okay.' I bite my lip, suppressing a smile. Martin hasn't changed at all. He wants to know why I have been summoned to the school. He wants all the goss.

Martin emerges from the Headmaster's office after about ten minutes. We walk down the corridor and go outside into the rain. Martin slows when we are halfway across the playground, in front of the wall which used to be 'home' during games of Kiss Chase. I had to explain the rules to my daughter because the political correctness of the present day has prevented Sasha from experiencing both the horror of being snogged by the class slug, and the shame of not being snogged at all.

The rain falls like water from a bucket. Martin fiddles with the press-stud and opens his umbrella, revealing blue and red canvas with *Thomas the Tank Engine* printed across it.

'I picked up the wrong one.' Martin hands it to me. Our fingers touch, very briefly, the contact like a shock of static. If he notices my reaction, he doesn't let on. 'Elliot will be climbing the walls when he comes home. The children will have wet play, which means they'll be indoors all day.'

Wet play? A classroom of kids playing Snakes and Ladders, and Dominoes? I glance at Martin's face, at the water dripping down his cheek.

The term 'wet play' conjures up a different image altogether.

'So what was that all about with old Dumbledore in there?' he goes on.

'Sasha has encouraged a gang of girls to fight against injustice.'

'The Avenging Angels.' Martin smiles. 'Cassie is on report, which I don't consider to be fair. They are only standing up for themselves and anyone else who is being bullied by Brooke and Tiegan.'

'The Head didn't mention any names.'

'Cassie has talked about them to me. I only wish I had taken more notice of her before.' Martin rubs the back of his neck. 'It's high spirits, that's all. There's no need to worry about our girls.'

But I do worry. Too permissive? Too tough? What kind of parent am I when my nine-year-old daughter believes that it is okay to set herself up as some kind of gangsta? She'll be running about with her mates and their mobiles, mugging people next. No, not really – but I thought I had taught her that you don't fight wrong with wrong.

I remember how Martin protected me, how he held my hand on my first day at school, walking me round and round the playground. We walk together now, sharing the umbrella. I link my arm through Martin's and we stroll along in companionable silence. Why companionable? Because we are friends. Just friends.

The rain settles to a light drizzle, and the sun tries to burn its way through the low cloud. It gives me an excuse to step away, to put space between us, because what is beginning to burn through my soul is not the warmth of friendship, but the fire of lust.

Turning the corner into the Parade, I hear shouting. Someone is in trouble. Martin runs on ahead, with me chasing behind him. Outside *Posies*, a group of three yobs with hoodies and baseball caps pulled down over their faces, are bouncing an invalid scooter, and the invalid is still in it, waving their stick.

'It's Gran!' I run at the yobs, stabbing the *Thomas the Tank Engine* brolly at them. 'Get away from her. Leave her alone.'

Two of the attackers run for it. Martin catches the third in an armlock.

'Who do you think you are, picking on a defenceless old woman?' he growls.

'Less of the old.' Gran is off her scooter now, tapping at Martin's prisoner around the ankles with her stick. 'I'll have you know that most of my friends are nonagerians.'

Martin's prisoner suddenly regains his strength and elbows him in the ribs. Martin doubles up, letting him go. The yob scarpers, but Martin is soon behind him, dodging the traffic to cross the road to reach the park beyond. He closes in, lunges, grabs him around the thighs and brings him down with a tackle of which Jonny Wilkinson would be proud.

'I've got the bastard.' Martin grimaces as he marches him with his arms behind his back across the road to us. The youth is cursing and kicking out his feet. 'Oy! That's enough!'

'Let's have a look at you then,' Gran says.

Martin tugs the hoodie down and pulls off the

156

cap, revealing a fifteen- or sixteen-year-old boy with a cruel attack of acne. 'What do you think, Lil?'

'He's just a baby.' Gran sounds surprised. 'How old are you, dear? Ten? Hang on a mo. Aren't you one of Nora Fulbright's great-grandsons?' The boy's face reddens as she continues, 'I shall have to have a word with your great-gran, tell her how you go around attacking people just like her on the streets.'

'No, no, don't do that. Please.' The hard man begins to cry, but I am not inclined towards compassion.

'We really should call the police,' I say.

'I think that Nora will handle it very well,' Gran says.

'She'll tell my dad and he'll kill me. I'm dead meat.'

'It may not be necessary to mention this little episode.' Gran's eyes flash with a wicked gleam. 'I've got a bit of gardening that needs doing. My borders must be dug before the summer, and I can't wield a spade any longer. Perhaps...'

'Yeah.' The boy nods. 'I'll get my mates to help out.'

'Gran! You'll have them nicking your stuff if you let them in your house.' I have visions of Nora Fulbright's shiny widescreen TV being recycled through the network of scamming and money laundering that it appeared from.

'If anything goes missing, I know exactly whom to speak to,' Gran says. 'Do we have an understanding?'

The boy nods.

'Off you go then, sonny. Let him go, Martin.'

I take Gran's hand. 'Are you okay?'

'I'm fine. It's Martin you should be looking after.'

'I'm all right.' He brushes his palms down the front of his jacket. 'You'd better come inside for a restorative cup of tea, Lil.'

'I'd prefer a brandy.'

'I'll see what I can do.'

I escort Gran out to the back room and sit her down on the chair at the table, while Martin pauses to select one of the miniature bottles of brandy from the shelves on the way. I overhear him talking to his mother before he joins us, and pours the contents of a bottle into one of the mugs from the draining-board.

'You don't mind not having it in a glass, Lil?' His shirt slips away from his chest, revealing his naked chest. My heart starts to beat more quickly. My blood runs hot.

'There's no need to stand on ceremony with me, young man.'

I can't help smiling to myself that my grandmother still thinks of Martin as a young man, although I suppose that he is half her age. She takes a swig of her drink, then frowns. 'Have you had to resort to ripping your customers off? Only if this isn't water, I'll eat my hat.'

'Which hat will that be?' Martin teases.

Gran considers for a moment. 'You can choose between my foldaway plastic rain-hood, my Ladies' Day at Ascot hat, or my funeral hat, the black one with ostrich feathers.'

Martin sniffs at the mouth of the bottle. 'It

158

smells like brandy.'

'Taste it.' Gran holds out the mug. Martin takes a sip from the opposite side of the rim that doesn't bear the imprint of her lipstick.

'Your hats are safe, Lil.' He looks towards me. 'We haven't received any complaints, have we?'

'We don't sell much brandy.'

Martin grins ruefully. 'That's because it's water, which is odd, because I'm always reordering that line.' He opens a second bottle. 'Thames Water with a hint of Cognac. Who has been tampering with the alcohol supplies?'

'Don't look at me,' I say, although I am beginning to wish that Martin would look at me in the way that a man looks at a woman he admires. I like to imagine a parallel universe in which Martin is unattached, and he fancies me like mad. 'I'll put the kettle on. Are you sure you aren't hurt, Gran?'

'I am as right as hatpins. Or should it be ninepins?'

'You mean ninepence.'

'Do I?' Gran pauses. 'Oh, I don't know what the world is coming to. I sometimes think that if I were twenty years younger, I'd emigrate.'

That is no idle thought, coming from someone who considers that anywhere south of Croydon and north of Watford is foreign country.

'My Teddy would have been ashamed to be out and about, turned out like those boys. My generation had pride in their appearance, and they knew that if they didn't behave, they'd get a clip around the ear.'

'Who's Teddy?' I ask Gran gently.

'Did I say Teddy?' Her lips quiver and her eyes fill with tears. 'I meant Jack, your grandad.'

'You'd better take Lilian home after she's had her tea,' Martin offers. 'It isn't that busy – you might as well take the rest of the day off.'

'You needn't talk about me as if I'm invisible,' Gran protests.

I am torn. I have taken an hour off already, chasing over to the school to talk about Sasha, and now I have a second relative who needs looking after when I should be working. I look at Gran, her hair ruffled up like a bird's nest, and her eyes dark with exhaustion. How can I leave her on her own after what has just happened? 'Thank you, Martin.'

I escort Gran home, jogging beside the scooter in my kinky boots, and panting out responses to her observations as she bumps and jerks along the pavements. I count three near misses, involving a streetlamp and two pedestrians.

'You have kept your insurance up to date?' I ask her.

'Of course.'

'Don't you have to have regular medical check-ups after the age of seventy, if you want to keep driving?'

'This isn't classified as a motor vehicle. It's a scooter.'

'Well...' I'm trying to be tactful. 'Isn't it time that you considered giving it up?'

'Driving?' Gran stares at me as if I have suggested that she jumps naked into the Wandle. 'How would I get out and about?'

'Look out!' I warn. She is heading straight for a

tree-trunk this time. 'Keep your eyes on the road.'

'Don't fuss, girl.' Gran steers sharply back onto a safer course, but maintains her concentration and silence for no more than half a minute before she's nattering again. 'So much for country air being the panorama for all ills. The city atmosphere suits you so much better.'

I leave Gran at her house a couple of hours later. She seems more chirpy, but I remain uneasy about the state of her health. What should I do? Leave my ex-mother in blissful ignorance, or give her a few sleepless nights worrying about her own mother? I decide to ring her, but first, I have to tackle Sasha.

As soon as we arrive home from school, I sit her down.

'I hear that your halo has slipped,' I say sternly. 'You've been winging it at school, so to speak.'

Sasha frowns. 'This is about the Angels, isn't it?'

'The Headmaster has said that gang membership is against school rules. Sasha, it has to stop.'

'We're saving lives out there,' she protests. 'We're protecting innocent schoolkids. We're exposing the bullies by writing their names on the walls and the whiteboards.'

'Graffiti?'

'And we punish them by taking their stuff.'

'Stealing?' I shake my head. 'What am I going to do with you?'

'Please, don't stop Cassie coming to my birthday treat,' Sasha says quickly.

'What birthday treat?'

'The Megasplash at the pool. Please, Mum. I've saved three pounds fifty from my pocket money and the cash Great-Granma's given to me.'

'I can afford to take you, Cassie and Elliot swimming.'

'Elliot as well?'

'Is it fair to leave him out? I imagine you know how that feels by now.'

Sasha nods thoughtfully.

'That's my girl. And I'll have my sunglasses back, if you don't mind.'

'You can't be a member of the Avenging Angels without shades.'

'Exactly.' I pause. 'If I were you, I'd have a bath, then make a start on my homework, knowing that I'd got off very lightly. I'm going to ring Nan.' I wait until I hear water running, then dial my ex-mother's number.

'It's Terri.'

'Let me guess – it hasn't worked out, cosying up with the Blakes, and you've decided that you need David's help after all,' my mother says. 'I knew you'd be back. The position of Entertainments Manager has been filled, but I expect we can find you a few caravans to clean.'

'I'm very happy here, and I don't need another job.'

'You want to apologise for your ridiculous outburst the other day?'

'No, I'm letting you know what happened to Gran today. I'm worried about her.'

'So am I,' Mum says sincerely.

'Do you think,' a sob catches in my throat, 'that this might be the beginning of the end?'

'The end of her building society account, I imagine.'

'What's that got to do with Gran dying?'

'She isn't dying. She's fitter than I am.'

'She seemed very confused.' I explain about the attack. 'She mentioned someone called Teddy when she was talking about Grandad.'

'We all do that, don't we? Even I get muddled up with names sometimes.'

'I know that, but this was different.' I hesitate. 'Gran's often hinted at some great family secret. I just wondered...'

'That is just your grandmother's sense of the dramatic. She has led a very ordinary life, apart from the war, and she likes to liven it up with little mysteries and intrigues. The mugging must have been a nasty shock, but she was on top form the last time I saw her. I hear that since I gave her that Digibox, she's spent all her spare time – and there's a lot of that between Bingo and the Lunch Club – surfing the shopping channels, buying all kinds of items, from Farmhouse Cheddar that gives her nightmares to jewellery that she'll never wear. All she has to live on is her pension, and I can't afford to bail her out if she overspends.'

'She might as well enjoy it,' I argue.

'But that's yours and Sasha's inheritance – at least, it will be eventually, after I've had my turn at it.'

I put the phone down on her. I don't need Gran's money, and someone is rapping at the door to the flat. Pat will be wanting his rent, but he'll have to wait till the end of the week, when Martin pays me again. If I can fend him off for a couple more days, I'll be able to settle up.

'Terri, are you there?' Pat knocks on the door

again, and again. What do the tough do when the going gets tough? I suppress a giggle as I curl up on the sofa. They hide.

Working for Martin was so much easier when I was fired up to resent him for the way he behaved towards me when we were teenage sweethearts. How impossible it seems now to act profession-ally and with restraint when I discover that I am in lust with him. I can think of a thousand reasons why I shouldn't be. Letitia. The children. My self-respect.

Martin is standing at the counter with his back to me, his shoulders shaking with laughter as he flicks through the order book. His T-shirt stretches taut across his shoulders, and hugs his waist as it narrows down to his hips. I'd like to sneak into the shop, grab a carnation from the staging, and stroke it down the back of his neck. I'd love to make him laugh, like I used to be able to do, then lead him upstairs by the hand...

I suppress my crazy impulse, then push the door open. At the sound of the bell, Martin looks round and smiles.

'Now that you're here – at long last – I'll go and fetch some milk for the coffee.' It's Val. She walks through with armfuls of roses and sticks them in the buckets on the staging. She pats the pocket of her tabard, which rattles with change. As she sails past us and out of the shop, she glances back. 'Don't do anything I wouldn't do.' Five minutes later, she returns with a carton of milk.

'I thought you might be hard at it by now,' she says slyly, or am I imagining that the atmosphere of calm is pricked with Val's suspicion? 'I've cut the ribbons for the pot mums for you, Terri. I've made a start.'

'You work too hard,' Martin says. 'Why don't you take the day off tomorrow?'

'I fancy a day out shopping in Croydon.' Val deliberates. 'No, I can't possibly leave you and Terri on your own here.'

'You don't have to keep an eye on me, Val,' I say. 'I know what I'm doing. I've had years of experience.'

'Indeed you have, but I shall continue to do my duty, much as it pains my poor old knees. I promised Letitia that I would take care of everything. Right – I'll keep an eye on the shop while you get on with the orders.'

I walk through to the back room with Martin, following the scent of fresh flowers, bruised stems and coffee. Martin clears a space on the table among the pot mums.

My job is to pop a pot into each basket with a piece of coloured tissue paper to show off the flowers, tie a bow of ribbon to the handle, wrap it all in clear cellophane and label it with the *Posies* logo. It is easy money, according to Val, who doesn't have to do anything but cut the ribbons.

Martin places four bottles on the table: three empty gift bottles and a lemonade bottle filled with a dark amber liquid. He flashes me a smile as he pours some of the liquid into each of the gift bottles via a funnel.

'I've added a secret ingredient,' he confides. 'Some of the pepper sweets I bought for the kids to use on April Fools Day. I've crushed up the

165

ones that are left and mixed them with some cheap brandy.'

'Is that wise?'

'I have my suspicions as to who is the thief, but he won't admit it unless I catch him in the act.'

'I'd be worried that the bottles you've planted will end up as gifts accompanying our customers' bouquets.' That would be disastrous.

'It's all right,' Martin says. 'I've marked all the labels.'

'Does your mum know about this?'

'You aren't accusing my mum, are you? She's teetotal.'

'You'd better show me where you're putting these bottles so that I know not to sell them.'

Martin arranges them at the front of the line of bottles on the shelves at the back of the shop.

'This is becoming more of a detective agency than a flower shop. Martin Blake, florist and superspy. How about that?'

'Daniel Craig has nothing on me.' Martin grins as he tightens the lids on the bottles.

'Martin! Your father's waiting,' Val calls through from the front.

'See you later.' Martin spins away, grabbing his mobile, notebook and wallet from the table, before racing out through the front of the shop. I follow him to fetch the order book from the counter.

Outside, the van is parked on the double red lines with its indicators on, but George must have spotted the traffic wardens, because he drives off, leaving Martin pacing up and down the pavement. The Poison Dwarf and her assistant lie in wait.

The van returns five minutes later and moves slowly along the Parade. Martin runs alongside, closely followed by the Poison Dwarf's assistant. Martin opens the passenger door, jumps in and slams it shut. The van's exhaust emits a puff of black smoke, and the Poison Dwarf shakes her fist in return.

I take the order book into the back room. When I open it, out falls a copy of the *Beano*.

'Martin has shown me the secret of happiness,' I tell Sharon when she rings in the evening. 'It's reading the *Beano*.'

'Very funny,' Sharon says drily. 'Well, I haven't discovered the secret of happiness, but I do have news of Robbie. Have you got a pen and paper handy to write down his number and current address? My brother gave them to me. I said that an old friend wanted to get in touch, nothing more.'

'Thanks.'

'You don't sound that grateful.'

'I am.' But also stunned. Numb. I scribble the information on the back of my hand in blue ink. 'What do I do now?'

'Dial the number, I imagine. What's wrong?'

'I didn't think that you'd find him this quickly. I thought that I would have more time...'

'To make excuses not to get in touch with Robbie,' Sharon finishes for me. 'Terri, I've always supported you, but I've had plenty of time to reflect. I guess it's because I've seen my children growing up with their dad. I can take them on the log flumes at the amusement park,

167

make up stories about talking trees, and throw them up into the air and catch them, but I can't do any of those things as well as Chris does.'

I remain silent, remembering how my father taught me to read, from the *Angling Times* and the *Sun*, making sure that we always skipped pages three and four; how he showed me the foreign coins that occasionally slipped through the till, and how he gave me a chocolate bar every Saturday morning for helping out with the papers.

'My brother says that Robbie's away for a few days on some training course at Hendon,' Sharon says eventually, 'so you have time to decide how you're going to introduce yourself.' She then changes the subject, asking after my grandmother, my job and my boss.

'I didn't come back for Martin,' I say defensively.

I can hear Sharon sniffing down the phone. 'I smell pants on fire.'

'I came so that Sasha and Gran could get to know each other.'

'And because you're a nosy cow.'

I tip my head to one side. 'And that too.'

'I still think that you made a mistake not stopping to chat up the firemen,' Sharon says. 'What if one of them turned out to be The One in Three and a Half Million? Why don't you join a dating agency, or take up a new hobby?'

'All I can think of is cycling.'

'So that you can be with Martin.'

'I wouldn't look good in Lycra though.'

'You'll have to accept that there'll never be any future for you and him.'

'Thank you, Trisha,' I say ironically. 'You've really cheered me up.'

'That is what friends are for,' Sharon says. 'To tell you what you don't want to hear.'

Chapter Eight

How will Robbie react? There is only one way to find out, and it takes me a few days to pluck up the courage to deal with it.

After her bath, I send Sasha off to bed, and hunt through all my paperwork, looking for Robbie's number. Several minutes pass before I recall that I tucked it inside a book, *Brief Encounters*, that I found in a box in the room that has become Sasha's.

Hugging the bear that Martin gave me, I stare at my phone throughout a whole episode of *East-Enders*. What if Robbie wants to play a large part in Sasha's life? What if he doesn't want to play any part at all? The first obstacle I didn't think of, is what to say if it isn't Robbie who answers the phone?

There's a woman's voice on the end of the line and a child wailing in the background.

'You'll have to wait until your daddy gets home to fix it.' The voice then launches into a tirade against cold-callers who pretend that they are operating from Birmingham, but turn out to be based in Bangalore. 'We've replaced all our uPVC windows with sustainable-wood frames, and I don't wish to make any further contribution to the destruction of the rain-forests by upgrading my mobile.'

'I'd like to speak to Robbie Ward,' I say, when I

finally manage to get a word in edgeways.

'About what?'

The receiver starts slipping in my hand. I say the first thing that comes into my head. 'I'm calling about an offer for free wine.'

'Ah, you're from the Wine Club.'

A lucky break, I think as the woman whom I assume is Robbie's wife, continues, 'He's out. Can I take a message?'

'I'll call back later. It sounds as though you're tied up.'

'We have a crisis.' The woman sounds more friendly now. 'We've bought a new Bionicle, and its brain has got stuck in the back of its head.'

'I have every sympathy.'

'My husband will be home by nine.'

'Thanks.' I give Robbie time to go home, greet his wife and children and fix the Bionicle, and try again. It is strange how, although I was with him for one night only, his voice is unmistakable. My toes curl with embarrassment.

'Please, please, don't put the phone down,' I say quickly, as he launches into a complaint about how he has ticked all the boxes to ensure that the Wine Club doesn't disturb him at home. 'It's Terri, Terri Mills from way back.'

There is silence, then, 'I don't think we have anything to say to each other.'

'This is about your daughter.'

'Amber? She's here with us, with me and Mel.'

'*Our* daughter.'

A woman's voice – Mel, I assume - calls in the background, 'Who are you talking to, Rob? Is that your mother?'

171

'It's the Wine Club – they've got a special offer on Californian Reds.'

'Darling, don't forget to mention the bottle that was corked, will you?'

'All right, I'll deal with it.' Robbie's voice is taut. 'So – Terri, isn't it – what is this going to cost me?'

'I'm talking about our daughter.'

'You can't be serious,' he says in a shocked whisper, then in a more controlled, and much louder staccato, 'That much? For a case?'

'I am.'

He swears, and lowers his voice. 'How do I know that you're telling the truth? It's been nine – no, ten years. I have a life. A wife. Kids. I don't need any complications.'

'She's called Sasha.'

'Sasha? That's the winemaker, or the owner of the vineyard?'

'What are you talking about, Robbie?'

'I have to pass these decisions to the Chancellor of the Exchequer.' He forces a laugh. 'My wife keeps popping in to check up on me. It's a strange name for a wine.'

'I like it.' I chose it from a book of babies' names. It means "Defender of Mankind." 'It suits her.'

'Why now? Why not ten years ago?' Robbie's voice fades then returns. 'A mature vintage, yes.'

'Sasha's been asking questions about her dad. I thought I was doing the right thing, trying to ignore it. I thought it was for the best.'

'It takes more than one night to make a wine,' Robbie blusters.

'One night was enough for us to become parents.'

'I don't want anything to do with this offer. I don't want to make a purchase. I don't want to hear from you again. I want to cancel my subscription. I won't do business with a company like yours again. Never!'

'Just ask yourself, why would I make such a story up?' But I am talking to a dead connection. I stab at the buttons to try again. All I get is some anonymous voice telling me that I can use ringback. What is the point? I've blown it. Unless... Unless I can think of a way to persuade Robbie to change his mind.

I doubt that I *shall* be able to convince him, but there is someone else who might...

I sneak into Sasha's room and hunt for her note under her pillow, trying and failing like the Tooth Fairy, not to wake her.

'What are you doing, Mum?' she says thickly. 'I like your perfume.'

'It's patchouli. Can I just borrow this so if people ask me what you'd like for your birthday, I can tell them?'

'Yeah, course.'

I notice that there are some additions to the list since she last read it out to me; a Tamagotchi and Scoubidous, a bicycle and rollerblades. I can't understand how an often poverty-stricken single parent like myself can have brought up such a materialistic child!

I fold the note up, put it in an envelope, print Robbie's address that Sharon gave me and stick on a stamp. I slip the envelope into the kitchen drawer, uncertain that I will really find the nerve to post it.

The morning after the night before, I caught Robbie rummaging through my handbag. He was perched on the edge of the wall outside in my garden with my chequebook.

'That won't be much use to you,' I said coolly.

He almost jumped out of his boxer shorts. He looked up, sheepish, pale and sweaty, and confessed that he was after my name, not my money.

'So ... T. Mills. Are you Teresa, or Tracey or Thea?'

'I'm Terri – my parents named me after the Chocolate Orange.'

We had a good laugh about it over bacon sandwiches and black coffee, and then Robbie left and that was the last I saw of him, apart from that brief interlude at the bus station, until Sasha was born. And then I saw him in her eyes, in the shape of her face, and the dimple in her chin.

How can I expect a man who scarcely knew my name to believe that I gave birth to his daughter, and especially after all this time?

It is ten years and forty-two weeks exactly, since I last saw Robbie. I know this because Sasha arrived two weeks after her due date, and the day before I was booked in to have my labour induced. My daughter is perched on the edge of the sofa, which is also my bed, her eyes flashing in the dark.

'It's past midnight, which means that it is my birthday and I can open my presents,' she says brightly.

'Happy Birthday.' I scrabble around on the floor for my watch, but I can't find it. 'What's the time?'

'Four o'clock.'

I pull my duvet up over my face. 'Go back to bed.'

'How can I, when I haven't got a proper one? Please, can I open my presents now, just one incey-wincey present?'

'Go on then.' I hope that she isn't disappointed. I bought lots of little bits and pieces – charcoal sticks, a pot in which you can carry your paintbrushes, tubes of glitter paint, textured paper – and wrapped them all separately. I can't afford to buy everything that Sasha's contemporaries at school appear to have. I'd love to get her a trampoline, a long, narrow one to fit in the garden, and a computer, a mobile phone and an iPod, but I can't.

By five-thirty, Sasha has created four pieces of artwork for the living-room walls. At ten, I am sitting back admiring them, when someone hoots from outside. I ignore it, but Sasha is at the window, leaning out over the sill.

'It's Martin's van. Cassie and Elliot are early for the Megasplash,' she says excitedly. 'I'll let them in.'

'No, no, I'm not dressed yet.'

'Yes, you are.' Sasha looks me up and down, and grins. 'In your nightie and your bedsocks. Why do you wear socks in bed in the middle of summer?'

'Because I get cold feet.'

'You didn't wear them when you were going

out with Russ.'

'You'll realise why when you're older, Sash. Just wait a minute. Please.' I grab the nearest item of clothing – a little red skirt that I bought from the jumble sale at the church hall the other weekend. I made the vicar an offer for it while he was sorting through the jumble during the girls' ballet class. It's brand new and still had the labels attached.

I slip into the skirt, tear off my nightie and select a clean T-shirt from the laundry pile. Then I run my fingers through my hair, squirt myself with perfume, gather up my duvet and stuff it behind the sofa. To finish off, I plump up the cushions and hide a couple of empty crisp packets on the windowsill behind the curtains. Slovenly, *moi?*

I suppose that I have been letting the housework slide. There isn't much incentive to look after a place when it isn't your own, especially when no matter how much lemon juice and bleach you use, it looks almost as scruffy as when you started. I would have been better off saving the salt and vinegar that I've used for cleaning to put on our fish and chips.

'You look like a princess,' says Sasha, making me realise that Gran isn't the only one to have noticed the glint of gold that spins through my hair, or the sparkle in my eyes, and the fact that I've taken to wearing my Wonderbra full-time. 'You look like a princess who is searching for a prince to marry her and help her live happily ever after.'

'Thanks, but I'm not looking for a prince.'

'What about a florist?'

'Definitely *not* a florist.'

'Why are you blushing then?'

'I'm not.' I wave her away. 'Go and answer the door.'

The next thing I hear is Sasha calling me from the pavement outside. I am curious, so I go out to the road where Martin is unlocking the rear doors of the *Posies* van. He stops when he sees me, and his eyes drift downwards to the little skirt, a scarlet strip of cotton, with a flounce that barely covers my thighs. I wish that I had chosen something more modest, like one of Val's tabards, because Martin's gaze lingers on my legs far longer than seems necessary. In truth, I'm flattered. I can't remember the last time a man considered my assets, unless you count the Official Receiver.

Suddenly, Martin grins. 'I like the socks.'

I suspect that my complexion has acquired the same hue as the third, eighth and thirteenth stripes down from my knee on my long, multicoloured socks. I try to shrug off my embarrassment – and, dare I admit it, my disappointment.

'You're very early,' I tell him. 'The Megasplash doesn't start for another hour.' I've arranged to take Cassie, Elliot and Sasha to the play session at the local pool for Sasha's birthday treat.

'We've come to put Sasha's present together,' Martin says. 'It might take me some time.'

'My dad is going to put it up in your room,' says Cassie.

'It's a–' squeaks Elliot.

Cassie darts behind her brother and claps her hand against his mouth. 'It's a surprise.'

Elliot's eyes widen as he struggles to escape his

177

sister's armlock.

'Let him go, Cassie,' Martin says meekly, but she doesn't release him until I tell her to. Elliot can't contain his excitement. Giving his sister a wide berth, he jumps up and down, and blurts out, 'It's a surprise bed!'

'No, Cassie,' I say as she makes to grab him again.

'Why do my kids listen to you when they fail to take any notice of me?' Martin complains.

'Because you're too nice to them.' I fold my arms across my breasts. 'You're too nice to everyone. You shouldn't have bought such a big present for Sasha.'

'It's secondhand. I paid for the mattress, that's all, so don't go on about it, Terri.'

The heat in my cheeks intensifies. 'It's a very generous gift.'

'It's the biggest present I've ever had,' says Sasha. 'I can't believe it.'

'Perhaps you having a bed will give your mum a better night's sleep in future,' Martin says.

'I doubt it,' I say quietly. It is Martin who keeps me awake – not in the flesh, sadly, but in my thoughts. He has made me restless. Unsettled. 'Was it Gran or Sasha who mentioned the fact that Sasha didn't have a real bed?'

'It was Lilian. Sasha wouldn't say anything, would she? She wouldn't have wanted you to feel bad,' Martin says. 'She's a very thoughtful person. Sometimes, it's hard to remember that she's only ten.'

I help Martin carry the bedstead, mattress and slats indoors to Sasha's room. The kids hinder our progress for a few minutes, until they become bored and disappear off to play in the garden, which gives me the opportunity to study Martin's physique as he bends over the pieces of the bed and starts fixing them together. His T-shirt is untucked. It slips to reveal an admirably flat belly, and firm loins.

I support the bedhead for him, holding on to the bulbous end of the upright at one end, while Martin tightens the nuts on the bedframe. My fingers trace its smooth curves, the solidity of the wood…

Martin looks up. 'Will you stop doing that.' He sounds as if he is trying to catch his breath. 'What you're doing, Terri? With the end of the bed? Just keep it still, please.'

'Okay.'

Beads of sweat form on Martin's forehead as he continues to fix the screws. He straightens for a moment and rubs at the small of his back, re-minding me that he is no longer an agile teenager, but a middle-aged man. An almost middle-aged man, I correct myself. If he is middle-aged, then so am I.

He swears softly. 'I hate DIY.'

'I've always found that it's more enjoyable when you have company,' I want to say, but I cannot. Brazen hussy! I scold myself for even thinking of it, yet my throat is tight and my mouth dry.

Martin wraps his hand around the end of the bed and jiggles it. The frame remains firm. He turns and lifts the mattress away from where we left it leaning against the wall, and lowers it onto the bed. 'How's that?' he asks. 'Go on, try it.'

I sit down, swing my legs round and lie back on the mattress. 'It's very comfortable.' To my consternation, Martin joins me.

'Shove up.' Grinning, he lies down beside me, so that our shoulders and hips are touching. 'What do you think?'

I'm trying not to think at all. That I am lying on a bed. With Martin. And the kids are occupied in the garden. And … I start to wonder if he can feel the throbbing of my pulse through the mattress springs…

'Terri…'

'We must go, otherwise we'll miss the Mega-splash session.' I sit up very quickly. The blood rushes away from my head to other places that I'd almost forgotten about. 'The bed's great, thanks. Fantastic. I'll call Sasha.' I move away, putting as much distance between myself and Martin as I reasonably can in a room that's eight foot by ten. It helps that all three kids turn up to admire Martin's handiwork, bouncing up and down on the mattress.

'It isn't a trampoline,' I warn.

'It won't fall apart,' says Martin. 'It's pretty firm now.'

I glance at Martin's face. His expression is perfectly serious. The innuendo is all in my head.

'I'll collect my swimming gear, and we'll see you back at *Posies*, Martin.'

'I have my goggles in the van, and a new pair of trunks.'

'Daddy's coming with us,' says Elliot.

'Did you think I'd miss out on the fun?' Martin smiles fondly at the children, and then at my

180

socks. 'Let's go.'

Martin drives the van. I take Sharon's car – I still think of it as Sharon's even though my name is now on the registration documents. At the pool, the girls and I find a cubicle in the family changing area, while Martin and Elliot grab the adjacent one as soon as it becomes vacant.

I wasn't bargaining on Martin deciding to accompany us to the pool. My body has weathered reasonably well, but I'm no longer a lithe and supple teenager.

I look down at my legs, exposed by a high-leg red-and-white polka-dot costume that I thought fabulous a few seasons ago in Debenhams, at the cellulite at the tops of my thighs, and the dark hairs that I've missed with the razor.

'Elliot's looking under the divider,' Sasha screeches.

Elliot giggles. Martin calls him back.

I emerge from the cubicle at the same time as Martin appears from his. I try to avoid staring at him, as he tries to avoid staring at me. I wish now I had suggested that we went ice-skating or bowling, some activity where you are required to keep your clothes on. I divert my attention away from the sight of his muscles that bulge and swell beneath his lightly tanned skin, by stuffing the girls' clothing into a locker.

'Where's Elliot?' says Sasha. 'He was here a minute ago.'

'Go and check the changing cubicle, Cassie,' Martin sighs.

'I wanna go swimming.'

'Do as I tell you, or I'll take you straight home.'

Cassie wanders off and Martin starts calling for Elliot. I look up and down the rows of lockers, but I can't see him. 'Where is he?' Martin asks anxiously, coming up behind me. 'He's disappeared.'

'You don't think...?' At the same time, we look towards the opening that leads to the pool beyond, where an enormous inflatable crocodile occupies most of the surface. There are people sliding out of its mouth and into the water.

'I told him to stick with us.' Martin's voice turns to panic. 'Where the hell is he?'

'I'll have a word with the lifeguard.' I don't think Martin hears me as he paces up and down the edge of the pool, looking for his son.

'Terri! Dad! We've found him. He's this way.'

Martin and I follow the girls back into the changing area. 'Where is he?' Martin repeats, as we block the passageway between two lines of lockers.

'He's behind you,' says Cassie.

Martin turns, the muscle at the side of his cheek tight, worry lines etched into his brow. 'He isn't.'

'Oh yes, he is,' Sasha says, smirking.

Suddenly, Martin relaxes. 'Oh no, he isn't.'

'Oh yes, he is.'

'Try Locker Number 72.' It is Cassie who gives the game away.

Martin pauses outside the locker that Cassie is pointing to. There's a muffled giggle from inside. The door flies open, revealing Elliot, all curled up in his goggles and Bermuda shorts that are far too big for him. His father grabs him by the arm and hauls him out.

182

'You are in big trouble, Ells. What do you think you were doing?'

'Playing,' Elliot says stubbornly.

'I told you to stay with us, you little toerag.'

'Don't be too hard on him,' I beg. 'This is Sasha's birthday treat.'

Martin squats down beside his son, takes his hand and says, more gently, 'I thought you'd been hurt, or someone had kidnapped you.'

'Like a pirate?' Elliot says.

'A pirate, or any other baddie. I couldn't bear it if anyone took you away.' Martin releases Elliot's hand. 'Come on, let's go and do what we're here for.'

'To have sweets out of the machine,' Elliot says.

'Maybe later. I'm talking about swimming.' Martin stands up, and now I have to look at him. The last time I saw him in swimming gear, he was wearing a pair of budgie-smugglers. Today, he is in navy shorts, quite clingy shorts which hug the contours of his thighs. I look up past the hint of a paunch to the dark triangle of hair that adorns his chest; not so little that it looks rather pathetic, but not so much that you would feel like you were pressing your face up against a gorilla.

'Off we go at last.' Martin smiles. A shiver runs down my spine, and it isn't because it is chilly beside the pool.

Cassie and Sasha head for the side and sit down on the edge, kicking their feet. Elliot and I aim for the steps. Martin swaggers off to the deep end, slips his goggles over his eyes, and dives. Show-off, I think, but that's only because I'm envious. I am like a fish out of water when I'm in water, if you see what I mean, whereas he splashes about as if it is his natural habitat.

He comes swimming down to join us. He ducks down under the surface as he approaches, then reappears right in front of me. There's something very sexy about a man with wet hair and water dripping down his face. Very primitive. I might only be in up to my middle, but with Martin, I am well and truly out of my depth.

'You can go off and do a few lengths if you like, Terri. I'll keep an eye on the kids.'

'I'm not that fit.' And then I wish that Martin would speak to me in his sweetest, huskiest voice, and say, 'If you want my opinion, you are the fittest woman I have ever met...' 'Swimming isn't my thing.' I've come over all weak and breathless and I haven't got my hair wet yet. I duck my shoulders under the water, to hide my nipples that are pert with cold.

Martin tips his head to one side. A droplet of water, suspended on the end of his nose, drops off. And then he's gone – I can sense the movement of his body through the water – sweeping Elliot up into his arms, lifting him high and throwing him back down into the water. Elliot screams with delight, and the girls, who were on their way back for a second go on the slide, return – Cassie wading, Sasha doing front crawl – to beg for a turn.

Martin can lift as well as any fireman, I think, as he manages to throw Sasha and Cassie in twice each before one of the lifeguards gives him a warning for breaking pool rules, and promptly evacuates the pool so that they can stop the pump that keeps the crocodile blown up. Gradually, it subsides to form a giant green lilypad on the surface of the water. At that point we decide to dry and dress, and after that, we head off in our separate directions. Sasha and I drive to Gran's, and the Blakes make for Val and George's place.

Like the children, I wish that we could all spend the afternoon together, and then...? I picture Martin taking me aside and murmuring into my ear, 'Do you think that you can arrange for us to spend the night together again?' And me reaching my fingers to his stubbled cheek and responding, 'I can arrange anything – I'm a florist.' But life isn't like that, and I find myself arranging candles instead, ten pink candles on top of a cake, in my grandmother's kitchen.

'I've got something for you.' Gran fetches a bag containing a set of green fleece towels and a packet of defrosting beefburgers.

'You've been watching the shopping channels again.'

'I've been skiing. Spending the kids' inheritance – we're always talking about it down at the Lunch Club. Old Dotty Donaldson went one better and signed over her house to Battersea Dogs' Home. Anyway, where was I? Oh, yes. I forgot that I'd already ordered towels, and I'm not sure why I chose the beefburgers because I'm not keen on meat that's been messed about with. I haven't got room in my freezer, and I thought that you and Sasha might be able to use them.' Gran presses the carrier bag into my arms. 'How I wish that I could have seen you all in the swimming pool. You, Sasha, Cassie, Elliot and Martin. You must have looked like one big, happy family.'

It's wishful thinking on Gran's part. Martin has his own family, and I must stop lusting after an as-good-as-married father of two, and start looking after my own.

Soon after Sasha and I have returned home to our flat, I take a quick guilt trip down to the postbox with the letter to Robbie.

Chapter Nine

What is love anyway, if not self-sacrifice? The more that I forbid myself from lusting after Martin, the more I want him. When I am away from him, life is like toast without cheese, a bap without the burger, and lettuce without vinaigrette.

My lips burn. I ache in places long forgotten. I wish ... I wish. If I should write a birthday list like Sasha did, all that would be on it would be Martin. Just Martin.

I wrestle with my conscience. Is it all right to lust after a family man, as long as you don't do anything about it? I realise it is a little late to start making New Year's Resolutions, but I resolve to do better.

I arrive at *Posies* at ten to nine on the Friday morning before the Bank Holiday at the end of May.

'Don't bother with fetching your tabard, Terri.' Val puts a bucket down alongside the others on the lower shelf of the staging. 'I told Del that I'd send you round to see what we can offer him in the way of window displays.'

There is a familiar green scooter parked outside the Funeral Directors. I open the door to a brief fanfare of organ music which brings Del Bickley out to the reception area.

'Terri.' He bows his head, revealing a small circle of white scalp on the crown. 'It's very kind of you to drop by, but I am tied up at present.'

'It's all right, Mr Bickley, we've finished,' Gran's voice calls from the room beyond. 'I'll sign on the dotted line, and then I'll be off. I want to do some shopping on the way to Bingo.'

'It's your granddaughter, Mrs Parkin,' Del calls back. 'This way.'

'What on earth are you doing here?' I ask, when I discover Gran sitting in an armchair in a small appointment room. She looks up from a heap of brochures on her lap.

'I'm on the brandy.' She raises a tiny glass.

Del offers me a drink as well.

'It's too early for me, thanks. I don't want Val sacking me for being drunk in charge of a pair of secateurs.' Not that there is any chance of any-one, even a long-term teetotaller, becoming the slightest bit sozzled on one of Del's measures.

Gran fumbles in her handbag for a pen.

'Are you sure that you wouldn't like me to run through the Platinum Plan once more?' Del asks.

'No, thank you, young man. You've been very helpful.' Gran signs multiple forms then, on the way out, she pauses at the stones lined up beside the desk in Del's reception area. I can't help noticing the pride in Del's voice as he invites us to take a closer look.

I lean forward to read the inscription on the headstone. *Mch Luvd & Sdly Mst*, it reads.

'Whatever next?' says Gran, shocked.

'The deceased lived for text messaging.'

Gran strokes the block of stone. 'I'd like one like this when I pop off.'

'You are a woman of taste, Mrs Parkin. That's

mock marble, Nero Marquinia, and it's already in your plan.'

'Don't look at me like that, Terri,' Gran says. 'You'll thank me when I've gone. Goodbye, Mr Bickley. See you soon, Terri, love. You'll have to pop round to see my new chair – it's due to arrive very soon.'

After Gran has gone, performing a serpentine along the Parade, I notice that Del has acquired a nervous tic. He fidgets with his shirt-cuffs, repeatedly tweaking at them so that they fall forward of his jacket sleeves. He clears his throat, looks at the floor, then tweaks his cuffs again. Suddenly, he stares me straight in the eyes, takes a deep breath and asks if I've ever thought about taking out a plan to pay for my funeral expenses.

'I couldn't possibly afford one at the moment.'

'Of course. You're a single mum. How foolish of me.' A solitaire board of beads wells up across Del's forehead. 'I apologise unreservedly for behaving in such an appalling manner, trying to sell my services to you when you are here to sell yours to me.'

'I understand that you'd like us to provide fresh flowers on a weekly basis?'

'We've always prided ourselves on keeping things simple, but my sisters and I have decided that the bowl of plastic lilies that we used to keep at Reception is inadequate for today's discerning customer. We're looking for something more natural, and more cheering – but not too cheering, if you see what I mean.'

'Lilies are always a safe option. White roses, asters, ivies...'

189

'I see that we are on the same wavelength. I hoped that we would be, and now I see that we are.' Del smiles for the first time. 'I shouldn't be surprised. We share common ground, after all. We are both expert at making arrangements – in our own ways, obviously.'

I wonder if Del has been on the brandy too. He seems to be talking in riddles, like a stranger in a bar who is trying to impress a new acquaintance, but isn't sure what to say.

'I'll come back later with some ideas,' I suggest, once I have ascertained that Del would like four arrangements, strategically placed – perhaps a bowl at Reception, two pedestals in the window, and a wreath and candle display in the corridor that leads to the Chapel of Rest.

'I'm looking forward to seeing much more of you.' Del reaches out one smooth white hand to shake mine, and the deal is done.

'You didn't have to hurry back,' Val says when I return to the shop. 'We're hardly rushed off our feet.'

'I can find plenty to do.'

'I expect that Del enjoyed your company. Such a lovely man. So deferential and respectful, un-like some people I could mention around here.'

'I hope that you're not referring to me,' I say, so deferentially and respectfully that Val is forced to concede an apology.

'When you go back again, just remember to make sure that you rotate the stock to keep the costs down, and keep a record of everything you use,' Val adds. 'In the meantime, I'm going to make George a strong black coffee.'

'Dad's feeling a bit liverish today.' The sound of Martin's voice takes me by surprise. I didn't realise he was going to be in today. I am not prepared. Get a grip, I tell myself.

He slips a light sweater off over his head, which messes up his hair, but he doesn't seem to care. His lack of vanity is one of the many things I love about him.

Love? Am I beginning to fall in love with Martin all over again? Is it possible?

'I don't know what's got into my husband,' Val says.

'Several pints of best bitter, I imagine.' Martin gazes towards the back of the shop as George comes shuffling through, rubbing at his forehead.

'I'm going down with flu,' he mutters.

'You're an old drunkard,' Val accuses him.

'Hey, missus, I'm the same age as my teeth, if you don't mind.' George sways slightly, his arm brushing against a mini-rose bush which sends a flutter of petals down to the floor. 'If I was drunk, which I am categorically not,' he slurs, 'it's because you've driven me to it.'

'Don't blame me,' says Val. 'I've been helping run the shop and look after our grandchildren too. I don't resort to alcohol to help me cope.'

Martin looks towards his father. 'You can give it up, you know.'

'I don't want to,' George says, appalled. 'I love it. It's my life. Always has been and always will.'

'George, you don't realise how long I've been waiting for you to admit your vice,' Val says.

'Hard work was never a vice,' George says. 'I was talking about the shop.'

191

After lunch, Martin and I are alone. He sits at the table while I spray the orchids on the staging with a mist of water to keep the humidity up. The Slipper Orchids are coming into flower, their exotic petals unfurling and deepening to purple. The mist settles, creating droplets of moisture that trickle down their stems.

I glance towards Martin who sits as still as a statue, deep in thought. I know that nothing can happen between us, that my conscience would never allow it, even if he wanted it to, which he wouldn't because he is an honourable man. But I love working alongside him, imagining how it could have been, if my mother hadn't been so obstructive, if she hadn't turned Val against my family by leading George astray…

I move to the counter and perch up on the edge, swinging my legs.

'I can't believe that my parents are still bickering after forty years,' Martin begins.

'I think it's sweet – that they've been together for so long, not that they argue all the time. I can't remember having a relationship that lasted more than forty weeks.' I pause, and pluck an aster from the vase that Val or Martin must have displayed on the counter the day before. I wish I hadn't put it like that. It makes me sound like a loose woman. 'That isn't true – I did live with someone for three years.'

'What happened?'

'I thought that he was The One, someone I could spend the rest of my life with.' Todd was a lovely guy, but it is only now that I realise the fatal flaw in my search for a partner. I have been

192

comparing every man I meet with Martin.

'I'm sorry.'

'It doesn't matter.' I pick a petal off the flower in my hand, catching it between my nails and letting it fall onto the floor. I continue to pick the petals off the aster. Sometimes a petal sticks and I have to blow it to dislodge it from my finger. I glance towards Martin. He loves me, he loves me not... *Not?*

No one knows how difficult it is for me to resist the temptation to take a second flower from the vase. I used to do the same as a teenager, picking daisies in the park, over and over until I found one that gave me the answer I wanted. He loves me, he loves me not, he loves me...

I smile to myself. How can the number of petals on a flower give me a definitive answer as to how Martin feels about me? Indeed, how can he feel anything for me when he is committed to Letitia, the mother of his children? I crush the remains of the flowerhead in my palm and throw it towards the bin.

Later, Val collects the children from school. She offers to cook their tea and keep an eye on them in the flat, so that Martin and I can look after the shop until closing time.

'Martin. Martin!' Val shouts from upstairs.

'Granny can't find the sausages.' Cassie comes running out through the shop in flip-flops, and a bikini.

'They're in the freezer,' Martin says.

'She can't find Grandad either,' Cassie adds. 'Have you seen him?'

'Not since lunchtime. I do have an idea where

he might be.' Martin moves over to the door, and slips the sign to *Closed*. Cassie and I follow him out to the alleyway where he opens the back of the van.

The light floods in. Lying on the bench that runs across the front of the compartment in the van is George, his cap across his eyes, his mouth wide open, one arm flopped down to the floor, his feet raised up onto the middle shelf of three.

'Martin! Is that you?' Val comes into view, holding a wooden spoon. 'Terri!'

'We came looking for Dad,' Martin says. 'He's in here.'

'I see,' says Val, her voice heavy with suspicion.

'There's Grandad.' Elliot jumps up and down beside his grandmother, with a castle-shaped bucket in one hand, and a plastic spade in the other. 'Come and look, Cassie and Sasha, Daddy and Terri have found him.' He frowns. 'Why is he in the van?'

'He's having a sleep,' says Val stiffly.

'He's always asleep,' says Elliot, concerned.

'It's because your poor grandfather is getting on in years, and he has to get up early to buy the flowers,' Val says.

'It's because he's drunk too much beer,' says Sasha. I give my daughter, who is wrapped in a beach towel, a hard stare, but she continues, 'That's what my mum says, anyway.'

'Mr Bickley says that you can tell the difference between someone who's dead and someone who's asleep, by holding a feather in front of their nose,' says Cassie.

'Don't you listen to that man,' Val snorts. 'Your

grandad is very much alive. Can't you hear him snoring?'

'I'll go and check. Sasha, we have to fetch a petal because we haven't got any feathers.' The girls return with a couple of leaves instead, and after poking them up poor George's nostrils, making him sneeze himself awake, they pronounce him very much alive, and Martin suggests that he takes his parents home, which leaves me to keep an eye on the children, and feed them.

'That's great,' Sasha says. 'That means I can finish my fridge magnet.'

'After you've changed out of those clothes, and eaten your tea. You must be frozen in that beach gear.'

'We're playing running a bar in Spain,' says Cassie. 'We're fine.'

'Then why are you shivering?'

The girls disappear off to change, and I head upstairs to the living room in the flat. It is in chaos. The coffee-table is covered with a plastic sheet and paintbrushes – Martin acquired a make-a-fridge-magnet kit from a box of washing powder. If I had known that Val had set the children up with such a messy craft, I might have found an excuse to take Sasha straight home. I don't know what Letitia will make of the state of her pale carpet. Not only is it skidded with grease from Martin's bike, it is now spattered with coloured paint.

It takes about as long as a hungry five year old takes to gobble down chicken fillets, carrots and mashed potato, followed by not one, but two yoghurts, for Martin to drop his parents home.

'Stay for a while. Let Sasha finish her magnet,' Martin says. 'I need a drink. How about you? There's lager or red wine.'

'Pleeeease,' my daughter says.

'It won't take long, will it?'

'Ten minutes?'

What is ten minutes? Time to drink a glass of wine. In the spirit of friendship.

'Wine would be lovely, thanks.'

Martin joins me and the children in the living room where they make a fresh start on their fridge magnets. I sit down beside him on the sofa, beside him, but apart, because there is no room elsewhere, and sip at my wine. It is a red: full-bodied, spicy and strong. Like Martin. I cross one leg over the other. Stop it, I tell myself.

'Elliot,' Sasha says, 'you've put your paintbrush in the blue without washing the brush first. It's gone muddy, and now I can't paint my blueberry face.'

'I didn't.' Elliot drips blue paint from the tip of his brush.

I glance towards Martin. It is up to him to have a word with his son about this blatant fib; it is down to me to pacify my daughter.

'Can't you paint it red instead, Sash?' I suggest. 'It would make a fantastic strawberry.'

'Yeah, a *really* fantastic one – it's the wrong shape, Mum.'

Cassie grapples with her brother. 'Now he's doing it with the yellow.'

Martin is gazing into the top of his lager can, as if he is expecting to find the answer to life itself in the bottom.

'Calm down, Elliot,' I say quietly, aware that some of his anger is down to frustration because his artwork isn't as good as the girls'. 'Let's go and clean the paintbrushes so that you can start again. I'll rinse the blue paint out, and mix some more.'

'No!' Lip trembling, he folds his arms.

'Pick up the paint-pot, please,' I say firmly.

'Go on, Ells.' Martin looks up at last. 'Do as Terri asks.'

Elliot picks up the pot and saunters out into the kitchen with me following along behind him. In the kitchen, he throws the pot into the sink.

'You can't tell me what to do. You're not my mummy.' I squat down and reach out my arms to hug him, but he bursts into tears and turns away. Has Elliot sensed that my relationship with his father has changed? That I am in some way a threat to his mother? I am not, but Elliot is more sensitive than he appears.

'I'm not trying to take your mummy's place.'

He continues to cry as if his heart is broken. 'I-want-my-mummy,' he gasps between sobs.

'I know, darling.' I warmed to Cassie immediately I met her, but I wasn't sure about her brother. It is a harsh fact of life – something to do with making a success of transferring your own genes down the generations – that you are never so fond of other people's children as you are of your own. However, Elliot's distress softens my attitude towards him. It isn't surprising that he is all mixed up when the grown-ups in his life – his mum and dad – don't know how to behave either.

I clean the brushes for him, watching the

pigment swirl down the plughole in the sink.

'Crisis over,' I say lightly when we return to the living room.

Martin sits still holding his can of lager, running his fingertip around the rim. He looks up and smiles, and my heart soars, and I want to say something, but I can't think of anything to say, no safe subject of conversation.

The phone rings. Martin kneels on the floor and rifles through the flotsam of family life – the odd socks, chocolate wrappers, pens, unopened post and toys – looking for the phone, but it is Elliot who finds it. He runs in from the kitchen, holding the receiver to his ear.

'It's Mummy,' he cries delightedly. 'Mummy, Mummy, Mummy! I've made a banana fridge magnet, and it's green.' He laughs. 'Granny cooked our tea, and Grandad was dead in the back of the van except that Cassie and Sasha found that he was alive. Daddy? He's invited his friend round to play. Terri, yes. I think she's his bestest friend ever 'cos she's almost always here all of the time.' Elliot pauses, his lips pursed. Vertical lines appear and deepen between his eyes. 'Yep, I'll hand you over to Daddy.'

I curl up in a ball on the sofa, hug my knees tight and press my heels against my bottom. Sasha is blowing on her fridge magnet to dry the paint. Cassie is watching her father, with her hand across her mouth.

'Terri? Yes, she works here,' Martin begins.

Elliot slips down off the sofa and runs away, shouting, 'Sasha, let's play pirates.'

'That's a boy's game,' Sasha says scornfully.

I notice how Martin's fingers tighten around the phone, how he forces his lips together so that the blood runs out of them. 'Cassie is in the same class as Sasha. Terri's just a mate.'

If I were Martin's girlfriend, he wouldn't convince me. I know how I would feel in Letitia's position, trapped in Spain away from my partner and kids by the vagaries of real estate, discovering that some woman, a blast from Martin's past, was here with him, innocently painting fridge magnets.

'Wendy was a girl in *Peter Pan*,' says Cassie. 'You can be Wendy, I'll be Peter, and Ells can be the crocodile.'

'I wanna be Captain Hook.'

'Then we shan't play, shall we, Cassie,' says Sasha.

'Stop arguing, will you?' Martin cuts in. I notice that his thumb is pressed against the mute button on the phone. 'Go and walk the plank, or something, anything but fight.'

'You can't be a pirate without fighting,' Cassie points out. 'That's what pirates do.'

'Go and be children then,' Martin says.

'They fight too,' says Sasha.

'Well, they shouldn't,' I say. 'Go on, off you go. Five more minutes and we're going home.' The Five Minute Warning works like magic. The children disappear, best friends once more, and peace descends.

Martin and I are alone again, apart from the fact that, with that phone call, Letitia has become a presence in her absence.

'Elliot really dropped me in it.'

'I'll clear this mess up,' I say quietly.

'You don't have to.'

'I want to.' I move everything from the coffee-table to the kitchen, and drop the empty paint-pots and newspaper into the bin, a stainless steel contraption that is almost as tall as Elliot. I glance at the coordinating canisters for tea, coffee and sugar, at the shiny smoothie-maker and the washing machine that bleeps like an electronic cuckoo at the end of each cycle. I guess that Letitia chose them.

I wipe down the worktops, wring out the cloth and hang it over the tap at the sink. On the win-dowsill behind it, there is an appointment card advertising a hair salon – *Tish Blake, full high-lights, 10 a.m.* on a date in August – last August, I assume. There is also a dried-out mascara wand without its lid, and a ten-pence piece. Letitia's things

I become aware of Martin behind me.

'I hope that me being here hasn't caused any trouble.' I don't look round. I cannot trust my expression.

'Between me and Letitia? She'll get over it.' I hear Martin crumple the can. 'She's sold the bar at last. She's on her way home.'

When I unlock the door to our flat, I glance up at the window above, where a silhouette of a woman with curly hair and a Cruella De Vil collar stands against a pink light. I shan't be able to sleep anyway, whether Pat and his Amateur Dramatics troupe are practising, or not. I've had better days.

'Hi there, Stranger,' Sharon says, when I ring

her after Sasha has gone to bed. Stranger. It's a throwaway comment, a hint that I haven't been in touch so often recently.

'Guilty as charged,' I say. 'I'm sorry.'

'Never mind. Did you speak to Robbie?'

'I messed it up. He put the phone down on me.'

'What did you expect? How would you feel if someone rang you up out of the blue and told you that you had a nine-year-old daughter?'

'All right, I know. Anyway, I've sent him a note, and I'm waiting to see if he replies.' I sit on the edge of the sofa with the phone tucked between my chin and shoulder, sewing the button back onto Sasha's polo-shirt while I talk. Sasha claims that the button dropped off, but there is a small tear which suggests that it became detached by more violent means.

'You sound a bit faint,' Sharon says.

'I'm multi-tasking. The phone slipped.' I smile to myself. 'I'm doing my impression of the perfect mother.'

'You don't have to do the impression. You *are* the perfect mother. You wouldn't catch me sewing a button onto a polo-shirt. I'd be down at Woolies buying a new one.'

'Well, needs must.'

'You're spending too much time with your grandmother. You'll be keeping your old clothes to cut up for rags next.'

'I would if I had any.' I pause. 'I can't help suspecting that my landlord has something to do with their disappearance. As far as I know, he's the only keyholder, apart from myself, and he does prance about in stilettos. He's an actor in his

201

spare time, apparently. He's always charming, and sounds so obliging that I almost believe him when he promises to drop in to repair the washing machine, replace the washers on the taps and fix the boiler.'

'Chris bought me flowers today,' Sharon says suddenly.

'What for?' For a moment I panic, wondering if I have missed a birthday or anniversary.

'Just to say that he loves me.'

'How sweet.'

'Have you found anyone to buy you flowers yet?'

'Of course not.' I try to laugh it off, but if I wasn't sure before, I am certain now. I have fallen in love with Martin, and now his long-term partner is on her way home, and I can no longer deceive myself that there is any chance that my love will be reciprocated. While Letitia was away, at least I could pretend that she might never come back.

Chapter Ten

The gerbera are bending towards the windows and the roses are flopping in the heat. It is a Thursday morning in June, and the temperature has already hit the eighties.

I take emergency measures to rescue *Posies'* stock, wrapping the gerbera stems in newspaper to straighten them, before switching the kettle on.

Personally, I don't like to use boiling water to shock roses, but Val likes it done her way. I probably wouldn't bother to shock them at all, but that is where I went wrong. When I had my own business, I threw the wilting blooms away, and paid for fresh ones. I didn't like to feel that I was short-changing my customers. Instead, I ended up short-changing myself.

I take a pair of secateurs and recut the stems of the roses, immerse the ends in boiling water for a couple of minutes, then plunge them into cold and leave them up to their necks for a couple of hours. It is like Viagra, perking them up so that they last a little longer.

A taxi pulls up on the double red lines outside. The driver unloads luggage from the boot: three coordinating scarlet suitcases, a trolley and a shoulderbag. He hands the latter to his passenger, a woman, who unzips it and removes a scarlet purse. She opens the purse and shakes her head. The driver gesticulates furiously, then stands with his hands in his pockets, watching the woman pick up some of her luggage and carry it towards *Posies*.

Who is she? I have no doubt. This woman isn't merely beautiful. She is stunning. Even carrying the weight of so much baggage, she walks with poise on high-heeled sandals with glittering straps. She taps the back of her fingers on the door. Grudgingly, I open it to let her in.

'Thanks,' she gasps. 'I thought I was going to drop my duty-free.' Her long blonde hair is loose around her shoulders. She wears a pale pink jacket, unfastened to show off her plunging cleavage, and a matching skirt that reveals much of the tanned and toned length of her thighs. It is tempting to describe her as a Barbie doll, with her big blue eyes and pouting lips, but there is nothing false or plastic about her physical appearance, apart from the eyelashes.

'Buenos dias!' She flashes a set of even white teeth at me, then drops her bags behind the counter, opens the till and counts out several ten-pound notes.

'Excuse me, but you can't do that.'

'Who says?' She rams the till shut. 'I have to pay the taxi driver.'

When she returns inside, she tweaks off the odd head that I missed between her long nails. She stalks around the shop as if she owns the place, which she does, I suppose. It is a painful realisation. Ironic too that someone who has little interest in flowers and the art of floristry has ended up joint owner of *Posies*. If *Posies* were mine, I would love it for its heart, not because it is a gold-mine.

'Where's that useless other half of mine?' she asks. Her other half? Why am I surprised that she refers to Martin as her other half? Martin *is* her other half.

'He's out with George.'

'And the children?'

'At school,' I say quietly. How can a mother not know that her children are at school?

'You must be the infamous Terri Mills, named after the *Terry's Chocolate Orange.*' Shock has the opposite effect on me as it does the roses – I feel myself wilting beneath Letitia's questioning gaze. She runs the fingers of one hand through her hair, teasing out the strands at her shoulder. 'You're much older than I imagined.'

'Letitia!' Val emerges from behind us. 'You should have told us when you were arriving, then George could have collected you from the airport.'

'I've put you to enough trouble already.' Letitia moves past the counter, evading Val's open arms.

'Come upstairs and tell me all about Spain. I'll make us a pot of tea.'

'I'm going to celebrate after all I've been through during the past few months. I'll open a bottle of Midori or Parfait Amour.'

'Not for me, or Terri, not while she's working, and make sure that George doesn't get his hands on the bottle.' Val looks out towards the front window. 'How many times have I told him not to stop out there?'

George stops for just long enough to drop Martin off and taunt the traffic wardens. Although the Poison Dwarf's assistant is wearing trainers instead of shoes this time, he still can't run quite fast enough to catch the van, and Martin becomes so embroiled in an argument with the Poison Dwarf that he doesn't notice Letitia until he is in the shop.

'Letitia!' He stands rooted to the floor, feet apart, elbows flexed, mouth open.

Letitia rests one hand on her hip. '*Hola, mi querido.* That means hello, my darling,' she adds, when Martin fails to respond with equal enthusiasm. 'Surprise!' She moves up to him, raises her hand to his cheek, then tilts her face and kisses him on the lips. 'Don't you like surprises any more?'

'The children will be over the moon,' Martin says quietly. He reaches for Letitia's wrist. She lets her hand fall away. 'You said you were coming back last week, then you said it wouldn't be until next Friday.'

'I thought I'd have a few more days on the beach, topping up my tan.'

She is joking, I think?

'And then I thought I'd like to get back and catch up with what's going on in the soaps. Well, I had to sell the TV and give up the satellite subscription, didn't I? I couldn't bring that back with me.'

'Come on,' Val interrupts. 'Upstairs. Martin, bring Tish's luggage, will you?'

Martin hangs back. 'Look, Terri, why don't you take the rest of the day off?' When I hesitate, he adds, 'I'll pay you anyway.'

That comment about the money hurts me more than seeing Martin with his girlfriend. I gaze towards the sunflowers that Val has put on special offer. I feel cheap. Used. It was convenient for them, taking me on while Letitia was absent. Now that she is back, my services are not required.

'We've dealt with today's orders,' he goes on. 'I'm going to close early.'

'Don't you trust me to look after *Posies* singlehanded?'

'It isn't that,' he says so gently that I think my heart will break all over again. 'I thought that as it was quiet, you might like to spend some time with Lilian. Letitia and I have some catching up to do.'

I turn away, and collect my bag and keys, before walking out onto the Parade. I can see why Martin fell for Letitia – physically, she is perfect. As for her manners, I am not so sure. Perhaps she is tired after her journey.

I am gutted. What is the point of trying to excuse her manners? Letitia is back. Any vain hopes I entertained, that the reason she was staying away was because she and Martin wanted no more to do with each other, have gone. I was kidding myself. While Letitia remained abroad, I could pretend there was a chance that Martin would fall in love with me all over again. Now that chance has gone. Wiped out in the time it takes for a 737 to fly from Malaga to London Gatwick.

'Letitia is back,' is the first thing I say to Sasha when I collect her from school later the same afternoon.

'That's great,' she says.

How can it be great? I want to blurt out to

everyone at the school gate. Martin's girlfriend is back, and she's gorgeous – and young. She is a double D to my A cup, and blonde to my auburn. Why say auburn? It is brown. My hair is *brown*.

'Cassie and Elliot will be so happy,' says Sasha thoughtfully, and I realise that I am being a selfish cow, thinking of myself, not the children. I wish that I could see Sasha and Elliot's faces, but there is no sign of Letitia or Martin outside school. I have missed them in the crowd.

'Have you heard from my dad?' Sasha says on the way home.

'Not yet. I warned you that it might take some time.'

'When do you think it will be?'

'How should I know, Sash?'

'You're an adult.' Her eyebrows disappear up under her hair. 'Today? Tomorrow? So, the day after yesterday, and the day before tomorrow are the same?'

'I don't know. How can I think straight when you're asking all these questions?'

'You're making excuses, Mum,' Sasha says sadly. 'Why won't you let me see my dad?'

I know what that feels like; that gnawing ache, that yearning for something or someone who is out of reach. If Sasha doesn't get to meet her father now, she'll always be searching for him, always wondering if one of the men she runs into on a train, on a bus or at work is her dad.

Letitia is back, is the first thing that I want to tell Gran, but she doesn't answer her doorbell when we stop outside her house on the way home after school. There is a pair of tubs overflowing with purple-and-white striped petunias outside the porch, and a heap of weeds and cigarette ends on the ground. I hope that Nora Fulbright's grandson has been using the spade that leans against the wall outside for legitimate purposes, not for battering pensioners.

Sasha and I hammer on the door, ring on the bell, and bang on the window.

'Do you think she's watching *QVC?*' Sasha peers through the glass.

Slightly apprehensive, I phone Gran on my mobile.

'Yes,' she answers eventually.

'Have I woken you?'

'I was just about to drink my cocoa.'

'We're on your doorstep, in case you hadn't noticed.'

A few minutes later, my grandmother is behind the front door, slipping the security chain and jiggling with the locks, before she can open it.

'You should have rung first.' She hangs back in the shadow of the hallway.

'Can we come in?'

'What if I'd been in the bath? It takes me hours to get out.' Gran gives a snort of annoyance. 'You know I don't like opening the door at night.'

'Great-Granma, it's still light,' Sasha says, amazed.

I am concerned. It is only four-thirty, and I thought she wanted to see us, that she'd love the opportunity to show off her new chair as soon as it arrived. I step through the door towards her. When my eyes have adjusted to the gloom, I realise that my grandmother is holding her left arm close to her chest as though she is wearing an imaginary sling. There is a red flare down her forearm. Her left eye is almost closed, and the surrounding skin is a livid mauve.

'What have they done to your eye? And your arm? You can't stop me this time. I'm calling the police.'

Gran grabs feebly for my hand. 'Don't do that, Terri. This has nothing to do with any youths. It was my fault. I've taken a little tumble.'

'From your new chair?' I am picturing one of those fairground bucking broncos that Sasha and I tried out a couple of times.

'From the loft.'

'What on earth were you doing up there?'

'Finding some papers. I wanted to make sure everything was in order.'

'I should call the doctor.'

'There's nothing broken.'

'But you must be in agony.'

'Nothing hurt, but my pride.'

'You must promise me that you won't go climbing again,' I say earnestly. 'You do promise?'

'Great-Granma, your fingers are crossed behind your back,' Sasha observes. 'We shan't tell you any gossip unless you promise.'

The lines at the corner of Gran's good eye crease with amusement for the first time since our arrival.

'Have you eaten today?' I ask her. She isn't sure, so I cook eggs on toast for the three of us, and then direct Sasha into the dining room to do her homework with Old Tom supervising, or rather interfering, by lying on her spellings sheet and playing with her handwriting pen. Gran and I sit down with mugs of cocoa in the sitting room, so that she can demonstrate her latest purchase.

Gran presses a button on the arm of her new adjustable chair. It whirrs and tilts so that she is leaning towards me.

'Spill the beans,' she says.

'Letitia's back.'

'Oh? That's good. Martin's children have their mother back.' Gran gazes at me. 'It's good for you too.'

'I know.' It means that I can stop wasting my time on daydreams. For a moment, I wonder if I have spoken those words aloud, because Gran says, 'You can pretend all you like, but you can't hide the fact that you are very fond of Martin. What you need now is stickability. Stick with it.'

'It won't make any difference. Martin is as-good-as-married. He has shown no interest in me, romantically anyway.'

'He can't until he ends his existing relationship. Martin has principles.'

'He won't risk losing his children by splitting up with Letitia. He adores them.'

'We'll see.' Gran's elbow catches on another button on the arm of her chair, sending it swivelling to face the fireplace, so that I can see only the wispy white hair on the top of her head above the back of the chair. 'It's simpler than operating this damned chair.' She stabs at the control panel, but nothing happens.

'Would you like me to move round there, so that we can see each other?'

She stabs again, and the chair whirrs her back

into her original position, but tipped back. Gran grins at me. 'I call this one the dental hygienist position, and I'm not sure how to get out of it. Give us a hand up, will you?'

I help her up, then together we run through the fifty-page instruction manual that the manufacturer sent with the chair, in order to find out how to return it to an upright position. It takes us half an hour. It would probably have taken Sasha two minutes, but I don't like to interrupt her homework.

'Thanks, Terri,' Gran says. 'I'm sorry if I was unwelcoming earlier.'

'It's all right. You aren't well.' I take her hand. 'Will you promise me that you'll make an appointment to see the doctor tomorrow? If you won't do it for yourself, do it for me, to put my mind at rest. Otherwise I'll be calling around here at all hours of the day and night to check up on you.'

My grandmother acquiesces remarkably meekly, so I take advantage of her accommodating mood and make her promise not to go climbing any more ladders. If she wants anything else down from the loft, she is to ask me to fetch it.

I can see that her fingers aren't crossed this time, but I am suspicious. Will she really take any notice of me? I expect that, inside her tartan slippers, she is busy crossing her toes.

'Martin doesn't love Letitia,' Gran says. 'If he did, he'd have been off to Spain to drag her back sooner.'

'He had a shop to run.'

Gran looks at me pityingly. 'I should have

212

thought from your experience of losing your business, you would have learned which was more important. Love, or livelihood?'

The Florist, His Mother and His Lover: yes, it could be the title of some arthouse film, but in fact it is a list of the people I find myself having to work with, because I discover from Val, on the day after her return, that Letitia has decided to rejoin the staff of *Posies*.

'I told her she didn't have to put herself out,' Val says, snipping out the heads of the blown roses on the staging, 'but she insisted on opening up the shop today.'

Letitia is on her mobile, and shaping her nails at the same time. She casts me a brief glance before returning to her conversation, but I notice that she is quite happy to cut it short when Kev walks in.

I am about to serve him, when Letitia takes over.

'I heard you were back.' Kev leans across the counter, going cross-eyed as he stares at Letitia's cleavage.

'Make the most of it. I'm considering my options, and researching the idea of running a diving school somewhere like Mauritius.'

'You always have been an adventurous woman.' Kev straightens.

'Not too adventurous, I hope,' Val interrupts. 'What are you after?'

'I'm not here to buy anything, not after what happened last time. I came to tell you my news. I'm going to be a dad.'

'Really?' The colour drains from Letitia's face. At least, her fantastic tan pales to the same shade of beige as the kitchen units back at my flat.

'You look as though you could do with a lie-down on my trolley.' Kev grins.

'I'm all right.' Letitia touches her chest. 'I'm exhausted. It's almost time for my siesta.'

Siesta? It's eleven-thirty, I think. I retreat to the back room.

Martin is already there, with a file of notes for the evening class that he takes on Wednesday nights, open on the table in front of him. The room is looking rather drab; there are cracks running down the walls, and the paint is flaking off the woodwork.

I sit down opposite him at the table, sidling my feet across the floor to avoid contact with his outstretched legs. He looks up, scissors in one hand and a stem of gypsophila in the other. He has a tiny piece of tissue stuck to his chin, and a nick above his upper lip where he has cut himself shaving. He smells of fresh aftershave and toothpaste.

'*Posies* could do with a refit,' I observe.

'Are you referring to me or the shop?'

'The shop, of course. You've weathered rather well.'

'We trade on our old-fashioned values. This is a traditional family business, and I'm determined to keep it that way. All *Posies* needs is a lick of paint.'

'Customer, Terri,' Val calls from the counter.

'Okay.' I reach out and pick a fragment of raffia from Martin's shoulder. It's a friendly gesture. Anyone would have done it, I tell myself. Anyone...

'One mixed bouquet, *Summer of Love* in the brochure. For Nigel,' Val elaborates when she appears with an armful of flowers, yellows and oranges and golds, and foliage. She eyes me suspiciously when she plonks them on the table beside me. 'Nigel's brought along a couple of items from his stall that you might like to look at.'

I make up the bouquet, wrap it in green cellophane and finish it off with a gold ribbon before taking it out to the till. It must be warm today because Nigel has cast off his overcoat, and rolled up the sleeves of his shirt.

'Take a butcher's at these.' He spreads a dark trouser suit with a single fabric button the size of a small saucer on the jacket, and kick-flared trousers across the counter. 'Val thought that a fashionista like yourself might appreciate a bargain.'

'It isn't really me.'

'You don't have to wear the trousers with the jacket. They are what I describe as multipurpose separates – you can dress them up, or dress them down.'

'Try it on,' says Val.

'Where on earth would I wear a suit like that?'

'When you're out and about with your beau,' she says, with a look on her face that I can't understand. I don't have a beau.

'Just look at the cut,' Nigel says. 'It's a snip at a fiver for the jacket, and seven for the trousers.'

'I'll stick with my jeans, but thanks for thinking of me.' As I make a hasty exit, I overhear Val apologising for my lack of taste.

'She's no Kate Moss, never has been. It's time that she started dressing in a style appropriate for

215

the more mature woman.'

'Like yourself, Valerie,' says Nigel, his tone of sincerity as faux as the designer labels on his clothing.

In less than the time it takes me to wire three roses, Val calls me out to the front again. 'Customer, Terri. Quick-smart. Service with a smile, please.'

A man stands at the counter. He must be in his fifties, and he wears a jacket which appears to have been woven from the same material as his ginger toupée. I imagine that my grandmother would describe him as a dapper young gentleman.

'I'd like my usual, please,' he announces.

'And what might that be?' I ask, politely and cheerfully, although I am wondering where Letitia has disappeared off to.

'The same as I had last time, and the time before that.'

'I haven't been working here for long.'

'In that case, I'll have to explain my requirement to you, which is very tiresome.'

I start to wonder if he is slightly peculiar.

'Six pink spray carnations, not fiddled about with, wrapped in paper, fully biodegradable, and a card made out to Ellen, my dear wife.'

'She's a lucky lady.' I select six stems and package them.

'There are some who might agree with your sentiment, considering the state of the world today, but I do not. My wife has been dead these past six years.'

'I'm so sorry.'

'How can you call yourself a florist when you

216

don't know that the gift of pink carnations means "I shall never forget you"?'

'People don't tend to worry about the meanings of the flowers they send nowadays. They choose them because the shape or the colour appeals to them.'

The man counts out three pound coins from his pocket, and hands them over. I don't like to upset him further by pointing out that the price has gone up since he last bought flowers. What can I do? I take a pound from my purse and put it in the till to make up for it. I don't know why Val couldn't serve him. The closest she seems inclined to get to floristry is leafing through one of her flowery romance novels.

'Where is Letitia?' I ask her.

'She's gone for a – what did she call it? A Brazilian.' Val keeps her nose in her book. 'It's a beauty treatment, I believe, but you wouldn't know much about that.'

I smile to myself. If I were inclined to bitchiness, I would add that Letitia seems like the type of woman who has had many Brazilians in her time, and not of the waxed version.

I return to Martin in the back room.

'Are you okay?' he asks.

'Gran isn't well – she fell out of her loft yesterday.' I find myself stroking the crinkled blooms of celosia or cockscomb that I am supposed to be using to make up the orders. A displacement activity, I think ruefully. 'It was lucky that she didn't end up in hospital.'

'I'll take her some flowers. What do you think of a dozen of those yellow roses?'

'She'd love them. Can I ask you a favour? Gran wouldn't refuse you if you asked to borrow her stepladder. You could stick it in the van, and forget to return it. That way, she won't be able to go falling out of her loft.'

'Consider it done. I'll pop over with the van sometime today. I won't go too late – I know she doesn't like opening the door in the evenings.'

'Thanks.' It is so quiet that I can hear the tick-tick-tick of my watch as I work. I snip and tear, wire and twist, glue and tie. *With Sympathy, Congratulations on Passing your Driving Test*, and a simple *I Love You*.

'Can I ask you a favour in return?' Martin scratches the back of his neck, raising an angry flare across his skin. 'You couldn't have Cassie and Elliot after school for a while, could you? Letitia and I–'

'It's fine,' I interrupt. I don't want to know about their plans.

'We won't be late.'

'It doesn't matter.' I say those words, but I am lying. The fact that Martin and Letitia are together again as a couple matters to me more than anything else in the world at this moment, and the radio compounds my regret, playing Daniel Powter's 'Bad Day'.

'Terri!' Val calls out. 'Your grandmother's here. I'll send her through.'

'Yoo hoo!' Gran turns up with her mac over her arm. She's wearing her Sunday best, a blouse with the brooch at the collar, and a pleated skirt.

'Hi, Lil,' Martin says awkwardly. 'Are you going somewhere special?'

'I've been to see the doctor. I just popped in to tell Terri how it went. I won't stop long.'

'I'll leave you two to it.' Martin stands up. 'I have a bridal appointment.'

'That's a pity,' Gran says. 'We haven't had a good old gossip for ages.'

Martin tilts his head to one side. 'I'm a busy man.'

'But not a very happy one,' Gran observes quietly, when he has gone. 'Where was I? I remember. I'm here to put your mind at rest, Terri – about me anyway. I've seen the doctor, and he can't find anything wrong.'

He can't be that good a doctor then, I think. 'Did he examine you? Did he listen to your heart?'

'His nurse was free at the time and she fixed me up to this Electro-Cardio-thingummy-jig to check my ticker.'

'What did she say?'

'She sent me back to Dr Holland, who said that my heart was in the right place, if nothing else.'

'Please don't joke about it, Gran.'

'I'm not joking. He was perfectly serious. He's referring me to see Mr Ayling, a consultant at the hospital, for more tests. He says I'll be able to have a go on his treadmill.'

A picture of my grandmother in a vest, shorts and trainers, pounding along to Peter Kay's version of 'Amarillo', flashes through my mind.

'I'll have to wait for a while,' Gran goes on. 'I'm not an urgent case.'

I beg to differ. She's in her eighties, she's struggling to look after herself, and sometimes

219

she can hardly breathe. If that isn't urgent, what is?

'Didn't he comment on your bruises or check your arm?'

'Terri,' Val calls.

'He asked me if Mike Tyson came out any worse.' She chuckles. 'That young man made me feel better straight away.' She raises one thin, wispy eyebrow. 'It's amazing what a young man can do, isn't it?'

'Terri!' Val calls again. 'This isn't a holiday camp. We are not paying you to stand around gossiping.'

'You and Martin will be together. One day, you'll marry the boy next door – I know you will. Trust me,' Gran adds in a low voice. 'I'm an octogenarian.'

I can't help smiling at my grandmother's forecast, even though it pains me because I am equally sure that it will never happen. I wonder about this particular octogenarian's credentials when it comes to predictions.

Letitia isn't all that reliable either. Cassie and Elliot's faces fall when they see me, not Letitia, at the school gate.

'Where's my mum?' Wild-eyed and panicky, Cassie searches the crowd for her mother.

'Where's Mummy?' Elliot's lip trembles. 'I want to give her this.' He holds out a picture of a big robot holding a little robot by one of its many projecting appendages.

'That's a fantastic work of art.' I try to cheer him up. 'Your mummy will be so proud of you.'

'Has she gone back to Spain?' Cassie asks anxiously.

'Your dad asked me to bring you home from school today. He and your mum had some things to do in town.' I can't understand why Letitia didn't warn them. Did she and Martin make last-minute plans? Did she not think about how her children would feel if she didn't turn up to collect them? Is she preoccupied with other concerns? She must, after all, be involved in certain financial transactions, selling up and moving away from Spain. Or is she downright selfish?

I am inclined to be charitable, plumping for the former option. I can't think of any mother, apart from mine, who wouldn't put their children's interests ahead of their own.

'Perhaps we could do something together when we get back,' I suggest.

Cassie brightens. 'Can we make a cake to welcome Mum home?'

'A ginormous one,' says Elliot. 'The biggest cake in the universe.'

It seems like a good idea to me, although I'm more accustomed to working with flowers than flour, because it will keep Letitia's kids' minds from the fact that their mum isn't here.

I shop for ingredients on the way back, but I haven't enough cash on me for Smarties as well as ready-to-roll icing.

'Why don't you buy a box of icing sugar like my granny does?' says Cassie.

'Because I'm no good at mixing it up. The last icing I made ended up around the cake, not on top of it.'

'We can use Martin's sprinkles,' Sasha suggests. In the kitchen in the flat above *Posies* Cassie

221

breaks eggs and their shells into the cake mix, Elliot sneezes into the flour, Sasha spills the cocoa powder, and I find myself wondering if I am taking the spirit of generous acceptance just a bit too far. How many other women would make a welcome-home cake for the girlfriend of the man with whom they are madly in love?

'Elliot, you've licked the spoon and put it back in the cake mixture.' Cassie wrinkles her nose.

Elliot giggles. Soon, we are all giggling. Cassie keeps praising my culinary skills, and Sasha is carried away by optimism that, because one errant parent has returned all the way from Spain, her father might be able to make the trip from Devon one day. Robbie is living just outside Exeter.

'It's only a drive up the motorway, isn't it?' she says. 'You have to fly from Spain.'

'Yes, darling.' I change the subject. 'Where's the skewer? We need one to test that the cake is cooked.'

While the cake is cooling on a rack, we turn our attention to the decoration. I roll out ready-made icing and the kids play with coloured strips. Cassie makes an effigy of her mum and Elliot, a footballer. Wayne Rooney has thick red legs, white shorts and a red shirt. We are somewhat limited by the choice of colours in the box. Sasha makes a zebra, a daddy zebra.

I lay the icing across the top of the cake and trim the edges. Sasha pours sprinkles onto the top from a great height, but the sheet of icing is so dry that they bounce all over the worktop. Elliot licks his fingers so that he can pick them up and press them into the icing, leaving cocoa-brown fingerprints.

The sound of voices interrupts our creative enterprise.

'It's Grandad!' Elliot wipes his hands on his shorts and runs down to escort George and Val up to the flat. To my horror, Val walks into the kitchen, carrying a cake double the size of ours, with a pink ruff and *Welcome Home Tish* written in neat letters across icing that is as smooth as a skating rink.

If Val's cake was a human being, you might assume that it had been away on a pamper day at a health farm. Ours looks like the victim of an assault.

'Hello, Cassie and Elliot. Oh, and Sasha.' Val glares at me. 'Where is our Tish?'

'She's out with Martin,' I respond. 'The children wanted to make a cake for her.'

George flashes me a sly wink. 'Val's been dealing with the fatted calf all afternoon. She's even splashed out on a new dress from Nigel's market stall.' He raises one eyebrow. 'I'm surprised you haven't complimented her on her outfit – you can hardly have missed it.'

'It's very striking.' What else can I say about the several metres of yellow and orange seersucker which billow from a band above Val's breasts.

'I admire your turn of phrase,' George says.

'We must go.' I drop my arms around Sasha's shoulders and hug her tight. It is too late though to avoid a confrontation with Letitia and Martin, who are just climbing the stairs. Martin nods to acknowledge me when he arrives, but doesn't speak.

'You'd better be off, hadn't you?' Val glances in my direction. 'I expect that you have an early start in the morning.'

'Terri and Sasha must have some cake,' George insists.

'We really have to go home,' I say awkwardly.

'Mum, please can we stay?' Sasha begs. 'I want to sample our cooking.'

I give in. Sasha wriggles out of my grasp to join Cassie and Elliot who are arguing over lighting the candles. The brother and sister end up holding one side of the plate each, and carrying the cake which lists dangerously, into the living room.

'Here you are, Mummy.' They place it on the coffee-table and grin proudly.

Letitia smiles. 'That's lovely, my darlings, but that blob isn't me, is it?'

'We didn't have any brown.' I guess that Cassie is referring to her mother's fantastic tan.

Letitia points to the second figure. 'Is that your daddy?'

'It's Wayne Rooney,' Elliot says, his tone suggesting, 'How on earth can you not know who that is?'

'That makes you a footballer's wife then, Tish,' George comments.

'Oh, George, you're a wag,' Val says.

'I'm not the WAG,' says George. 'Tish is.'

'Very funny.' Letitia's tone suggests that she is referring to George, not his attempt at a joke. At least that is what she sounds like to me, but then, I am biased.

'Shall I cut the cake?' offers Martin.

'Just a small piece for me,' says Letitia. 'Cake is

a red light on the GI diet.'

I watch Martin cut a tiny sliver, and hand it on a paper napkin to Letitia.

'Thank you, darling,' she says.

'How about you?' Martin turns to me, but I cannot trust myself to meet his eyes, or open my mouth. I shake my head.

'I can't think why you left Addiscombe in the first place, Tish,' George says.

'George, you loved the Costa Brava,' says Val.

'Only because of the traditional English pubs. Anyone for a brew?' Without waiting for an answer, George heads out towards the kitchen.

I leave Sasha to sample the cake, and join him. While I am stacking the dishwasher, I notice how he slips his hand into his jacket pocket and pulls out a small bottle of brandy, one of the 'added extras' from the shop. He unscrews the lid and pours a generous splash into his mug.

'It's just a snifter.' He nods in the direction of the sitting room. 'I can't watch that woman pushing that piece of cake around her plate until it's crumbs. It's like that film, *The Mummy Returns* – and the sooner she goes, the better. Why do you think she's come back? I'll tell you.' George's sideburns quiver. 'To take my grandchildren away.' He slaps his mug down, sloshing tea on the worktop. 'Over my dead body.' He throws his arms around me and gives me a squeeze. 'You're a great girl.'

'I'm hardly a girl any more,' I say quietly.

'You'll always be a girl to me.' He releases me and steps back. 'For what it's worth, that woman next door is nothing compared with you.'

How can George's opinion be worth anything to me when Martin clearly doesn't – and cannot – share it?

George grabs his mug and raises it to his lips. As he drinks, his eyes seem to bulge from their sockets and his mouth twists into an anguished grimace. He rushes to the sink, hawks and spits, before wiping his chin with the back of his hand.

'I've used one of Tish's herbal teabags by mistake. What's in those bloody things?'

Martin appears in the doorway.

'I'll let your son explain.' I pick up the brandy bottle and hand it to him as I pass by. 'Your dad needs help.'

Back at the flat, Sasha collects up the post.

'It's all for you, Mum.' She hands me a sheaf of envelopes from the letterbox. I examine the only one that isn't obviously a bill: my name and address is printed beneath an Exeter postmark. I find my fingers trembling as I tear it open. It can't be the Inland Revenue because they mark their envelopes, but it reminds me of some of the solicitors' letters that I received when my business went bankrupt. Has one of my creditors caught up with me at last?

'What is it?' Sasha queries.

'Oh, more advertising.' I scan the letter while I'm cooking our dinner of beefburgers, potato waffles and peas. It is signed by a solicitor on behalf of Mr and Mrs R. Ward. Is it a good sign that Robbie and his wife have decided to present a united front?

My clients, it reads, *are unhappy about the length of time that has elapsed between the alleged incident of conception, and the occasion of your making allegations that Mr Robert Ward was present at the alleged incident, and may indeed be the father of your daughter.*

Not unreasonably, your approach has caused some difficulties within my clients' marriage, and they regret that you did not make it through a solicitor.

My clients accept that if this child is Mr Robert Ward's daughter, then she should have some contact with her family, conditions to be acceptable to both parties. However, they insist on a paternity test to confirm or disprove any genetic link with Mr Ward.

If you wish to proceed further, please respond in writing within 30 days.

The beefburgers blacken and start to smoke under the grill. I turn it off and stir the peas, frantically scraping them off the bottom of the saucepan.

How am I going to tell Sasha? 'Listen, darling, your father has contacted me, but he isn't sure that you're his daughter so you'll have to have a DNA test.' It sounds like a dilemma straight from the *Jerry Springer Show.*

I trim the blackened coating from the beefburgers. What should I do? I can't decide.

When it is quiet and Sasha is asleep in her birthday bed, I spread my fingertips and push her door open. I walk over to her, rearrange her duvet and stroke my daughter's hair. My heart cramps with pain, as I finally admit how selfish I have been, trying to keep her all to myself. She is my daughter, and Robbie's.

Chapter Eleven

Letitia is on tenterhooks. How do I know? She must have reapplied her lippy at least six times since I arrived at work, and I've only been here ten minutes. *Posies* looks amazing. All the stock seems to have been brought from the back room into the shop. You can almost hear the staging groaning with the weight of flowers; glorious sunflowers, fragrant English roses and enormous flower heads of hydrangea, and you can hardly move without brushing against a bucket of carnations or gerbera.

'Are you expecting Royalty?' I ask Val who is at the till, reading a novel, another romance, with a photo of a clean-cut, blond hero on the front cover, visible between her fingers. Not my kind of hero though. I can't imagine fancying anyone else except Martin. I have tried to divert my attentions, but neither Ewan McGregor nor Brad Pitt can distract me.

'As good as.' She looks me up and down. 'You're turned out nicely today.'

'Oh? Thanks.'

'It's wonderful what make-up can do. I can't spot a single blemish.'

Okay, I think. Serves me right. In trying to outdo Letitia in the beauty stakes, I've gone overboard with the foundation.

'Letitia has arranged for a top designer to come and discuss the refurbishment, and,' Val hugs her ample breasts and her face contorts with glee, 'she's booked a celebrity in for an appointment to discuss wedding flowers with Martin. Letitia and Martin make such a good team. Things happen when Tish is around.'

'Who is this celebrity?' I ask, slightly disappointed that my connections are so lacking that my only claim to fame is that I once arranged some flowers for the wedding of someone who claimed to be a descendant of Genghis Khan. As Sharon pointed out to me at the time, there must be a lot of them around.

'It's Simone Simmonds,' Letitia interrupts.

'Simone who?'

Letitia stares at me as if I am an alien, just landed on Earth. 'How can you not know, Terri? Don't you watch television or read the papers? Don't you even read *Hello!* or *OK!?*'

I used to when my parents ran a newsagents, but I find them an expensive luxury since I had Sasha, and I read them only out of date in waiting rooms.

'There is no shame in admitting an interest in popular culture,' Val says superciliously.

'What does she do? Is she an actress? A pop-star?'

'What does she do, Tish?' Val echoes.

'I can't believe that I'm standing with the two people in the solar system who don't know how Simone became a celeb.' Letitia pauses for effect, her hands on her curvy hips. 'Simone Simmonds is famous for stripping naked on one of those Big-Brother-style television programmes.'

I'm not sure whether Letitia admires celebrity,

or envies it.

'Where did you meet her?' Val asks.

'In Spain. She was doing a photo-shoot there, modelling for a lads' mag. I invited her back to the bar for drinks. Martin and I are hoping that this occasion will give *Posies* and *Martin Blake* the same kind of exposure in the national press as Simone gave herself on the telly,' Letitia goes on.

'I think you mean as much exposure, rather than the same kind,' Val says. 'I'm afraid that Martin is stuck in traffic on the Purley Way. He rang a few minutes ago to say he was running half an hour late.'

'Why didn't you say so before?'

'Relax, Tish, imagine that you're lying on the beach with a tequila cocktail.'

'I can do it,' I offer. 'If Martin isn't back, I can talk to Simone.'

'We could do it together,' says Val.

'What about me?' says Letitia.

Val looks at her, as if she is looking at her for the very first time, appraising, and considering her opinion. 'How can you take an order for wedding flowers? You can wrap a couple of bunches of daffs together in a piece of cellophane, but you haven't the eye of a florist. You can't wire a rose, or tie a ribbon, although, heaven knows, I've tried to teach you often enough.' Val turns to me. 'Help me set out some samples on the table, Terri, while Tish does a stint behind the till.'

Val and I choose a selection of flowers from the buckets in the back room, judging their freshness and appeal to a celebrity bride. I wonder at Val's change of attitude towards me. I make the most of it. I don't suppose that it will last.

'I didn't think that I would ever say this, little Miss Chocolate Orange, but it is a relief that you are back here working at *Posies*. You are more capable than I imagined, and now that Tish is back in the family fold, I shan't have to worry about the fact that, as well as having an eye for the flowers, you have your eye on my son.'

Val pulls a white chrysanthemum from one of the buckets. White, for the truth. I cannot admit it. Why should I? Yet, I cannot deny it either.

'Was that the bell?' Val says, breaking the tension. 'Is that Simone?'

I chase Val out to the front of the shop where Letitia is greeting a woman at the till. The woman drops her handbag onto the counter and rests her hands on top. She closes her eyes and takes deep breaths, her shoulders rising and falling inside a mannish red jacket.

Suddenly, her eyes pop open. 'What a fabulous scent!' she exclaims.

'This is Flinty Maxwell of the FM Design Company,' Letitia says, introducing us.

'Delighted to meet you.' Val pushes in to greet Letitia's eminent designer, who has her hair tied back tightly in the style of a Croydon facelift. I am not convinced that Flinty Maxwell's choice of clothing bodes well for *Posies'* future. Black linen trousers, a white shirt and tie and flat brown bowling shoes make her look frumpy, not cool. She appears to be younger than me, but not by much.

Flinty is gushing. Everything is fantastic. In fact, she is so complimentary about the existing shop that I can't believe that she would want to change anything. However, she summarises her plans for nipping the heart out of *Posies*, and creating something more appropriate to the twenty-first century.

She makes a couple of sketches, charcoal on stark white paper, representing structures created from brushed steel and surfaces faced with granite.

'It looks expensive,' says Val.

'You can't put a price on art,' says Flinty.

I refrain from observing that I'm sure that Martin can ... and probably will.

'I don't like to put you on the spot,' Flinty goes on, having given a rough estimate of the cost herself, 'but my services are in great demand at the moment. I'm always busy. Buzz, buzz, buzz.'

Letitia stares at her, but apparently deciding that all great artists have an element of madness in their character, relaxes and asks Flinty when she can start work.

'If you're happy, I'll make up the designs over the weekend, call my team together, and we can make a start on Monday. If you'd like to sign the agreement...' Flinty pulls out some papers and a gold pen from her handbag. Letitia signs on the dotted line and Flinty countersigns. Having exchanged air kisses with Letitia, Flinty leaves *Posies* several minutes in advance of Martin's return.

'Have I missed Simone?' he asks.

'She must be caught in the traffic too, thank goodness,' says Letitia. 'Can I get you a cold drink, love? Iced water with a slice of lemon, or a glass of sangria?'

'What have you gone and done now?'

'What do you mean, *mi querido?*'

'The last time you offered to make me a drink, you had just bought the bar over the Internet, without seeing it first. Haven't you learned anything from that experience?'

'It's nothing as drastic as that,' Letitia says breezily. 'I've booked the designer for the refurb. Her fee isn't nearly as much as I expected, and the estimate of the labour and materials seems very reasonable.'

'As estimates tend to be,' Martin sighs. 'You should have requested a fixed quote.'

'It's too late now – I've signed the contract.'

Martin's jaw drops. 'What!'

'You're so cautious, you'd take a day just to make it across the road outside. Anyway, it isn't your shop, Martin. It's *our* shop.' Letitia scrapes her nails along the counter.

'Why didn't you discuss it with me first? Why didn't you at least wait until we'd obtained a couple more quotes?'

'I had to make a snap decision. Flinty hinted that there was a problem with her availability, and I didn't want us losing out to someone else.'

'I hope we aren't going to have this hanging over our heads until next year.'

'She can bring her team in to start as early as next week.'

'A problem with her availability?' Martin grimaces. 'I'd say that there is. She's far too available for my liking. It doesn't sound as if she has any existing clients at all. Letitia, have you seen her portfolio?'

'Her model-shoot piccies?'

Martin's mouth curves into a mocking smile. 'No, a portfolio of Flinty Maxwell's *work* – photos of projects that she's already designed.'

'She's done a shop-window display for one of the top London stores.'

'Which one?'

'She wouldn't say – she has to be discreet.' Letitia reaches up to Martin's collar and unfastens his tie. 'That is *so* not cool. Undo your top button. That's better. And didn't you remember that I told you not to shave this morning? I read somewhere that Simone likes her men *au naturel.*' She turns to me with a wicked smile on her face. 'I guess that's how we all prefer them, eh, Terri?'

'Speak for yourself,' I say lightly. I pick up a piece of cellophane which floats across the floor, as what George might describe as a kerfuffle breaks out at the front door.

There are two women, making their way into the shop, one hustling the other ahead of her under the canopy of a multi-coloured umbrella. The woman who is doing the hustling glances nervously behind her before she closes the door and, once inside, hands the brolly over to me as if I am some kind of porter, or doorperson.

'You can't be too careful,' she says. 'There are so many of them walking our streets. Stalkers, dognappers, the Press, my ex-husbands. The world is a dangerous place.'

The combination of shades, brolly and mac with the collar turned up, when it hasn't rained for days, seems an odd way of trying to ensure that you don't attract attention to yourself. The

234

younger woman, who was hiding beneath the umbrella, also wears a fur muff. She must be about twenty years old. She has moody brown eyes, and long dark hair which touches the curve of her buttocks.

I drop the umbrella into an empty bucket at one end of the staging.

'Do be more careful with that umbrella, Terri,' Letitia whispers.

I smile to myself for not giving Simone's belongings the respect that Letitia thinks they deserve. It is only an umbrella, and it reminds me very much of one that I saw in a recent Argos catalogue.

'Welcome to *Martin Blake*, florist to the stars.' Letitia steps forwards, all smiles. 'Can I take your coats, and your fur?'

The fur bares a set of white fangs.

Letitia jumps back, clutching her chest. 'It's a dog! How cute!'

'Do you have CCTV?' The older woman is checking through the plants.

'One camera,' says Letitia, 'for security purposes, not snooping.'

'I'll have the tape when we've finished here. Simone has contracts for exclusive photos with several newspapers. We don't want anyone else saturating the market with pictures.' She smiles fondly at the woman I assume is Simone. 'We have to think of our pensions, don't we, darling. Allow me to introduce myself. I'm Amanda, Simone's mother, agent and manager.'

Amanda is very similar to her daughter, dark-haired and dark-eyed, but her facial features are rather less mobile and her lips slightly more full, the effect of cosmetic enhancement, perhaps. 'Let me take Pepi for you.'

Simone transfers the dog to her mother's arms, while Letitia assists her in slipping off her mac to reveal a lacy top through which I can see her bra, and tight white trousers through which I can see her pants. Amanda wears a more demure frock and shortsleeved jacket, the kind of clothing that I always wished my mother would wear, instead of showing me up in her miniskirts and boob tubes at school, and out shopping.

'Can we offer you both a drink?' Val sweeps across the floor, holding the wings of her skirt. For a moment, I am afraid that she is going to curtsey to Simone and her mother, but Simone's suggestion that they have a glass of champagne brings her to an abrupt halt.

'Isn't it a little too early for champers, darling?' Amanda asks, then glances at her watch, a Rolex, I guess, not that I have seen enough Rolexes in my lifetime to have become familiar with their appearance. 'Oh, why not?'

Val whisks out through the shop and grabs a bottle of unchilled champagne from the shelves.

'We need a cushion for Pepi too,' Simone adds.

Val returns with glasses of champagne on a plate, and one of Letitia's mohair cushions from the sofa upstairs. 'What a cute little dog. What breed is he?'

'He's a designer dog,' Amanda says.

'One of those puggles?' says Val.

'A Pekinese crossed with a poodle,' says Simone.

'Peke-a-poos are all the rage at the moment,'

the proud grandmother says.

Val leans down to pet the dog. It yaps and lunges towards her.

'He does seem to have some anger management issues.' Val makes a hasty retreat to a safe distance.

'He's seeing a canine psychologist,' Amanda says.

'For his gender identity crisis, Mother, not aggression.' Simone places the dog on top of the cushion on the counter. It looks more like a dog now, with tightly curled hair as if it's had a 1980s perm, a ribbon tying its fringe from its eyes, and a black patent collar. 'Poor Pepi, you almost scared him to death, ducking down like that.'

'Letitia, you look after the till.' Val wipes her hands on her tabard. 'Terri, out the back. I'm going upstairs to put my poor old feet up for a while.'

'It must be time for *Neighbours*,' Letitia observes. Does Val hear her? If she does, she doesn't let on.

I head out to the back room, where I stop for lunch, a ham sandwich and an apple. From where I sit, with the door into the shop propped open with a bucket of foliage, I can watch Martin with his client. I am not sure who is supposed to be getting married; Simone, or the dog. It sits, chewing the fluff from the cushion throughout the appointment, and everything Martin suggests has to be approved by a sniff or a meaningful look from Pepi.

I overhear snippets of conversation which drift through the air like petals on a breeze. Simone is thinking Lady Diana's dress, then Sandra Bullock's cowboy boots. How about snow leopards, fur and ice sculptures? Amanda covers Pepi's ears at the mention of fur. How about releasing doves as a symbol of love? Pepi might chase them, and photos of a peke-a-poo with a dove limp in its mouth would make a stir of the wrong kind in the Press.

'Although it would probably make the nationals,' Amanda muses aloud.

I can't understand why they haven't decided on a theme beforehand. I can't understand why, when faced with a wedding to organise, high-flying, independent women suddenly become incapable of making the smallest decision.

The appointment lasts three hours, by which time just about every reference book, bridal and celebrity magazine, and Martin's portfolio of wedding flowers has been scrutinised, judged and discarded. The table behind the counter is covered with samples of materials, flowers and foliage.

Val decides that she will collect the children from school because Letitia has an appointment for a respray to top up her tan. Martin calls me through to see if I can focus Simone's floral requirements in any particular direction.

He introduces me as his right-hand woman. 'Terri has been arranging flowers since she was three years old.' He smiles, and my heart turns over. Will I ever succeed in suppressing my responses to Martin? I am beginning to doubt it.

'Cream roses look fantastic against Simone's colouring.' Martin continues. He holds a single, perfect bloom against Simone's cheek, and I feel a brief wrench of jealousy. 'What do you think? Roses and dark foliage. Simple. Traditional.'

'I like the sound of that,' says Amanda.

'It sounds rather boring.' Simone turns to her dog. 'What do you think, Pepi?' I wonder about the fiancé, whether he realises how much competition he has from Simone's canine baby.

'Help,' mouths Martin.

My prince, I think, sticking my hands in the pockets of my tabard, rustling the piece of cellophane I picked up earlier, but forgot to throw in the bin. It isn't very often that I experience one of those flash-of-lightning moments, but this is one of them.

'How about a fairytale theme? The prince and princess. A folly in the grounds of a castle. You could have a walkway, banked on either side with roses, and the path scattered with scented petals. It would look stunning.'

'It would make a great photograph for the magazines,' says Amanda.

'Yeah,' says Simone, 'but what does Pepi think?'

I rustle the cellophane in my pocket. The dog looks up in my direction, his brown eyes on the alert, his tongue sticking out of his mouth. I rustle the cellophane for a second time. Pepi whines.

'Oh Pepi, that's a yes.' Simone whisks him up and hugs him, kissing his fur.

'Thanks, Pepi,' I murmur under my breath. Martin sits back, smiling.

'That was easier than I expected,' Simone says at last. 'A wedding with a fairytale theme. What more can a girl ask for?'

'At least another fifty thousand for the pictures. I'll contact the mags, and see if I can trigger a bidding war.' Amanda shuffles around in her designer handbag, and pulls out a phone.

'Not now, Mother,' Simone sighs. 'I want to go home.'

'We have an appointment at the milliners, and then we're going to take tea with Lady Helena to talk about the reception.' Amanda flashes a smile at Martin. 'How much do we owe for the deposit?'

After Amanda has paid over a sum that seems incredible to me – I mean, I've never dealt with this level of celebrity, nor seen an order for so many flowers – she and Simone leave with Pepi to continue the quest for the perfect wedding ceremony.

The shop door closes and the jangle of the bell fades away. Martin and I are alone.

'Thanks for your inspiration. I was beginning to wonder if Simone would make a decision on the flowers before her wedding day. She's getting hitched in less than three weeks' time.' He smiles. 'That was a great trick with the dog. I don't think that even Victoria Stilwell could have done better.'

'It all depended on Pepi.'

'No, it was you. I don't know what I'd do without you.'

'Thanks.' I turn away, my eyelids pricking, but it is too late.

'Are you okay?'

I turn back to him and brazen it out, blinking hard. 'It's a touch of hayfever.'

He moves towards me. 'I didn't know you suffered from hayfever.'

'It's the f-freesias. Pollen overload,' I stammer, stepping back until I bump up against the counter. 'I'll be fine.' At least, I would be if Martin was more offhand, not swamping me with concern. The atmosphere of *Posies*, the warmth, Martin's musky scent combined with rose and lavender, the way the carnations and chrysanths seem to lean in from the staging, forcing their colours swirling into my vision, makes me feel claustrophobic. I take a deep breath. I have to get away.

'Where are you off to?' Martin asks as I take a step towards the door.

'Del's. I should check on the arrangements I delivered the other day. I'll see you later.' I force myself to walk, not run.

Del offers me tea and biscuits while I am freshening up the displays. I tweak sprigs of rosemary, a symbol of remembrance, remove faded roses and fill in the gaps with new ones, while Del paces back and forth across the carpet, his gleaming shoes squeaking with each step. He pauses to mop his brow with a black handkerchief, and remove his jacket. He takes a coathanger out of a drawer behind his reception desk, slips his jacket onto it and hangs it over a door.

'I am a most particular man, you see?' he says.

'Indeed.'

'You appear to be a most particular kind of woman, in the way that you are so precise in placing the flowers into your arrangements to make them pleasing to the eye.' I notice how his oh-so-smooth hands are clenching into tight fists. Clenching and unclenching. A tremor of unease works its way down my spine.

241

'I was wondering,' he clears his throat, 'if you would consider another kind of arrangement?'

'A cross, perhaps, in the corner over there?' I suggest helpfully.

'No, no, no.' Del stamps one foot softly on the carpet. 'I was talking of a more personal arrangement.'

'Like letters spelling out MUM or UNCLE?'

'Terri, this has nothing to do with flowers. I am asking you if you would do me the honour of accompanying me on a weekend away.'

Has Del's profession made him ultra-sensitive to his own mortality? Doesn't he realise that women like to be wooed over the course of a few dates before they're ready for the dirty weekend?

'It's the Annual Funeral Directors' Convention in Warwickshire next month,' he continues hoarsely. 'It's like a house-party As well as the business and promotional side, there's a gala dinner, music and dancing. Everyone who is anyone in funerals will be there, and I'd like you to be there too. If you are agreeable.' The clock ticks on the wall. 'I take it from your silence that that is a negative. It's all right. I had my suspicions that a pretty face like yours was already taken.'

'I'm not actually seeing anyone, and you're a lovely guy, but I couldn't be interested in you as anything more than a friend.'

'Val implied that now Letitia was back, your affections were no longer engaged.'

'Val was out of order,' I say fiercely. My face burns even though the misunderstanding was not my fault. At no time have I encouraged Del Bickley's attentions. 'I hope that you find someone else to go with you. Now, I must get back. Goodbye.'

Del bows his head respectfully, and I feel sorry for him. I think of Martin, and how much easier life would be if we were able to choose with whom we fell in love.

On the way home, I collect Sasha from school and stop by at the supermarket for emergency rations as there is no food left in the flat, apart from Gran's beefburgers, a box of cornflakes and a live yoghurt that is so out of date that it must be well and truly dead by now.

Sasha chooses kiwi fruit, potato waffles and peas, while I buy ice cream. I pick up the triple chocolate, because as I discovered too late, like making love, once you've tasted the luxury version, you can't possibly go back to vanilla. I'm thinking of Martin here, not Robbie.

'What do you know about genes?' I ask Sasha on the way home. It's time to tackle a tricky subject.

'They come in pairs.'

That sounds reasonable, I think, until she adds, 'From the *Next* catalogue.'

'I mean genes with a g.'

'I know about the Jeans for Genes Day at school, when you take a pound and wear jeans to help save lives.' Sasha pauses. 'I know that I've inherited some genes from you, and some from my dad.'

'If you want to meet your father, you need to take a test.' There – I've said it.

'What? Like SATs?'

'Don't worry, you don't have to do anything. All you have to do is give a sample of your spit,

243

or a scraping from the inside of your cheek, and we'll send it off to a special laboratory who will test it and return the results.'

'What is the point of that?'

'It's just routine.' How can I tell her that Robbie refuses to see her unless she has the test? That he doubts me?

'I'll do it then.' Sasha skips on ahead of me.

The outcome of the paternity test is a foregone conclusion, although I find opening the envelope containing the result very much like opening the letter which gave the results of my O Levels, as they were then. I send Robbie a copy, although I know that he will have received the result separately, to remind him that Sasha is waiting for him to respond.

Robbie is Sasha's dad. The question is, will he want to do anything about it?

Chapter Twelve

It's early July, and Flinty Maxwell's team has failed to materialise so far to make a start on the refurbishment, due to what she describes as 'unforeseen circumstances'. Which is odd because just about everyone else, apart from Letitia – who has a blind spot where celebs of any kind are concerned – could foresee her circumstances perfectly.

I can't help wondering where Letitia went wrong, taking so long to sell the Blakes' Spanish bar, considering the business skills she demonstrates while working at *Posies*. She is ruthless, and well-versed in management-speak.

I am supposed to be making up the orders for the day, but George, Letitia and Martin are holding an animated discussion in the middle of the shop in front of several customers. Letitia wears a short linen jacket, cropped trousers and heels, but no tabard, I notice. (Val's opinion is that it would be a shame to cover up that healthy glow of hers.)

George stands, wringing his cap in his hands. 'Corporate branding, company logos, and process improvement,' he snorts. 'Since when have you elected yourself Personnel Manager, Tish?'

'It's called Human Resources nowadays,' Letitia says sharply. 'And I'm not acting in that capacity. This is a Health and Safety issue – for my health and your safety.' She taps the end of a pen against the counter, leans forward and growls, 'You're fired!'

'You're no Alan Sugar, and I'm not your bloody apprentice.' George turns to Martin. 'She can't sack me, son, not over a minor kerfuffle.'

'There was no kerfuffle. It was a sackable offence.' Letitia looks at Martin, demanding alliance. 'Two customers – one ordered flowers to mark the reopening of his wife's shop in new premises, and the other ordered a wreath to put on the grave of a close relative.'

'*With Deepest Sympathy,* and *Best of Luck on Your Relocation?* I see.' I notice how Martin's lips curve into a small smile.

'So no harm done then,' says George. 'It won't happen again.'

'It won't, because you won't be making any more deliveries. That's right, isn't it, darling?' Letitia steps up to Martin and touches his chest. 'Thanks for being so supportive.'

Martin pushes her back with his hands against her shoulders. 'I won't sack my dad.'

'We're doing him a favour, releasing your father to enjoy his well-deserved retirement down at the Claret or the Cricketers, or wherever he prefers to hang out.'

'I didn't want to retire in the first place,' George says. 'I missed the shop, and my mates down the market.'

'I'm sure that Val would love to have you back at home,' says Letitia.

'She says that I get under her feet.'

'Letitia, you aren't listening,' Martin says. 'I am

246

not going to get rid of my father. He and Mum have helped keep this business going for years. If they hadn't been here when you were away, I don't know what I would have done. *Posies* would have gone under. Not only that, how am I going to manage trips to the market, and the deliveries, and everything else?'

'We'll talk about it later!' Letitia's cheeks glow with suppressed fury beneath a layer of foundation that is a little too pale for her tan.

'Am I reinstated then?' asks George.

'No,' says Martin.

'Thank you, *mi querido.*' Letitia rests one hand on her hips, and gives George a condescending wave with the other.

George hangs his head in defeat.

'Dad, I said no, you are not reinstated because you were never sacked in the first place. Is that clear?' Martin frowns at Letitia. 'Haven't you got anything better to do than interfere in my business?'

'I was under the impression that it was *our* business.' Letitia tips her head to one side, tugs at a lock of her hair, and twists it. Can she wrap Martin around her little finger, or will he see past his girlfriend's double-edged gesture and stand up to her? You could cut the atmosphere with a floristry knife.

Martin's voice is almost inaudible when he responds, 'Of course.'

'Yoo hoo!' Gran's arrival breaks the tension. 'I can see that you're all busy. I would offer to make the tea, but for my poorly arm.' She wanders past the counter, and along the corridor of foliage and flowers towards the back room, where she halts. 'Is that my ladder? Have you finished with it yet?'

Martin winks at me. 'Do you mind if I hold on to it for a bit longer?'

'As long as it isn't too long,' she says sternly. 'I hope this isn't a little scheme you two have plotted between you to take my belongings away. That ladder, Terri, belonged to your grandad. Very fond of it, he was.'

'Seriously?'

'No, I think I used it more than he did, but a little emotional blackmail might hasten it back to me.'

'You mustn't go climbing ladders any more, Gran.'

'That's your opinion. On a good day, I am as nimble as Sir Edmund Hillary when he conquered Everest. I didn't finish tidying my loft, and I want to get it straight so that you don't have to when I'm gone.'

'You're not going anywhere yet.'

'Life is like a game of Bingo – you never know when your number will come up.'

'Lil, I'll bring the ladder back as soon as I can,' says Martin. 'Then I'll help you clear your loft.'

'Thank you, but I believe that you have your own house to put in order.'

As I watch the muscle in Martin's cheek tauten and relax, I wish that Gran would be more tactful.

'I *insist* on helping you,' he says, but kindly.

'You're a love.'

Not mine though, I muse sadly, as I watch him head up the stairs to the flat. It is time that I began to accept that he never will be. I shall have to be content with memories.

Gran drinks a mug of tea. I offer her a second, but she declines.

'You look as if you could do with a break, Terri,' she says. 'Why don't I have Sasha on Saturday night?'

'I'm fine.'

'You'd be doing me a favour. Saturday nights aren't what they used to be. I'd love a girls' night in, as you youngsters call it, with my great-granddaughter.' She gets up and rinses her mug under the tap, and leaves it turned upside down on the draining-board. 'You can go out to see a film, or stay in and have a long, hot soak in the bath.'

The long, hot soak without interruption from Sasha sounds appealing. How many times have I ended up in the bath with Sasha perched on the edge, chatting while I try to read a book? My daughter's conversation is wide-ranging – from an analysis of the ingredients listed on chocolate wrappers, to the contribution I am making to global warming by bathing instead of showering. The way that she goes on, anyone would think that I am melting the polar ice-caps all by myself.

'That's settled then,' says Gran. 'Drop her round to me at about six with her pyjamas, and I'll give her her tea.'

'Thanks.'

'I can feed you as well, Terri. In fact, I think that I should. You're as skinny as a bean. A nice piece of liver will put some colour back in your cheeks.'

I weigh up the idea of a plate of steaming liver and onions, compared with a microwaved chicken tikka masala for one. The chicken wins.

In the meantime, I escape from my inner turmoil inside *Posies*. I find peace among the flowers. This morning, there are new arrivals in the back room: roses the colour of whipped cream, the edges of their petals tinted pink as if an artist has taken a paintbrush and painted wet on wet; Turban Buttercups which appear to have been made with layer upon layer of tissue paper; dramatic spikes of Red Hot Poker.

Who can resist curly bamboo combined with golden calla lilies against a contrasting background of dark foliage? Maybe Letitia is right when she finally reappears and suggests that I have made up too many bouquets of that particular combination for one day.

'You'll have to take them apart again, or put them on special offer.'

'Isn't that up to Martin?' I say coolly.

'While he's out, I am in charge and I make the decisions. He's picking the children up after he's seen the Headmaster.' Letitia hesitates. 'You don't have any idea what it's about, do you? I asked him, but he was in a hurry – he didn't want to be late for school. I assume that Elliot has been playing up.'

'Cassie and Sasha are on report.'

'Martin didn't mention it. Neither did Cassie.' Letitia chews her lip, and I feel rather smug, as I continue with information to which Letitia has not been privy

'Dumbledore – that's Martin's nickname for the Head – describes the year as "having some peer-group issues". The girls have formed a gang

250

to protect themselves, and others, against two bullies. You wouldn't know them – they're called Tiegan and Brooke.'

Letitia swears softly. 'I know Tiegan's mother. I used to push her around when I was at school before she took up kickboxing. I'll have a quiet word.'

'I don't think that will be necessary,' I say quickly. 'The school are managing the situation.'

'Managing?' Letitia flexes her perfectly delineated biceps.

'I really would prefer to deal with it through the proper channels.'

'That will take for ever. I'll get it sorted, all right?' Letitia pauses. 'I'd like Cassie to leave on a good note.'

'Leave?' The hairs on the back of my neck prickle with suspicion.

'To go and live abroad.'

'I thought you were showing off when you were talking to Kev the other day about diving schools.'

'You didn't think I'd given up, did you? Once Flinty and her team have refurbished the shop, we'll put it on the market, sell up and fly away.' Letitia snakes her arm through the air, mimicking a rather turbulent flight. 'The premises alone are worth a small fortune. What do you think?'

I can't think. I am in shock. Sell *Posies*? It would be a tragedy. I picture our lost heritage, *Posies* turned into an Indian take-away, or, like *Flower Power*, a kebab shop.

'By the way,' Letitia goes on, 'the kettle needs descaling when you have five minutes. My tightwad other half is too mean to buy a new one.'

Bossy cow! I don't say it. I bite on the inside of my cheek, and my mouth fills with the taste of iron.

Later, Letitia catches me as I am rearranging the teddybears on the shelf.

'What exactly are you to *mi querido?*' she asks. 'Only I can't help noticing the way you look at him.'

'And what way is that?' I give nothing away. I am surprised that Letitia is bothered about what I feel for her partner since she is decidedly more glamorous than I am.

'Like a small kid might look at one of those teddies – kind of desperate.'

'I'm desperate to keep my job, that's all.' I appeal to her maternal instincts – if she has any. 'I'm a single mum.'

'That's what I'm worried about, that you're looking for some sucker of a bloke to provide for you and Sasha.'

'You're quite safe. I am not about to give up my independence for anyone else's boyfriend.'

'Perhaps you should try speed-dating.'

'I don't need to.' I lower my voice. 'In fact, I was chatted up only the other day.'

'Nigel chats everyone up,' Letitia says dismissively.

'It wasn't Nigel.'

I have piqued her curiosity. 'Who was it then? Tell me.'

I tell her of Del Bickley's invitation to the Funeral Directors' Convention, and immediately wish that I hadn't, although it does have the

252

desired effect of putting her off the scent of linking me with Martin in anything more than a boss-employee relationship. I don't enlighten her that I turned him down, because it will make me feel less jumpy around Martin, reassured that Letitia isn't going to interpret every conversation I have with him as a threat to their relationship.

While Letitia wanders about chatting on her mobile, I descale the kettle and make one last hand-tied bouquet of bamboo and lilies just to spite her. George is shuffling about behind me, whistling 'Amazing Grace' above the tinny sound of the radio. Val is relaxing at the counter with a book.

The bell jangles. 'Customer for you, Terri.' Val moves away to give me access to the till when I join her at the front of the shop.

A lanky man with thick lenses in his glasses that magnify his eyes, asks for sweet peas, giftwrapped with a card dedicated *To the Sweetest Pea of all*.

'Who's the lucky lady then?'

'My partner.' He smiles. 'Michael.'

Me and my big mouth. I'm not concentrating. My gaydar, as Sharon used to call it, isn't working. I process his credit card through the chip and pin reader, and send him on his way.

'Your mother didn't used to think before she spoke, either,' Val observes, walking up behind me. 'Very free and easy, she was. I don't suppose that she's changed all that much.'

'You know what it's like. When you get to your age, you become set in your ways.'

'I heard that the sea air didn't suit your father.'

I nod slowly. That is true. He suffered an attack

of bronchitis, and died.

'And then your mother remarried with unseemly haste. Let me see if I remember correctly: your grandmother described June's new husband as a much older man who made his fortune out of some tacky mascot,' Val goes on spitefully. 'He must be in a nursing home by now.'

'David is very much alive,' I say, 'and the kids at the holiday park adore Marky the Mackerel, and his friends in the Rockpool Cavern.'

It is as if Val realises that she has gone too far in condemning my parents.

'I liked your father – he was a kind man,' she says eventually. 'Right – I suppose that I'd better pop out to buy something for the children's tea. Sasha can stay, if she'd like to.'

'Not today, thanks, Val.' Not *any* day, now that Letitia is home.

At five, I go upstairs to fetch Sasha who is playing with Cassie and Elliot while Val babysits. I don't know where Martin is now. Is he avoiding me, or Letitia, or both of us?

I come across Elliot on the bottom of the stairs, holding a doll which is wrapped in a pillowcase.

'I hope you're being gentle with that doll,' I say, assuming that he has to be strangling or suffocating it.

He looks up, and strokes the doll's face. 'I'm cuddling her.'

'What's happened to your light sabre, Darth?'

'I'm not Darth Vader.'

'Have you just rescued that baby from an inferno, Fireman Sam?'

'No, I'm a daddy today.'

'Is that your baby?'

'It's Terri's.' He looks back behind him up the stairs. 'Terri, your baby's here. I found her running away.' The baby drops from his hands and thumps down the last step.

'You've dropped the baby!' wails Sasha, rushing down past Elliot to pick her up. 'Poor Daisy.'

'I didn't mean to hurt her.'

'You've broken her skull. Look.' Sasha presses the plastic head with her fingers and thumbs in an imitation of a violent form of cranial massage. 'Real dads don't break their babies.'

'I didn't break her,' Elliot insists. 'The stair did.'

Cassie, never far away, joins us. 'I don't want to be a little girl any more,' she says mutinously. 'I want to be Mum.'

'Let's both be mums,' Sasha says diplomatically. 'Elliot can still be Dad. What's your name, Elliot?'

'Daddy.'

'You have to have a name as well. Your dad's called Martin. Why don't you be Martin?'

'Okay,' Elliot agrees, apparently happy at the concept of being involved in a love triangle. I worry that although I did my best to suppress my feelings, all three children – not just Elliot – seem to have assimilated the idea that I was more than a friend to Martin, as Cassie goes on, 'I'll be Letitia. Let me look after the baby while Terri cooks the tea.'

'What shall I do then?' says Elliot.

'I dunno. What do dads do?' says Sasha.

There is a moment's silence.

'They go to work, and they get grumpy. And

255

they fart.' I stifle a giggle as Elliot continues, 'And my daddy, he does DII.'

'I think you mean DIY,' Sasha cuts in.

'I know, they go to the pub,' Cassie pipes up. 'Off you go, Martin, and don't show your face till teatime.'

Elliot hovers.

'Go on, get out from under my feet,' Cassie goes on. 'The pub's in your bedroom. If you hurry, you might meet Grandad there before he falls asleep.'

'I'm sorry to spoil your game, but Sasha and I have to go home for tea,' I say gently, and for once, Sasha doesn't protest.

'I don't like Cassie's mum much,' she says on the way back to the flat.

'Why is that?'

'She won't let anyone have any fun. Elliot isn't allowed to play with his light sabres in the sitting room, and Martin can't have ice cream for breakfast, not even for tea.'

I can't help recalling the sight of the three children playing happily together without adult interference, without restriction, or prejudice. Whatever happens between Martin and Letitia, someone – maybe all of us – is going to get hurt.

When Sasha and I finally arrive back at the flat, there is, among the post on the doormat, a package. It's quite thick, and addressed to me. I take it into the kitchen and open it as Sasha unpacks her schoolbag to find her lunchbox for tomorrow.

Terri, if you're sure, the letter inside reads, *please give this to our daughter.* Having read the letter, I find myself opening a bottle of wine that I have kept in the cupboard for some time. I am not sure whether I fancy a drink to celebrate the fact that Sasha's dad is in touch with her, or to commiserate with myself that I am no longer truly a single parent. Yes, I shall keep full custody of our daughter – at least, that is how I anticipate the future, but I accept that Robbie will want some input. How much though? Christmas and birthday cards – or interference in my decisions about Sasha's upbringing?

Although Robbie and I did once go all the way – and Sasha is proof of that – he doesn't appear to be the going-all-the-way kind of man. The tone of his letter is kind and thoughtful, not at all demanding.

'Sasha,' I call. 'There's a letter from your...' I find myself unable to form the words 'your father' but Sasha has already guessed who it is from without me having to tell her. She throws her lunchbox skidding across the worktop into the sink, grabs the package and rips it open.

I don't know whether to laugh with her, or cry.

There are photos of Robbie with his other children. I glance apprehensively over Sasha's shoulder. Robbie's pudgy face smiles out from every picture. In most of them, he wears a yellow and black rugby shirt over his belly that is swollen like a bee's. Would I recognise him if I met him on the street? I don't know. I wish that he'd sent a close-up so that I could match some of Sasha's features with his.

'I don't look like my dad,' Sasha says flatly.

'There is some resemblance. Your hair is the

same colour.' I'm not doing very well, am I? 'Why don't you read his letter?'

Sasha reads out snippets to me right up until bedtime. Robbie wants to meet her. She can't wait. He supports a rugby team, Exeter Chiefs. He hates swimming. He loves Marmite. Sasha changes her mind about wanting to meet him.

'That is disgusting.' Sasha screws up her face. 'I hate Marmite. How can he be my dad?'

'You like strawberry jam, but I can't bear the stuff, and you have no trouble accepting that I'm your mum,' I point out. 'Are you going to write your reply before you go to bed?'

Sasha shakes her head. 'I don't know what to say.'

'That's unusual for you.' I pause. 'Why don't you have a bath, change into your pyjamas, then we can sit down and I'll help you.'

An hour later, Sasha sits beside me on the sofa, chewing on the end of a pen while the paper resting on a book in her lap remains blank. 'Dear Sir or Hi Robbie, or Hello Dad? What do you think, Mum?'

'I think that it's time for bed.'

'I haven't finished my letter.'

'You haven't started it, so it'll have to wait.'

'Everyone else at school stays up till ten. Letitia says that Cassie and Elliot can go to bed whenever they like.'

There is no way that I am going to be outdone by Letitia. 'You can stay up for ten more minutes.'

'Okay.' Sasha snuggles against me, her body warm and scented with raspberry bubblebath, her damp hair drying to ringlets. Eventually, after I have drunk a third glass of wine and the paper remains blank, I send her to bed, but she wanders back an hour later, waving a piece of paper, hand-written on both sides.

'I couldn't sleep until I wrote my letter. I've said "Dear RD" – that's short for Real Dad.'

'And?' Sasha has taken so long to write her reply that I had half hoped that something in Robbie's letter to her had put her off getting in touch with him.

'I've decided that I'm going to say that I'll meet him, Mum – if that's all right with you.'

'Of course it is, darling.' A hangover is on its way; I am light of head, and heavy of heart.

Chapter Thirteen

The long, hot summer progresses. One stifling night, I am sleeping the sleep of the innocent. I can say that because, just lately, I have been so tempted to revealing the depth of my love for Martin, but have resisted. I am glad that I didn't.

The sound of the phone ringing cuts into my consciousness, and I scrabble about in the semi-darkness to find it on the floor beside the sofa. I press the button on the receiver. I am connected.

'Gran, are you all right?' I say quickly.

'Terri.' It's a deep, masculine voice, husky with sleep.

'Martin?'

'Little Red Riding Hood,' he growls. 'It's the Big Bad Wolf here.'

I can't help smiling. 'You've been reading too many fairytales. What are you doing? It's four in the morning.'

'And less than eight hours before the Wedding of the Year. Is there any chance of you coming to the aid of a florist in distress?'

'What kind of aid?' I ask suspiciously.

'Have you ever wired a mushroom?'

'Zillions.' I'm serious – I've wired just about everything you can think of in my time as a florist.

'Great. I was going to make a start on Simone's flowers two hours ago, but I overslept, and I must have bought the wrong kind of mushroom. Terri, please, I'm desperate.'

'You haven't asked me to work with you for a while.'

'I know, and I'm sorry. I've been stupid and insensitive, and I'm utterly shattered, thoroughly pissed off, and I never want to see another mushroom – no, another flower of any description for the rest of my life – which won't be very long, if I don't get these arrangements finished by mid-morning. Please, I need you now!'

I should be so lucky, I think. I wake Sasha, who is delighted at the idea of an early start to playing with Cassie and Elliot, and we walk round to *Posies* at dawn. Sasha skips through the shop and up to the flat to snuggle down with Cassie for a while, since it's too early to wake the whole household, and I join Martin in the back room.

At first, I can't see him for crates and boxes of flowers, fruits and fungi, coloured sands, ferns and hundreds of roses.

'Martin?' I say softly.

'Over here.' His head appears above the top of the table. 'I'm running out of diamanté pins.' He smiles briefly. 'I'm glad that Letitia made me clear everything out for the workmen, even if they haven't done any work yet, and you don't know how happy I am to see you.'

The feeling is mutual, but my happiness at seeing Martin is tempered with regret that he is pleased to see me only because I am an extra pair of hands.

'It isn't like me to mess up. I should have knuckled down and done more yesterday.' He nods towards the ceiling. 'I tried to wake the scarlet harlot, but she's enjoying her beauty sleep.'

I assume that he's referring to Letitia and infer from his tone of voice that 'scarlet harlot' is not a term of endearment, that there is some kind of trouble between them.

'What can I do?' I study Martin's drawings for table decorations and the bride's bouquet, and trace the outline of a tower of exotic fungi with the tip of my finger.

'The tower was Simone's idea,' Martin says. 'I made the most of it, I hope.'

'It all looks somewhat subterranean.'

'Middle Earth.'

'I can't help wondering if the bridegroom might be a frog.'

'Gollum.' Martin chuckles as he continues to assemble exotic mushrooms together with a glue-gun. 'Simone felt that she had to do something quite way-out to attract the Press to the wedding. The venue is ideal – a stately home which has a castle-like folly in a woodland clearing.'

'Do you know what she's planning to wear?'

'I'm sworn to secrecy, but I can give you a hint. Think Princess in a diaphanous blue dress. Think tall pointy hat.'

'Sounds more like a witch.' I collect an armful of lemons from one of the crates that is open on the floor, and plonk them on the table where they roll about, settling against a heap of foliage.

'In blue, with voile draped down from the point to create the effect of a veil.' Martin picks up one of the lemons that reaches him, and hands it back to me, dropping it into my hand. Our fingers touch very briefly, and desire begins to flicker through my soul, like the pulse of a crash victim returning to life.

I have lost the thread of the conversation. I sit down, keeping hold of the lemon. I feel a bit like a lemon myself. No, more of a gooseberry, not that Martin and Letitia appear particularly affectionate towards each other, not for a couple who were forced by circumstance to live apart for several months.

I take a piece of wire and stab the side of the fruit, just above the base, pushing it through so that it sticks out the other side. I force a second wire at right angles to the first. Juice trickles out onto my fingers as I twist the four ends of wire into two stems so that I can attach the lemon to the body of the swag later.

'How is Sasha?' Martin asks. 'We haven't seen so much of her recently.'

I mumble some excuse about how busy we've been, but the truth is that I am not comfortable sending Sasha to play at the Blakes' any longer. How can I, when Letitia always manages to make her feel unwelcome? 'I'm taking Sasha to meet her father soon,' I go on. 'He's arranged to meet us in Croydon.'

'The Real Dad? I guess you're apprehensive. I would be.'

'He talked about offering financial support for Sasha, but that wasn't why I contacted him.'

'It'll work out.'

'I wish that I had your conviction.'

'You're forgetting how resourceful, how strong you are, Terri. I couldn't have coped being a single parent for a few months, let alone years. I would never have managed to run my own business with a toddler in tow, and without the support of my family.'

'Oh, stop it.' I can't help smiling. 'You're making me sound like Mother Teresa.'

'You are – you've saved my life.'

The wedding arrangements are beginning to take shape out of the chaos. The pedestals flare with foliage and coloured roses. The table-top disappears beneath rows of corsages, buttonholes and table decorations, vases of striped layers of sand, fruit swags, and circlets of fungi. The air fills with the scent of strong coffee, roses and citrus. By nine-thirty, Martin and I are loading the *Posies* van, and a second hire van which George is to drive.

'I hope that we aren't too late,' Martin says. 'Simone has to have her bouquet before she walks down the aisle.'

'Will there be an aisle in the grounds of a stately home?'

'Some of those pedestal arrangements are to flank a special walkway, laid with Astroturf, and that carpet of rose petals that you suggested. Fresh, not freeze-dried.'

'Martin, shouldn't you be somewhere else by now?' Letitia appears down the stairs, stops and rests one hand on her hip. She has her hair tied back in a ponytail, and is dressed in a vest top and joggers as if she's about to leave for the gym. 'I'm so looking forward to Simone's cheque. It's high time we had a new car. I'm thinking a sporty number, a soft top with no room in the back for the kids.'

'You'll be lucky,' says Martin, stowing another box. 'It won't cover the cost of the refurbishment.'

'I can't believe that you're about to waste this opportunity to break into the celebrity circuit, *mi querido*. Actually, on second thoughts, I can believe it.'

'I'm not sucking up to anyone.' Martin hands me two smaller boxes. 'I don't need to.'

'You couldn't even get us an invitation to the wedding,' Letitia taunts.

'Perhaps I'd have more time to network if you worked a bit harder.'

She bridles. 'Don't go blaming *me* for your deficiencies.'

'Letitia!' I watch the muscle in Martin's cheek twitch with annoyance, as she continues, 'You'll have to manage without me today. I have appointments with Flinty Maxwell and Big Dave.'

'Oh dear, I was hoping to take you with me,' says Martin sarcastically. 'Someone else will have to accompany me to Simone's wedding instead. I didn't get round to telling you, but we have an invite to have drinks with the guests before the main reception. Do you mind, Terri?'

Do I mind? I shall be rushed off my feet, distributing the arrangements according to Martin's plan of the venue, glueing and tying last-minute breakages into place, and giving the flowers one last tweak. The pressure will be on – Martin expects nothing less than perfection. However, I would love to see our work in the setting it was designed for, to see how the bride and her guests respond to it.

Letitia's eyes flash with fury. 'She can't possibly represent *Martin Blake*. Just look at her! Mutton dressed as lamb.'

'Better than the other way around,' Martin mutters.

'What did you say?'

'That I'm looking at Terri, and I can't see anything wrong with her. Far from it, in fact.'

At this, Letitia makes a great show of mulling through her options. 'I suppose I could cancel Flinty,' she begins, but Martin interrupts.

'I'm taking Terri,' he says sharply. 'Come on, let's finish getting the vans loaded. Where's my dad?'

Once we are on the road, Martin pushes the *Posies* van to its limit as though he can't get away from the shop fast enough.

'I meant what I said back there, Terri. You look great. You *always* look great, but if you like, we can stop round at yours so that you can change.'

'There's no need.' I finger the hem of my *Posies* tabard. 'No one will be looking at me, will they? All eyes will be on Simone.'

Simone is a vision in cornflower blue. She sits stiffly in a position that has clearly been staged for maximum photographic impact, one arm outstretched along the back of an open carriage, her skirts carefully arranged to show off the jewels on her designer wedding shoes. The four white horses which draw the carriage at a spanking trot, along a sweeping drive to the foot of the ruins of a fairytale castle, toss their coordinating

266

plumes and ribbons. A group of wandering minstrels play a fanfare to announce the great Simone's arrival to the scores of guests who await her presence in a mocked-up grotto behind the castle wall.

The grotto is beautifully tacky. An aisle of fresh rose-petals curves up to an altar-like arrangement of concrete stones with what appear to be ancient runes carved into the surface. A waterfall pours down the stonework behind the altar, its spray caught and split into rainbows by spotlights which are recessed into more rocks on either side, and disguised by hanging ferns, pillows of moss, and towers of exotic fungi.

A footman springs from the carriage as it pulls up, and helps Simone down onto the gravel. Martin steps forward with the bride's bouquet, an enormous flurry of electric-blue roses, delphiniums and irises, with masses of foliage. The weight seems to take Simone by surprise.

Martin makes a couple of final adjustments to the flowers for the benefit of the Press Pack – one reporter and a photographer – and Simone sets off towards the grotto with her ridiculous hat and flowing tail of voile. She has had her hair recoloured – it's blonde now, not dark – and had extensions added so that it reaches down to her calves.

'Which fairytale is it?' I whisper to Martin when he returns to join me, watching from a distance as we haven't been invited to the ceremony.

'*Beauty and the Beast.*' He grins. 'I've just seen the groom.'

'Martin.' I give him a friendly dig in the ribs.

267

'That's unfair.'

'Simone can't have kissed him yet – there's still time for him to turn into a prince.'

'I think that she's modelled herself on Rapunzel. "Rapunzel, Rapunzel, let down your golden hair..."'

A second carriage, not quite as elaborate as the bride's, drawn by two dapple greys, pulls up behind the first. Simone's mother, in an ice-blue dress and tiara, a man, and several girls ranging from ages of about four to twenty-four, dressed as pink fairies, descend from the carriage. Another footman in blue livery trots along holding the end of a lead, dragging Pepi, the peke-a-poo, who sports a ruff of pleated netting, and pompoms.

'I think that Simone has lost the plot,' I observe. 'What are all those men doing? The ones in black?'

'They're bouncers. Amanda is afraid that the competition will crash the wedding. The photos have to be exclusive, you see.'

'Is the groom a celeb too?' I have kept my tabard on over my T-shirt, and my arms are bare. When Martin sidles closer, whether by accident or design, his arm touches mine, raising goosepimples over my skin. I step abruptly away.

'He's a Hugh Grant lookalike, and chat-show host on daytime TV.'

Simone and her new husband finally emerge from the grotto to the cheers of several hundred people.

'How can anyone possibly keep up with that many friends and relatives?'

'Just think of all the presents.'

'And the thank-you letters,' I add. Martin's hand creeps around my back, and rests on my hip. I don't move away this time. Why shouldn't I enjoy the contact? The caress of Martin's fingers, roughened with peeling glue and callused by too much wiring and cutting and tying, against the naked skin between the waistband of my jeans and the hem of my T-shirt; the rise and fall of his chest that I am watching out of the corner of my eye; his scent of the outdoors, bruised leaves and citrus...

I shiver as a cloud spreads across the sun. I am loving it all far too much.

'Most of Simone's guests will be her hired help – cleaners, personal trainer, personal shopper, hairdresser, gynaecologist and vet,' Martin says eventually.

'Do you really think that she'll try to throw that bouquet?'

'Try, yes, but probably not succeed, unless she's been doing exercises to increase her upper-body strength.' A chuckle wells from Martin's throat then dies again. 'I did warn her about the weight of those flowers, but she insisted on having that outsized bouquet to counterbalance the height of her hat.'

'Perhaps she'll ask one of the bouncers to throw it for her.'

Martin grasps my arm. 'Let's not stop to find out.'

'What about the photographers? What about Letitia? She'll be furious if you don't get your face on the same page as Simone.'

'They'll be hours taking pictures of all this lot.'

Martin raises one eyebrow. 'Well?'

'You have a point.'

Martin releases my arm. 'Let's go.'

As he drives us back towards Addiscombe, his easy manner seems to fade. I find myself talking about my grandmother to fill the awkward gaps in our conversation.

'Gran says that she is better, but it's all bravado. She's exhausted. She keeps falling asleep with her mug of coffee in her hand.'

'I thought coffee was supposed to keep you awake,' Martin jokes, and I can't help smiling back. Then he says, 'I can't bear the thought of going back to the shop just yet.' He pulls into a pub car park, leaving the engine running. 'I feel like bunking off for a while.'

I am uncomfortably aware of the gearstick that throbs between us, of the heat that radiates from Martin's body, of the length of his thigh, just inches from mine.

'Terri, I'd like to...' The words seem to catch in Martin's throat. 'I really want...' A pulse starts to pound, filling my ears so that I can hardly hear what he is saying. I am suddenly afraid that he is going to confess that he wants to make love to me, and if he did, how could I resist?

I force myself to picture Cassie and Elliot's faces, their innocent smiles as they welcome me back to *Posies* later on today. It has to be the children, because I can no longer respect Letitia as Martin's partner. She is a self-centred, spoiled child herself, and I hate her for making Martin miserable, for making him look less of a man for not standing up to her.

Martin takes a deep breath, and the desire that clouds my judgement dispenses.

'Can I buy you lunch?' he asks.

'Shouldn't we be back at *Posies* by now?' I say gently. 'I should be working.'

'Call it an early finish – you've done a full day already.' Martin turns the key in the ignition, switching off the engine.

Once inside the pub, I decline his offer of lunch, but accept a white wine soda. He buys a bitter shandy for himself. While he pays at the bar, he slips Amanda's cheque for the balance of the wedding flowers into his wallet.

'I wonder if we'll be invited back.' He hands me my glass.

We? Back? It takes me a moment to realise that Martin is referring to us, and Simone's next wedding.

'She's getting hitched for the money,' he goes on. 'Next time, when she's faded into obscurity – because there are only so many times you can take your clothes off on national TV – it might be for love.'

We sit outside on a bench set in an arbour of fragrant climbing roses, watching a couple of swans necking on the river at the end of the field beyond.

'Swans pair for life, don't they?' Martin observes.

'I think so.'

He is uncomfortably close to me. Once again, my pulse quickens, my powers of thought falter. He gazes at me for a long time. Heat creeps up the back of my neck and spreads across my cheeks.

271

'You're straying,' I tell him quietly.

'I haven't touched you.'

'You don't have to. It's in your eyes.' I assess the deep flush that clothes his cheeks. 'I want you to take me back to work.'

Martin stretches one arm along the back of the bench and slips his fingers behind my neck, stroking my skin. It would be so easy to give in. This is what I have yearned for, after all. This is what I wanted. For Martin to pay attention to me, to fall in love with me all over again...

It is too late. It cannot be. I find my fingers tightening around my glass.

'You have a wife, and two lovely kids.'

'Wife?'

'Longterm girlfriend, partner, mother of your children then. You're as good as married.' I reach for the van keys at his side, pick them up and throw them at him. 'Now, take me back.'

Martin drives me back to *Posies*, silent and apparently chastened.

The way that he looked at me just now... What on earth was he thinking of?

When can you be sure that you have settled into a new life? I have acquired a ticket from Croydon Libraries, and enrolled Sasha in a course of trampoline lessons since she has decided that she is not going to be the next Darcy Bussell, after all. Much to Val's disappointment, Cassie has joined her. Those flexible ankles, wasted!

I have also stopped ringing the best friend I left behind twice a day. Sharon and I still have plenty to chat about, but perhaps not quite so much as before I left Devon for Addiscombe.

Sasha is at Gran's again tonight – I am not sure who is looking after whom. I tried to cancel our arrangement because I didn't want to tire Gran out, but both she and Sasha were so disappointed that I changed my mind.

Alone in the flat, I start to run a bath. I mix a few drops of essential oil of lavender with a bubblebath base, and pour the mixture into the flow of the hot tap. The foam swells up over the side, and slithers down onto the mat. I turn the tap off and light three scented tealights, scatter the petals of a scarlet rose around the edge of the bath, and fetch a book that I have borrowed from the library.

I strip off my clothes – T-shirt and bra, cropped trousers and pants – then test the water with one elbow, a habit that I acquired when Sasha was a baby, and haven't yet discarded, as if I am hanging onto those days when she didn't answer back, or have an opinion on what clothes she should wear.

The temperature is perfect for once. A glass of sparkling white wine bubbles on the tiled surround. I step into the bath and slide down beneath the foam, tip my head back and close my eyes. I picture Martin, his face, his smile ... then blow him like a bubble, out of my vision, only for him to come drifting back again...

Out of all the dodgy appliances and fittings in Pat's flat, the one gadget I can guarantee will work reliably every time is the doorbell, which plays an electronic version of what I think is 'I Hear You Knockin'. I squeeze my eyelids tight and hold my

273

breath, hoping that whoever is ringing it, will go away. I haven't ordered from either the Bettaware or Avon catalogues that have come through the door. I haven't requested a prayer appointment with the Jehovah's Witnesses. I haven't phoned for a pizza. And I don't owe Pat any money.

Whoever it is, is determined, and I eventually drag myself out of the bath, fling on my towelling dressing-gown and, dripping water along the hallway, slip the chain across the front door before I pull it open.

A man in a cycle helmet and the tightest Lycra suit that leaves nothing to the imagination removes his goggles. 'Terri?'

'Martin?' I slide the chain back and open the door.

'I'm sorry. I've disturbed you,' he says awkwardly, swivelling his eyes away from the shadow between my breasts where the dressing-gown gapes. 'I didn't mean...'

'Just a mo – I'll go and get dressed.'

'Don't bother. I mean, I'll be in and out in a jiffy.'

And it is here that I wish I could tip my head to one side, let my robe gape open just a teensy bit more, and sigh, 'Oh Martin, come inside and ravish me.' I wish I could reach out and tug him towards me, press my face against the bare skin at the base of his neck and inhale his scent of eucalyptus, traffic fumes and fresh air.

'What on earth are you doing here at this time of night?' It crosses my mind that he is about to sack me, to tell me that my services are no longer required at *Posies* and *Martin Blake*.

274

'I've come to look at your kitchen tap. Your gran said you had a drip that needed fixing.' Martin's face is in shadow, his voice clean of pretence. If there has been any dishonesty on Gran's part in persuading him to visit me, I am confident that Martin is not involved. He looks at me closely. 'You haven't, have you?'

Now get out of that, I think.

'The drip that Gran was referring to was my landlord Pat. He's supposed to be a property developer but he is almost as unenthusiastic about DIY as you are. I asked him several times to replace the washer in the tap, and guess what, he came round earlier this evening and dealt with it. Sorry, Martin. What am I going to do with my grandmother?'

'Lil means well,' Martin says. 'She wasn't to know that your landlord had been round. Actually, we do need to talk. This might be a good time.'

'Would you like a drink? I've opened a bottle of wine.'

I fling on some jeans and a clean top, and find a second glass. I sit on the sofa while Martin leans against the windowsill, the curtains wafting gently behind him, the sounds of the street drifting up through the window – the rustle of the leaves of the tree outside, the phut-phut-phut of a moped, the purr of a car engine, doors slamming, laughter and farewells.

'For someone so intent on talking, you seem very quiet,' I say.

'Yeah.'

'I'd like as much notice as possible, Martin. I

realise that I haven't got a formal contract, but if I'm going to lose my job, I need time to find another one.'

'What makes you think I'm going to fire you?' Martin frowns. 'I wouldn't have been able to manage without you.'

'That was then, and this is now,' I say cryptically. 'I suppose that Letitia will take up where she left off. *Posies* can't possibly support two families.'

'The shop itself can't, but *Martin Blake* can. Letitia is great with the customers but she has no flair for flowers.'

'I guess that it is a case of last in, first out.' I must be brave. 'Don't spare my feelings because of Gran.'

'Of course not.'

'I shan't grovel.'

'You're just like your daughter, going on and on.' Martin moves closer, his expression briefly teasing. 'Terri, if you don't shut up, I *will* sack you.' The sofa creaks as he sits down beside me.

There's something I need to know.

'Gran wanted me to ask – I mean, we've both been wondering, Martin, if you and Letitia are planning to sell the shop once Flinty Maxwell's team have finished.'

'Finished? They haven't started yet,' Martin snorts. 'No, Terri, I will never sell *Posies*. You and Letitia are right – the shop does needs a revamp, but *Posies* will remain a traditional florists. It's been increasingly difficult with competition from the supermarkets and garage forecourts, but there's still a niche market.'

'Is that how you would describe the church

276

ladies?' I ask lightly. 'And Nigel?'

'Nigel pays in kind, keeping my mother up to date with the latest fashions.' Martin grins. 'I'm being ironic.'

My skin grows hot. I am sitting with my former lover side by side, my thigh touching his, very lightly, where the dip in the sofa's cushions has forced us together. We are alone. My heart misses a beat. Anything could happen, and no one would know except the two of us, but my conscience would not allow it.

Martin shifts along the sofa. I am aware of his fingertips walking back and forth across my forearm, but I can't feel any sensation, just numbness. My heart screws up into a tiny ball. Tighten and tighter, until it feels as if it will implode.

'I am truly sorry about the other day, in the van. It was a moment of madness on my part. You are a...' He stumbles for the right words. 'You're a great friend, very attractive ... and I guess, well, we have history, and ... I went too far. It will never happen again – you have my word.'

Does he expect me to jump up and down, and scream with gratitude? A leaf trembles on the potplant on top of the television – an orphan which I discovered dehydrated and neglected among Martin's tax files, and brought home to revive. Martin presses his lips together and swallows hard. The leaf drops.

'Cassie and Elliot have persuaded Letitia that Addiscombe is home from now on,' Martin adds in a low voice, and my heart plummets further. Letitia is staying.

'That's great,' I say flatly.

'They missed their mum like mad.'

'I know.'

Martin leaves his glass on the floor at his feet and stands up, his muscles rippling beneath his leggings. 'I'd better get back.'

'Sure.'

'Goodnight, Terri.'

'Goodnight, and thanks for dropping by.' Once I have closed the door behind him, I lift the corner of the curtain in the living room and watch his flashing bike lights twinkle into the distance. I try not to think of his pumping thighs...

When I return to my bath, the tealights have gone out, the water is cold, and the bubbles turned to a flat scum. I stretch out on Sasha's bed, the bed which Martin bought for her birthday, and draw a picture of which Sasha would be proud.

It is a portrait of Letitia. I should be glad that she is staying, that the Blake family are reunited, and I know that children are usually better off with their mum – but *Letitia?* I scribble some yellow highlights into her hair, stabbing at the paper, until the tip of the felt pen disappears inside the shaft. I shall have to own up, and buy Sasha a new set.

The next morning, I am up early to fetch Sasha from Gran's house because I couldn't sleep for thinking about The End of the World. Does that sound melodramatic? Martin has made his decision. He has chosen Letitia. That's all.

'We've had a great time.' Sasha hugs me. 'Gran's been giving me rides round the block on her scooter. We've been bumping up and down on the pavements.'

'Isn't that a little irresponsible, Gran?'

'It was just a bit of fun, and I can't drive any faster than eight miles per hour, since Martin interfered with it.' Gran is wearing support tights that are the colour of Werther's Originals, with a burgundy skirt and scarlet blouse. She has the brooch that she always wears on a Sunday pinned to her collar.

'He didn't do it out of malice. I'm sure it was for your own safety.' I accept my grandmother's offer of coffee.

'Did you enjoy your evening?' she asks.

'What do you think?' I respond.

'Did Martin fix everything?'

'Martin?' Sasha cuts in.

'He dropped by to mend a tap,' I say quickly, unsure whether Letitia knows about Martin's errand of mercy, and unwilling for Sasha to be the one who reveals it to her, if she doesn't.

'Did he fix it?' Gran repeats.

'No, he failed,' I say abruptly.

When we walk back to the flat, Sasha says that she'd like to stay with Gran again soon, so that they can take the scooter out again and try it on the skateboard circuit in the park.

'Did you do anything else?'

'Great-Granma and I had lemonade and sweets, and we played Monotony – the old-fashioned version with the top hat and the dog and the battleship. Great Granma put the dog away so it wouldn't frighten Old Tom.' Sasha pauses. 'Sometimes, she treats me like I'm about five.'

'Who won?'

'Great-Granma bought a hotel for Mayfair and took all my money.' Sasha's bottom lip juts out. 'She cheated.'

I don't try to defend my grandmother. If it wasn't for her, Sasha and I would not be living in Addiscombe. Far from being an innocent old lady, there is more to Mrs Lilian Parkin than meets the eye. It has been quite a shock to me to discover exactly how devious she can be.

Chapter Fourteen

A recent survey has found that florists are happier in their work than dentists and architects. Why is that, when they earn far less money for their efforts?

While Sasha is sitting in the dentist's chair in what Gran would call the 'dental-hygienist position', the sound of a drill on the other side of the wall goes straight through me. I notice too how Sasha's eyes widen and her knuckles turn white.

Now I remember why dentists are paid more than florists.

The dentist glances in my direction. 'I can't wait until those workmen are out of here. It's a masonry drill for walls, not patients, so you can both relax. Have you been cleaning your teeth twice daily, Miss Mills?'

Sasha nods.

'But you also like sweets and fizzy pop?'

Sasha nods again.

'Don't we all.' The dentist's smile is almost as brilliant as Letitia's. 'You have two tiny cavities in your back teeth. I shall fill them today, and check again in six months. In the meantime, you mustn't eat sweets more than once a week.'

'I don't give Sasha sweets,' I butt in.

The dentist's eyebrows shoot up behind his floppy fringe. 'Do you have sugary treats between meals?'

'Sometimes I have ice cream for breakfast,' she says when he removes his pick and mirror from her mouth.

'I think you should stick with cornflakes or unsweetened porridge in future.'

At the end of the treatment – which is brief and mainly painless – he offers Sasha a choice of sticker from a plastic tub. Having had a good rummage, and having first pulled out Postman Pat and Winnie the Pooh, she declines.

'I'm too old.'

'If I was ten again, I would choose that one.' Mr Nasiri points to one of Postman Pat's black and white cat. Sasha gazes at it, her mouth twisted with indecision. 'You can change your mind.'

'Okay.' She takes the sticker, then remembers her manners. 'Thank you.'

On our way out, I say, 'It must be Martin who's been feeding you ice cream for breakfast.'

'He used to.' Sasha corrects me. 'I don't have breakfast with Cassie and Elliot so often now that their mum is back, and anyway, she won't let them keep ice cream in the flat. She says that it makes Martin fat.'

'Has someone been giving you sweets? Is it Great-Granma?'

'I can't answer that,' Sasha says. 'It isn't right to lie, is it, and I don't want to get her into any trouble.'

'So she does?'

'It's a game that we play in the park. Great-Granma says that the troll hides sweets behind the bushes and under the benches for us, but we know that it's her. Please don't tell her that we know, Mum, because she'll be upset. Elliot asked why we couldn't see the troll, and Great-Granma said that it was because he'd nipped out to the pub, and she told him that if he didn't believe in the troll, then he wouldn't find any sweets.' Sasha tips her head to one side. 'It's exactly what you say about Father Christmas.'

I don't deny it. I smile ruefully. I do wish that Sasha still believed in Santa. I wish she still believed in fairytales, and that the one about her meeting her dad and living happily ever after comes true.

When I arrive outside *Posies*, the Poison Dwarf and her associate are ticketing a dirty white pick-up. I saw a van like that in the dentist's car park earlier: they seem to be everywhere this morning. I stop just inside the shop door. There is no sign of Val, George or Martin, and the lights are off. However, the sound of voices carries through from out the back. I tread softly towards the door into the back room, which has been left ajar.

'Mrs Blake, you are a tease,' growls a male voice that most definitely isn't George's.

Val – a tease? In those sexy chintz blouses? Who knows what passions might beat beneath a winceyette nightie?

'You don't think I'm married to that grumpy old sod, do you?'

'You're behaving like a married woman,' the voice goes on, 'on the lookout for a bit of fun on the side.'

'You wish.' The woman giggles – it's Letitia.

'Stop playing with your end and push it up against the wall. No, no, into the corner.'

'Like this?'

'That,' grunt, 'is a perfect fit.'

'It might be for you, but for me, these dimensions are hopelessly inadequate.'

The man swears lightly. 'They don't call me Big Dave for nothing.' There is a tearing noise followed by rustling. 'Have a feel of that, love.'

'Mmmm... Very smooth.'

'Is that firm enough for you?'

'Oh, yeeesss...'

There are a few seconds of silence, then the male voice returns, quite matter-of-fact now. 'There really is no way that I can make this room accommodate a double draining-board and two rows of wall units without blocking access to the stairs to your flat.'

'They fit perfectly on Flinty's drawings.'

'Sketches, you mean. They aren't proper lay-outs,' Big Dave says. 'A kid could do them better.'

'But Flinty–'

'You don't want to listen to her, love. She's got some degree in Art and Design, but she doesn't know her arse from her elbow when it comes to putting theory into practice. It's like all this chrome she's suggested – it's impossible to work with, and costs an arm and a leg. If I were you, I'd go for a bit of MDF. If you really want it all silvery-like, I'll get my mate, Little Pete, to give it a squirt with some spray paint.'

'Are you sure?'

'Leave it to the experts,' says Big Dave. 'Trust me.'

I push the door open wide. 'Hi.'

'Terri!' Letitia turns. Her hand flies to her throat

284

and slides down to cover the butterfly flush across the swell of her breasts. Is she wearing a bra under that tiny top? I fear not, but I'm not coming over all prim and proper like my grandmother. I am thinking of Martin.

Big Dave steps back towards the window and bends down to sort through his toolbox. He reminds me more of a surfer than a carpenter, or 'chippie' as he prefers to be known. He has cropped hair with the tips dyed blonde, blue eyes, a deep tan and a gold stud in his left earlobe. His neck is broad and corded with muscle, and his shoulders are pumped up like balloons. He wears vests, ripped jeans, and steel toe-capped boots.

He is good-looking in a square-jawed kind of way; you know the type – the one who wears the hard hat, boots and ripped boiler-suit in a troupe of male strippers.

I glare at Letitia. Do I detect a guilty conscience? What does she think she is doing, flirting with the builder when she is supposed to be refurbishing her relationship with Martin?

'I didn't expect you to turn up so early,' she says brazenly.

'I'm late,' I point out as the bell jangles behind us.

'Aren't you going to see what they want?'

'I have to condition the new stock. I thought that you were supposed to be at the till when Val wasn't here.'

'Can't you see that I'm tied up?' Letitia smiles ever-so-sweetly towards Big Dave. 'I have decisions to make.'

I wish that she would decide to leave Addiscombe. I wish that she would stop tormenting Cassie and Elliot with her inconsistent behaviour, and leave Martin in peace. Sometimes, I believe that the Blakes would be better off without her.

Biting my lip, I head back out into the front of the shop where Maureen and Ella are waiting with their shopping trolleys.

'Morning, Terri. No Martin again?' says Maureen.

I let her down gently, understanding her disappointment. Little does she know... 'He's visiting a trade fair today. Don't worry though – he'll be back.' I hear the sound of heavy footsteps behind me. It's Big Dave with his toolbox in one hand and keys in the other.

'Morning, ladies.' He smiles. 'What are you after today?'

'Lilies, mainly.' Ella waves towards the staging.

'I don't understand it myself,' says Big Dave. 'A flower is a flower is a flower to me.'

'Young man,' Maureen simpers, 'flowers have their own language. For example, the cattleaya orchid symbolises mature charm, like mine. And, when I hand you one of these delphiniums, it demonstrates my ardent attachment.'

'Flight of fancy, you mean,' says Ella, but Maureen will not give up.

'If you pop into the church one day soon, I shall be more than willing to continue your education.'

'I'll bet you can teach me a thing or two,' Big Dave says, making a rapid escape past the shopping trolleys. 'See you later.'

'How marvellous,' Maureen says.

'He doesn't mean it,' says Ella. 'It was a figure of speech.'

We watch Big Dave rip the ticket off the windscreen of the pick-up outside. He screws it up and tosses it into the gutter.

'Litter lout,' Ella grumbles.

Maureen runs her fingers through her hair, which is all shades of silver.

'Mind your set,' Ella says quickly.

'I don't usually go for blonds.'

'I shall have to pray for your soul,' Ella sighs. 'You are incorrigible.'

Letitia brings me a mug of coffee, and loiters about at the till once the church ladies have left.

'This place is such a dump,' she complains. 'I can't wait to see it once Flinty has finished with it.'

'If she ever does. I overheard you and Big Dave – er, talking.' It takes an effort to form the word, because I can't believe that talking was all they were doing. 'How does he measure up then? And don't try to tell me that he was using a ruler and tape.'

Letitia's cheeks grow pink, like the blushing double blooms of lisianthus in the buckets on the staging.

'Does Martin know?' I continue.

'We were just having a laugh.'

'I meant, about the deadline? Martin thinks that he's going to have the shop back by the end of the week.'

'That's what I thought you meant,' Letitia says quickly. 'Of course he knows – he must guess anyway, from the state of the back room.' She laughs softly. 'Don't look at me like that, Terri. We aren't that different. We all exploit situations to our advantage, don't we? You and Martin – while I was away, helping him out with the children, making yourself indispensable. I'm no airhead. I know about your teenage crush on the boy next door. I know why you came back, but don't kid yourself. You have no chance.'

She turns and struts away on her heels, leaving me speechless and frozen to the spot. I feel sick. Caught out. Even though nothing has happened between me and Martin.

Gradually, I recover my composure. The shop is very quiet. There are no customers. What can I do? I need to occupy myself, otherwise I'll go mad. I get sweeping.

Should I raise my suspicions about Letitia and Big Dave? Would Martin believe me if I did?

After work, I drop round to Gran's with Sasha so that I can discuss the situation with her. Her petunias are wilting in the sun.

'I'll water them later,' says Sasha.

'That's a kind offer.' I knock at the porch door.

Gran appears at the inner door, and looks us both up and down before she lets us in.

'You can't be too careful nowadays. We've just had a lovely talk by a policeman down at the Lunch Club about crime prevention.'

'My dad's a policeman,' Sasha says. 'I'll show you his photo.'

Gran winks at me. Sasha has shown her the picture of Robbie that she keeps on her person at all times. Today, she takes it out of the pocket of her summer dress.

'This father of yours is rather corporal,' says Gran, examining the photo.

'He isn't,' says Sasha. 'He's a Detective Inspector.'

'I know, love. I meant that he's rather a chubby chap.' Gran sounds a little breathless as she leads us through to the sitting room where we can hardly get inside the door for cardboard boxes. Sasha slides a couple out of the way to create a route through to Gran's chair.

'You haven't been vaulting into your loft again, have you?'

'These are the boxes I brought down the other day. I fetched them in from the bedroom because I want to sort through them.' Gran pauses. 'Is that chocolate? For me?'

'We've brought you some sweets,' Sasha confirms.

'You shouldn't have.'

'They aren't from us,' I say. 'They're from the troll that lives in the park.'

'I see,' Gran says slowly.

'Sasha had to have two fillings.'

'Oh? Oh well, I don't suppose that the troll will be buying any more sweets then.'

'It would be better for him to spend his money on beer,' I say as sternly as I can.

'Indeed.' Gran smiles, her lips disappearing into her mouth.

'I'll go out and buy us some dinner,' I suggest. 'Make sure you slip your teeth in by the time I get back.'

I pop out shopping, leaving Sasha to Great-Granny-sit, as she calls it, and help Gran go through the contents of her boxes. I choose three ready meals of stuffed cannelloni, plus some garlic bread and fresh parsley. I'm not cooking today, but if I heat the meals up in Gran's conventional oven so that the smell permeates the house, and I scatter some herbs on the side, she won't know the difference.

'Didn't they have any of those stuffed hearts down at the butchers?' Gran asks on my return.

'They were closed. I had to go to the super-market.'

'You should have taken my scooter, going all that way.'

'I enjoyed the walk.' I change the subject quickly. 'What have you found in the boxes? No, let me guess. The Parkin family's long-lost heir-looms, a golden chalice, and pieces of eight.'

'Almost.' Sasha's face is radiant with excite-ment. 'It's like Christmas. We've found Great-Grandad's medals from the war, and your first pair of shoes, Mum, that you had when you were a baby. And look at this.' She waves a jam jar which, on closer inspection, contains a desiccated worm-like spiral. 'It's Nan's umbilical cord, the one you have when you're inside your mum's tummy.'

'I know what it is, Sasha. You don't have to give me the gory details. The contents of that jar are quite gruesome enough, especially just before tea.' I turn to my grandmother, who has arranged several bundles of letters tied up with ribbon on the arm of her chair. 'Why on earth did you keep that?'

'It's history.' Gran smiles fondly. 'Something to

help me remember the time that has gone by all too quickly.'

'Can we open this one now?' Sasha wraps her arms around the last box, which still has its string and sticky tape seals intact.

'I'll go through it later.'

'I'll start on the tea then,' I say. 'When we've eaten and cleared up, we'll leave you to rest. I'll drop by in the morning.'

'I'm going to meet my dad at the weekend,' Sasha says.

Gran reaches out for her hand and gives it a squeeze. 'You've told me that several times already. I'm sure that he'll be delighted to meet you.' She glances in my direction and adds, 'After all this time.'

'Sash, didn't you say that you'd water Gran's flowers?'

'Did I?'

'There's a watering can, a plastic one on the kitchen windowsill.'

'That's tiny – it'll take me ages.'

'You'd better get started then.'

'Okay.' Sasha looks from me to Gran and back again. 'You aren't going to talk about anything interesting while I'm out of the room, are you?'

'No, of course not,' Gran and I say at the same time.

'Who do you think we are, darling?' Gran adds.

'A pair of old chatterboxes.' Then Sasha skips off to look for the watering can, leaving me to take advantage of her absence.

'What's the gossip, Terri? Is it Martin?'

'It's Letitia.'

'I heard that,' Sasha says, whizzing past the open door with a watering can, and spilling water on the way.

'Hop it, Big Ears,' I call out. 'I don't know what to do, Gran.' I tell her about finding Letitia with Big Dave. 'Should I mention it to Martin, or not? I feel that I should, but I don't want to be accused of making it up for my own ends. Would it be a gesture of friendship, or the machinations of a spiteful old cow?'

'I'll tell him,' says Gran.

'You mustn't say anything.'

'You leave it to me.'

'Promise me you'll keep quiet. I'll deal with it in my own way, in my own time.'

'Deal with what, Mum?' Sasha rushes into the sitting room. She leans against Gran's chair. It whirrs and tilts until Gran is almost upright. Sasha laughs and stabs the buttons, sending Gran back to her original position.

I leave them to it, turning my attention to our meal. Gran fails to spot that I didn't cook from scratch, and I have to remain curious about what might be hidden in that last box. What family secrets can she be keeping in there?

I could give Sasha a list of *One Hundred Subjects Not To Mention In Front of Your Father*, but she'll never remember them all, so I plant the seeds of the most important ones to avoid, dropping them into our conversations leading up to the great day. They include the fast-food freak, the toyboy, Todd, bankruptcy and my ex-mother.

We take the tram. Sasha sits beside me, holding

a rectangle of cardboard with *Robbie* printed across it in black felt-tip pen. She has a few summer freckles across the bridge of her nose.

'Is my hair all right?' she asks.

'It's fine.' She's ten. What is she going to be like when she's a teenager?

'What do you call a dad who drinks too much beer?'

'I don't know.'

'An alcopop.' Sasha twirls a lock of her hair around her finger. 'I wish that you'd let me bring those cans of lager as well as the fountain pen.'

'Not all dads drink lager. The dad on the beach in shorts, socks and sandals, holding a can of drink, is a cliché.'

'Well, I hope that he's just like Martin.'

'Does he wear socks with sandals?'

'Sometimes.'

I smile to myself. Does it matter if Martin lapses in sartorial elegance occasionally? He makes up for it in his Lycra cycling kit. And then my heart sinks again as I recall Martin's revelation the other night; that Letitia is staying; that they have made a commitment to making their partnership work.

'Letitia says that she won't be seen dead with Martin in his socks.' Sasha grins. 'Especially his Crystal Palace or his Father Christmas ones. Mum, Martin has promised that me and Cassie can be waitresses at the launch party.'

'At the what?'

'When *Posies* has been redecorated, Letitia wants to throw a party for all the customers. Martin says that he'll pay us. It'll be my first proper job, and I'll be able to give you some money so that you can pay Pat, and I'll spend the rest on gel pens.'

'Sasha, I do love you.'

'Love you too, Mum.'

We disembark in the centre of Croydon, opposite East Croydon station. Sasha skips across the tram rails and over the road in her pale blue dress with butterflies embroidered around the hem, and sandals with a tiny heel. However, once we reach the station, she slips her hand into mine. I respond with a reassuring pressure.

Inside the concourse, Sasha runs ahead, checking the overhead screens for details of arrivals and departures.

'We had better wait here,' I say. 'I'm not sure which platform Robbie's train will arrive at.'

'Where will he come from?'

'Victoria or Clapham Junction, I'm not sure.' I suck on a mint which clashes with the taste of cherry gloss on my lips. I am beginning to wish that I had worn my heels, as my tendons are beginning to ache, but otherwise I am comfortable in an ethnic-style aqua top, and a crinkle-cotton skirt.

'If he's lost, he won't need to ask for directions because he's a policeman.'

'If he knows where he's going, he won't get lost,' I point out, quite gently, because I realise how much Sasha is looking forward to meeting her father; she's depending on it. However, there is always a chance that Robbie will be late, or have an attack of cold feet and not turn up at all.

A group of people swarm up one of the walkways from the platforms, having disembarked from a train. Sasha shades her eyes with one hand, and holds out her board with the other.

'Do you think he'll be wearing his helmet?' Sasha asks, but doesn't wait for a reply. 'Robbie!' She runs up to one of the men who is walking past the ticket barrier towards us. He stops, and smiles.

'Pleased to meet you. You must be Sasha.'

I needn't have worried about not recognising him. There is no mistaking the similarities between father and daughter when you see them together in the flesh.

'Robbie, Robbie, come and meet my mum. She's over there.' Sasha pauses to take a breath. 'Normally she wears her kinky boots which she bought for fifty pee in a charity shop.'

Thanks, Sash, I think. Have you ever wished that life was like a DVD-player, that you could press rewind and start all over again?

Robbie glances towards me and nods nervously. 'It's okay, Sasha, we have met before. Hello, Terri. There, I remembered your name this time.' He stops abruptly, blushing furiously.

'Thanks for turning up,' I say. We don't shake hands.

Robbie's navy shirt and stone-coloured chinos are slightly creased from his journey, but I imagine that Sasha would describe his appearance as pretty cool.

'Have you brought your handcuffs?' Sasha asks, her eyes on the carrier bag that Robbie has with him.

Robbie grins. 'Someone stole them.'

'No, they didn't,' Sasha flashes back. 'If they had, the Chief of Police would have given you the sack.'

'I hope that you don't let her watch programmes like *The Bill*, Terri,' Robbie says, quite seriously.

'No.'

'Mum doesn't know that I sometimes watch from behind the door when she's eating chocolate,' Sasha says.

'Do you like chocolate?'

'I love it.'

'Can I buy you some?'

'Yes please!' Then Sasha's face falls. 'No, actually, thanks because the dentist told me I mustn't eat sweets in the middle of the day. Look.' She slips her finger into her mouth and opens wide. 'I had to have two fillings because of Great-Granma and the Troll.'

'It's a long story,' I cut in.

'I haven't given you your present.' Sasha looks at me. I unfasten the clip on my handbag, and pull out the gift that Sasha has wrapped. It takes Robbie a while to break through the layers of sticky tape.

'Thank you very much,' he says, examining the pen.

'I was going to buy you a notebook as well, but Mum said that you probably had lots of them at work. Do you have a car with flashing lights, like they do in *Traffic Cops?*'

'I don't. Does your mum really let you watch programmes after the watershed?'

'Sometimes,' Sasha says at the same time as I

deny it.

'We don't have a television set,' he informs us. 'My wife won't allow it.'

'What do you do in the evenings?' Sasha says, appalled.

'We make our own entertainment.'

'Don't your other children miss *Tracy Beaker?*'

'They are younger than you, Sasha. Amber is eight, and Ryan is six.'

I take a step back now that I can see that Sasha is comfortable with her father. I can see too why Robbie and I would never have worked out. When I look at him, I feel no flicker of interest in my heart, no smouldering attraction. He is Mr Nice Guy, Mr Amenable – a wuss.

Luckily for Sasha, she didn't inherit her father's feet. He has flat size twelves, policeman's feet. Her feet are like her grandmother's, with high arches and long toes.

'I could do with a drink and a pastry.' Robbie pats his rather large stomach. 'Do you like pastries, Sasha?'

'I prefer doughnuts.'

'Which way to the doughnut shop?' asks Robbie. 'Do we proceed in a northerly, southerly, easterly or westerly direction?'

We end up in an Italian café in the Whitgift Shopping Centre. I sip at a cappuccino and watch Sasha with her father. Robbie has brought letters and small gifts, including a bracelet from his wife and family. Sasha is transfixed by his descriptions of her half-brother and -sister, of his house, and her new grandparent, Robbie's father.

I don't find Robbie's anecdotes quite so

297

arresting. In fact, I can see that his jolly attitude would become annoying if you had to live with him. For me, this meeting has confirmed what I already know – and perhaps Martin doesn't, because try as I might, I can't see any reason why anyone would want to live with Letitia – that you can't force a relationship for the sake of the children.

After coffee, we wander down to Woolworths, where Robbie gives Sasha a fiver to buy more art materials. While she is choosing – I suggested that she buys felt-tip pens because I haven't had the opportunity to replace the pen that I destroyed in performing two-dimensional Voodoo on Letitia – Robbie takes the opportunity to ask me if it would be all right if he invited Sasha to stay with his family for a few days this summer.

I don't know how to respond. I have a vision of Robbie walking away with my – I mean, *our* daughter – and never coming back. My chest tightens at the thought.

Then: is this why Martin wants so much to keep his family together? I ask myself. Because he can't bear to have his children taken away from him to live with their mother?

'I realise that this is difficult for you,' Robbie goes on quietly. 'You can't change the past, but you can shape the future. I'm not asking for much, Terri. Just a few days. If only I had gone after you, instead of going off on that rugby tour. As it was, I was relieved that you rushed off...'

What can I do?

When Sasha returns with a packet of felt-tip pens, she looks from one to the other of us.

'You've been talking about me.'

'Robbie has invited you to his house later in the summer.'

'Wow,' she breathes. 'Can I go, Mum?'

'Yes, of course you can.'

Sasha moves over to Robbie and flings her arms up around his neck.

'This is the best day of my life.' She hesitates for a moment. 'Can I call you Dad?'

'Of course you can.' When Robbie wraps his hands around her back and hugs her, I have to turn away to hide my tears. It is as if they have known each other all their lives.

Chapter Fifteen

According to Big Dave, the carpenter on Flinty Maxwell's team for the refurbishment, he has been on the job for over two weeks now. On which job, though? No one, least of all Big Dave himself, seems to be sure. Big Dave and Little Pete, the decorator, appear regularly, bringing ladders and sheets of MDF, various fittings, tools and paints, then turn up to take them away again.

Outside the shop, the pavement shimmers beneath a midday sun. Inside, Val has a fan running on the counter beside the till. In this heat, it is difficult to keep the flowers in good condition. Stems droop, leaves wilt, and petals stiffen and turn brown.

Letitia stands in the stream of air blowing from the fan, while Val sits on the far side of the till, fanning herself with an open paperback.

'How can I get on with anything, with that pair of comedians under my feet?' says Val. 'How many times have I bashed my poor old shins on their ladders and paint-pots?'

'Are they working today, or has another of their close relatives died?' I ask. Either Little Pete has many decrepit aunts, or one who has passed away more than once.

'Big Dave has a dental appointment,' says Letitia.

Val snorts. 'That's the second time in the past

week. He must have terrible teeth.'

'He has great teeth. He looks after them.' Letitia's lips curve into a small smile. 'Anyway, I'm confident that Flinty's team will finish eventually. They make me feel as if I'm back in Spain – quite chilled, as if nothing matters quite as much as it did in England. *Mañana*, that's what tradesmen call it out there.'

Val throws her book down on the counter. 'Here's Nigel. At least I can rely on him to turn up when he's wanted.'

Nigel, laden with clothing wrapped in clear cellophane, pushes the door open.

'Good morning, ladies.' He spreads the clothes across the counter. 'I have a selection of fancy dresses here for your perusal, as you requested, Valerie.'

'Have a look at them, Terri.' Val smiles. 'Cinderella *shall* go to the ball.'

'Ball?'

Nigel slips the cellophane from one of his items of clothing to reveal a sheath of yellow satin. 'This one is the "Cate Blanchett at the Oscars" look.'

'I haven't got an invite for the Oscars.'

Val takes it by the hanger and holds it up close to my face. 'The colour isn't right. You can't wear yellow. How about the jade?'

'You mean the green,' says Letitia.

'No,' says Val. 'It's too low-cut.'

'The green is too fussy,' Letitia goes on. 'Look at all those frills.'

'My Betty chose one of those for her tea dances.'

301

'That does it then,' I say firmly. 'Not the yellow or the green. I don't wear dresses.'

'You should,' Val says. 'It's a shame that women have to go about in tight jeans, flashing their loins as if they are on a building site. On younger girls like Letitia it might look attractive, but on a middle-aged siren, it looks tarty.'

'I hope that you aren't referring to me.'

'Valerie was making one of her sweeping statements.' Nigel winks at me, and goes on, 'I have to admit that I rather appreciate the sight of a few inches of bare naked flesh betwixt waistband and bodice. If I can't interest you in one of my exclusive outfits, Terri, perhaps I can show Valerie a real bargain, perfect for a party on a cruise-liner.' He extracts a long gown, made from purple viscose and smothered with enormous multicoloured sequins which remind me of Marky the Mackerel's scales.

Val fingers the dress covetously, then shakes her head. 'I can't see George and me travelling the world this year. He isn't well.'

'I am sorry,' says Nigel. 'What's wrong with him?'

'He has a problem with his balance.'

I glance towards Letitia. It's the first that I've heard of it.

'It isn't all the time.' I notice how Val glares at Letitia, but she won't be silenced. 'Mainly in the evenings, at Last Orders.'

'Tish, that's no way to talk about your father-in-law-in-waiting.'

'He'll have to wait a very long time,' Letitia says coolly.

'I'll never give up hope that one day the Blakes will celebrate the Big Wedding between you and my Martin.' Val turns back to Nigel. 'Do you do hats?'

Half an hour later, Nigel leaves with a mixed summer bouquet and without the sequinned gown.

'You two had better hurry along too,' says Val. This afternoon, it's the school sports day, and Letitia and I have been given time off to attend.

'Are you sure that you won't come with us?' says Letitia.

'I'd love to have come, but it's too hot for me. I expect they'll have air conditioning at this convention you're going to, Terri.'

'What convention?' I purse my lips. Have I missed something? A floristry trade fair?

'Letitia mentioned it to me,' Val goes on. 'I hope that I'm not breaking a confidence. You really should have bought that suit off Nigel the other day. Sober, yet classy, it would have been perfect. The dress, in retrospect, would have been too bright for a funeral directors' dinner-dance.'

'Oh, you mean Del! I'm not going anywhere with him,' I say immediately. 'He invited me, but I turned him down.'

'That was a little hasty, wasn't it? Offers don't come along very often at your age.'

'I am not prepared to compromise.' I am aware that Letitia is looking at me. Is she annoyed that I didn't explain that I turned down Del's invitation?

'You made the right decision,' she says. 'I wouldn't be seen dead at a Funeral Directors'

Convention either.'

'*The Florist and the Funeral Director*. Alas, the story remains unwritten. Such a pity,' Val sighs. 'Anyway, wish the girls all the luck in the world from me, won't you?'

'I think Sasha will need it more than Cassie,' Letitia says meanly. 'Cassie and I have been practising handing over the baton in the park. She's a natural sprinter.'

'Not everyone can run like Kelly Holmes,' I say, sticking up for my daughter. 'Sasha has a talent for art.'

'Like that Tracey Emin?' says Letitia. 'The one who made that bed. Huh!'

'I think that was the point. That she didn't make it.'

'Oh?' Letitia gives a smile that is clearly more brilliant than her mind when it comes to the concept of modern art. '*Vamos!* See you later, Val.'

I carry my bag, shades and a rolled-up parasol, while Letitia strolls along with a blue coolbag over one shoulder. Her hair is tied back and streaked with silvery-blonde highlights. It is twenty-eight degrees, and she still manages to look cool in shorts, a vest top and trainers, while the sweat trickles down between my shoulder-blades, clamping my T-shirt to my back. How does she do it?

The school playing-field is crowded with parents, grandparents and carers, all suffering from the heat.

'We should have arrived earlier.' Letitia parks the coolbag between two parties of spectators as if she is bagging her territory on the beach. 'Anyone would think it was the London Olympics.'

A woman with flabby upper arms and a crocheted cotton top grudgingly shifts her sandals to give us more space between her and another group of mums.

'Well, if it isn't Letitia, the boyfriend-snatcher,' says one. 'I remember you from school – primary, secondary and afterwards. Wherever I went, you turned up.'

'This is Tiegan's mother, Alex,' Letitia says. 'Alex, this is Terri.'

The kickboxer, I assume from Alex's appearance. She is muscular, wide-shouldered and narrow-hipped. Her hair is dark and shaved, apart from the fringe which is stuck up from her forehead with sweat and gel. She wears two vests and loose joggers. As my grandmother might say, 'I shouldn't like to meet *her* on a dark night.'

'Are you still with that old bloke, the florist?' Alex enquires.

'Martin Blake. Of course.'

'Only I've heard a rumour that you've left him.'

'I've been in Spain for the past year, living in a villa with a private pool, sun-terrace and access to the beach.' Letitia sits down on the grass, stretches her legs, out in front of her and smiles sweetly. I am beginning to recognise that smile. 'That's the advantage of having a rich old bloke as a partner. Are you and Tiegan still living with your parents?'

'It's only temporary.'

'Five years is an interesting definition of temporary.' Letitia looks towards the children being led out in a crocodile from the school.

Sasha's polo-shirt is greyer than Cassie's, and idly I remind myself to try out a different brand of washing powder. As they pass us and head for the startline, Cassie ducks out to see her mum.

'Cassie!' A teacher – not Miss Hudson because, according to Sasha, she is on maternity leave – calls her back. 'You must stay with the rest of the class.'

'I wonder if Miss Hudson has had her baby yet,' I comment.

'Oh yeah, you might be interested to know who the father is, Letitia,' Alex cuts in. 'I don't expect you to remember every bloke you ever slept with, mind.'

'Get real,' says Letitia. 'I didn't have half as many as I could have done.'

'How restrained,' Alex says sarcastically. 'Anyway, Miss Hudson has been spotted in Croydon with Kev Prior pushing the pram. What is it about Kev? Is it his caring, sharing attitude? Spreads himself about, doesn't he?'

'Oh, f*** off,' Letitia snaps. 'It's ancient history.'

'See you in the Mothers' Race,' Alex says. 'We're going to hit the shade.' Her group gather up their belongings and traipse off towards the hedge at the perimeter of the field.

Letitia sits in silence, chewing her lip. Eventually she says, 'I hope that Kev makes a better job of being a father than someone else I could mention.'

'Martin? He's a brilliant dad.'

'He could have planned his appointments more carefully. One day he'll regret missing out on his children's special days.'

'Didn't you do the same, staying away like that? It wasn't as if you could pop back from Spain for Cassie's ballet show, or Elliot's nativity play.'

'Yes, and I am sorry that I wasn't here. If I had been, I would have made a much better job than Martin of Elliot's donkey mask, and I'd have got Cassie to practise her dance just one more time, so that she wouldn't have gone the wrong way in the Naughty Little Mice routine.' She looks at me. 'Martin could have torn himself away from work, and come with me today. You know, Terri, there have always been three of us in this relationship.'

I turn away, my hands slipping on the parasol as I try to dig the end into the ground to make it stand up on its own, but I flatter myself if I imagine that Letitia is referring to me because she continues, 'If it wasn't for that bloody flower shop, we'd all be living in Spain by now. It's so important for children to have the opportunity to immerse themselves in a different culture.'

I give up on the parasol because the earth is too hard. 'What, fish and chips, and traditional Brit pubs on the beach?'

'You can eat paella as well as pie and mash. Sasha would love it.' Letitia sits back and turns to the coolbag. 'Squash?' She pulls out a lemonade bottle, filled with ice, small chunks of orange with the peel left on, and a red liquid. She hands me a plastic mug and pours. 'Get that down you.'

'Thanks.' I sip. Choke. 'That's never black-currant.'

I catch a draught of coconut suncream as Letitia leans towards me and whispers, 'It's a

307

taste of Spain. I want to make sure you don't beat me in the Mothers' Race.' Grinning and flashing those brilliant white teeth of hers, she pulls her shades down over her eyes. 'I won last year and the year before, so I'll have my sangria later.' She holds up a sports bottle and clashes it against my mug. 'Cheers!'

I don't respond, secretly admonishing myself for falling for Letitia's trick. Letitia gives nothing away, unless it is to her advantage.

Cassie wanders down to the startline for the sprint.

'There's no need to warm up today, Mum,' she calls out. 'I'm boiling already.'

'You do some stretches,' Letitia calls back. Cassie bobs up and down on the startline, ready to run at the sound of the Headmaster's whistle. The start is delayed because two of the older children are still trying to untangle a knot in the finishing tape, and by the time the Headmaster starts the race, Cassie is in the middle of performing a limp-legged cartwheel. In spite of her slow start, she chases after and catches up with her competitors. Letitia is on her feet, yelling encouragement. Cassie overtakes the leaders, her chin jutting out, her elbows sticking out like chicken wings, and her head held high. With one last effort, she speeds up and breasts the finishing tape in first place.

She receives a sticker, a red paper dot on her T-shirt for winning, then looks shyly to her mother for approval.

'That was rubbish! You almost lost that!' Letitia shouts, and like the ladybird escaping beneath the blades of grass at my side, I want to crawl away and hide. 'There's still the Beanbag Race. Perhaps you'll do better at that.'

A few minutes later, I watch Sasha and Cassie patting their bags down on their heads. The Headmaster blows his whistle and off they go. As Cassie runs, the beanbag slips off her head. She picks it up, plonks it back on, then sets off again, her hands hovering near her ears to catch it again and again. Sasha has a chance. She is in front. I cross my fingers, my toes, everything, willing that bag not to fall off.

Sasha crosses the finishing line while Cassie is still halfway back up the track. Realising that she is going to be last unless she does something about it, Cassie grabs her beanbag, holds it on her head, and runs at the same time.

'I don't believe it.' Letitia is livid. 'You know what's happened. Martin's only gone and washed her hair last night in the shower. I'll bloody kill him.'

'Not many dads would think of washing their daughter's hair.'

'He knew that it was Sports Day today.'

'It really isn't that important, is it?' I feel for Cassie. Just because she didn't win the Beanbag Race doesn't mean that she'll fail her SATs.

Letitia pours me another mug of sangria and I am feeling comfortably numb when the Headmaster tries to round up as many volunteers as possible for the parents' races.

How can I run when I haven't brought my games kit? I have a sore eyebrow. I'm not wearing a fitted sports bra. How many excuses can there possibly be?

'Oh, come on, you mums,' the Head says. 'Let's be having you.'

Sasha runs over and takes my hand. 'Please, Mum. The Mills family is depending on you.'

Letitia doesn't hesitate. She is on her feet, and off across the track, challenging Tiegan's mother to beat her.

I find myself on the startline between the two of them.

'I hope your daughter hasn't been picking on my little girl again.' Letitia performs a couple of stretches.

'Not since your Cassie's mate stuffed her Games Kit down the toilet and made it look like it was Brooke who done it.' Tiegan's mother glowers at me.

Not Sasha?

'Your Sash wouldn't dream of doing a thing like that, would she, Terri?' Letitia says.

I'm keeping out of this, I think, taking a step back from the startline.

'I shall be having another word with the Headmaster,' says Tiegan's mother.

'There's no need to involve a higher authority.' Letitia lifts her leg and holds the toe of her trainer behind her. I jog on the spot, and when the whistle blows, I set off at a gangling lollop, unsure what to do with my arms, uncertain where to look.

Letitia and Tiegan's mother are ahead of me, and then they aren't. I find myself flat on my face with the breath knocked out of me. What did I trip on? A tuft of grass? Thin air? Pain shoots through my ankle, but it doesn't hurt anywhere near as much as my pride.

When I look up, Letitia is jumping up and down. Tiegan's mother is walking away with her head bowed.

'You always were a loser!' Letitia shouts after her.

The Headmaster trots over in his grey flannel trousers.

'How can the school be expected to instil a spirit of sportsmanship and fair play when the children see adults behaving like that?' he complains as he helps me up and walks me back to my place. I sit down and hold the ice-block from the coolbag against my leg. I avoid Sasha's gaze.

In spite of my public mishap, there are plenty of volunteers for the Fathers' Race. There is Cuddly Dad – like Robbie – in a T-shirt that is far too tight, and shapeless shorts. There is Office Dad in his suit and tie. There is Sporty Dad, looking tanned and muscular in a vest and running shoes.

Once the fathers have raced like knock-kneed ostriches with beanbags between their legs, the children start chanting for a Teachers' Race. The Head looks at his watch, and guess what – they've run out of time.

'What did you have to go and do that for? And in front of the whole school,' Sasha says crossly, when we are reunited after she has changed and retrieved her schoolbag from the cloakroom.

'I didn't choose to fall over, did I?'

Sasha and I walk back to *Posies* with Letitia, Cassie and Elliot. Val goes home, leaving me to shut up shop at five-thirty. Martin still hasn't returned from his appointment, and Letitia is supposed to be meeting the carpenter to compare samples of the materials he could use in the refurbishment.

'Reconstituted marble or granite? Veneered chipboard or solid wood? Mr Bean or Orlando Bloom? Would you mind having the children, Terri? I won't be long. An hour, max.' Letitia waits while I consider. It would be pretty spiteful to say no, wouldn't it? Especially as I have drunk the equivalent of at least a bottle of red wine in her sangria.

'Okay,' I agree.

'You can wait upstairs in the flat,' she says, as though giving me special dispensation. 'Elliot will find the remote for you if you want to watch the television.'

The girls and Elliot play pirates upstairs in Cassie's bedroom while I sit reading one of Letitia's magazines filled with celebrity gossip. Towards the back, there is a mention of Simone Simmonds's wedding, about three column inches, with more of a snapshot than a photo of her holding her bouquet, under the predictable headline of *Simone's Fairytale Wedding*. There is no mention of *Martin Blake*.

There is a crash and a scream, and Cassie comes charging downstairs.

'Terri, Terri, Elliot's broken himself.'

My heart misses a beat. Broken? Unconscious? Dead? I start to panic.

'Elliot,' I call. 'Elliot!'

The scary silence is terminated by the sound of Elliot wailing, and I run upstairs to find him.

'What was he doing?'

'He was walking the plank off the top bunk,' Cassie follows me. 'He's bruised his arm.'

When I dash upstairs to examine Elliot, I discover that Cassie's assessment of the injury was a little optimistic. His arm is kinked between his wrist and his elbow, and he refuses to let me touch it.

'How many times has your dad told you not to jump about on the top bunk,' I say reproachfully. 'I'm supposed to be looking after you. He'll be furious with me.' I could cry. I do cry, and Elliot cries too, and I feel sorry for him with his tear-streaked cheeks and his hair messed up. I touch his shoulder very gently. 'I'm going to ring your mummy and daddy, and then we're going to the hospital to see a doctor about your arm.'

I leave messages on Martin's and Letitia's mobiles, toy with the idea of contacting Val and decide against it. I can't bear the thought of the recriminations. How can I accuse Letitia of being an unfit mother, when one of her children has broken his arm while in my care?

I call a cab to take me, Elliot, Cassie and Sasha off to the hospital.

'Can't you call the 'copter, Terri?' Elliot asks more cheerfully. 'I need the 'copter.'

'He means the air ambulance,' Cassie interprets for me.

'That won't be necessary. We'll wait outside for the taxi – are you able to run and jump into the car if the parking officers are patrolling the red route?'

'I don't think so,' Elliot says.

'You haven't hurt your legs,' says Cassie.

The cab arrives, and the Poison Dwarf – yes, she is there, as if she has been waiting all day for this moment – tells us that we will have to walk around the corner and up the road until we reach a kerb without parking restrictions where the cab driver can stop, otherwise he will receive a ticket.

'This is an emergency,' I say hotly, as the cab driver moves off.

'No exceptions,' says the Poison Dwarf. 'If I make an exception for you, I have to do the same for everyone.'

'What happens if I call an ambulance?'

'I do have some discretion, as long as the casualty is in a serious condition.'

I think of Letitia, of Simone, and everyone else who manages to get their own way. Of how Amanda tries to manipulate the media.

'I'll ring the papers.' I take my phone out of my pocket. 'They love a human interest story, how a little boy–'

'I'm not little.'

'Shut up, Ells. A boy of five years old was forced to walk several miles with a broken arm and who knows what other internal injuries because of some over-zealous traffic warden.'

The Poison Dwarf looks down her nose at Elliot. 'Has he really hurt it? Only, members of the public make up the most ridiculous excuses for parking on my red route.'

'I can assure you that he is *not* making it up.' I spot the cab returning around the corner. 'Now, are you going to let us jump into the car, or am I going to have to call the Press?'

'You can go this time, but don't expect me to believe the same excuse twice.'

'We won't be breaking any more arms, I can promise you. Come on, kids. Jump in.'

'You've passed the hospital, Mr Cab Driver.' Sasha points to a sign en route. 'It says *Body Repairs* are that way.'

'That isn't the hospital, love,' he chuckles. 'It's a garage that mends cars, not people.'

In the A&E Department, I switch off my mobile, according to instructions, and sit worrying about how Elliot's parents are going to get in touch with us. We wait. And wait. And wait. Elliot decides that he wants a drink and I send the girls to buy him one. They return with three Cokes and a cold coffee.

'Guess who we saw,' says Cassie.

'Your dad is here?' My sigh of relief is premature because Cassie shakes her head.

'Guess!'

'I've no idea.'

'That friend of Mum's. My mum's. Kev. He was pushing a trolley, and it had a body on it, covered in a white sheet.'

'A dead body,' adds Sasha in a macabre voice.

'Do you mean Kev, the hospital porter?' I think back to one of my first customers at *Posies*, and the kerfuffle of the wrongly delivered bouquets. Oh no! I am beginning to sound like a Blake.

'I've seen that man before,' says Sasha. 'He used to collect Miss Hudson from outside school when she was pregnant.'

'Kev did?' So Tiegan's mother wasn't merely winding Letitia up, I muse.

315

'I think that Miss Hudson was in love with him,' Sasha says seriously, 'because she held his hand.'

'You must remember Kev, Elliot?' Cassie goes on. 'He gave you five pounds and we played that game, the Secret Gang, where we weren't to tell Dad that Kev had visited Mummy at the house.'

'Mum took me to *Toys 'R' Us* – we buyed a light sabre with it.'

I am curious. I thought that Kev had been an ex long before Letitia met Martin, yet their acquaintance has continued long enough for the children to have met him. The history between them appears more modern than ancient.

'Was this when you were living away from the shop?' I ask.

Cassie nods. 'Me and Ells had ice lollies while Kev and Mum played in the paddling pool to cool down.'

'Did you see Kev very often?'

'A few times,' says Cassie. 'We went to his house once, but Mum got into a fight with the lady who answered the door, and we came home.'

How could she, I think. Not only did Letitia involve Cassie and Elliot in lying to their father to cover up for her infidelities, but she was prepared to row with strangers in front of them as well. She's like an old banger of a car, frequently re-sprayed and waxed, high mileage and decidedly used.

I have to admire Martin's determination to keep his family together in spite of his partner's affair. I couldn't have been so forgiving if I were in his position.

I am worrying about whether or not I can give my consent for Elliot to have his arm X-rayed when Martin arrives.

'Daddy! Daddy!' Elliot squeals. 'The floor hurt me!'

'You hurt yourself,' Cassie says.

'That's enough, Cass.' Martin squats down to speak to Elliot. 'How are you, little man?'

'I'm not little,' Elliot protests again.

I don't know what it is – the sight of Martin's face, pinched with worry; the responsibility of it all; the after-effects of the sangria, but I burst into tears. 'It was my fault. I should have been watching him.'

Martin looks up at me. His brow furrows then smooths again. 'What do you mean? Where the hell is Letitia?'

'She had an appointment with the carpenter, something to do with choosing materials for the refit.'

'Big Dave?' I hear Martin's breath catch in his throat, see his eyes darken. 'I thought we'd settled on the MDF. I wish she'd leave the plans alone, so that Flinty Maxwell's team can get on with the work.' Martin pulls a handkerchief from his pocket, takes my hand and presses it into my palm. Keeping the contact, he gazes into my eyes. My throat tightens as he continues, 'I don't blame you, Terri. We all know that Elliot is an accident waiting to happen.'

Trembling, I draw back.

'You don't have to hang around here,' Martin continues softly. 'I can look after the boy now. I'm sure that he'll be fine.'

317

'I hope so...' What if it had been Elliot's neck, not his arm? I am ashamed at myself for drinking before six o'clock, in the heat of a full sun, and on an empty stomach. I have no self-control. Look at me, still trying, and failing to convince myself that I don't feel anything for Martin. I revel in him holding my hand. The warmth and reassurance in his gesture banishes my loneliness. I don't want him to let go.

'I'd like to stay.'

'Why don't I give you the keys to the van?'

Why doesn't Martin realise that he is not inconveniencing me by letting me stay?

'You can drive back,' he continues, 'and I'll ask my dad to return here to collect us. We're going to be some time.'

'I can't drive. I've been drinking.' I cringe. Now Martin will assume that I was drunk in charge of his children. 'I had a couple of glasses of sangria at the school Sports Day.'

'That must be why you fell over, Mum,' Sasha says. 'Did you know, Martin, that she fell over in the Mum's Race?'

'I do now.' He gives a wry smile. 'I'll pay for a cab to take you and Sasha back to the flat. It's the least I can do.'

Later, I phone Martin to find out how Elliot is feeling. Martin confirms Cassie's diagnosis that her brother has broken himself.

'Elliot thought he was going to get away without baths and showers for the next six weeks, but the nurse has told us about some waterproof cover that you can use to protect the cast.'

318

And Letitia, I want to ask, has she returned from her tête-a-tête with the carpenter? I bite my tongue.

'I'm glad he's okay,' I say. 'Goodnight.'

'Goodnight.'

I sit back on Pat's sofa with a throbbing head and sore ankle. It has been quite a day. Low point: I am still in love with Martin. High point: Elliot and I have both been plastered.

Chapter Sixteen

It is easy to forget that material goods are not as important as love and security when faced with a trampoline and what Sasha describes on the phone, using Elliot's language, as a 'completely ginormous' paddling pool.

It is a Saturday morning in August, and Sasha is away, visiting the Real Dad. Martin and I are in the van, returning from the church where we have prepared the flowers for a much more traditional wedding than Simone's.

'I'd love to see the photos afterwards,' I comment as Martin turns down into the alleyway behind *Posies*. 'Red and white. Strawberries and cream.'

Martin glances towards me. His hair is rumpled, his face unshaven, and his eyes dark with shadows as if he has been up all night, which he probably has. I don't need to fathom why; it is painfully obvious to me. Him and Letitia, and all that 'catching up' they have to do.

'It isn't anywhere nearly as romantic as you think,' Martin says, and for a heartstopping moment, I wonder, if he can read my mind. 'The groom is a Man United fan, so the bride chose flowers in the team colours.'

'It must be love.'

'Yeah.'

Martin locks the van, and we wander indoors,

into the back room.

'This is more of a mess than Cassie's bedroom.' Martin chucks the van keys clattering onto the steel table in the centre of the floor. The wall with the door into the shop is bare of plaster. The ceiling is cut with empty holes for spotlights. It is like a battlezone: florists versus builders. Fresh flowers, containers and glue-guns line up along one wall; paint-kettles, ladders and Stanley knives on the other. At the moment, neither side appears to be winning.

The stench of fresh paint and glue is overwhelming. I find myself yearning for the beach, for the aromas of candyfloss and frying chips, and seaweed steaming in the sun. I didn't think I'd miss Paignton all that much. I swallow back the sob that threatens to well up in my throat. I miss Sharon. Most of all though, I'm missing Sasha.

Today, I received a card from Sharon with *Still Flirty at Forty* written inside, and a framed picture of Sasha's which I particularly admired: a red and cream tram hurtling down an impossible slope through lollipop traffic-lights. She wrapped it herself, finishing it off with a gold ribbon that Val let her have from the shop, and left it on her bed for me to find.

'I almost forgot.' Martin struggles past a couple of ladders and dangling lengths of electrical flex, to hand me two envelopes he's picked up from the new worktop, a gleaming black altar to the god of wastefulness and bad taste, and edged with chrome. 'Happy Birthday.'

'How did you know?'

'I remembered, from before.' He blushes. 'I sent Sasha next door with Cassie before she left to choose a card, and they came back with two because they couldn't decide between them.'

'Thanks.' I bite my lip as I read the cards, one a picture of a hot-air balloon from Sasha, and the other a photo of a row of brightly coloured parasols lined up beside the sea from the Blakes.

Martin is very close to me. 'It's nothing.'

Nothing? To me, this small kindness means everything.

'I'll be glad when this refit is over,' Martin begins and, when I don't respond, he continues, 'I'm not sure about the colour scheme. What do you think?'

I hesitate.

'Be honest.'

'It doesn't feel like *Posies* any more.'

'Letitia wants to change the name to *Martin Blake*.'

My heart sinks. 'I suppose that it does advertise your personal expertise.'

'I hate it,' he says emphatically.

'Life doesn't stand still.' I'm trying to comfort myself, not Martin.

'You're beginning to sound like your grandmother.' His lips curve into a brief smile. 'How is she?'

'Gran is fine.' Why did I say that? She isn't fine. She has a heart condition. I clear my throat, and rub my eyes to stop the tears that are threatening to well up and give me away.

I feel Martin's arms around me, drawing me close. I catch sight of a stray yellow sprinkle stuck

322

to his dark T-shirt, evidence perhaps that he is rebelling against Letitia's healthy breakfast directive. I pick it off and discard it in a practical 'Martin isn't really hugging me right in the middle of the back room' manner.

Martin's arms fall away and his hands grip my upper arms. He ducks his head to look up at my face. 'Is there anything I can do?'

'Not unless you can perform a heart transplant.'

'I wasn't talking about Lilian. I was talking about you.' He smiles again. 'Can I help *you?*'

I shake my head. It's too late. I feel as if my ribcage has been bound with wire, and my heart pounds so hard that it might be me who needs a transplant. I gaze into Martin's eyes. He moves closer and presses his lips to my cheek, then straightens and steps back. 'If there is anything...'

'I'm having a Bridget Jones moment,' I try to joke. 'It's my birthday, Sasha is off with her dad, and my best friend lives miles away.' My lip wobbles.

'I can crack open one of those bottles of brandy that my dad is so fond of,' Martin says lightly. 'Or give you some of my mum's Prozac?'

'I didn't think you cared.'

'I do, more than you imagine.' Martin smiles and says softly, 'I can still remember your fifth birthday party. You wore a yellow dress, the same colour as those sunflowers over there, and your gran made you a rainbow cake.'

I love you. The words are on the tip of my tongue.

'Dad!' Cassie appears at the top of the stairs to

the flat. I bite my lip and take a step back as she continues, 'Elliot's playing pirate ships in the bath, and he isn't wearing the cover for his plastercast.' Then she adds, 'I'm not telling tales – I thought you should know.'

'How many times do I have to tell him? I'm not going to spend another six hours down at the hospital, waiting for him to be replastered.' He grins at me. 'That's the third cast he's had already.'

'I think you should be grateful that it takes the medical staff six hours – it's going to be six years before Big Dave gets round to doing any plastering, at this rate. You'd better see what's going on up there.'

'It's a bad habit of mine, leaving everything too late.' As Martin runs up the stairs, taking two steps at a time, I wonder if he is merely referring to Elliot's cast.

I have that tight, sick feeling in my stomach. I recognise it from the past, the incurable suffering of unrequited love. I know now – as if I had any doubts before – that Martin is, and always will be, the man for me. He is The One, and, if he is by any small chance living a lie, then so am I, pretending that it could be otherwise.

I head out to the front of the shop to find the order book. Letitia is sitting on the new counter, swinging her long brown legs and flicking her pink mules against the soles of her feet. Her hair is loose around her shoulders, her shades are perched on the top of her head. With her skimpy top and shorts, she looks as if she is on holiday, which I suppose she might just as well be, with the tiny contribution she makes towards the running of the shop.

'Hiya all.' Big Dave comes marching through in a vest, shorts and boots, showing off a spectacular pair of legs. 'Sorry about the late start – I had a dental appointment.'

'Again?' I can't help it. It just slipped out.

'Oh, you poor man,' says Letitia. 'Would you like some paracetamol?'

'I'll tough it out,' he says with manful gravitas.

'I don't know how you can stand the sound of the drill,' Letitia says. 'When I had a filling, I had to be sedated.'

'I can handle a bit of drilling now and again.'

I suddenly think back to Sasha's visit to the dentist, to the masonry drill on the other side of the consulting-room door, and that dirty white pick-up in the car park ... but I don't say anything. It can wait.

'I won't have any painkillers, but I'll have a glass of your blackcurrant squash. That'll do the trick.' Big Dave gazes towards Letitia's cleavage with his mouth open and a wad of gum visible on his tongue. Letitia rearranges her décolletage, tweaking her bra to give her breasts just a little more lift, before jumping down to the floor.

'Back in a mo,' she says, leaving me and Big Dave alone.

'I don't suppose there's anything I can do for you, Terri? On the side, like. Flinty – in my opinion, that's short for skinflint – makes a bloody fortune, taking advantage of craftsmen like myself and Little Pete. I don't mind doing a bit of moonlighting for cash in hand – know what I mean?'

I haven't got my own place, so I can't take

advantage of Dave's offer to do any building work as such, but there is something he could do for me. 'Can you make a bed?'

Big Dave raises one eyebrow, which is incomplete, like a row of dashes. What does he think I am suggesting?

'I mean, build a frame, not rearrange the duvet.'

He grins. 'I reckon about a hundred quid for a basic structure, but if you want it with knobs on, extras like under-bed storage or a four-poster, it'll be a bit more.'

'I'm sure you can let me have the whole caboodle – without the posts – for a hundred, Dave.'

'What do you think I am, love?'

'Don't you "love" me. I know about your moonlighting, your frequent appointments with the dentist. If I happen to let slip to Martin the real reason why you're hardly ever here to work on the refurbishment...'

Big Dave pulls a pencil out from behind his ear and fiddles with it, rolling it between his fingers. 'Okay,' he says eventually. 'It's a deal.' He hands me the pencil. 'You'd better give me your address.'

Letitia looks from me to Dave and back again when she returns with a jug, rattling with ice cubes, and glasses on a tray.

'Dave's asked for my details.' I hand him a piece of *Posies'* headed notepaper with my details, and smile sweetly at Letitia. 'Is one of those glasses for me?'

'I thought you'd prefer coffee.'

'Oh no, I'm celebrating. It's my birthday.'

Letitia pours the drinks. Big Dave hands one to me. As I suspected, the squash is more grape than blackcurrant, and is accompanied by slices of orange and the faint aroma of alcohol. I am sucking on an ice cube when Martin joins us.

'If you want a cold drink, you'll have to go and make some more,' Letitia says rudely, oblivious, it seems, to the fact that Martin has just been upstairs, checking on Elliot.

'Have you got to go to the hospital, Martin?' I ask.

'No, but someone else might have to.' Martin looks towards Big Dave. In spite of their difference in height, Big Dave appears to shrink in the face of Martin's angry stare. 'How much longer is this going to take? You said five days at most, and that was two weeks ago.'

'That is what Flinty said. These arty-farty designers have no idea how long anything takes.' Big Dave looks towards Letitia. I see that look, even if Martin doesn't. 'You can't rush these things.'

'Where's the decorator?' Martin says.

'Here he is.' Big Dave waves towards the window. Little Pete is struggling along the pavement in white overalls, with a ladder and two tubs of paint. I open the door for him.

'I had to park a couple of miles away,' Little Pete grumbles. Yes, he really is little, five foot one and a quarter, he claims, although Big Dave says he finds that hard to believe when Little Pete has to stand on a ladder to paint the skirting. He reminds me of one of the Chuckle Brothers on *Chucklevision*, one of Sasha's favourite programmes, although she won't admit it now. 'How am I going to work in here? I'll have to throw a couple of dustsheets over that new counter, and those buckets of flowers will have to move. I don't want pollen sticking to my paintwork.'

'Can't you make a start on the back room today?' says Martin.

'I haven't quite finished the plastering out there,' Big Dave cuts in.

'This is bloody brilliant,' Martin growls.

'I'm a little behind schedule,' says Big Dave.

'And I'm a little ahead,' says Little Pete.

'Terri and I need to get on with making up the orders. This is driving me mad.' Martin runs his hands through his hair in desperation. 'The refurbishment is going to run weeks late. Simone's cheque has bounced. What next?'

'If you hadn't been such a stubborn old fool, *mi querido*,' says Letitia, 'we could have been rid of the shop by now, and running the bar in Spain.'

Martin turns to her, his eyes flashing dangerously. 'Using the money to prop it up, you mean? That bar was like a multi-storey car park, a concrete monstrosity, and it was in the wrong place.'

Letitia crushes an ice cube between her teeth. 'Change the record, Martin. It's boring.'

Big Dave swallows his gum, and taps the buckle on his belt. 'I'd better get on.'

'You do that,' Martin says. 'I'll shift the buckets. Terri, you can do the orders upstairs in the flat.'

Letitia opens her mouth to protest, then shuts it again when Martin scowls at her.

I carry what I can up to the kitchen. I have to clear a space amongst the dirty crockery on the worktop before I can start, and load Martin's Lycra cycling kit into the washing machine. I take a sneaky peek in the living room as well; there is a duvet plonked on top of the coffee-table, and at least three of Martin's dirty socks on the floor. Martin works fulltime, and Letitia merely dabbles with employment, so I would expect her to do at least some of the housework, but obviously, it isn't one of her strong points. In fact, I don't believe that she has any.

What did Martin ever see in her? The question goes round and round in my head, like lights from a spinning disco ball.

I can hear what Letitia and Big Dave are saying in the back room, if I concentrate on their conversation. I'm not sure if Letitia has sought him out again, or the other way round.

'I've always fancied running a bar.' Big Dave is sawing something, timber or MDF. 'A bar on the beach with sunbeds and parasols.'

'It isn't all it's cut out to be. It was bloody hard work.'

'I thought you said—'

'I know what I said, but I'm never going to admit to Martin that he was right. I'd never hear the end of it.'

Martin isn't that kind of man, I want to shout out. I look down at the rose in my hand. I have stripped it of its petals, and torn them into tiny pieces. I make up my mind. During my lunch-break, I write my letter of resignation.

Dear Martin or *Dear Mr Blake*. It reminds me of writing those love letters all those years ago. *I cannot bear to work at* Posies *any longer,* or *I regret that I am unable to continue my employment with you.* Because? *Because I am in love with you, and you are apparently committed to the mother of your children, which I perfectly understand.* Cross out *perfectly* because I don't understand at all.

How can someone like Martin live with someone like Letitia?

I give myself a stern telling-off. It is none of my business. Not any more.

I decide to hang on to my letter of resignation until the launch of the newly refurbished shop so that Sasha can enjoy her moment of glory as a waitress. In the meantime, I shall have to look for another job, within a small radius of Addiscombe so that I can remain living near Gran until such a time as she doesn't need me any more. And then? What will be left to keep me and Sasha here in South London?

As if to prove that there is nothing wrong with her, and that she is more than likely to live another eighty years, my grandmother shuffles up and down the hallway of her house at great speed, bringing me the parcels she has stashed away under her bed for my birthday.

She sits on her adjustable chair in the sitting room to watch me open them.

The first is a Luxury Foot Massager, the second a Cloisonné Musical Egg Box, and the third is a set of tinted blue wineglasses.

'You shouldn't have done.'

'You deserve to be spoiled a little.'

I don't, I muse, not when I'm guilty of falling in love with an as-good-as-married man, but Gran

330

continues, 'I don't think all that much of those glasses myself, but they're cheap and cheerful, and it won't matter if Sasha smashes a few of them. In fact, I wonder if they wouldn't be more suitable for Knickerbocker Glories than wine.'

'Thanks, but there really was no need to waste your pension on me.'

'I'm all right. I have a little extra coming in now that my allowance for my supplies of intercontinentals has gone up.'

It would seem ungrateful to lecture my grandmother about obtaining money by deception, so I offer her the cheese, biscuits and chocolates that I've brought with me to celebrate my birthday.

'I won't have any cheese, dear. It makes me dream and I can't get to sleep as it is.'

'You must eat to keep your strength up.'

'There's no need to fuss. I'm enjoying looking like an advert for a slimming club. It's a first for me.'

I look around the sitting room, noticing the traces of dust on the skirting, and a cobweb dangling from the corner where the walls meet the ceiling. I wonder if I will hurt Gran's feelings if I offer to help her with some housework. I decide to keep silent.

'I don't fancy cheese, but I'd love a tipple. How about a nip of brandy?'

'What about the warfarin in your heart medication?'

'To hell with it.' Gran presses a button in the arm of her chair. It whirrs and tilts so that she looks like Sasha used to, waiting at the top of a slide in the playpark for me to catch her at the bottom. 'I've spent years trying to avoid putting down rat poison for the mice in my porch, and now the doctors are telling me that it's good for me.'

'I'll go and get the brandy.'

'I can do it.' Gran slips off her chair, rubs her hip as she straightens, and takes a few deep breaths before setting off down the hall again. She returns with two glasses (the ones she uses for Sasha's squash), a spirit measure and a bottle of brandy. 'Have you hurt your face?'

'You've lost me.'

'Your cheek – you keep touching it.'

'No, I'm fine.' I clamp my hands to my thighs. How ridiculous. It was just a kiss, a birthday kiss.

Gran pours a generous measure of brandy into each glass and passes one to me. She sits back in her chair and raises her glass.

'To the future.' She downs her brandy in one.

'To the future,' I echo.

'I'll have a top-up, if you wouldn't mind.'

I pick up the bottle and pour more brandy into Gran's glass, bypassing the measure altogether this time.

'I'm no fool,' Gran says. 'You're completely besotted by Martin, and he is in love with you.'

Am I? Is he?

'Don't look at me like that, all doubtful and patronising. You'll end up like your mother.'

'I'm sorry, but–'

'I must have always seemed old to you,' Gran interrupts. 'You youngsters forget that us oldies did once lead interesting and exciting lives.'

I feel a pang of guilt for believing otherwise. I

mean, I always think of her in the kitchen, making jam, her fingers and lips stained with blackcurrants, or in the garden, enveloped in the scent of broken geranium leaves as she pots up seedlings from trays into tubs.

'I gave up too easily, and I've always – no, that isn't fair – I've *often* regretted it. I was a feeble young woman.'

'What are you talking about?'

Gran blinks several times, then presses one of the buttons on her chair, It swivels, enabling her to put her glass down on a copy of a newspaper on her occasional table, and pick up an envelope instead. The paper looks soft, as if it might crumble.

'You know, I always cry when I watch that film where old what-his-name falls in love with you-know-who.' She hums a tune that is fracturing and out of key, but still recognisable as the theme to *Casablanca*.

'Humphrey Bogart and Ingrid Bergman.'

'Who, dear?'

'Humphrey and Ingrid.'

'Such a beautiful couple.' Gran opens the envelope and pulls out a wedge of tissue paper. With trembling fingers, she unfolds it and spreads it across the palm of her hand, revealing its contents: two-dimensional teardrops of translucent, faded ochre. 'Pressed violets. They were a present to me from a very special man, not Jack.'

The brandy kicks at the back of my throat, making me choke.

Gran passes me a hankie. 'Your manners are worse than Sasha's.'

'That's strong stuff,' I say, breathing more easily again. (I'm not referring to the brandy.)

'I met Teddy during the war. Your grandad was away and I didn't know where he was, or whether or not he was coming home. I'm not making excuses, but times were different. When I went out shopping, I didn't know if our house would still be there when I got back. It was tempting to live for the moment.' She tilts her head to one side. 'I married Jack because I loved him, but the man who returned from the war wasn't the man I married. He retreated into a world of his own, a place where no one, including his wife and child, could reach him, and that's where he stayed for the rest of his life. It didn't have a name back then,' Gran continues. 'Now, they treat soldiers for post-dramatic stress.'

I hadn't thought about it before, but I understand now why my grandfather hated loud noises: the sound of a car backfiring; fireworks; me, running around as a child, banging doors. They scared him, and in his turn, he frightened me.

'I had to choose.' Gran sighs. 'I think I'll have another brandy.'

'Perhaps a cup of tea would be more appropriate.' I go off to make it and, by the time I return, Gran is nodding off. I touch the back of her hand. Her skin is cool. 'I'll help you to bed.'

'I can manage.'

'I want to make sure you won't suddenly decide to nip out in your buggy. Imagine getting arrested for being drunk in charge of that scooter.'

'I am insured.'

'That's no defence if you cause an accident, or

end up in the Wandle.' I pause. 'You were saying, about Teddy and Grandad?'

'Was I?'

I can't help feeling that Gran has deliberately lost the thread of her conversation on this occasion.

'You said you had to make a choice.'

Gran sips at her tea, then, as if it has revived her memory, she says, 'I gave up too easily. I followed my head, not my heart. You have the advantage of youth. Don't give up. Don't repeat the mistakes of the past.'

As I walk home in the evening, still missing Sasha like mad, I realise that my grandmother was referring to Martin, and that her confession has raised more questions than it has answered.

'Did Robbie pass the dad test?' It is a few days since Robbie dropped Sasha off at the flat at the end of her stay with him and his family. She is curled up on the sofa beside me with a chocolate milkshake, and this is the first time that we have sat down quietly to discuss how she expects her relationship with the RD to proceed.

'I think so.' Sasha screws up her face as if she is considering. 'He tells really funny jokes and is good at cooking pancakes.'

'Oh?'

'He can sing great karaoke. Did you know they've got a karaoke machine?'

'Yes, you've told me that several times already.'

'And about the trampoline and the pool?'

I nod. 'Perhaps you'd like to go and live with him?'

'No,' she says quickly, boosting my morale. 'I want to live with you, Mum.'

She chatters on about how Robbie's wife insists that their children take a daily dose of fish oils for their brains, and how Robbie wears odd socks, and makes his children play *Trivial Pursuit* instead of watching television. They are not endearing traits in a perfect father, obviously. 'I love you, Mum.'

I kiss the top of her head and smile to myself. Life is never all bad. Sasha should be prescribed as an antidepressant. 'I love you too, Sunshine.'

I retire to bed, happy. Big Dave has created a simple box from MDF – where the MDF came from, I didn't ask. The mattress arrived today; I found it in the free ads, still in its original wrapping. Pat has dumped the sofa for me – hiding it under a tarpaulin at the end of his garden – because the room is too small for both a sofa and a bed. I hope that he isn't planning to keep it for the next occupants of the flat.

I strip the mattress and manhandle it onto the base, ignoring the ominous creak, then make the bed up with clean linen. It almost looks too good to sleep on.

I slip into my shortie pyjamas, turn back the duvet and lie down. The room sways slightly, and I haven't been drinking. I tuck the duvet up around my ears, and lie very still. I close my eyes, and drift off...

I have recurrent nightmares about my teeth falling out, and tidal waves – signs of insecurity and feeling overwhelmed respectively, according to Gran – but I've never dreamed about an earthquake before.

When I wake in the morning, I discover that I am sleeping on a slope with my pillow on the floor, and my legs in the air, the mattress bowed beneath me, and the bed in pieces. I should be furious, jumping up and ranting about Big Dave's incompetence, but the blood has rushed to my head.

It isn't all that funny, I tell myself sternly when I try to get up.

Martin, having had words with Flinty Maxwell, has managed to get the refurbishment on track. Big Dave and Little Pete have proved that they can transform something out of *DIY SOS* into a finished project like those on *Grand Designs* in the time it takes to perform a *Sixty-Minute Makeover*.

Preparations for the launch are well under way. I should mention the quality of Big Dave's workmanship to Martin and Letitia, but I don't want to be accused of trying to ruin the party.

Chapter Seventeen

It is the end of August, and the forecast is mixed. Will the launch of the new-look *Posies* coincide with blue skies for Martin and his family? And what about me and Sasha? What of our future? I foresee storms ahead when she finds out about my resignation, which is why I haven't been able to bring myself to tell her just yet.

Sasha runs into the shop ahead of me to find Cassie and Elliot, and to collect an apron for her waitressing duties.

Inside, the counter gleams brightly beneath the curly stems of an overhead light-fitting which remind me of twigs of contorted hazel, but the remaining features of Flinty Maxwell's redesign are invisible, hidden by masses of flowers, foliage, and feature plants. I move past the new circular table with matching chairs, past the shelves of teddies, chocolates and other extras, into the back room, following the scent of garlic, tomatoes and anchovies. Val is preparing canapés upstairs in the flat, and the appetising aroma floats downstairs.

Martin is unpacking champagne flutes from a cardboard box onto the characterless expanse of brushed steel that has taken over from the old pine table. He looks up, his eyes reflecting the shade of his shirt; a warm Mediterranean blue.

'Welcome to the madhouse.' He smiles and my heart misses a beat, then another, until I fear that

I am about to have a cardiac arrest. I fiddle with the clasp on my bag, giving myself time to get over it. It is better that he doesn't know how I feel about him. He has enough to deal with already, without contending with a lovesick employee – almost ex-employee.

I respect him for committing himself to his family. He must love Letitia almost as much as I love him, to forgive her for the way she has behaved towards him and the children.

I pull the envelope containing my letter from my bag, and hand it over. It is supposed to be a dramatic gesture, an acknowledgement that our relationship – as boss and employee, as friends, as childhood sweethearts – is over, but I notice with a stab of disappointment that Martin puts it down, unopened, beside the till.

'Dad is still unloading the van. I decided to rebel against Flinty Maxwell's concept of minimalism, and see how many flowers we could pack into *Posies*.'

Just then, Letitia saunters downstairs on high heels. She struts up and down the back room like a model on a catwalk, showing off a dress in geometric black-and-white print, with a plunging neckline and asymmetric hem.

'This one, or the Alberta Ferretti? What do you think?'

'I'm stunned,' says Martin.

'Oh?' Letitia sounds surprised. 'Thanks.'

'By the price tag,' Martin goes on. 'Couldn't you have gone to Nigel?'

'I have a reputation to live up to.'

'Oh, I realise *that*.'

Letitia glances in my direction, as if suddenly aware of my presence. 'Martin, you're supposed to have finished that twenty minutes ago.' She wipes her forehead with the back of her hand, revealing her red lacquered nails, like claws that have ripped out my heart.

'You do the drinks then,' he says. 'You're the one who knows how to run a bar – allegedly. I'll stick with what I'm good at – the flowers.'

Letitia grabs Martin's arm. 'Actually, I wanted to have a word with you about those arrangements in the window.'

'Why? I finished them by eight, according to your orders.'

'Yes, but they aren't quite what Flinty suggested, are they?'

'Good morning, darlings!'

I notice how Martin's face falls at the sound of Flinty's voice.

'Come through!' Letitia calls.

Flinty Maxwell, dressed in a grey linen suit, greets Letitia, kissing her on both cheeks, not once, or twice, but three times. 'Tish, that dress is absolutely fabulous.' She tips her head forward in a gesture of apology. 'I don't like those arrangements in the windows though. I abhor flamboyance of any kind.'

'I told you so, Martin,' Letitia says.

'What happened to my theme?' Flinty goes on. 'Let's whip those flowers away from the windows.'

'You can't relaunch a florists without flowers!' Martin exclaims. 'I've never heard anything so ridiculous.'

'Martin!' Letitia warns. 'Let Flinty have her say.

We've invested a lot of time and money to get this right for our clientèle.'

Martin turns to his girlfriend. 'To get it right so that you can put the shop on the market, you mean? I am not unaware of your scheming.'

Letitia flushes more the colour of the purple dahlias that grace the new stainless-steel staging, than the offending scarlet poppies in the window.

'Champagne, Flinty?' she says, and I notice how she continues to ally herself with the designer, not Martin, which seems a little odd considering that if I were in Letitia's cute red heels, I should be showing my gratitude to my partner for deciding to give our relationship a chance. I would slip my arm through Martin's and defend his arrangements to the death. Well, almost...

'Oh, that would be fabulous, darling. I'm absolutely gasping.'

'Martin, crack open a couple of bottles, will you?' Letitia says.

'After I've fetched the corsages and button-holes for the guests, and organised some parking.'

'You'll be lucky to find parking within five miles of here.' Letitia turns towards the window of the shop, following her husband's gaze. Six, no seven, mobility scooters move sedately in a row across the park towards the Parade. Gran is at the front, resplendent in her turquoise mac in the hot sun. 'Where did you dig that lot up from?'

'It's Lil and some of her buddies from the Lunch Club.'

Gran must have seen Martin wave as she approaches the road, for she waves back. Her scooter swerves to one side then the other, ending up with its front end bumped against the post that supports the traffic-lights for the crossing. Martin dashes out to marshal her into reverse, then organises a row of double parking for scooters on the pavement, right in front of the traffic wardens. I admire his tact and patience. The Poison Dwarf can do nothing but shake her head.

Martin accompanies my grandmother into the shop, looks up at me, and smiles. My chest tightens. I wish... Oh, what is the point in wishing? I have done it now. In a week, I shall be gone from *Posies*. Gradually, very gradually, Martin will become a memory as he was before. I shall stop looking for him in a crowd. My heart will stop jumping whenever I catch sight of a man who reminds me of him, because I used to see Martin everywhere – in the supermarket aisle, cycling past the hairdresser's window, walking in the park. My emotions will return to normal, and I will be able to continue my life as a rational human being.

Gran is right: out of sight is out of mind.

'You should have invited the Gestapo in for the launch.' A piece of costume jewellery, a circlet of paste flowers, flashes from the breast of Gran's navy polka-dot dress.

'The Poison Dwarf and her assistant would have interpreted that as an attempt at bribery. Besides, they aren't allowed to drink on duty.'

'I can't see anything wrong with a little bribery and corruption.' Gran smiles in my direction, her false teeth slipping about on her gums.

The rest of the OAPs shuffle into the shop, and

Gran introduces us to Raymond, the only man in the group, whose green-and-yellow striped blazer blends in with the clashing patterns of the women's dresses.

Letitia calls the children down from the flat, and asks them to take any coats the OAPs have brought with them and put them upstairs out of the way. I am surprised that she doesn't ask them to take the OAPs as well.

'What do you think of the new *Posies*, Lil?' Martin asks.

'I find it hard to think of the shop as *Posies* any more. It is a little less homely than before.'

'You can be straight with me.'

'If you want my honest opinion, it reminds me of a public convenience.'

Not *quite* that honest, Gran, I think. Don't hold back, will you? I must have expressed my sentiments aloud because Gran turns to me.

'I heard that, Terri. You're right, Martin. Life *is* too short to shilly-shally about. You have to say what you mean, and mean what you say.' Gran has regained some of her colour during the days since she fell out of the loft. She raises her arm stiffly above her head and clicks her fingers. 'Let's get this party started, shall we? I've been looking forward to a good old knees-up.'

Seeing my grandmother looking so happy compounds my guilt. I haven't told her about my resignation either.

I slip into the back room ahead of the crowd. Flinty is sitting on the table. She nibbles on a cocktail sausage, then slenches champagne straight out of the bottle. When she sees me, she swivels round, wiping bubbles from her chin.

'Just testing that the champers isn't orf.' She hiccups, and tilts the bottle up against her lips to take another gulp. She wrinkles her nose and pumps her cheeks with her mouth closed, and swallows again. 'Bread and apples.'

At first I wonder if Flinty has strange tastes in food as well as interior design, but she enlightens me.

'The flavour. Bread and apples.'

'Cox or Braeburn?' My flippant remark sends Flinty back to the bottle for more, after which she pronounces that the bread is wholemeal and the apples are Granny Smith.

'This champers,' she takes another swig, 'is one that improves on drinking.'

I take an unopened bottle from the crate beneath the table – I imagine that Flinty will need the space there by lunchtime. I pop the cork, and start pouring into the flutes on the tray that Martin arranged earlier. I call the children down to perform their duties. Cassie and Sasha have changed into party dresses with white aprons, and Elliot is dressed in a long black cape, his arm still in plaster, a ragged appendage which is due to be removed very soon. George turns up too, asking if it's Happy Hour. Val brings down platefuls of canapés.

'Where are the sausage rolls, love?' George asks.

Val looks down her nose at him. 'This isn't some do in a room above a pub. I want everyone to know that the Blakes are pushing the boat out.'

'You aren't going on about the cruise again?'

'Now that Letitia is back, and Terri's working under Martin, I can't see any reason not to book the tickets and buy yourself a decent outfit. Look at you,' Val scolds.

George fastens the top button of his shirt and tidies his tie.

'That's better. Now, make sure you behave yourself.'

'I'll have a beer to set me up.'

'There isn't any beer,' Elliot interrupts. 'Mummy said we mustn't have any because it makes Grandad fall over.'

'She didn't?' says Val.

'And it makes him burp.' Elliot giggles.

George gives him a gentle clip around the ear. 'I thought you were supposed to be Head Waiter today.'

'I am.'

'Cassie and I are handing out the fizzy drinks,' says Sasha.

'But I want to,' says Elliot.

'You'll drop them,' Cassie says.

Elliot takes a swipe at his sister with his plastercast, his fourth, and misses.

'Let Elliot take the crisps,' I suggest firmly.

'They aren't crisps,' says Cassie. 'My mum says that they're speciality, handmade potato chips, with sea salt, chili seasoning and black pepper.'

'Posh crisps for anyone?' Elliot wraps his good arm around the bowl, and lifts it off the table. Before he hands any crisps over, he takes a fistful and stuffs them into his mouth. I wasn't sure about him when I first met him in his Darth Vader guise, but I have come to admire him. Like me, he is a survivor.

I open a second and third bottle of champagne.

'Doesn't anyone prefer a soft drink?' Letitia aims this at me as if it is all my fault that her guests prefer a glass of bubbly.

'I find that alcohol is rather harsh on an empty stomach,' says Gran. 'I take it that we help ourselves to the nosh.' This is a sign for the OAPs to surge forwards and help themselves to food, piling paper plates high with anchovy toast, chicken satay on sticks, salmon bites, and puff pastry parcels filled with goat's cheese and sun-dried tomatoes.

'This is so much more fun than that trip we had down to Eastbourne. I'll never forget Ethel doing the Can-Can on the pier, throwing up her skirts so that everyone could see her wherewithal. I hope that you don't mind us all turning up like this, Letitia, but Martin said—'

'The more the merrier,' Martin interrupts.

All the Blakes' old associates turn up – George's mates from the market, his drinking companions, Nigel and the church ladies, the people who owned the electrical shop in the days when it was a greengrocers, and friends of Martin's from way back. Customers drop by too, along with Big Dave and Little Pete.

Posies is becoming rather crowded. An arrangement of dahlias, and a couple of champagne flutes hit the floor. It is Ella who offers to help me clear up.

'Thank you, but I can manage,' I say, but she grabs the broom from the back room, and starts sweeping the pieces of glass into a bucket turned on its side.

'Look at Maureen,' Ella mutters. 'She's all over the poor vicar – she had him by the hollyhocks in church last Sunday. He's a lovely man, but he doesn't seem to be able to say no.'

'Who can't say no?' Big Dave relieves Ella of the broom and bucket, and sticks them outside the shop. By the time he returns inside, Maureen has abandoned the vicar.

'Hands off my builder.' Letitia elbows Maureen out of the way.

'He's a babe magnet,' Maureen coos.

'I'm so glad you could make it, Dave,' Letitia says.

'You know me. I can make anything if I put my mind to it.' He flexes his biceps and turns to me. 'Are you sleeping any better?'

'Your bed collapsed.'

'Oh dear.' Big Dave strokes his chin. 'What were you doing? No, don't tell me. I can come round later, and add some crossbars to the frame.'

'That won't be necessary, thanks. Sasha and I have fixed it.' I'm telling a white lie because I don't want Big Dave hanging about in my flat for another couple of days. The bed was beyond repair, and I had to ask Pat to help me move the sofa back in from the end of the garden.

Del pops in from next door, then, having spoken with my grandmother, introduces himself to the rest of the OAPs, his head bowed respectfully.

'What's he doing here?' Letitia shudders. 'He's like the Black Death in that suit, plaguing them to sign up to his funeral plans.'

'The presence of an undertaker does rather put

the dampener on the mood of a party,' Flinty agrees tipsily.

'This has to be the worst day of my life,' Letitia goes on. 'My future mother-in-law's dressed up as one of her cakes.'

I follow Letitia's gaze to where Val stands at the foot of the stairs, displaying her latest creation, a mountain of sponge, decorated with sparkling sugar balls and purple icing, on the table. It is indeed possible that Val took inspiration for the cake from the gown she is wearing, the one which reminds me of Marky the Mackerel.

'Is there any more of that champagne?' Gran asks me.

'What about your drugs?' I remind her gently. 'You're not supposed to drink alcohol with them.'

She turns to Martin. 'Did you know that the doctors are trying to kill me?'

'I'm more worried that you're going to kill yourself, driving that scooter about with no hands.'

'You have to let your hair down while you still have some,' she says sternly.

Martin laughs. 'You look very well, Lil.'

I wonder if he has read my letter yet, whether he is light-hearted because I have saved him the trouble of asking me to leave.

'It's those antidiabolicals that the doctor prescribed. They've done me the power of good. And so has this marvellous party.'

Sasha tugs on my sleeve. 'When's the reporter from the paper coming?'

'Soon.' I don't know for sure, but Letitia keeps looking at her watch as though she is expecting some fresh arrival at any moment.

'Cassie,' she says, 'will you put some of that food aside for the Press and our celebrity who is going to launch the opening? Stick it in the fridge upstairs.'

'Another celebrity?' Flinty cuts in, implying that she should be celebrity enough for such an occasion. 'Whom might it be, Tish?'

Letitia taps on the side of her nose.

'Who is it, Mum?' says Cassie. 'Is it one of the *Blue Peter* presenters?'

'Mummy, Mummy, is it *Spongebob Squarepants?*' Elliot brandishes his light sabre, but I don't think Letitia notices. I dread to think how far Elliot has to go before his mother pays him any attention.

'Is it Willy Wonka from *Charlie and the Chocolate Factory?*' says Sasha.

'Johnny Depp has been held up in Hollywood, and Freddie Flintoff is practising in his nets, so you'll have to make do with...' Letitia pauses for effect '...Simone Simmonds!'

'Who's he?' says Cassie.

'She!' Letitia exclaims.

'My definition of a celebrity is someone I've heard of before,' Gran joins in. 'I've never heard of Simone Simmonds.'

'You don't watch the right channels,' I say. 'Simone is one of Martin's clients. We did the mushrooms for her wedding.' My face grows warm at the memory of that day, of Martin's unguarded approach...

'Mushrooms?'

'It's a long story.' To make amends for being

slow to settle her account with us, Letitia persuaded her to come and reopen the shop. 'Her claim to fame is that she bared her breasts on national TV.'

'And a lot more besides,' says Letitia. 'I mean, she does a lot more than strip. She's an extra as well. So far, she's walked the cobbles of *Coronation Street*, the lanes of *Emmerdale*, and the pavements of *EastEnders*. She's also recording an album of cover songs.'

'If she's that busy,' says Gran, 'how on earth will she have time to launch your new-look shop?' She yawns. 'It's time I took myself off home to check those shopping channels.'

There are murmurs of agreement among the ranks of the OAPs. The champagne is running dry, and they don't see the point in hanging about for the reporter to come and take their picture with someone they've never heard of.

'There's no need to rush off. I'm sure that I can persuade Del to pick up some more champagne from the offie and stick it in the back of his hearse.' Letitia is desperate. Without the OAPs, she will appear to have been stood up.

The murmurings die down and, before they can change their minds, a stretch limo draws up outside the shop.

'Make way, please. Make way.' In spite of Letitia's criticism of Del, she might just as well be modelling her obsequiousness on him. Grovel. Crawl. She is almost on her knees.

Suddenly, though, she is pushing her way back through the shop at great speed, her eyes wide with panic. As her footsteps fade up the stairs to the flat, Simone Simmonds appears, accompanied by her mother. Pepi, the peke-a-poo, in a chav Burberry coat and shades, trots in beside them on a jewel-studded lead, pausing to cock one leg up on the new staging just inside the door.

Simone stands in the centre of the shop with the guests in a circle around her. She runs her hands through her hair, then rests them on her hips as if she is modelling her outfit, which looks very familiar – a dress with a geometric black-and-white print, a plunging neckline and asymmetric hem.

'I thought Letitia would be here to greet her,' says Martin from beside me.

'She will be,' I say and on cue, Letitia returns in a strappy sundress which complements the flush on her cheeks.

Val elbows her way between Martin and me. 'Dear Tish, she could wear a binbag and still look stylish. Haven't you forgotten something. Martin? The red carpet? I thought we were going to scatter scarlet rose petals across the floor.'

'Simone is only a C-list celebrity, Mother.'

'I'd be surprised if she's on any list at all,' Gran interrupts.

'Before she married, she slept with...' Martin lowers his voice so that I can't catch the name. 'Allegedly.'

'In my day, people were celebrities because they made a difference to people's lives, not because they slept around with famous men,' Gran says. 'I don't know why Letitia asked her along. *You* should launch the party, Martin. *Posies* is your shop, your business.'

'And who Martin chooses, isn't yours,' I cut in gently. Or mine…

Two men follow Simone into the shop, one with a camera bag slung over his shoulder, and the other wearing a crumpled shirt with dark patches of sweat under the arms. I search Elliot out, and ask him to find the photographer and reporter a cold drink.

'Yep, I can do that. Can I give them canopies too?'

'I'm not sure that there are any canapés left.' I try not to smile. I don't want him to think that I am laughing at him.

'We've got some spare ones upstairs in my bedroom. Cassie and Sasha are planning a mid-night feast.'

'Why don't you offer him a piece of your granma's cake?'

'Because,' Elliot whispers, 'Big Dave's eaten it all.'

'He hasn't?'

'Mummy says that he has a ginormous appe-tite.'

I fear that, like a sponge – of the marine, not the cake variety – Elliot absorbs far too much information.

Val ties a piece of red ribbon across the door to the shop, then realises that everyone is on the wrong side of it for the formal opening, but the photographer says that he is in a hurry, so not to worry. Simone can cut the ribbon from the inside of the shop.

After Letitia and Martin have posed with

Simone, Val suggests a photo of the Blake dynasty. Martin calls for George, Cassie and Elliot, but his father fails to turn up.

'I'll have a look for him.' It doesn't seem right for Letitia to take all the glory when, without George and his father before him, there wouldn't have been a flower shop here at all.

However, when I do find George, he is going nowhere. He is sprawled out in the back of the van, his head on a folded sweatshirt, his eyes closed and his mouth open, beside a bucket of poppies that must have been left behind earlier. I don't need to use Del's Feather Principle to check that he is still breathing because the scarlet petals tremble delicately with each rumbling snore. Oblivion.

'Your dad is indisposed,' I tell Martin quietly.

He smiles wryly, and my heart twists with regret. 'We'll do the photo without him.'

After a while, people begin to drift away. As Martin says farewell to Nigel, evading his offer of seven silk handkerchiefs for one of the arrangements in the window, Elliot tugs on his father's trouser leg.

'Daddy, Daddy, I've just been upstairs to find my dinosaurs and, do you know what? Mummy and Big Dave are fixing the bed.'

'What bed?' Martin frowns. 'What do you mean by fixing it?'

'Yours and Mummy's bed. Big Dave is making it squeak.' Elliot turns and runs off. 'Come and see.'

Martin follows Elliot. I follow Martin. As we run up, the stairs creak as they always have done, but there is an additional sound that doesn't tie in with the rhythm of our footsteps. One flight. Two flights. I am gasping for breath and, so it seems, is Big Dave, for when Martin shoulders the bedroom door open, almost forcing it off its hinges, Big Dave is under the duvet with Letitia, his boots sticking out from the end of the bed.

'What the f*** are you doing?' Martin growls.

Big Dave slides out of the bed on the far side, landing on his knees with a thud. 'That did the trick.' His mouth is smiling, but his eyes are not. 'It needed a minor adjustment. You'll sleep well at night now.'

'I don't sleep in here. I've been sleeping on the bloody couch.'

I hold on to Elliot's hand, holding him back, as Big Dave stands up and heads towards the bedroom door.

'I reckon that I'll sleep better than you will.' Martin pops him on the nose, and Big Dave falls back on the bed, clutching his face.

Letitia scrambles out from beneath Big Dave, and helps him sit up. Blood trickles from between his fingers and down his chin.

'I'm sorry.' Letitia starts to cry. 'I didn't mean for this to happen.'

Martin doesn't appear to be listening. He ducks forward and grabs Big Dave by both straps of his vest, hauls him up and marches him out past me and Elliot, and down the two flights of stairs. Letitia trots after them with me and Elliot in close pursuit.

'Are you okay, Ells?' I ask him. He doesn't respond.

Martin shoves Big Dave out through the shop

to the pavement outside, then turns back to face Letitia. 'I thought we'd agreed not to mess the kids about.'

'What's the point in pretending any more? Why this charade of playing Happy Families when we've already agreed that we're going our separate ways?'

The OAPs stop gossiping. The reporter sniffs a human-interest story. Elliot waves a dinosaur. Sasha and Cassie stare.

'I came back for our children's sake.'

'You came to take them away from me!' Martin flashes back.

'I came to see if we could make some arrangement. A mutual agreement. I am not the Mother from Hell. I'm not a bad person.'

'You have just been sha–'

'That's enough!' I push myself between Martin and his wife as Raymond and Gran hustle Sasha, Cassie and Elliot out through to the rear of the shop. 'Why don't you take some time to calm down, and talk about this in private?'

Martin is not listening. 'You're a two-faced slag, Letitia!' he explodes.

Behind me, I hear Letitia's voice, clear and controlled. 'You aren't exactly Mr Perfect yourself, Martin Blake. When I return from Spain, completely stressed out from dealing with the sale of the bar on my own, I find you shacked up with a single mum.'

'What are you talking about?' Martin swears softly and runs his hands through his hair.

'Terri. Very convenient. As soon as I'm out of the picture, you take up with a woman who can help you bring up our kids.'

'You're wrong. Terri and I weren't shacked up, as you call it.'

How I wish though, that we had been. All this time, I have been fighting my responses to Martin, assuming that he and Letitia were working to save their relationship, when it turns out that they have had no intention of staying together. They have been sleeping in separate beds. I feel numb.

'I've had enough of you treating me like a doormat,' Martin growls. 'Go, Letitia. Get out of my sight.'

'N-now?' Letitia stammers. 'I haven't had a chance to find a place to stay yet.'

'I'm sure that your boyfriend can find room for you.'

'Boyfriend?' Letitia's complexion is pale, yet her cheeks and neck are splashed with livid blotches of colour.

'Don't tell me: Big Dave is a just a mate,' Martin says sarcastically. 'I refuse to put up with your lies any more. It's like Carlos and Gilberto, and the bloke who became a regular customer – our *only* regular customer – at the bar after you did your pole-dancing act. All *mates.*'

'Okay, okay,' Letitia says. 'I'll go, but I'll be back for my stuff.'

'Not the children,' Martin says hastily.

Letitia shakes her head. 'I'll have to stay at my sister's. There isn't room for the kids.'

'Who's leaving?' George comes stumbling through the shop, catching his shoulder on the shelves that Big Dave put up, and sending them crashing to the floor. 'I thought I heard someone talking about leaving, and I'd like to give them a big hug before they go.' He looks at us. 'Am I missing out on all the fun? Oh hello Terri, you look blooming – blooming marvellous.'

I look towards Val, assuming that she will take responsibility for her husband, but she is sitting in one of the new chairs, fanning herself with a sheet of giftwrap folded in half.

'Come with me.' I take George through to the back room, stepping over the shattered shelves, the teddybears, shards of glass, and plaster. I sit him down on the bottom step of the stairs with a dose of strong black coffee, aware that Gran and Raymond are chatting to the children in the flat above.

'I'm fine, Terri. There's no need to fuss.'

George's hands are shaking, and his nose is red and puffy. It is time that someone, and it might as well be me, told it straight.

'You're drunk.'

'I'm stone cold so–'

'Stop right there!'

George shrugs in defeat. 'I'm stone cold sloshed. There, I've admitted it in a roundabout way.' Holding his empty mug by the handle, he rests both hands on his knees. 'I, George Blake, am an alcoholic.'

I fetch Val. When he sees his wife, George struggles up, sways and hangs on to my shoulder. He raises his mug. 'I am an alcoholic.'

'Let's go home, love.' Val has tears – genuine ones, not reptilian – in her eyes. 'The party is well and truly over.'

Val and George leaving is a sign for the rest of

the guests to leave too. I don't know whether to let Martin and Letitia sort out their differences in peace, or stay to clear up. Martin decides for me.

'Don't worry about the wreckage. Go home.'

'Daddy, can we go swimming now?' It is Elliot, complaining that he is too hot.

For a moment, I expect Martin to stamp his feet and yell at Elliot to shut up, but he takes the grown-up course of action for the very first time in this whole débâcle. He grabs his son, picks him up and throws him over his shoulder. 'Let's run you a bath. I'll bring you the cover for your plastercast, and a couple of buckets and you can pretend you're at the seaside.'

'Can I have sand in the bath?'

Martin pulls his son back down so that the boy has his arms around his dad's neck, and his legs around his waist. They look each other in the eye.

'What do you think?' says Martin.

Elliot grins and rubs his nose against his dad's. 'I'll have bubbles instead.'

I leave them to it. Poor Martin. How must it feel, the certainty that almost everyone in your acquaintance knows that the mother of your children has succumbed to the throes of carnal lust with the builder you employed to refurbish your business? And not a very good builder at that.

I catch my grandmother out when I visit her the next morning to see how she is. I don't mean that she's invited a builder into her home to share her bed. She isn't dressed.

She answers the door in her dressing-gown and

358

slippers, her face glistening with moisturiser. 'I thought you were Martin bringing my ladder back. He promised me faithfully that he'd bring it today.'

'Faithfully' isn't a good word, I think, considering the events of the weekend.

'What time is it?' she asks sleepily.

'Elevenish.'

'I must have overslept. I'm still recovering from the party.'

'That's what comes of trying to dance both the Lindy Hop and the Lambada.'

Gran smiles weakly. 'Would you mind putting the kettle on?'

In the kitchen, Old Tom winds around my calves, mewing and twitching her tail, making me wonder if Gran has remembered to feed her. I feed her anyway, from a tin of gourmet-type cat food: tender beef pieces in gravy with vegetables. I am concerned that the cat appears to be eating better than my grandmother.

I find tomatoes in the fruit bowl in the kitchen, punnets of them on the worktop, and when I open the fridge for the milk, I find tomatoes in there too.

'Were tomatoes on offer?'

'There's no need to shout,' Gran says from the doorway, dressed now in a blouse and skirt. 'I can always use them for chutney.' She watches me empty her bin into the rubbish outside, and chuck away a few rotten tomatoes.

'I don't want to be a burden. Go home and do your own housework.'

'Everyone needs a little help now and again.'

'You must have people queueing up to have a friend like you.'

'Your tea's ready. Why don't you sit down and drink it while it's hot?'

Gran doesn't argue. She lets me do some dusting while she sits in her adjustable chair. I work along the mantelpiece: the modern bejewelled clock; a velvet ring box; a small casket that you might find round at Del Bickley's with a blank brass plate on the front. I pick it up and wipe it down. As I replace it on the mantelpiece, it slips from my grasp and rolls across the carpet.

'Butterfingers!' Gran exclaims.

'I'm sorry.' I rescue the casket.

'You've just dropped Grandad.'

I almost drop the casket again. 'I thought you scattered his ashes in the Garden of Remembrance at the crematorium?'

'Tell the truth, Terri, I burned a few of Jack's papers, and kept a handful of ash for that occasion. I kept Jack himself up in the loft for safe-keeping.'

'Why on earth would you want to do that?' I am confused.

'Because I needed time to think. It was such a shock when he passed away.' She gazes up at me from her mug. 'I did him a terrible wrong.'

I can hear my heart beating above the relentless electronic ticking of the clock.

'What did you do?'

'Jack was a good man, loyal and loving, in his own way.' Gran's mug wobbles, so I lift it from her and put it down. 'It's taken me a long time to recognise that. He could have turned me out on the street, but he didn't. There's many a cuckold who wouldn't take on another man's child.' Gran gulps in a deep breath. 'Don't look at me like that, Terri. You used to ask your mother why she was called June when her birthday was in April. Try working back forty weeks.'

I take a seat on the carpet in front of Gran's monster television. The family secret is out. Jack wasn't my mother's father. My grandfather, the man I thought was my grandfather, wasn't. 'Does Mum – I mean, June – know?'

Gran shakes her head.

'You have to tell her!'

'Do you think it'll make all that much difference to Saint Peter when he gives his judgement at the Pearly Gates?' My grandmother slips her hand down inside the arm of the chair and takes out a set of letters tied together with ribbon, like the ones she unpacked from her boxes with Sasha the other day.

'You give them to your mum. You tell her for me, Terri.'

'It will be better coming from you,' I say firmly. 'I can't tell her – I haven't got a mother, if you remember.'

'You and June are both as stubborn as each other. I must be losing my touch. I thought that this was the perfect way to get you two back together.'

'I don't need the extra hassle of having a mother, thank you. It's difficult enough being one.'

'You must think very badly of me.'

'I can understand why you wanted to protect her from the truth, but she suspected that something wasn't right, didn't she? She's always gone on about how she felt different, an outcast.'

'To all intents and purposes, Jack was her father. Teddy, my lover, was what might have been, whereas Jack was what *was*.' Gran gazes towards the casket that I have placed back on the mantelpiece. 'I've chosen a plot with room for two.'

'I wish you wouldn't keep on about dying.'

'Terri, love, we're all dying from the day we are born. I've lived my life, and I've been happy. How many people can say that?' Gran tips her chair so that she is leaning closer to me, and smiles gamely. 'What about you? There's something you haven't told me.'

I can't believe her unerring vision, her gift for reading my mind.

'How did you know?' I ask softly.

Gran smiles. 'I didn't, but now you can tell me. A problem aired, and all that.'

'I've handed in my resignation.'

Gran thinks for a moment. 'You'll have to go and withdraw it then.'

'I've made up my mind.'

'How will those poor children of Martin's cope with having a second mother figure abandoning them? They might never recover.'

'It's no use trying emotional blackmail this time. Do you really think that I'd fall for it again?'

Gran screws up her face. 'I believe that you would, if Martin had anything to do with it. What would make you happy, Terri?'

I take a step back. I see that I have to reconsider my plans for the future. Should I stay, or should I go?

Chapter Eighteen

Why is the new staging installed by Flinty Maxwell's team lined up on the pavement outside the shop? Why is there a strong smell of fresh paint inside, and what is Little Pete doing up a ladder with his roller, turning the wall by the window pale green?

Have I stepped into a parallel universe in which the launch of the new-look *Posies* has not yet taken place? Did I dream it all up? Especially the parts where I handed Martin my notice, and Letitia walked out.

Am I in a dream inside a dream? I doubt it. Sasha is with me and she seems real enough.

'What day is it today, Petal?'

'Tuesday.'

Val is talking to Del and a woman I don't recognise, at the counter. The woman – in her late thirties like me, I'd guess – has black curly hair which contrasts with her pale complexion. She wears a black miniskirt and opaque tights even though it's 28 degrees outside.

'What's going on?' says Sasha.

'Martin has had the furniture nipped out before it falls apart, and Little Pete is returning *Posies* to her former glory.' Val sighs. 'Letitia wanted the launch to be an event that is talked about for years, and it will be – for all the wrong reasons.'

Del gazes in our direction. 'Val and I were just

finishing our post-mortem.' His presence makes me feel slightly awkward, but he nods and smiles in greeting. 'It wasn't much of a party compared with the Funeral Directors' Convention. It was a shame that you couldn't be there, Terri, but I had the good fortune to meet a delightful young lady who has consented to be my wife. Allow me to introduce Verbena.'

'Congratulations.'

'I believe that we're perfectly suited.' Del takes Verbena's hand in his oh-so-smooth and well-preserved fingers. 'She operates the cremators at a crematorium only half an hour's drive from Addiscombe. How about that?'

'I hope that you'll be very happy together.'

Del clicks his heels together, and bids us farewell. Verbena accompanies him, keeping her lips pressed mournfully together.

'Does she speak?' I comment, wondering at the same time if Martin has read my letter, or where he would have left it if he hasn't.

'Not much. I've been talking to Del's sister, and rumour has it that Verbena sleeps in a coffin. She's also offered to lend me a vampire romance, but I declined.' Val grimaces. 'All that blood-sucking... Oh dear, I hope that poor Del isn't in any danger.'

'It's fiction,' I point out. 'Although Verbena does look rather drained.'

'You have turned out to have more wit than I imagined.' Val smiles, then becomes serious again. 'Still, nothing is funny to me any more. I knew that it would end in tears.'

'You've lost me.'

364

'Martin and Letitia,' Val huffs. 'They weren't really suited. Anyone could see that. After all that effort I put into baking my cakes, she would nibble at the icing and push the rest aside. I saw her. I knew what she was up to all along, crumbling sponge between her fingertips to make it look as if she'd eaten most of the slice. And now she wants half of *Posies*.'

I can offer no consolation. I cannot afford to enter into a partnership – a business arrangement – with Martin. My credit rating remains at zero.

'Come on, there are buckets to scrub and poppies to seal.' Val hands me a box of matches which I slip into the pocket of my tabard. I head out to the back room past Little Pete's ladder. Elliot is tipping a bucket upside down. It drips dirty water across the floor.

Keep calm, I tell myself. 'What are you doing in here, Fireman Sam?'

Elliot looks up. 'I'm not a fireman any more. I've lost my T-Rex.' His cheeks are smudged with grime, and his T-shirt is smeared with what could be jam.

'I'll help you look for him, as long as you promise not to tip any more buckets out.'

'Okay.' Elliot nods, and watches me while I search, lifting and shaking out Little Pete's dust-sheets. 'Guess what?'

I don't need to guess because he goes on to tell me anyway.

'My mummy has gone to stay at her sister's, which isn't very far away on the tram. It'll be better,' he intones, 'because she won't be at home to argue with Daddy, so it will be much more peacefuller, but we'll see her lots and lots because she won't be living in Spain.'

Thanks for that information, Ells, I think to myself. It means that I don't have to ask.

'There's my dinosaur!' Elliot dives forward and picks up T-Rex and an envelope which fell out of the last dustsheet.

'That's mine.' I reach out for the letter, but Elliot hangs on to it, peering at the writing on the front. 'Give it to me.'

'It's a message for my daddy.' Elliot runs off upstairs, giggling. 'I'll be Postman Pat.'

I follow, catching up with him in time to see him handing the envelope to his father.

'For me? Thanks, Ells.'

'Actually, I'd rather...' I say, but it's too late. Martin tears the envelope open and takes out my letter.

I wait, hardly able to breathe, as he scans my note. Elliot watches too, clutching T-Rex to his chest.

'What's it say?'

Martin looks up at me, his face dark with emotion. 'Terri,' he says in a low voice, 'we need to talk.'

'Letitia's here,' Val calls up the stairs. 'Cassie and Elliot, your mum's come to see you.'

'Mummy!' Elliot's eyes light up and my heart sinks. What is Letitia up to now?

'I'll catch you later,' Martin murmurs aside to me, before following his son as he runs back downstairs as quickly as he can.

I tell Cassie, who is playing in her room with

Sasha, that her mother is here, in case she hasn't heard.

'So?' Cassie's eyes flash from the shadows on the bottom bunkbed. I can understand her angry indifference. There have been occasions recently when I have been torn between venting my fury against my ex-mother when she phones to speak to Sasha, and accepting that she is who she is, and that I still hold some affection for her.

'You might regret not seeing her.'

'I might. Then again, I might not.'

'I'll come down with you, Cassie,' says Sasha. 'Your dad might let us cut some more pieces of ribbon for the dolls.'

Letitia acquires quite an audience in the shop. It includes Kev who stands in the doorway, blocking the entrance. Val leans against the counter, Little Pete continues to paint, and Martin surveys the scene from where the staging is supposed to be, testing the sharpness of a floristry knife on a stalk of foliage, twisting it around the blade and slicing through it until it is in tiny pieces on the floor.

'Cassie and Elliot, my darlings.' Letitia bends and kisses her children in turn, revealing what looks suspiciously like a strawberry love-bite across the top of her left breast. 'Do you remember Kev?'

Cassie folds her arms and bites her lip.

'He taked your dress off once, Mummy,' says Elliot, ''cos it was dirty.'

'You do exaggerate sometimes.' Letitia gives a nervous giggle as she glances towards Martin. 'Anyway, Kev has just bought a flat, a new conversion near Mitcham Common. We're moving in together.'

'Our landlord is a property developer,' Sasha pipes up. 'He's called Pat. Sometimes he wears a dress, and other times, red braces.'

'Red braces?' says Letitia. 'Is he quite good-looking?'

'He isn't very good at mending things,' Sasha says.

'I should make sure that you have a full survey, and check that all the appliances are working properly,' I cut in.

'Too late,' says Letitia. 'We've just picked up the keys.'

'I didn't realise how much a hospital porter earned nowadays,' Martin interrupts.

'An elderly cancer patient I once had on my trolley left me a considerable legacy.' Kev looks very smug in a designer T-shirt, shorts and deck shoes.

'She must have been off her trolley to leave her money to someone like you.'

'I was kind to her in her last weeks.'

'Smarmy git!'

'Martin!' Letitia warns. 'Let me fetch my suit-cases and I'll be off.'

'Mummy, when can we come and see you?' says Elliot.

'I thought you were staying at Auntie Kirsty's,' says Cassie.

'You can come whenever you like.'

I glance towards Martin. Letitia is revelling in her ability to land butter side up like a piece of toast; she is enjoying making him look like a fool.

'I've just had a thought, Letitia,' I say. 'If you need any work done on your new flat, you can always ask Big Dave. He'll do *anything* for you.'

As I hoped, Kev, being a liar and a cheat himself, is quick to catch on.

'Who's this Big Dave bloke?' he cuts in. 'You never mentioned any Big Dave.'

'He's Letitia's builder,' I explain.

'He was just a mate,' Letitia protests.

'You haven't been lying to me, have you?' Kev steps up behind her and rests his hands on the curve of her waist.

'You know me,' she says.

'I'm afraid that I do,' Kev says quietly. 'If ever I find you messing me about, you can find some other–'

'Some other mug to look after you,' Martin finishes for him. He glances towards me and a smile crosses his face, very briefly, like clouds uncovering the sun.

'How is your baby?' Sasha asks. 'What have you done with Miss Hudson?'

Kevin blushes for the first time. 'Miss Hudson and I fell out. I couldn't live with her. She's just too bossy.'

'What did you expect?' Letitia says. 'She's a teacher.'

'We don't all take our work home with us,' says Kev. 'I don't push you around, do I?'

Letitia raises one eyebrow, then changes the subject. 'I won't make a song and dance about dividing the furniture, Martin. Kev and I are making an expedition to IKEA. I've had a word with Flinty, and she's suggested some contemporary design ideas.'

'Great,' Martin says with sarcasm. 'Fantastic.'

'It's all your fault. What did you expect me to do? Struggle through life, working all hours as well as looking after the kids and a boring old man like you?'

'I thought you loved me.'

'I did, at first, until I realised that you were in love with another woman. Don't pretend otherwise, Martin. No matter what I did, I could never match up to *her*.' She gazes at me. Me?

She means me! Is it true that Martin never fell out of love with me? A lump catches in my throat. Hands shaking, I turn away and retire to the back room to scrub buckets.

It sounds dull, but it is the kind of occupation I need right now. The buckets have to be kept clean because the presence of bacteria – bad ones, in this case – shortens the life of cut flowers. I scrub and rinse, as Letitia and Kev come and go with suitcases, the same ones as she brought back with her from Spain.

Once all the buckets are upside down on the double draining-board in the back room – a feature of Flinty Maxwell's design that Martin won't have removed, I'm sure – I turn my attention to the poppies which Val has left in containers on the table beside two buckets of fresh water.

I sit down with the matchbox, remove a match, strike it, and watch the flame burn down until it catches my fingers. I wave it, blow it out, and drop it onto the table where it continues to smoulder and smoke. What a mess.

The poppies range in colour from fiery oranges to assertive reds, each bloom's dark centre suggesting hidden depths. All is not lost. What can I do to make it better?

I become aware that Val is watching me, her big arms folded across her bust.

'You did get your fingers burned messing about with my boy all those years ago, didn't you?'

I pick up a second match and strike it, pick up a poppy stem and hold the match to the end until it is blackened, then blow out the match and stick the stem into clean water. 'I don't know what you're talking about.'

'I know why you came back – you're still fond of him.' Val's voice softens slightly. 'Do you remember when you were a little girl, and you first saw me searing poppies? You gave me merry hell for playing with matches.' She is about to continue, but the bell jangles in the shop. 'I expect that's Nigel – he's going to drop by with some of his new winter range of cardigans.' As she bustles back out again, Martin appears at the foot of the stairs.

'She's gone,' he says simply.

'Where are the children?'

'Playing schools – you can tell it's the end of the summer holidays.' Martin's shadow falls across the table.

I light a third match and pick up a stem which drips milky sap across the steel surface of the table. I gaze up at Martin, his eyes dark and soft like the velvet depths of the poppy, and my pulse quickens.

I pass the end of the stem through the flame

from the match, creating a seal of charcoal.

'There is a burner somewhere – it's quicker than lighting matches.' Martin clears his throat. When he next speaks, his voice quavers. 'Please, don't leave. Give it a few weeks to see if you can feel any differently about working here, about me. I beg you.'

'I shan't stay because of the job, or because of your children,' I say quietly.

'Terri...'

'There you are, Martin.' It is Val again. She looks from her son to me, and back. 'It can wait.'

Martin and I listen to her footsteps fading as she bustles back into the shop. I can just hear her chatting to Nigel, but not the subject of their conversation.

'What were you saying?' Martin starts again.

'I shall stay because of you.'

'Thank you.' Martin reaches out his hand and cups my chin.

'I d-don't think you understand,' I stammer.

'Shh.' He leans down and presses his lips against mine. Slowly, he probes my mouth with his tongue. He's kissing me, and I am sixteen again, and I don't want him to stop.

'Terri, I am so excited!' It's Val again.

'You and me, both,' Martin whispers, pulling away, his breathing ragged as his mother returns.

'Look at this. Nigel had two left, and I snapped them both up; one for me, and one,' Val shakes out a saggy cardigan in a shade that reminds me of the mushrooms that Martin and I wired for Simone's wedding, 'for you, Terri.'

'For me?'

'Take it.' Val thrusts it into my hands. 'Try it on. I won't take no for an answer.'

Reluctantly, I slip it on.

'What do you think of that?' Val says.

Martin looks me up and down. 'Unbelievable,' he says with a twinkle in his eye.

'I saw it, and thought of Terri.' Val beams like a giant sunflower, confirming what I have already guessed: that the cardigan is a genuine gift, not some malicious gesture to get back at a member of the Mills family.

'Thanks, Val,' I say, but she is concerned for her son.

'Are you coming down with something?' she asks, pressing the back of her hand against his forehead. 'You look feverish.'

Martin grins. 'I've never felt better.' Then: 'Why don't you give that cardi to your gran?' he whispers once his mother has returned to the counter. 'Talking of Lil, I haven't seen her since the launch. She didn't come in yesterday on the way to Bingo.'

'I was going to ring her this morning, but I didn't like to wake her.'

'Ring her now.'

I do, but there is no reply. Apprehension pricks up my spine like the thorns on a rose.

'Something is wrong,' I say. 'I know it is. I'm going to her house.'

'I'll take you.' Martin picks up his keys.

Why didn't I phone my grandmother last night? Why didn't I drop by this morning? I feel so guilty.

Martin calls Del who says that she probably slipped away not long after I left the day before. I visited her two mornings and evenings in a row, but skipped today, thinking that I would take Sasha round to see her after school.

'Oh, poor Gran,' I sob into Martin's shirt. 'I left her sitting alone in her chair all night.'

Martin rests his chin on the top of my head and holds me tight.

'She did say that it was a particularly comfortable chair,' he says softly.

Sunshine and showers. That is how the children react to the news of Gran's passing. Sasha is in a sunny mood as we sit, a few days later, in the office of Dugdale & Townsend, Solicitors and Commissioners of Oaths.

'Why did Great-Granma die again, Mum?' Sasha asks me.

Martin slips his arm around my waist and gives me a comforting squeeze.

'Because her heart had worn out.' I bite my lip, praying for no further questions.

'Cassie said she died of a man's best friend, but that's a dog, isn't it, and you can't die from a dog.'

'Not unless it bites you,' says Martin.

'Pneumonia is an old man's best friend, that's what the doctor called it,' I say gently.

'Pneumonia is a very long word. How do you spell it?'

'Sasha, you are impossible. Come and sit down.' I pat the seat of the ladder-backed chair beside me, but Sasha chooses the chair next to my mother.

Mr Dugdale is playing golf, and Mr Townsend is lunching with a client, but we don't have to wait for them, because Gran left instructions that Martin should undertake the reading of her will. He takes the seat on the opposite side of the solicitor's desk and chews his lip, apparently deep in thought as he scans the envelope that Mr Dugdale's secretary handed him on our arrival at the office.

Then Martin looks up and gives me a small sad smile. Sometimes I forget that he is grieving for my grandmother too.

'I realise that it is a family matter, and I don't belong here, but Lil requested that I read out her instructions. So, here we go.' He reads from the front of the envelope. *'For the Attention of my Executive, Martin Blake.* I think she means Executor.' Martin opens the envelope, removes the papers inside and unfolds them, pressing them flat. *'Here is the last will and testament of...'*

'Go on,' says the woman who is no longer my mother, the woman who ruined my life, except that she didn't because I have been given a second chance of happiness – as long as I am bold enough to take it.

My ex-mother is dressed in black. Her mascara is smudged, and her sheer tights snagged. She looks old and weary, as if she has suddenly taken Gran's place as the matriarch. The oldest surviving member of the family. My family. I wonder if she is remembering my father's death.

'Don't keep us in suspense.'

'Now that you have both of my stubborn so-and-sos

375

sitting together in the same room', Martin glances up, 'they're Lil's words, not mine, *you have my blessing to knock their heads together.'*

I avoid looking at my ex-mother, as Martin continues, *'I leave my house, and the monies from my small insurance policy to The Addiscombe Cat Rescue and Rehabilitation Society.'*

My ex-mother makes to stand up, then sits down again. 'That isn't right!' she exclaims.

'Gran was devoted to Old Tom, and all the Old Toms before her,' I say softly, sorry not for myself because I don't need anyone's money, but for my daughter.

'Your great-grandmother's inheritance would have set you up for life, Sasha.' My ex-mother's voice sounds rather faint. 'It would have paid for your education, should you have decided to go to university to learn more about the Egyptians and marry an impoverished Professor. It would have meant that you could put down a deposit on a home of your own. How could my mother do that – disinherit her own flesh and blood!'

'Imagine how many cans of cat food the Rescue Society will be able to buy,' Sasha says, looking on the bright side.

'Sh!' says Martin. 'There is a codicil. If my daughter and granddaughter agree to a permanent reconciliation, the house will pass to my granddaughter, Terri, to live in for as long as she is alive, and it will then pass to my great-granddaughter, Sasha, who may dispose of it as she sees fit.'

'Crafty old devil,' says my ex-mother. 'She's left us with Hobson's choice.'

Martin continues to read. *'There is a bottle of brandy in the sideboard, unopened. Help yourselves.'*

I look to Martin. What would he do? I don't have to ask. I should be ashamed of myself.

'Let's go, Mum,' I say. Life is too short.

'Thank you, Terri.' My mother picks up her handbag from the floor and walks across to give me an awkward hug.

'Where are you and David staying?'

'At the Croydon Hotel in Lower Addiscombe Road. It's very convenient.'

'Why don't you stay at the house?'

'Thanks, Terri, but I couldn't bear to stay there. I grew up there, remember?'

I link my arm through hers, and head for the door.

'You've forgotten something.' Martin calls us back. 'The key.' He stands up and drops Gran's keys into my palm across the desk. 'Here's the rest of the paperwork. Sasha, you come with me. Cassie's expecting you.'

My mother and I walk to Gran's house, unlock the door, and pick up the post from the mat. My throat tightens when I read the name of the addressee: *Mrs L. Parkin.* I unlock the door into the hallway, and push it open. Old Tom appears at the bottom of the stairs and mews, her tail curved like a question mark.

'The poor creature must be hungry,' says my mother.

'I thought you hated cats.' I bend to stroke the purring animal, who now belongs to Sasha and me.

'I wish that you didn't have such a low opinion

of me. Mothers make mistakes. You've done it yourself, imagining that by keeping Sasha from her father, you were protecting her, as I was trying to save you from being hurt by Martin Blake all those years ago.' Mum pauses. 'Where's that bottle of brandy? I need a drink.'

I look around – at the silver teaspoon with the emblem P for Parkin on the end which hasn't been put away where it belongs with the best cutlery; at the enormous widescreen TV; at the empty tartan slippers that lie beneath the coathooks in the hall. It doesn't feel like mine and Sasha's house. It still belongs to Gran.

I open the brandy, pour out two glasses and sit down in the dining room, while my mother reads through the rest of the paperwork from the solicitors.

'She's left me that damned scooter,' she says eventually.

'Perhaps it will come in useful one day.'

'I refuse to drive one of those things. I shall sell it – Mother will never know.'

A gust of wind through the open window catches the corner of one of the curtains, knocking over a photograph of my mother as a girl in school uniform.

'Won't she?' I say. 'I wouldn't be too sure of that.'

'That was no ghost. It must have been the cat.' My mother is of the 'never mind, you just have to get on with it' school of dealing with grief, not the 'curl up in a corner and cry'. I find our differences difficult to deal with.

'Nothing will scare me into keeping that

scooter,' she goes on.

'You won't get much money for it, with all its dents and scrapes.'

'One reckless lady owner? I shall have to give it a provenance. Do you remember that car that once belonged to the Pope? It went for a fortune.'

'The buggy has no Catholic connections.'

'I'm sure it wouldn't be beyond us to discover one,' Mum says. 'We could persuade Sasha to employ her artistic talent to create some extra paperwork for it.'

There is a small sum of money to pay back the allowance that Gran claimed for her incontinence pads – her conscience must have caught up with her eventually. And thinking of my grandmother's conscience, I recall her refusal to tell her daughter of her origins. The letters! They are still on the arm of the adjustable chair which no one has touched since...

I fetch the letters and the ring box and hand them to my mother. She drains her glass. I fill it up again. Thank goodness my grandmother had the foresight to buy a litre bottle, not one of those miniatures that you can stash away inside a handbag.

Mum unwraps the crushed violet petals first, then wraps them up again. She opens the jewellery box and removes the contents – a band of silver with a single sapphire.

'I don't recognise this,' she murmurs. 'I thought she kept all her sparklers in the safe in the sideboard. And what are these? Love letters? A note from Mother...' She opens a piece of paper, lined and torn from an A4 pad of paper – one of

Sasha's, I suspect. There is a brief message in a beautiful, copperplate hand. My mother scans it several times, then screws it up and tosses it away, not caring where it lands. There are tears in her eyes. She wipes them away with a tissue, and sniffs. 'I used to envy the way she would open up to you, not me.'

'I didn't know until very recently. I wanted her to tell you herself.'

'I suppose she did, in her own way, scribbling that last-minute note.' My mother smiles wryly. 'I knew already that Jack wasn't my biological father because he told me so when I was about to leave home at seventeen.'

'Were you very hurt?'

'At first. I tried to find the man who wrote these letters. I searched for years, but never found him. Jack supported me through the ups and downs. He was my real family.' My mother sips at her brandy. 'We are all human. Your grandmother wasn't all good, just as I am not all bad. Tell me, what's happening with you and Martin?'

Silence hangs between us. I glance out through the net curtains at the rear garden beyond, where Sasha will be able to have a trampoline at last. I wait for my mother to give me some clue as to what she is talking about, as she sits dry-eyed now, and increasingly pie-eyed, at Gran's dining-table.

'Mother mentioned that you were engaged.'

'She must have been confused,' I say, but my mother carries on talking as if she hasn't heard me.

'I have never met a single man who would be

good enough for my daughter. Or a married one.'
I detect a note of humour in my mother's voice.
'Whenever I see Martin, I think of George and
what might have been. I've been a bloody fool.
Terri, I mean it. You could do a lot worse.' She
pours another brandy and raises her glass. 'To
Mother.'

'To Gran,' I murmur.

'I'll bet she's giving Saint Peter merry hell at
the Pearly Gates.'

It wouldn't surprise me, considering the trouble
she managed to stir up during her lifetime. Me?
Engaged to Martin? Where did Gran get that one
from? He has given me no hint, apart from that
one kiss, that he expects us to become more than
friends.

Chapter Nineteen

It is the little things that catch me out, like the hops that come into *Posies* from Kent with their sharp, beery scent, the sound of the theme tune to *Casablanca*, the sight of a figure trundling along on an invalid scooter, and the smell of hot custard.

'These don't fit.' Sasha limps around the kitchen in the flat in a pair of shiny black shoes.

'Let me check them.' I bend down and press on the toes. 'You have plenty of growing room.'

'I'll have outgrown them by the time I go back to school.'

'You go back the day after tomorrow.'

'Yes, but...' Sasha's voice trails off. She knows when she's defeated, which is more than I do. If I knew for sure that Martin wasn't interested in me, I would walk away. I need to find out first, and I have had some ideas as to how to do it. For the first time since I received that bankruptcy order, my brain has cleared, and I can see exactly what is going on. I can take back control of my destiny. And Sasha's.

'You're just saying that those shoes are too tight because I wouldn't buy you the ones with high heels.'

Caught out, Sasha grins.

'I wouldn't let Cassie have them either.' I took all three children shopping for new school uniforms as a favour to Martin to make up in some small way for all that he has done for me since Gran's death.

'Cassie would like to come and live with us because her mum and dad are being horrid to each other.'

'That wouldn't be a good idea.'

Sasha slips the shoes off. 'You could foster her.'

'You mean, she'd be like your heroine, Tracy Beaker?'

'Except there would be a happy ending, and she'd live with us forever and ever.' Sasha hesitates. 'Her mum and dad are officially splitting up.'

'Cassie and Elliot will spend time with both of their parents. Splitting up doesn't make you an orphan, Sash.'

The thought of poor children made parentless by death, makes me think of my dad and my grandmother, and I burst into tears.

'Why are you crying, Mum? I thought you'd be pleased that Martin and Letitia are splitting up because it means that you can marry Martin, and then you'll be Cassie's mum – well, stepmum anyway.'

'I'm not crying because of the Blakes.'

My daughter looks at me, her expression unbearingly solemn, and says, 'You're sad about Great-Granma, aren't you?'

It is true. I am also upset and apprehensive about having to finish clearing out Gran's house tomorrow.

'Why don't you ring Sharon? She'll cheer you up.' Sasha pauses. 'I won't listen. Promise.'

We shake hands on it, and I call Sharon. Half a minute into our conversation, Sharon disappears. I gaze into the receiver. I haven't pressed the mute button by mistake. I tap the phone and give it a little shake. Sharon returns, giggling.

'I'm sorry about that – I dropped the phone into the bath. It's almost bedtime.'

'It isn't that late.'

'For the twins, not me.' Sharon hesitates. 'Are you holding something back? You sound different somehow. Distant.'

'I am almost two hundred miles away,' I say lightly. 'Is it my South London accent?'

'There's something that you're not telling me. Is it Martin?'

'He kissed me. I didn't tell you before – it was just before Gran...'

'I see.' There is silence, then rising hysteria on the other end of the line. 'Oh my God, that's fantastic!'

'I thought you might disapprove. Martin and Letitia have only just parted company.'

'We know now that they weren't in love any longer,' Sharon says. 'The situation is completely different.'

'It was only a kiss,' I say regretfully.

'Go for it, Terri.'

'Oh, I shall.'

'Just make sure that you keep me updated, good news or bad.'

'What about your news?' I ask.

'If you and Martin should ever set a date for a wedding, you must avoid January next year. I'm pregnant with number four.'

'Congratulations. That's wonderful.'

'And five,' Sharon adds. 'It's twins. Chris and I will have to hire a minibus when we come to see you and Sasha. We are still planning to.'

'We'll have more room for you to stay soon.' I realise I am beginning to accept that, although Sharon and I will always be friends, our lives are changing. Sasha is happy. I know that because she is looking forward to returning to school. Devon is no longer home. Our home is here, in Addiscombe.

Later, when I am sitting on Pat's sofa with a small glass of wine, Sasha bounces her bottom down beside me.

'Are you in love with Martin?'

'Of course not,' I say defensively.

'You do like him though?'

'Where's your pencilcase, Sash?'

She raises one eyebrow, a trick of hers, meaning 'I know where it is, but do I really have to fetch it?'

'I thought you wanted me to help you mark your new pencils with your name.'

'If you aren't in love with Martin, why did you let him kiss you?' Sasha frowns. 'I overheard you telling Sharon.'

'Hey, Big Ears.' I grab a cushion and bop her on the head with it. 'What did I tell you?'

She grins. 'You don't tell me anything – that's why I have to listen in to your phone calls.'

I take a sip of my wine. 'I'm fond of him, that's all. We kissed. So what? It isn't a big deal.' But it is, isn't it? 'Go and find your pencilcase while I pop upstairs to see Pat.'

'I want to come with you.'

'I won't be more than five minutes.'

'Can I ring the RD?'

'That's a great idea. Just don't tell him that I've left you home alone for hours, like you did last time.'

Pat answers the door to his flat – at least, I think that it's Pat. He is in full make-up, and wearing a geometric black-and-white print dress with a plunging neckline and asymmetric hem. Behind him, in the hallway, stands a clotheshorse with various items of underwear hanging from its rails.

'What do you think?' He gives me a twirl. 'I bought it from a charity shop.'

I think that the dress looked very much better on Simone Simmonds, and even – I hate to admit it – on Letitia, but I refrain from voicing an honest opinion.

'What are you performing next? *The Importance of Being Earnest?* You make a great Lady Bracknell.' Pat stares at me. 'How did the panto go? You never mentioned it again.'

'That was a little fib, Terri. I enjoy dressing up – it's quite harmless, just a hobby, like stamp collecting or T'ai Chi. I don't want to *be* a girl. I just like wearing women's clothes.'

'Including my pants.' I take a deep breath. 'It was you, wasn't it? I've seen them on your washing line and, if I wasn't certain before, I am now. I imagine that those pants on the clotheshorse – the big ones, in shocking pink – are about my size, and, if I looked at the label, I'd find that they were from M&S.'

Pat backs away. 'Oh no, they are not.'

'Let's cut the panto, shall we? Sasha and I are leaving the flat next Sunday, and I'd like my deposit back.'

'What about your statutory notice?'

'I'm not paying a penny more rent, or shifting the Blu-tack stains, or taking responsibility for the state of the boiler.'

'Are you trying to ruin me?'

'I thought that a successful property developer like yourself with flats to rent in Addiscombe, and for sale in Mitcham, would hardly notice a few hundred quid. I have friends in the police force,' I go on, thinking of Robbie, 'and they would be very interested in interviewing you for petty theft, and for letting a property in an unsafe condition.' I made the last offence up, but far from being the bold and assertive businessman that he makes himself out to be, Pat isn't prepared to take any risks. 'I'd hate to see you get your comeuppance like one of Cinderella's Ugly Sisters.'

Today, I go commando, but it isn't because I have any hope of getting laid. It's because, thanks to Pat, I couldn't find any pants. It is Sunday morning, and I am round at *Posies*. Why? Because Martin has invited Sasha over to play with Cassie until after lunch when he is bringing the children to meet me at my grandmother's house – it will always be Gran's – to help me move the last of her possessions.

When Sasha runs off to find Cassie, I stand in the front of the shop and take a deep breath. The scent of roses is heavy on the air. There are hundreds of them, in buckets on the floor, on the counter and on the staging. There are yellow and pink carnations too. The Blakes must have been spending all the profits down at the market.

'I see that you can't keep away, Terri.'

'I wasn't expecting to see you here, George.' He looks remarkably lively for ten o'clock. 'What's with all the flowers? Have you started opening on Sundays?'

'Val and I offered to help Martin out – he's planning a busy week. Val's cooking a roast. You will join us?'

'No thanks, I have a lot to do.'

'Never mind. Another time.'

'How are we going to make a decision on which cruise to book?' Val says, entering the shop from the back room.

'As long as there are enough soft drinks and lifeboats to go round, I'll be happy,' George says.

'It's thanks to you, Terri, that we're able to take off at all,' Val says.

'We'll be casting off, not taking off,' George teases.

'You know what I mean. I was just saying before my good-for-nothing husband interrupted, that we're grateful that you changed your mind about leaving us. George and I are confident that Martin can manage the shop with your assistance – not that we're intending to rush off immediately,' Val says. 'I don't want to miss anything that might happen here.'

George gives her a nudge, as if Val has spoken out of turn.

'I'll see if Martin wants a word before you go,'

she says.

'There's no need to disturb him.'

'He won't mind.' Val bustles out. 'Martin!'

I wait amongst the flowers with George. For once, he is lost for words.

Martin turns up, rubbing at his wet hair with one towel, and with another wrapped around his middle.

'George, you come with me,' Vat calls. 'Potatoes don't peel themselves.'

'Funny,' says George, wandering out past Martin. 'I thought she'd bought ready-prepared.'

'Hi,' says Martin.

'Hi.' It is all very well, going for it, as Sharon, and Gran in her way suggested, but it is far more difficult than I imagined when the object of my desires is pretty well naked in front of me. However, I walk around the table and perch my bum on the edge. Why isn't he transfixed by the sight of my décolletage, a low-cut top and a hint of lilac bra strap? Why isn't he choking on the half-bottle of patchouli perfume that I poured onto my pulse points this morning? *Look at me*, I am screaming inside. *Look at me!*

'Are you okay?' he asks.

'I'm fine. How about you?'

'Letitia's been giving me more hassle. Having said that she's quite happy for me to have custody of the children, she's changed her mind.'

'Do you really think she'll try to take them away from you?'

'She can try, but she won't succeed. I'll dress up as Spiderman and dangle from Big Ben if that is what it takes. What's up?'

'I'm sorry...'

'Don't apologise, Terri. What is it?'

'I'm trying not to imagine you in a catsuit.' Am I being too flippant? Too pushy? Have I overstepped the mark? I watch Martin's eyes. His expression is sombre, but then he smiles for the first time.

'I'd wear my cycling gear,' he jokes, then says seriously, 'Letitia's using the kids as a bargaining tool to try to screw some money out of me. She wants half of *Posies*.'

'Your mum mentioned it. If there was any way I could help out, I would.'

'I know, but it doesn't matter – I can always take out a loan if I need to. I'd rather give Letitia a fixed settlement and make a clean break – financially, I mean. I want her to continue playing her part in bringing up Cassie and Elliot.'

Whatever that is, I think. Letitia's idea of motherhood is a walk-on role. Walk on, and walk off.

'You're too good,' I say gently.

Martin arches one eyebrow. 'If only you knew,' he says, and that is all. Then he turns away and goes back upstairs to the flat. I leave for Gran's with a heavy heart. Does Martin fancy me at all? If not, why did he kiss me? How long will it take for me to work out the answers to these questions? I fear that I am in for the long, slow burn.

Above me, the children are charging around playing Tag in the empty, echoing bedrooms, reminding me of the elephants dancing at Miss Cora's ballet classes. The sun streams in through the window of Gran's sitting room, across the last of her treasures. I sit on the carpet with them in front of me: my first shoes, a locket containing a curl of my mother's hair, and that jam jar of desiccated umbilical cord.

Martin's shadow falls across them. I don't look up.

'How can I possibly throw them away?'

Martin kneels beside me and reaches one hand to the back of my neck. I close my eyes and tip my head back, leaning into the caress of his fingers.

'Lil wouldn't have expected you to keep everything. You have her photos, and her rings – surely, they are enough?'

I open my eyes and turn to him. 'It seems wrong to bin everything.'

'Well, you can't auction old body parts on eBay, can you?' he says lightly. 'How will you fit yours and Sasha's belongings in here, if you've kept all your gran's?'

I remain unconvinced. Tears prick my eyelids. While I have her precious possessions with me, I can pretend that when I walk into the house, she will be here.

Martin takes both my hands in his. 'You have to let her go.'

'I know.'

'They aren't your memories,' he continues. 'We have to make our own.'

We? I hold Martin's gaze. My pulse throbs with hope, real hope this time. I like to think of myself as a capable, independent woman, but with Martin at my side, I could do anything. To my disappointment though, he changes the subject.

'Let's get this finished. The children can't wait to get back to *Posies*.'

I glance up towards the ceiling. 'It doesn't sound as though they're in any great hurry.'

Slowly, I pick up Gran's treasures and place them into the cardboard box, marked *SKIP*. Martin lifts the box up and carries it outside to the skip that is parked on the roadside. I watch him from the window, in his blue fleece and dark trousers, lowering the box onto the top of the rubbish – the cardboard boxes and wrapping from Gran's shopping channel acquisitions – gently, and with respect. On the way back into the house, he stamps his feet in the porch, calls for the children, then rejoins me.

'We're going, Mum,' Sasha yells from the front door. 'I've put biscuits and fresh water down for Old Tom!'

'Come on, Terri,' Elliot shouts. 'We've made a surprise for you at *Posies*.'

'Shh, shut your big mouth,' Cassie hisses.

'We can't do any more here today,' says Martin. 'I have to make a start on packing our belongings in the flat, not that there are very many of them.'

'There will be six binbags and two suitcases full, plus a few bits and pieces that we've bought here in Addiscombe. And a bed,' Sasha says.

'You must come back for tea and cake first,' Martin insists.

I agree, for Sasha's sake, because she looks so downcast when I suggest that we go straight home to the flat.

At *Posies*, the flowers have disappeared from the

392

front of the shop. It is like a desert of pale green paint and empty shelving, but the children don't appear to be surprised by this.

'Remember what you promised,' says Martin, addressing this mainly to Elliot.

'We'll put a DVD on and stay out of the way,' Elliot says.

'I bags *Nanny McPhee*,' says Cassie.

'I wanna see *Herbie: Fully Loaded*.'

'I vote for *Nanny McPhee*,' says Sasha.

'That isn't fair.' Elliot stamps his foot.

'What else did you promise me?' asks Martin sternly.

The three children look up at him, and speak in unison. 'That we wouldn't argue about which DVD we were going to watch.'

'Go on then,' Martin says. 'Scarper.' He turns back to me, looks me up and down very slowly, his gaze lingering on my face, then the curves of my breasts, then my legs, and my heart starts to beat faster.

'Where's this surprise that the kids have been so excited about then?' I ask. 'I was expecting to see the world's first truly black rose at the least.'

'Surprise?' Martin's brow furrows. 'What surprise?'

'I must have misunderstood.'

Martin's eyes flash with amusement. 'Gotcha, Terri. Follow me.' He takes my hand. 'Close your eyes, and promise me you won't peek.' His voice, like the children's, is taut with anticipation and expectation.

'I promise.' My mouth is dry. What exactly is Martin up to?

'This way.'

I walk no more than six small steps, tripping against Martin's feet before he asks me to stop. I hear the sound of a door opening, the familiar creak of the door to the back room swinging on its hinges, and it is as if a complex floral perfume has been sprayed into the air around me. Martin tugs on my hand. I take two more steps forwards.

'You can look now.'

I take a deep breath and open my eyes, only to find myself overwhelmed by a rush of colour: showy reds and burned oranges; soft pinks and acid greens; sunny yellows and shy violets. There are roses, carnations and gypsophila; lisianthus, freesias, and birds of paradise. I have never seen so many flowers gathered into such a small space.

'You did this for me?' I reach out and brush my fingertips through the nearest blooms, a mass of solid-coloured and striped carnations in a bucket on the back-room table. A lump catches in my throat, and the colours begin to blur in front of my eyes.

'I thought that you needed cheering up.' Martin moves closer and slips his hands around my waist. 'A formal or informal arrangement? What do you think?'

I can't think. All I can see is his face. All I can hear is him breathing.

'I didn't come here to arrange flowers,' I say doubtfully.

'I'm not referring to the flowers. I'm asking you about the future.' Martin's voice fractures with impatience. 'I love you, Terri. I've always loved you.'

Tears prick my eyes. 'I love you too.'

'Do you? I mean, will you marry me?'

Marriage? So soon? My heart misses a beat, then another. 'Oh, Martin!'

'I haven't been able to think about anything else, and I'm not going to let you escape a second time. Please, don't turn me down. I couldn't bear it.'

Smiling, I select a carnation from the bucket, a red one, not a striped one which would indicate a refusal. I hand it to Martin. He frowns.

'Are you saying yes?'

'Of course.'

I can feel the tension drain from his body. His face lights up.

'I thought you were going to turn me down, Miss Independent.' He presses his lips to my forehead. 'I remember that scent now – it isn't one of the flowers, it's patchouli. That takes me back.'

'It used to drive you wild.'

'It still does.' His breath blows hot against the side of my neck, my cheek, then my lips...

'They're kissing!' It is Sasha's voice that breaks the spell. 'Look at my mum and your dad!'

Martin and I start guiltily, like a pair of teenagers – in fact, just like we used to when Val caught us snogging in the very same back room at *Posies*. I guess that, with three children between us, we're going to have to get used to the interruptions.

Sasha and Cassie are peering around the banisters at the foot of the stairs.

'That's disgusting,' Cassie squeals.

'Yucky, yucky!' Elliot joins in, leaping around

the room with his light sabre in one hand and his old woollen comfort blanket in the other. He has taken to carrying it around with him again – I suppose that it is for security since his parents split up.

Martin winks at me. 'Actually, it's rather pleasant.' He kisses me again.

Elliot sits on the floor with his blanket on his head. 'Are you going to be our stairmother one day soon, Terri?'

'Stairmother? It's a stepmum, you dimwit,' crows Cassie.

'Not now,' warns Martin.

'My friend Tom at school has a stairmother and a mum, and they both buy him presents at Christmas. He had a remote-controlled Dalek and a Dr Who.'

'I don't think that Terri will be your stepmother by Christmas.' Martin smiles. 'Not officially, but we are engaged to be married.'

'Next Christmas then?' Elliot asks hopefully.

'We hope so,' I say, lingering on the word *we*. We. Martin and I.

He takes me in his arms, holding me close and tight. I rest my head against his chest, listening to the regular march of his heartbeat. His lips brush the top of my head, his breath warm and slightly damp. This is where I belong, where I have always belonged, in Martin's embrace.

'I've already decided which bedroom I'll share with Cassie,' Sasha pipes up. 'Martin and Cassie and Elliot are going to live at Great-Granma's – I mean, at our house – with us.'

'Are they?' I can't help smiling as I look up into

Martin's eyes.

'If you'd like us to,' Martin says.

'We'd love it,' I say, softly.

'I can't believe that I'll have two dads,' says Sasha. 'Do you think the RD will mind?'

'Will Terri have a baby?' asks Elliot.

'Ells,' says Cassie, 'you don't get a baby by kissing.'

'I'd like it to be a boy,' says Elliot. 'If I have a little brother, I won't be mean to him, like Cassie is to me.'

'Are you sure that you want to become Mrs Blake?' Martin takes my hand and interlinks his fingers through mine.

Sasha, Cassie and Elliot fall silent, listening for my answer.

'We'll be on our best-est behaviour,' Elliot says. 'For ever and ever.'

'We promise,' says Cassie.

'For as much of the time as we can,' says Sasha, more realistically. 'Please, Mum, say yes.'

I gaze at my new family, too choked to speak. Martin squeezes my hand. I turn to him, and slip my arms up around his neck.

'After waiting for so long? Of course I do.'

'They're kissing again,' Cassie says.

'Yuck,' says Elliot.

'Let's leave them to it,' says Sasha. 'Let's play Sardines.'

The children's footsteps fade away, and time seems to stand still, as we begin making up for those years apart. I am aware of Martin, just Martin, of the pressure of his lips, his tongue and his teeth, of his taste of sweet tea and biscuits, of his smell of aftershave and musk.

Eventually, the vague scent of talc and rosewater seeps into my consciousness, and I can hear my grandmother saying, 'Told you so, Terri. I always knew that one day, you would marry the boy next door.'

The publishers hope that this book has given you enjoyable reading. Large Print Books are especially designed to be as easy to see and hold as possible. If you wish a complete list of our books please ask at your local library or write directly to:

Magna Large Print Books
Magna House, Long Preston,
Skipton, North Yorkshire.
BD23 4ND

This Large Print Book for the partially sighted, who cannot read normal print, is published under the auspices of

THE ULVERSCROFT FOUNDATION

1	21	41	61	81	101	121	141	161	181
2	22	42	62	82	102	122	142	162	182
3	23	43	63	83	103	123	143	163	183
4	24	44	64	84	104	124	144	164	184
5	25	45	65	85	105	125	145	165	(185)
6	26	46	66	(86)	106	126	146	166	186
7	27	47	67	87	107	127	147	(167)	187
8	28	48	68	88	108	128	148	168	188
9	29	49	69	89	109	129	149	169	189
(10)	30	50	70	90	110	130	150	170	190
11	31	51	71	91	111	131	151	171	191
12	32	52	72	92	112	132	152	172	192
13	33	53	73	93	113	133	153	173	193
14	34	54	74	94	114	134	154	174	194
15	35	55	75	95	115	135	155	175	195
16	36	56	76	96	116	136	156	176	196
17	37	57	77	97	117	137	157	177	197
(18)	38	58	78	98	118	138	(158)	178	198
19	39	59	79	99	119	139	159	179	199
20	40	60	80	100	120	140	160	180	200

201	211	221	231	241	251	261	271	281	291
202	212	222	232	242	252	262	272	282	292
203	213	223	233	243	253	263	273	283	293
204	214	224	234	244	254	264	274	284	294
205	215	225	235	245	255	265	275	285	295
206	216	226	236	246	256	266	276	286	296
207	217	227	237	247	257	267	277	287	297
208	218	228	238	248	258	268	278	288	298
209	219	229	239	249	259	269	279	289	299
210	220	230	240	250	260	270	280	290	300

301	310	319	328	337	346
302	311	320	329	338	347
303	312	321	330	339	348
304	313	322	331	340	349
305	314	323	332	341	350
306	315	324	333	342	
307	316	325	334	343	
308	317	326	335	344	
309	318	327	336	345	